Tom Lake

ALSO BY ANN PATCHETT

Novels

The Patron Saint of Liars

Taft

The Magician's Assistant

Bel Canto

Run

State of Wonder

Commonwealth

The Dutch House

Nonfiction

Truth and Beauty

What now?

This Is the Story of a Happy Marriage

These Precious Days

Children's

Lambslide

Escape Goat

Tom Lake

A Novel

Ann Patchett

HARPER LARGE PRINT
An Imprint of HarperCollins*Publishers*

This is a work of fiction. Names, characters, places, and incidents are products of the author's imagination or are used fictitiously and are not to be construed as real. Any resemblance to actual events, locales, organizations, or persons, living or dead, is entirely coincidental.

HarperCollins books may be purchased for educational, business, or sales promotional use. For information, please e-mail the Special Markets Department at SPsales@harpercollins.com.

FIRST HARPER LARGE PRINT EDITION

ISBN: 978-0-06-334772-4

Library of Congress Cataloging-in-Publication Data is available upon request.

23 24 25 26 27 LBC 8 7 6 5 4

For Kate DiCamillo
who held the lantern high

Tom Lake

1

That Veronica and I were given keys and told to come early on a frozen Saturday in April to open the school for the *Our Town* auditions was proof of our dull reliability. The play's director, Mr. Martin, was my grandmother's friend and State Farm agent. That's how I was wrangled in, through my grandmother, and Veronica was wrangled because we did pretty much everything together. Citizens of New Hampshire could not get enough of *Our Town.* We felt about the play the way other Americans felt about the Constitution or the "Star-Spangled Banner." It spoke to us, made us feel special and seen. Mr. Martin predicted a large turnout for the auditions, which explained why he needed use of the school gym for the day. The community theater production had nothing to do with our high school, but seeing as how Mr. Martin was also the principal's insurance agent and very likely his friend, the request was granted. Ours was that kind of town.

We arrived with our travel mugs of coffee and thick paperback novels, *Firestarter* for Veronica and *Doctor Zhivago* for me. I liked school fine but hated the gym and everything it stood for: team sports, pep rallies, vicious games of kickball, running in circles when it was too cold to go outside, formal dances, graduations. But on that Saturday morning the place was empty and strangely beautiful. The sunlight poured in through the narrow windows just below the roofline. I don't think I'd ever realized the gym had windows. The floors and the walls and the bleachers were all made of the same strips of pale wood. The stage was on one end behind the basketball hoop, its heavy red curtains pulled back to reveal matte-black nothingness. That's where the action was scheduled to take place. We had instructions to set up one banquet table and five folding chairs in front of the stage ("Close but not too close," Mr. Martin had told us) and then ninety-two feet away, under the opposing basketball hoop, we were to set up a second banquet table right in front of the doors to the lobby. That second table was for registration, which was our job. We wrestled the two folding tables from the storage closet. We brought out folding chairs. We were to spend our morning explaining how to fill out the form: *Name, Stage Name if Different, Height, Hair Color, Age (in categories of seven years - please check one), Phone Number.* The hopefuls had been asked to bring a headshot and a résumé, listing all the roles they'd played before. We had a cup full of pens. For people who arrived without résumés there was space to write things in, and Veronica was prepared to take a Polaroid of anyone who didn't have a headshot and then paper-clip it to the form. Mr. Martin told us we weren't to make anyone feel embarrassed for having less experience because, and this was what he actually said, "Sometimes that's where the diamonds are."

But Veronica and I were not theater girls. Theater girls had not been asked to do this job in case they wanted to try out for a part. We were regular girls who would've had no idea how to make adults feel judged based on their lack of theatrical experience. Once we had the person's paperwork, we were to hand over the pages they would be asked to read from, which Mr. Martin told us were called "sides," along with a number printed on a square of paper, and then we would direct them back out to the lobby to wait.

When the doors opened at eight o'clock, so many people flooded in that Veronica and I had to hustle back to our table to get ahead of the crowd. We were instantly, overwhelmingly at work.

"Yes," I assured one woman and then another, "if you read for Mrs. Gibbs, you'll still be considered for Mrs. Webb." What I didn't say, though it was rapidly becoming evident, was that if you read for Emily you would still be considered for Emily's mother. In a high school production it was not uncommon for someone fifteen to play the parent of someone seventeen, but community theater was a different cat. That morning the hopefuls were all ages, not just old men looking to be the Stage Manager, but college types who came to read for Emily and George. (The Emilys wore too much makeup and dressed like the Amish girls who sold cinnamon buns at the farmer's market. The Georges slyly checked out the other Georges.) Bona fide children approached our table announcing they were there to read for Wally or Rebecca. Parents must have been looking for childcare because what ten-year-old boy announces over breakfast that he wants to be Wally Webb?

"If all these people come back and buy a ticket, they'll have a smash on their hands," Veronica said. "The whole production can go straight to Broadway and we'll be rich."

"How does that make *us* rich?" I asked.

Veronica said she was extrapolating.

Mr. Martin had thought of everything except clipboards, which turned out to be a real oversight. People were using our table as a desk, creating a bottleneck in the flow of traffic. I tried to decide if it was more depressing to see the people I knew or the people I didn't know. Cheryl, who worked the register at Major Market and must have been my mother's age, was holding a résumé and headshot in her mittened hands. If Cheryl had always wanted to be an actress, I didn't think I could ever go to the grocery store again. Then there were the rafts of strangers, men and women bundled in their coats and scarves, looking around the gym in a way that made it clear they'd never seen it before. It struck me as equally sad to think of these people driving for who knew how long on this frozen morning because it meant they were willing to keep driving here for rehearsals and performances straight into summer.

"'All the world's a stage,'" Veronica said, because Veronica could read my mind, "and all the men and women merely want to be players."

I accepted a résumé and headshot from the father of my friend Marcia, which she pronounced Mar-*see*-a. I had sat at this man's dinner table, ridden in the back seat of his station wagon when he took his family for ice cream, slept in the second twin bed of his daughter's rose-pink bedroom. I pretended not to know him because I thought that was the kindest course of action.

"Laura," he said, smiling with all his teeth. "Good morning! Some sort of crowd."

I agreed that it was, then gave him his number and the sides and told him to go back out to the lobby to wait.

"Where's the restroom?" he asked.

It was mortifying. Even the men wanted to know where the restroom was. They wanted to fluff up their hair that had been flattened by sock hats. They wanted to read their part aloud to themselves in the mirror to see how they looked. I told him the one by the Language Arts Center would be less crowded.

"You girls look busy," my grandmother said. She came up from behind us just as Marcia's father walked away.

"Do you want a part?" Veronica asked her. "I know people. I can make you a star." Veronica loved my grandmother. Everyone did.

"I'm just here to take a look." My grandmother glanced back to the table in front of the stage to indicate that she would be sitting with Mr. Martin and the theater people. My grandmother, who owned Stitch-It, the alterations shop in town, had volunteered to make the costumes, which meant that she'd volunteered me to make the costumes as well since I worked for her after school. She kissed the top of my head before crossing the long, empty stretch of the basketball court towards that faraway table.

Auditions were to have begun promptly at ten, but thanks to the clipboard situation it was past ten-thirty. Once everyone had been registered, Veronica said she would cull out small groups according to their numbers and the roles they had come for, then herd them down the hallway to wait. "I'll be the sheepdog," she said, getting up from our table. I would stay and silently register the stragglers. Mr. Martin and my grandmother took their seats with three other people at the table in front of the stage and just that fast the gym, which had been booming all morning, fell to silence. Veronica was to escort the would-be actors down the hall and up the stairs, through the backstage, and right to the edge of the stage when their names were called. The actors waiting to audition were not allowed to watch the other auditions, and the actors who had finished their auditions were instructed to leave unless specifically asked to stay. All the Stage Managers would go first (the Stage Manager being the biggest and most important part in the play) followed by all the Georges and Emilys, and then the other Webbs (Mister and Missus and Wally) and the other Gibbses (Doctor and Missus and Rebecca). The smaller roles would be awarded on a runner-up basis. No one leaves home hoping to land the part of Constable Warren, but if Constable Warren is what you are offered, you take it.

"Mr. Saxon," Mr. Martin called out. "You'll be reading the beginning of the second act." All the Stage Managers would be reading the beginning of the second act.

That I could hear the light shuffle of Mr. Saxon's footsteps crossing the stage surprised me. "I'm first?" Mr. Saxon had failed to consider that this would be the outcome of arriving at a high school gym half an hour before the doors opened.

"You, sir, are the first," Mr. Martin said. "Please begin when you're ready."

And so Mr. Saxon cleared his throat and, after waiting a full minute longer than what would have been merely awkward, he began. "Three years have gone by," he said. "Yes, the sun's come up over a thousand times."

I continued to face the lobby as I had all morning, though now those two sets of double doors were closed. Mr. Martin and my grandmother and the people sitting with them were far away, their backs to me, my back to them, and poor Mr. Saxon, who was dying a terrible death up there, was doubtlessly looking at the director and not the back of a high school girl. Still, as a courtesy, I did not turn around. He went all the way to the end of the page. "There! You can hear the 5:45 for Boston," he said finally, his voice flooded with relief. The reading lasted two minutes and I wondered how anyone could have thought it wise to have picked such a long passage.

"Thank you very much," Mr. Martin said, his voice devoid of encouragement.

Such a sadness welled in me. If Veronica had been there we would have played a silent game of hangman, adding a limb for every word Mr. Saxon hit too plaintively. We would have refused to look at each other for fear of laughing. But Veronica was in the hallway, and no one had come in late the way we'd been so sure they would. As it turned out, the auditioners had all had the same idea: arrive promptly, register, and stand in line as directed—thus proving themselves to be good at taking direction. Mr. Martin called out for the second hopeful, Mr. Parks.

"Should I start at the top of the page where it's marked?" Mr. Parks asked.

"That would be just fine," Mr. Martin said.

"Three years have gone by," Mr. Parks said, and then waited three years in order to underscore the point. "Yes." He paused again. "The sun's come up over a thousand times."

Mr. Parks was playing to Maine, not New Hampshire. Were I to turn around I no doubt would have seen a man in a yellow slicker, a lobster tucked beneath his arm. Silently, I reached into the backpack hanging from my chair and felt for my copy of *Doctor Zhivago.* This had always been the plan: they would audition and I would read, and when we got bored Veronica and I would swap our posts so she could read. Mr. Parks was nowhere near the end of the page. The good thing about *Doctor Zhivago* was that the plot was sufficiently convoluted so as to require all of my brain. I didn't much like the novel but I wanted to see what would happen to Lara. Still, by the sixth time some aspiring Stage Manager announced that the sun had come up, I realized Pasternak was no match for my circumstances and I turned my chair around.

One after the other, the Stage Managers walked out onto the proscenium and began. The awkward ways these men held their bodies, and how the paper trembled in their hands, were things no high school girl should ever see. Some of them had decent voices, but tip them off the side of a boat and they would go down like anchors. Zero buoyancy. Others were okay in their bodies, pacing around with one hand stuffed in a pocket, but they sounded out each word phonetically. The dichotomy was neck-up neck-down: Some had one and some had the other, but no one managed both and several managed neither. Put together, the Stage Managers were a car crash, a multiple-vehicle pileup, and I could not look away.

Despite all evidence, it was nearly springtime in New Hampshire. My junior year was seven weeks from its completion but I kept thinking that this was the first day of my true education. None of the books I'd read were as important as this, none of the math tests or history papers had taught me how to act, and by "act" I don't mean on a stage, I mean in life. What I was seeing was nothing less than how to present myself in the world. Watching actors who had memorized their lines and been coached along for months was one thing, but seeing adults stumble and fail was something else entirely. The magic was in identifying where each one went wrong. Mr. Anderson, a loan officer from Liberty Bank, had brought a pipe, a prop that may have been all right to hold, but which he kept clenched between his teeth. A person didn't have to act to know that the ability to separate one's jaws was helpful in speaking, and yet I knew it and he didn't. Then, in the middle of the two-minute speech, he folded the sheet of paper he was reading from, slipped it into the inside pocket of his suit jacket, pulled a box of wooden matches from the patch pocket of that jacket and lit the pipe. The puffing it took to pull the fire into the tobacco, the little flame flashing up from the bowl, it was all part of his audition. Then he put the box of matches and the spent match back in his pocket, removed the page of script, unfolded it and resumed his performance while the sweet pipe smoke drifted towards the rafters and worked its way back to me.

That Mr. Martin didn't just stand up and say forget it, I have no interest in directing *Our Town*, was a testament to his fortitude. Instead, he coughed and thanked Mr. Anderson for his time. Mr. Anderson, nodding gravely, departed.

Every Stage Manager came with an unintended lesson: clarity, intention, simplicity. They were teaching me. Like all my friends, I was wondering what I should do with my life. Plenty of days I thought I would be an English teacher because English was my best class and the idea of a life spent reading and making other people read appealed to me. I was forever jotting down ideas for my syllabus in the back of a spiral notebook, thinking how we'd start with *David Copperfield*, but no sooner had I committed myself to teaching, I wrote off to request an application for the Peace Corps. I loved books, of course I did, but how could I spend my life in a classroom knowing that wells needed to be dug and mosquito nets needed to be distributed? The Peace Corps would be the most direct route to doing something truly decent with my life. Decency, a word I used to cover any aspect of being a good person, factored heavily into my thinking about the future. Being a veterinarian was decent—we all wanted to be veterinarians at some point—but it meant taking chemistry, and chemistry made me nervous.

But why was I always reaching for six-hundred-page British novels and hard sciences and jobs that would require malaria vaccinations? Why not do something I was already good at? My friends all thought I should take over my grandmother's alterations shop because I knew how to sew and they didn't. Their mothers didn't. When I turned a hem or took in a waistband, they looked at me like I was Prometheus coming down from Olympus with fire.

If you wonder where the decency is in alterations, I can tell you: my grandmother. She was both a seamstress and a fountain of human decency. When Veronica spoke about the jeans I diverted from the Goodwill bag by tapering the legs, she said, "You saved my life!" People liked their clothes to fit, so making them fit was helpful, decent. My grandmother—who always had a yellow tape measure hanging around her neck and a pin cushion held to her wrist with a strip of elastic (the pincushion corsage I called it) taught me that.

Watching these men recite the same lines so badly while polishing their glasses with giant white handkerchiefs really made me think about my life.

"Wait, wait, wait, you wanted to be a vet?" Maisie shakes her head. "You never wanted to be a vet. You never said that before." Maisie will begin her third year of veterinary school in the fall, if in fact there is school in the fall.

"I did for a while. You know how it is in high school."

"You wanted to be a pediatrician in high school," Nell says to her sister in my defense.

"Could someone explain to me what any of this has to do with Peter Duke?" Emily asks. "What does sewing have to do with Duke?"

My girls have directed me to start the story at the beginning when they have no interest in the beginning. They want to hear the parts they want to hear with the rest cut out to save time. "If you think you can do a better job then tell the story yourself," I say, standing, though not in a punitive way. I stretch my hands up over my head. "The three of you can tell it to one another." God knows there's work to be done around here.

"Shush," Nell says to her sisters. She pats the sofa. "Come here," she says to me. "Come back. We're listening." Nell knows how to move people around.

Emily, the eldest, sweeps her magnitude of silky dark hair over one shoulder. "I just thought this was going to be about Duke. That's all I'm saying."

"Stop flipping your hair," Maisie says, irritated. Maisie had her father cut her hair short in the spring and she misses it. Her little dog Hazel stands up, turns three awkward circles on the couch then falls over into a comfortable ball. They tell me they're ready.

All three girls are in their twenties now, and for all their evolution and ostensible liberation, they have no interest in a story that is not about a handsome, famous man. Still, I am their mother, and they understand that they will have to endure me in order to get to him. I take back my place on the sofa and begin again, knowing full well that the parts they're waiting to hear are the parts I'm never going to tell them.

"Duke," Emily says. "We're ready."

"I promise you, he doesn't get here for a while."

"Is that all the Stage Managers?" Mr. Martin said finally, his voice tired.

Veronica's dear head popped out from the edge of the curtain. "That's all of them," she called, and then her eyes caught mine. She jerked her head back a split second before starting to laugh.

Mr. Martin picked his thermos off the floor and unscrewed the cap while his cohorts whispered among themselves. "Onward," he said.

While the Stage Manager is a solitary character,

George and Emily exist in relation to each other and to their families, so the Georges and the Emilys auditioned in pairs. Again, Mr. Martin had chosen readings from the second act, which, in my opinion (and the high school girl at the back of the gym was newly loaded with opinions) was the practical choice. The first short exchange showed off more of Emily and the second one showed more of George, unless you were taking into account a person's ability to listen, in which case the primacy was reversed.

I wondered if the pairs had been put together based on any two people standing next to each other in line, or if Veronica was back there doing something funny, because the first George looked to be about sixteen, and the first Emily, not that I knew, looked every hard day of thirty-five. Rumor had it certain women wanted to play Emily forever. They criss-crossed New Hampshire town to town, year after year, trying to land the part. This one wore her hair in pigtails.

Mr. Martin asked if they were ready, and straightaway George began.

"Emily, why are you mad at me?" he said. I had the page from the script in my lap.

Emily blinked. Clearly, she was mad at George, but she struggled to decide whether or not to tell him. Then she turned and looked at Mr. Martin. She shielded her eyes with her hand the way you see people do in the movies when they're talking to directors out in the audience, but since there were no stage lights to squint into, the gesture failed. "I wasn't ready," she said.

"Not to worry," Mr. Martin said. "Just start again."

I imagined him talking to people about car insurance, life insurance, how State Farm would be there if their home burned to the ground. I bet he made it easy for them.

"Emily, why are you mad at me?" George said again.

She looked at George like she might kill him, then turned back to Mr. Martin. "He can't just *start* like that," Emily said. "I have to be ready."

I didn't understand what was happening, and then I did: She had lost. Like a horse that stumbles straight out of the gate. She hadn't even started and it was over.

"We can do it again," Mr. Martin said. "No matter."

"But it *does* matter." Would she cry? That's what we were waiting to see.

The boy was tall with a crazy thatch of light-brown hair that looked for all the world like he'd cut it himself in the dark. The expression on his face made me think he'd been working over some aspect of baseball in his head and just now realized he was in trouble. "I'm awfully sorry," George said, exactly the way George would say it—sorry and concerned and slightly buffaloed by the whole thing. In short, this guy was going ahead with his audition, and Emily knew that, too.

"I want to get back in line," she said, teetering. "I want to read with someone else."

"That's fine," Mr. Martin said, and before she had so much as turned, he called out in a louder voice, "We need another Emily."

We were rich in Emilys. So many more Emilys than Georges. I knew that from registration. The Emily going out passed the Emily coming in, a girl some fifteen years younger whose yellow hair was loose and shining. She put a little swish in her hips so that her pretty skirt swayed. It was scary to see how fast time goes. I knew the first one would not be getting back in the line.

That George though, I liked him. The Stage Managers had set a very low bar. That George stayed through three more rounds and each time he did something different, something particular that was in response to the Emily he was reading with. When the Emily was shrill, he was matter-of-fact. When the Emily was timid, he was quietly protective. The third one—who knew how she managed it so quickly—started to cry. Just a few tears at first, impressive really, but then she lost control of herself and was bawling. "George, *please* don't think of that. I don't know why I said it—"

George pulled out his handkerchief. Did they all

carry one? He dabbed at her face, making a single shushing sound that somehow, miraculously, shushed her. At the back of the gym I shivered.

Many of the Georges who followed read their lines as if they were trying out for Peter Pan. The older they were, the more they leapt in a scene that did not call for leaping. The Emilys were tremulous, emotive, cramming the breadth of human experience into every line. They were *Angry* and *Sorry* and *Very Moved.* I started to wonder if the part was more difficult than I'd imagined.

Listen to yourself, I wanted to call out from the back of the gym. Listen to what you're saying.

A mediocre George could stay through three or four Emilys simply because he was needed, though if he was hopeless he stayed for only one. The Stage Managers had embarrassed me, and the Georges, at least after the first one, bored me, but the Emilys irritated me deeply. They were playing the smartest student in her high school class as if she were a half-wit. Emily Webb asked questions, told the truth, and knew her mind, while these Emilys bunched up their prairie skirts in their hands and mewled like kittens. Didn't any of them remember what it was like to be the smart girl? No high school girls had come to try out for the part, at least no girls from my high school, probably because there would be too many rehearsals on nights better spent doing homework or waiting tables for tips or hanging out with friends. No one had come to speak for our kind.

And so when Emily and George left the stage, in the moment before the next Emily and George arrived, I turned my chair around. For a minute I told myself I would go back to *Doctor Zhivago,* but reached for a registration form instead. It wasn't that I wanted to be an actress, it was that I knew that I could do a better job. *Name* the form said. *Stage Name if Different.* I printed my name: *Laura Kenison.* Other than my address, phone number, date of birth, I had nothing to offer, no way to turn my after-school job at Stitch-It into theatrical experience. I listened to the audition behind me. "Well, UP un*TIL* a YEAR ago I *USED* to like *YOU* a LOT," Emily sang. I folded up the registration form and put it in my copy of Pasternak, then took a fresh sheet and started again. This time I spelled my name L-A-R-A, tossing out the "u" my parents had given me at birth because I believed this new spelling to be Russian and worldly. I decided Mr. Martin had been right. I decided that I would be the diamond.

2

"You had a 'u' in your name?" Emily looks at me skeptically.

"For sixteen years."

"Did you know she had a 'u'?" she asks her sisters, and they shake their heads, mystified by what I've withheld from them.

"There's a lot you don't know," I say.

Hazel the dog looks at me.

"I didn't know it was going to be funny," Maisie says.

"No idea," Nell says.

"It isn't funny," I tell them. "You know that. It isn't a funny story except for the parts that are."

"Life," Nell says, dropping her head against my shoulder in a way that touches me. "Keep going. I'm thinking the hot George is still going to be there."

I waited for the George and Emily on the stage to finish before going out to the lobby, the application in my hand, the Polaroid camera around my neck. Somehow I'd forgotten there would still be so many people waiting to try out for the other parts: the Gibbses and the Webbs. Men and women and children were pacing, silently mouthing the words on the pages they held. I was one of them now. I was about to tell George I was disappointed in him because all he ever thought about was baseball and was no longer the boy I considered to be my friend.

A scant handful of Georges and Emilys sat in the hallway that went back to the stage. Everyone had a chair except for Veronica and the first George, the good one. They were sitting together on the stairs and he was making her laugh, which, I can tell you, was not the hardest thing in the world to do. Her black hair swung down across one flushed cheek, and I realized that we should have swapped our posts two hours ago. I had forgotten because I'd been studying at the school of theatrical auditions, and she had forgotten because she'd been talking to George. You really couldn't hear the stage from the hallway, which was why she stayed close to the door, propping it open just a little bit with her fat Stephen King novel. Whatever else was going on, Veronica never stopped paying attention to the stage.

When she looked up and saw me there with the camera she raised one magnificent eyebrow. Veronica's eyebrows were thick and black and she tweezed them into delicate submission. She could get more information across with an eyebrow than other people could with a microphone. She knew I was going to read for Emily, and that I would get the part. I used to say Veronica could never play poker because her thoughts passed across her forehead like a tickertape. She realized that she could have read for Emily, and then she could have been the one to come to rehearsals with this guy. They could have practiced their lines in his car, and raised their clasped hands above their heads at the end of every performance, bowing one more time before the curtain came down. But Veronica almost never got to go out at night because her mother was a nurse who worked the second shift and her stepfather was long gone and she had to look after her brothers. We both had two brothers, yet another bond between us, though mine were much older and hers, technically half brothers, were little kids. If it hadn't been for those brothers, Veronica would have made a truly great Emily.

"Really?" she asked me.

I nodded, handing her the camera. She stood to take the clip out of my hair.

"You have to go last," she said. "No jumping line. If Jimmy's still around he can read with you."

Jimmy looked me dead in the eye and reached out his hand. We shook on it. "No place I'd rather be," he said.

I went back down the hall and took my seat. I didn't want anyone to think I was getting preferential treatment, which, of course, I was. I didn't have to run to the bathroom with Veronica to know what she was doing. Mr. Martin needed to find an Emily in a field with no contenders. All his hopes would be pinned on whatever girl came last. I had audited over four hours of AP acting classes, which didn't mean I knew how to act, but I sure as hell knew how not to. All I had to do was say the words and not get in the way.

When the last pair had gone and it was just me and Veronica and Jimmy-George in the hall, I asked Veronica to braid my hair.

Jimmy-George shook his head and Veronica agreed with him. "It's prettier down," she said.

I was wearing jeans and duck boots and my brother Hardy's old U. New Hampshire sweatshirt. Go Wildcats.

"You would have told me, right?" Veronica said. "If this was always the master plan?"

"You know I never have a plan." Why did it feel like I was leaving her?

She cocked her head like you do when you hear the sound of a door opening somewhere in the house, then she put her arms around me and squeezed. "Kill it," she whispered.

The gym was the gym again, site of all humiliations: the running, the kickball, the dancing, the play. I wanted to teach English, join the Peace Corps, save a dog's life, sew a dress. Acting had not been on the list. When I handed my form to one of the men who stood to take it, I very nearly cried out from the fear. Was this how the Stage Managers felt? Was this the reason they lit their pipes and fiddled with their hats? The Georges leapt, the Emilys twirled their fingers through their hair like they were practicing the baton, all because they knew they were going to die up there. My grandmother was watching, and I knew she must be so afraid for me. I closed my eyes for one second, telling myself it would all go so fast. Jimmy was George and I was Emily and we knew our parts by heart.

"Emily, why are you mad at me?" George said.

"I'm not mad at you," I said.

It was a simple conversation between two childhood friends who were about to fall in love. I said the lines the way I'd heard them in my head all morning, and when we were finished, Mr. Martin and my grandmother and the three men who were with them stood and clapped their hands.

I look at my watch. It's easy to forget how late it is because the sun stays up forever in the summer. "We're switching to montage now," I tell the girls. "I won't put you through any more of high school."

"But what about the play?" Emily asks, her impossible legs over the back of the couch. Emily has never been able to sit on furniture like a normal person. I lost that fight when she was still a child. Whoever installed her interior compass put the magnet in upside down.

"You know all about the play, and anyway, it comes up a lot. We have to pace ourselves."

"What happened to Veronica and Jimmy-George?" Maisie asks. "I've never heard a word about either of them."

"We lost touch."

Maisie snorts. "There is no such thing as losing touch." She pulls her phone from the pocket of her shorts and wags it at me like some wonderful new invention. "What are their last names?"

I look at her and smile.

"You can at least tell us which one of you ended up with him," Nell says.

"We all ended up with ourselves."

The girls groan in harmony. It's their best trick.

Emily reaches over and tugs on my shirt. "Give us something."

We will be back in the orchard hours from now. If they don't go to bed soon they'll be worthless tomorrow, though I don't tell them that. I labor to tell them as little as possible. "The play was a big success. We were scheduled for six performances and we got extended to ten. A reporter came from Concord and wrote us up in the *Monitor.*"

My picture was on the front page of the weekend section. My grandmother bought five copies. I found them stacked in the bottom of her blanket chest after she died.

Nell asks who played the Stage Manager. Nell is an actress. She has to see the whole thing in her head.

The Stage Manager. There had been so many Stage Managers. I have to think about it. The bad ones are all so clear in my mind, but who got the part? He was good, I know that. I try to picture him walking me to the cemetery. "Marcia's father!" I cry, because even if I don't remember his name, I see his face as clear as day. The brain is a remarkable thing, what's lost snaps right into focus and you've done nothing at all. "He was trying out for Doc Gibbs but he was better than the other men so Mr. Martin made him the Stage Manager." He lacked the hubris to believe that he should have the lead, that's what made him good. Marcia was humiliated by the thought of me spending time with her father. She avoided me through all the rehearsals and then the play, wouldn't sit with me at lunch, wouldn't look at me, but when we came back in the fall for our senior year we were fine again.

"And Jimmy was George?" Emily asks.

"Clearly, Jimmy was George," Maisie says.

"Jimmy was George," I say.

"Was he as good a George as Duke?" Emily asks. Oh, the look that comes over her when she says Duke's name. I wish I'd had the wherewithal to lie about everything, continuously, right from the start.

"Duke never played George."

Maisie raises a hand to object. "Who was he then?"

"He was Mr. Webb."

"No," Nell says. "No. At Tom Lake? Duke was George."

"I was there. None of you were born."

"But all three of us can't have it wrong," Emily says, as if their math outweighs my life.

"You remember it that way because it makes a better story if Duke was George and I was Emily. That doesn't means it's true."

They mull on this for a minute.

"But that means he played your father," Maisie says.

As if on cue, their own father walks in the back door, his pants bristling with chaff. Hazel raises her head and barks until Maisie shushes her. Hazel barks at the entrance of any man.

"Workers," he says to us, clapping his hands. "Go to bed."

"Daddy, we're old," says Nell, the youngest. "You can't send us to bed."

Emily, our farmer, Emily, who plans to take all of this over when we are old, looks at her watch. "Mom was just about to switch to montage."

"What's the story?" he asks, pulling off his boots by the door the way I've asked him to for years.

The girls look at one another and then at me.

"The past," I say.

"Ah," he says, and takes off his glasses. "I'll be in the shower. No excuses in the morning though."

"Promise," we all say.

And so I endeavor to take us through the boring parts as quickly as possible.

My senior year I signed up for drama club. I played Annie Sullivan in *The Miracle Worker* with a very small seventh grader named Sissy who had to be reminded not to break the skin when she bit me. We slung each other all over the stage. The big spring musical was *Bye Bye Birdie*, and I played Rosie DeLeon. No one would call me a singer but I didn't embarrass myself. I got into Dartmouth and Penn without financial aid. I went to the University of New Hampshire, where the yearly bill, including tuition, room, board, books, and fees, came to just over $2,500 after my merit scholarship. In college, I was no closer to knowing what I was going to do with my life than I'd been in high school. The University of New Hampshire didn't offer fashion design and I still hadn't signed up for chemistry. I kept the application for the Peace Corps in my desk. My grandmother had given me her beloved black Singer for graduation, a war horse, and I made pocket money shortening the corduroy skirts of sorority girls. The days filled up with British Literature and Introduction to Biology and piles of sewing. I fell asleep in the library, my head turned sideways on an open book. Acting never crossed my mind.

Or it didn't until my junior year, when I saw an audition notice for *Our Town* tacked to a cork board in the student center. I was there to tack up my own notice: *Stitch-It, Speedy Alterations.* My first thought was that it would be fun to register people for the play, and my second thought was that I could try for Emily. There would be so much pleasure in saying those words again, and I understood the metrics by which one's social sphere was enlarged by theater. Even as a junior, most of the kids I knew in college were the kids I'd gone to high school with.

In any given year more girls who had once played Emily attended the University of New Hampshire than any other university in the country, all of us thinking that we had nailed the part. What I wouldn't have given to be in the room for their auditions, but this time I lacked a plausible excuse. I waited in the hallway with my number, wearing my brother's Wildcats sweatshirt for luck.

Luck was everything.

Bill Ripley was in the audience on the night of the third performance. He was a tall man with perpetually flushed cheeks and a premature edge of gray in his dark hair that gave him an air of gravitas. He sat in the fifth row with his sister, his voluminous wool dress coat draped over his lap because he hadn't wanted to wait in line for the coat check.

I called him The Talented Mr. Ripley because I'd seen the paperback once in a bookstore and liked the title. I thought of it as a compliment. Everyone in my family referred to him as Ripley-Believe-It-Or-Not. Both sobriquets contained an element of truth, which is not to suggest that Ripley was a sociopath, but rather that he had an ability to insert himself in other people's lives and make them feel like he belonged there. The believe-it-or-not part was self-evident.

People don't get scouted in Durham, New Hampshire, and Ripley was no scout. His sister lived in Boston, and he'd come to visit for her birthday. What she wanted, what she'd specifically asked him for as a present, was that they drive up to Durham so that he could see his niece, her daughter Rae Ann, in the role of Mrs. Gibbs. Ripley's sister believed her daughter had talent, and she believed her brother owed her the consideration of a look.

I hadn't known Ripley's niece before the play, and even after a slew of rehearsals and three performances I still wouldn't say I knew her. She played my mother-in-law, and like every other girl in that production, Rae Ann had wanted to be Emily and so held my success quietly against me. That she won the role of Mrs. Gibbs spoke in her favor, and that she was completely flat in the part was hardly her fault. It's tough for a nineteen-year-old to be successful as a middle-aged mother pantomiming the feeding of chickens. Ripley cut her plenty of slack and still, he never turned his eyes to her. He hugged her after the curtain call and told her she was magnificent, then sent her off to the cast party with her mother, saying he would be along shortly. He loitered in the hallway with his coat, and when a girl came along he asked her where he could find Emily.

Nineteen eighty-four was nothing like what Orwell had envisioned and still it was a world nearly impossible to explain. A strange man in a suit knocked on the door to the dressing room before I'd had the chance to change back into my own clothes, and when I stuck out my head he said he wanted to talk to me and could we go somewhere quiet for a minute? I said sure, like a child taking instructions from an adult, which was the case. A small rehearsal room down the hall had a piano in it and a couch and a couple of folding chairs. I knew no one would be in there so late. I opened the door and ran my hand over the cold cinder block wall, feeling for the light switch. What was I thinking? That's the part I can't retrieve.

But this is a story about luck, at least in the early years, and so my luck continued to hold. Bill Ripley had not come to rape or dismember. He sat down on one of the folding chairs, leaving the couch for me. He told me he was a director. They were casting a new movie and this movie had a part for a girl, a critical part, really, but they hadn't found the right person yet. They'd been looking for quite some time but they hadn't found her.

I nodded, wishing I'd thought to leave the door open.

"You might be the girl." He was looking at me hard, and because I'd just come offstage and was not feeling particularly shy, I stared back at him. "What I mean is, I'm pretty sure you are her. I need you to come out to L.A. and take a screen test. Can you do that?"

"I've never been to Los Angeles," I said, when what I meant was, my family went to Florida once for spring break when I was ten and that was the only time I'd been on a plane.

He wrote a number down on the back of a business card and told me he was staying with his sister in Boston, and that I should call him the next morning at nine.

"I'm in class at nine." I could feel myself starting to sweat in Emily's long white dress.

He looked at his watch. "They're going to wonder where I am." He stood up and held out his hand so I shook it. "Let's keep this between us for now," he said.

"Sure," I said, wondering who I shouldn't tell.

"Rae Ann is my niece." He answered my question as if I'd asked it.

"Oh." Rae Ann. That made me feel better somehow.

"Tomorrow," he said, and I said, "Tomorrow" like I was a myna bird.

I did not lie awake in my dorm room that night wondering if I'd get the part. I wondered how many quarters I'd need to call someone in Boston during peak rates. Where could I get enough quarters? I wondered how much a plane ticket to Los Angeles would cost in terms of pairs of pants hemmed, and then on top of that the cost of the taxi from the airport and the hotel. Of course all of that was taken care of, though not as quickly as one might think. Bill Ripley straightened everything out, for a while at least. I had dithered around trying to decide what to do with my life for such a long time that he stepped in and made the decision for me. I was going to be an actress.

"Show me where the decency is in that!" Nell shouts, and we all break up laughing.

All three of our girls are home now. Emily came back to the farm after she graduated from college, while Maisie and Nell, still in school, returned in March. It was an anxious spring for the world, though from our kitchen window it played out just like every other spring in northern Michigan: wet and rainy and cold, followed by a late heavy snow, a sudden warm spell, and then the spectacle of trees in bloom. Emily and Maisie and Nell ignored the trees and chose to chip away at their sanity with news feeds instead. I finally put an end to the television being on in the evening because after we watched it, none of us slept. "Turn your head in one direction and it's hopeless despair," I told them. "Turn your head in the other direction—" I pointed to the explosion of white petals out the window.

"You can't pretend this isn't happening," Maisie said.

I couldn't, and I don't. Nor do I pretend that all of us being together doesn't fill me with joy. I understand that joy is inappropriate these days and still, we feel what we feel.

As we moved into summer and blossoms gave way to fruit, our circumstances shifted from *Here are our daughters and we are so glad to have them home*, to *Here are our daughters, who spent their childhood picking cherries and know how to do the job when only a fraction of our regular workers have come this year for seasonal employment.* Their father identified the girls sprawled across the furniture pecking at their phones as the hand-pick crew he needed.

"I went to college so I wouldn't have to pick cherries," Nell said.

"College is closed," Joe said. "College can't protect you now."

3

"Good night, good night, good night," they sing, knocking against one another purposefully on the stairs. The three of them are younger when they're together. They regress.

"Mama's going to California to be a movie star," Nell says to her sisters. "And we'll still be locked up on the farm."

"At least someone got out," Emily says.

I promise to tell them all about it tomorrow.

Maisie yawns, stretching up her hands to touch the doorframe, Hazel at her heel. Hazel is some kind of yellow terrier with a crooked front leg and fine, irregular hair that stands up in patches. Maisie got her from the animal-control shelter where she worked during her second semester of veterinary school. The staff labeled the cages with folksy names—Opie and Sparky and Goober and Bear—subliminal promises of how good these dogs would be. Hazel had long been kenneled in a row of enormous brutes who bit the metal bars day and night in hopes of eating her, and Hazel in turn picked up so many bad habits that one of the staff had scrawled the word "WITCH" above her name with a fat black Sharpie. Those bad habits, along with the bum leg and what appeared to be mange, had rendered her unadoptable, and after several weeks at the shelter, Maisie saw the tag on Witch Hazel's kennel indicating her time was up. She kept going back to slip biscuits between the bars. Last biscuits.

"Watch your fingers," her supervisor had said when Maisie announced her plan to take Hazel home for the weekend. But as soon as she reached into the kennel the dog began to howl, disbelieving that good fortune could arrive so late in an unfortunate life. Students were counseled against the dangers of sentimentality but for that day Maisie chose to ignore the lesson, and the mangy little terrier thumped a grateful tail against her.

Emily comes back downstairs with her book, some manual about branch grafting. She says it knocks her out, by which she means puts her to sleep. Emily lives in the little house at the edge of the north apple orchard. She picks up a flashlight from the basket by the back door, the basket of flashlights and sock caps and mittens and bug spray.

"I'll walk you halfway," I tell her.

She laughs. She comes back and kisses me. Emily kisses me. "Good night," she says.

I watch from the window above the sink until I can no longer see her steady beam sweeping over the road, then I turn out all the lights and go upstairs.

Their father is sound asleep. Because he cannot wait for me, he's left the lamp on the nightstand burning and folded back the covers on my side of the bed. One hand is on his heart, as if the last thing he did was check to see if it was still beating, the other is out of the bed, his fingers nearly brushing the floor. Nothing can wake him in the summer. After dinner, he goes back out to the barn, saying he has just a few more things to finish, then winds up putting in a second day. I picture the farm as a giant parquet dance floor he balances on his head, the trees growing up from the little squares. The fruit that must be picked, the branches that must be pruned, the fertilizer and insecticide (just try growing cherries without it), the barn full of broken machinery along with the new tractor we can't afford and the goats that seemed like such a good idea five years ago when Benny first suggested them for weed management and cheese, the workers whose children are sick and the workers who need money to go home to see their children and the little house whose roof leaks and the stacks of twenty-pound plastic lugs with *Three Sisters Orchard* printed on the side, and me and Emily and Maisie and Nell, all of it is on him. We try to be helpful but it is his head this place rests on. He carries it with him to our bed at night.

I put on my nightgown and crawl in beside him, covering the hand that covers his heart. Live forever, I say to myself.

Veronica didn't get to go to the University of New Hampshire. She had to stay home because no one else was there to watch the boys. Her plan was to do two years of community college and then transfer her credits. Everyone has plans, and by the time we graduated from high school she wasn't telling me hers anymore. She was the one who started out with Jimmy-George, by which I don't mean sitting on the steps at the end of the hall, talking. He was older than us, twenty-two, though no one believed it. Veronica asked to see his driver's license when he told her and she still thought he was lying, just like the guys in the outlet stores thought his ID was fake and then sold him the beer anyway. He lived two towns over and was doing his student teaching. He said the kids in his class had laughed that first day of school when he wrote his name on the blackboard. Jimmy-George was going to be a high school math teacher, and that in itself made him a valuable asset because he did our math homework for us. He did other things. Six years older would be nothing later on, but at the time it was an unimaginable distance. We couldn't believe how lucky we were when he reached for us, an adult who played a kid onstage.

Veronica told me how she felt about him, and later she told me what they did. Two nights a week he came to her house after he'd finished rehearsal and she'd put the boys to bed. He would curl around her in her single bed so they could go to sleep like married people, then he would get up in the early dark and drive back to the room he rented and get ready for school, all before her mother finished her shift at the hospital. Veronica said that his eyes never left hers the entire time. She said she was pretty sure no one had ever really looked at her before, not in her entire life, and maybe that was true, but it was also true that that was just the way Jimmy-George looked at people. Onstage he looked at me like someone had dropped a giant Mason jar over us and we were alone in the world. He was the one who taught me how not to look away.

"We should be spending time together," he said one

night after rehearsal. "You know, be George and Emily, have a strawberry phosphate or something."

But we were George and Emily and Veronica. "I don't think so," I said.

"I thought you liked acting," he said. "I'm just talking about us being more convincing."

I told him that I thought we were pretty good already, when what I should have said was, Back up. He stood much closer when we weren't on the stage, when no one else was around.

He touched one finger to the side of my neck. "Chemistry," he said. "That's what George and Emily have."

I couldn't say he was wrong about that. I hedged for a couple of days before climbing into his car, telling myself this thing between us was all in the name of theater. We passed Mr. Martin in the parking lot one night while he was standing beneath a street light in a wool hunting jacket, smoking a cigarette. I could tell he was trying to calculate the potential for damage.

"Fifteen will get you twenty, Mr. Haywood," he said finally, his voice neither leering nor scolding, just a helpful piece of information passed along. Jimmy's last name was Haywood.

Jimmy-George removed his hand from my waist and laughed, so I laughed too, even though I had no idea what Mr. Martin was talking about. Years later, I heard the expression again on a set and it made perfect sense. Mr. Martin had been concerned for Jimmy Haywood's safety.

For a while we really did just run our lines in the back of his car, and then those lines were lightly punctuated with kissing. One night he asked if I knew a place we could stretch out, something I hadn't done before, something my body felt keenly attuned to wanting, something Veronica said was amazing. I had the keys to Stitch-It, and so I unlocked the door and took him up the stairs without turning on the lights, past the sewing machines and thread racks, past a thousand buttons and god only knew how many zippers hanging from oversized safety pins, right to a couch where my grandmother sometimes napped. Nobody caught us, and since Veronica was the only person in the world I would have told, I told no one. But god, it ruined everything: the rehearsals, the play, my grandmother's shop where I'd been the very happiest, and my best friendship. While the math teacher was pulling my sweater over my head, I failed to take into account that Veronica would still be able to read my mind.

I wish I'd thought to ask him why he picked us. I know he wasn't much more than a kid himself, but if high school girls were his thing, why did he feel the need to drive two towns over to see what was available? He had four classes of math students to choose from. But then of course I realized he must have been sleeping with the math girls, too. He was a good-looking kid, and he knew everything about eye contact, and he could act. Truly, he was the best George I ever saw. This could just as easily have been a story about my having slept with Jimmy-George Haywood who then went on to be a stupendously famous actor, though I'm pretty sure he went on to be a math teacher somewhere in New Hampshire.

I blame myself for what happened. I was hideously disloyal to the person I loved in order to be with a person I didn't love at all. But I was also sixteen, and as sure as fifteen will get you twenty, sixteen doesn't stand a chance against twenty-two.

Maybe I should have told my girls this part of the story, but they would have needed to hear it before they turned sixteen for the information to do them any good.

Joe lets us sleep in after all, or Maisie and Nell and I slept. On the far side of the orchard, Emily had set her alarm so that she could start the coffee and make egg sandwiches before she and her father meet for work. Emily, twenty-six, had been a senior in high school when she started saying she would come back after college and help us with the farm. She said that when we were ready to retire she would run the place herself.

"You can do anything in the world," I said, channeling my grandmother. "And you might want to do something else."

"You might want to do something else," my husband echoed, but what he meant was Yes and Please and Thank you. The farm is either the very paradise of Eden or a crushing burden of disappointment and despair manifested in fruit, depending on the day. I would love to leave my child Eden. The other stuff, less so.

"This isn't a monarchy," Maisie said. "It's not like you get the land because you're the oldest. What if I want to run the farm?"

"Then we run it together," Emily said. "That's easier anyway. Do you want the apples or cherries?"

Maisie's future was never going to be in fruit, but that didn't mean she wanted her sister to win. Even though no one would believe it now, Emily had once been the harbinger of misery for all of us. Nell certainly didn't want the farm. She'd been pricing tickets to New York since seventh grade. Of our three girls, only Emily found fascination in the profits of sweet cherries versus tarts. She paid attention to trees the way Maisie paid attention to animals and Nell paid attention to people. Even as a child, she was the one to notice the first traces of brown rot. Emily liked to work outside while her sisters slapped at mosquitos. She was good with her hands while they cut themselves on leaves. She liked to sit in the fruit stand and talk to the people who stopped to buy peaches and jam. Maisie and Nell did not go near the fruit stand.

But in her day, Emily had been a beast, a teenage girl so riven with hormones and rage that her two younger sisters decided it would be easier to just be good. Emily had raised sufficient hell for all of them put together. We worried that her devotion to the orchard might be some latent penance for bad behavior. She was trying to make it up to us long after we had ceased to be hurt.

"Take your time," we'd say when she talked about the farm. "You don't have to decide now."

But she had decided. She signed up for a horticulture major at Michigan State. She signed up for an agribusiness management minor. Her father shook his head when she told him about the minor. "Someone's been paying attention," he said.

When I go down the hall and find Maisie and Nell asleep in their twin beds, I see them both as they are and as they were: grown women and little girls. The forced-air heat blew weakly from floor vents on the second story before we updated the HVAC system, and every winter morning they begged to spend a single day warm in bed, and every morning I dragged them out, telling them to wear their bedspreads over their nightgowns and get dressed in front of the stove. Parts of the house date back to the 1800s. It was warm only in pockets. The girls referred to the *Little House on the Prairie* books as the stories of their lives.

But we are in the full glory of summer now—the windows open, the room bright, and still these daughters, twenty-four and twenty-two, sleep on.

"You promised your father," I say, because that's what gets them.

"Take Hazel out, please," Maisie says into her pillow.

When I go to lift the little dog from under her arm, Hazel shows me her teeth, even though she doesn't mean it. She, too, yearns for a day in bed. I carry her because her front leg doesn't work on stairs. I put her out the kitchen door and she squats beside my pot of geraniums then trots away.

Emily had been fourteen when she first informed me Peter Duke was her father. She'd been slamming around the house for weeks, her head bent beneath the weight of her interior darkness. When I asked what was wrong she said *nothing* in the same voice one would say *go fuck yourself.*

Where was everyone? It was early March and the snow was blowing sideways while I sat next to the fireplace with a pile of mending. Sometimes I wondered if the girls bit the buttons off their shirts just to give me something to do. I put my hands in my lap. "Where did you get that idea?"

Her eyes opened up as if she were finally fully awake. "You don't even deny it."

"Of course I deny it. I just wonder what could have made you think it."

"Because it's true."

"Emily, it's not true."

"How would you even know?"

I don't remember ever looking at my mother this way, like I could eat her down to the bone then wipe my bloody mouth on her hair. Emily was genuinely frightening, and at the same time I wanted to laugh for the sheer lunacy of it all. Fear and laughter: the two worst reactions in the absence of logic. "I would know because I would have been there."

"But you'd lie about it. You lie about everything."

A pause for reflection read as guilt, but the accusation was so strange I was having a hard time being nimble. "What did I lie about?"

"Knowing. Him." Plunge-plunge, like an ice pick.

"I never lied about that."

"Well, you never talk about it."

"That isn't the same thing as lying."

"Why won't you tell me?"

"Because there's nothing to tell."

"That's a lie."

"Emily, I'm not lying to you."

"Just give me his phone number."

"I don't have Duke's phone number."

"Of course you do! You just want to keep me from him. He has the right to know he has a daughter."

How many daughters must Duke have out there in the world? One wondered. "Your *father* has a daughter," I said. "Your father has three daughters. With me. Your mother." I went on to say that she should consider the feelings of her father who had conceived her, loved her and raised her, before setting out to construct a new origin story.

"Don't say *conceived*." She put her hands over her ears to block my voice retroactively. "That's disgusting."

"Think about this for a minute."

"I can find him myself." She was crying now and trying hard to stop.

I stood to go to her, my daughter who was losing her mind.

"Sit down!" She was screaming.

"Just tell me what's happened."

"I don't belong here! Maisie and Nell belong here, you and Daddy belong here, but I do not belong in northern *fucking* Michigan. I'm supposed to be with Duke."

Fire leapt off her, like the fire in the fireplace spitting and cracking behind me. The snow came down and covered the fields. I wanted to take my sweater off, wrap her up. I wanted to roll her around until the fire was out. "Honey, I knew Duke for one summer, years and years before you were born. I didn't know him very well then, and now I don't know him at all. He's not your father."

"Then what about my hair? How can you explain that?" Screaming.

Joe must have driven Nell to dance class. That's where they were. Maybe Maisie had gone along for the ride. The girls loved to be in the car when it was snowing. "Your hair?"

"Tell me I don't have Duke's hair." She held a hank of it up for me to see, dark and heavy and straight. I'd never had the thought before but her magnificent head of hair was not wholly dissimilar to Duke's.

"Your hair is beautiful and it's yours, not Duke's. Nothing in our lives belongs to Duke."

This scene goes on forever but I'll stop it here, the details best forgotten. Emily's belief that she should be living in Malibu with the movie star she deemed to be her father came over her like a fever. For days and even weeks it would recede, only to flare again at the times we were most vulnerable. She was telling me how sick she was of us, that she hated being a teenager, hated her body, didn't want to be stuck on a cherry orchard, that she had bigger ideas of the world. But she didn't have words for any of that, not even words she could say to herself. She could only experience the wracking pain of her circumstances, inflict it on us, and then demand that Duke was that pain's only solution. We all became so sick of it I considered tracking down Duke's brother Sebastian so that Duke could send her some sort of document of liberation, a headshot signed, "To Emily, I am not your father. Love, Peter Duke."

Joe took all of this better than I did, but what else was new? Joe took everything better than I did. Emily seemed able to treat him as her father while at the same time endlessly declaring that someone else was her father. She wanted them both. Two fathers and no mother would have been the dream. To some extent, Joe blamed himself for the whole situation. And to a lesser extent, I blamed him, because it had been Joe who unleashed Duke on our girls. I certainly had no intention of telling them I dated a movie star for a summer in my twenties before he was a movie star.

Had it been before or after we took the kitchen wall out to make a family room that Joe told the girls about Duke? It must have been after. Emily must have been twelve, which would mean that Maisie and Nell were more or less ten and eight. Maybe it was Christmastime.

I know it was winter. Maisie had dug *The Popcorn King* out of what we referred to as the movie basket. They had seen it who knew how many times before and that's exactly what made the experience appealing to them, the repetition, the pleasure of anticipating what came next. They chimed in on the best lines, *No BUTTER?* and cracked themselves up. Winters were so long, and we leaned into the movie basket and the books on the low shelves beneath the window to save us. Yes, this was definitely after the expansion because I remember standing at the wide white sink doing dishes while the three girls braided their hair into a single fat rope. Their conversation consisted of one of them telling the other two to hold still, and then another one complaining the others were pulling and would mess everything up. The movie's soundtrack became their soundtrack, the insistent violins that lagged half a beat behind Duke's feathery alto. Mostly his voice was lost to the water running in the sink and the girls' laughing, though every now and then I heard him sing the word *Popcorn!* quite distinctly. He'd done a lot of family movies after the cop show, after the astronaut movie, before he reinvented himself as a Very Serious Actor, though the popcorn movie was already old on the night of this particular viewing, and he was already a Very Serious Actor. We'd lost the cardboard sleeve to the VHS tape. This was the only one of the family movies in which he'd been made to sing and dance, and while he didn't do either of those things naturally, the immensity of his charisma provided sufficient cover.

I knew the movie as well as the girls did. I knew that we were at the scene where he was dancing on a floor covered in unpopped kernels, dancing and sliding, arms windmilling wildly, nearly falling and never falling, his perfect physicality overwhelming in its abandon. I used to watch that scene and wonder how many times they'd made him dance on popcorn. How many days did they ask him to do it again so that there would be enough footage to splice the number together? On that night I struggled to scrub a crust of lasagna off the bottom of a pan. *Baked-on, burnt-on mess.* What was that a commercial for? Some tool meant to free me from labor. I did not turn around to watch him in his bowler hat and pearl-gray suit. I was staring out the window above the sink. I did not turn towards his voice, nor, had I been facing in the direction of the television set, would I have turned away. Duke had been famous for as many years as we had been apart. Had every sight or sound of him sent me off on a pilgrimage of nostalgia or excoriation I would have lost my mind years before. We coexisted peacefully, Duke and I, or I coexisted.

Into this scene of braiding and scrubbing and movie

and dancing came my husband, stamping the snow from his boots. He stood behind the couch where our three girls were firmly tethered together as one daughter, Nell facing the television and Maisie and Emily each facing out to the side, the backs of their heads touching. They were thrilled by what they had accomplished, the end of the braid secured by a rubber band. Joe stood and watched the screen with them for a minute. The kernels beneath Duke's feet were just starting to pop and he scooped up handfuls and flung them into the air like snow. That was when Joe said, "You know your mother used to date him."

Imagine braiding the tails of three mice and then throwing in a cat. I don't think he realized their heads were fastened, or that they would all begin to scream and claw so violently in an attempt to separate themselves and get to me. I don't think Joe was thinking. He had seen Duke dancing on popcorn as often as the rest of us, but for whatever reason on that night he offered commentary. One of the girls, I'd bet it was Maisie, thought to tug off the rubber band, and in a matter of seconds they were apart, their long hair flashing into shields. They were loud in that piercing way of girls, and Joe, as if to amend his poor judgment, picked up the remote and paused the movie, thus silencing not the children but the topic of discussion. Duke froze there, the bowler nearly slipping off his loose, dark hair, his mouth open, his eyes half-closed in a moment of mock-sexual ecstacy I could have done without. Emily said that Daddy was making it up. Nell wanted to know if Duke and I had gone to school together. Maisie asked when he was coming to our house, the very thought of which lit the three of them from within, their favorite movie star soon to arrive on a winter night because why else would their father have picked this moment for the great reveal? *When is he coming?* they cried.

What was it Lear says at the end? *Never, never, never, never, never.*

We might as well have cut each girl a heavy slice of chocolate cake soaked in espresso, then stood back to watch them lick the plates. They were relentless. How had it happened, they wanted to know. Why hadn't I married Duke instead?

On that long ago night our girls were still years away from having boyfriends of their own. I tried to remember what I thought dating meant when I was their age: ice cream, movies, walking home from school, the dread and desire that surrounded the mystery of kissing. In summer stock, Duke slept in my bed because I had the infinitely superior room—a closet, a dresser, a window that looked out over Tom Lake, my own tiny bathroom with a shower we could just barely fit into together. We lay in that double bed and ran each other's lines. We lay in that bed. When ambition overcame us, we played tennis or swam in the lake. We got drunk after shows or got high. We ate the pita bread I kept in the nightstand for the times we were hungry and couldn't bear the thought of getting up. Sometimes he would go for coffee and bring it back to bed, or I would go. We were on the stage or in that bed, forgotten cigarettes burning down to the filters in the ashtray. We were dating.

My three little girls stared at me, paralyzed by expectation. Winter, and they had seen every movie in the basket three dozen times. It appalled them to think there was a story in this house they didn't know.

"We were in a play together," I said. Truth. And they already knew that for a brief time when I was young I had wanted to be an actress. We had a VHS of that as well.

"So you didn't *date* him," Emily corrected. "You knew him."

I shrugged. The girls believed we were so old then, their father and I, that they took into account we might not remember our own lives. "We dated while we were in a play."

He carried my books. He walked me home. We kissed.

When they finally went back to watch the end of the movie, Duke was no longer just the Popcorn King. He was the man who had once eaten ice cream with their mother. "Don't you want to watch with us?" Maisie asked.

"I've seen it," I said.

"That doesn't make any difference," she said. "It's good."

"Maybe it's upsetting to her," Emily said in a stage whisper, though it was Emily who insisted they start the movie over once it had ended because she wanted to be able to think about Duke as someone I knew in the first part of the film as well as the last. In the beginning, Duke is the banished King of Popcorn who returns in disguise so that he might overthrow the interloper and reclaim his rightful place. That always struck me as the most ludicrous part of the story, the idea that, despite the newsboy's cap and ragged jacket, anyone would fail to recognize Duke.

Nell looked away from the screen to see how I was holding up. She mouthed the words *I love you*, information not intended for anyone else.

Joe said it too, when, after more and more of the same, we at last wrestled our children into bed.

"I may have to kill you just to make sure it never happens again," I said to him, pulling my sweater over my head, that terrible moment when the warmest article of clothing comes off.

"I don't think a mistake of that magnitude could be made twice."

"Let's not find out." I was shaking with cold and he took me in his arms.

"I had no idea they would care," he said. "Or at least I didn't think they would care that much."

"Or you didn't think at all. You just said it."

I could feel his chin nodding against the top of my head. "That's what it was."

The high tide of Duke hung around the house for weeks after that, and while it slowly receded, it never went away. The girls began spending their allowance on *People* magazine, Duke being a reliable fixture for paparazzi: at the opening of the Met season, coming home from the gym with a duffel bag slung over his shoulder, with an admirable mutt on the beach, with an admirable starlet on the beach. The girls started watching his cop show, *Rampart*, in reruns. They devoted themselves to the Duke movies that were already in the basket because I refused to buy more. Their favorite was a boneheaded remake of *The Swiss Family Robinson* called *Swiss Father Robinson* which featured a mostly shirtless Duke on a gorgeous desert island, his snug pants tattered just above the knee. His wife claims that Duke, an internationally famous architect, scarcely knows his own children, and so she stays in Zurich while he takes their four adorable offspring on a sailing adventure by himself. After the brief inconvenience of a shipwreck, he builds his family a chalet in the trees, with a slide that drops the plucky little ones into the bay when they need a bath. A bright red parrot with a yellow breast sits on his shoulder while he splits open coconuts for breakfast, the toddler secured to his back with a sarong. Despite his complete lack of experience, Duke turns out to be a miracle of a father, teaching the children to read and love the land and master carpentry. The most disappointing scene in the movie is when his wife finally shows up to rescue them from paradise. Disappointment, the children learn early on, is embodied by the mother. Two years later, Emily decided Duke was her father, Maisie decided Emily had been possessed by Satan, and Nell decided she wanted to be an actress who would never come home again, though that might have happened anyway. Thanks to his ubiquitous presence in the world, the man I'd spent a summer with took up residence in our home, and still I thought of him remarkably little.

4

Hazel's yellow head pops up in the tall grass. She's come back to wait for Maisie but when she sees me she decides I am enough. Together we take the dirt road past the wall of hemlocks and white pines to the barn. The cherry trees are so burdened that I don't know how we'll get the fruit picked before it rots. Most of the crew trailers are empty, three families down from the usual ten or twelve. Joe has divided the acres and given everyone their parcel to work. We wave to each other at a great distance. I leave a tray of sandwiches at the sorting table in the morning and pick up the empty platter at night. Emily's ever-helpful boyfriend, Benny Holzapfel, is no help at all since he is working sixteen-hour days on his own family's farm. Holzapfel—meaning crab apple, or the crabby people who hang out near sour little apples—is a selling name but does not suit our warm and generous friends. You could spend years in a New York apartment never knowing the people who live two feet away from you, but live on an orchard in Michigan and you will use the word *neighbor* to refer to every person for miles. You will rely on them and know their children and their harvest and their machinery and their dogs. The Whitings have an old German shepherd named Duchess, though she could have just as easily been Princess or Queenie. Despite her wolfish appearance, she is a sweet girl. Duchess has been known to walk all the way to our back door in the summer. I give her a bowl of water and some biscuits, and after a nap on the warm flagstones, she heads off again.

Past the pond there is a place where the two farms touch, ours and the Holzapfels. My husband used to joke that someday one of our girls would marry a Holzapfel, but when Benny started showing up in our kitchen his senior year of high school, Joe dropped the joke for fear of scaring the boy away. Since then my husband has whispered his dreams to me alone, in the winter, in our bed late at night: Emily and Benny would marry and join the farms. We would fix up the little house, put on a proper porch, a new kitchen, a real master bedroom, everything on one floor. Joe and

I would move to the little house and give our house to Emily and Benny so they could have children here, children who may one day marry the children of the Otts or the Whitings nearby, weaving together an ever greater parcel, because even if a person can't work the land they have, they will still want more. It has been years since Emily was bewitched by Duke, and years since the enchantment was broken and our daughter returned, and while we love her and rely on her, we've never completely gotten over being afraid of her. She says that the farm is her life, and of course she's going to stay here. She says it with Benny standing beside her in the kitchen, both of them barefoot, shucking corn for dinner.

Benny has been riding his bike down the path that links our farms since he was a child, and by the time he was in high school he was showing up in our kitchen to talk to Joe about his 4-H projects. We called Benny the Man with the Plan—heirloom apples, high-density apples, club apples—he made a dinner presentation out of every pamphlet the Michigan Farm Bureau sent. The constant chatter about apples was mostly cover for his nerves because clearly it was Emily he had come to see. Even before he left for college he made it clear he was coming back to work with his parents. Benny hadn't missed the fact that other lives were available to him, it was just that the choice he liked best was the one that sprang to life beneath the tires of his bike, the one that might include Emily if she were interested.

But Emily had always been interested in the farm, and she had always been interested in Benny, and over time those two interests slowly pushed Duke aside. Or maybe it didn't have anything to do with the farm, maybe she just outgrew him. She came home from East Lansing to work the harvest every summer. She said we needed to think about building our own cold storage so that we wouldn't have to outsource refrigeration, and that maybe we could build a big one and split the cost with our neighbors. The investment would pay for itself when we started selling more sweets for the fresh market.

Where was Duke in all these plans?

He was nowhere.

Hazel heads up the hill to the cemetery where generations of my husband's people are buried behind a low iron fence, and for whatever reason I follow the dog. A plush vegetation is knitted over all the graves, and I think of how meticulously Joe's aunt had kept things here, but this is not the summer for weeding. The cemetery is the highest point on the property and would have been the logical site for a house, the way it overlooks the trees and the barn and all the way to the edge of the lake, but those first settlers gave the best land to their dead, the very first a two-year-old named Mary. One by one they followed her up the hill until twenty-nine of them were resting beneath the mossy slabs, and there they wait for us to join them. That's what life was like back in the day, you buried your children, your husband, your parents right there on the farm. They had never been anywhere else. They had never wanted to be anywhere else.

I look down from the hill until I can see Emily in her green Michigan State cap, and a minute later I see Maisie and Nell walking out to the barn. Hazel picks up the distant scent of Maisie in the breeze and darts off to thank her again for her life.

Benny Holzapfel had long professed his faith in fresh-market sweet cherries as part of a healthy system of cash flow. He was still a sophomore in high school when he talked my husband into pushing out the plums at the east end of the upper orchard and putting in forty acres of dark sweets. I hadn't been in favor of taking the advice of our fifteen-year-old neighbor at the time. I said we needed more trees like we needed more goats, which had also been Benny's idea. You can't shake sweet cherries mechanically. You have to take them by hand and they have to come off perfectly, as if every last one was employed by the Michigan tourism board.

Tarts are frozen and later boiled down to juice or jam or sold for pies. They're dried into sturdy cherry-raisins and no one cares what they looked like. The problem with tarts is that distributors make a down payment on delivery and don't pay the balance until they sell them, and because the cherries are already frozen or dried, there's never any rush. You could work yourself to death bringing in tarts in July and not see your profit until December, or next July. Sweets, on the other hand, don't freeze. Early in the summer they last two weeks in the cooler, and by the end of the season when the sugar is high the turnaround is considerably faster. Of course the brines become maraschinos, and some other sweets wind up in yogurt, but most of them we sell through an agricultural co-op for cash, and the co-op in turn sells them to grocery stores and CSAs. The money we make off those pretty cherries put Nell through the University of Michigan and is now subsidizing Maisie's veterinary education.

Thank you, Benny Holzapfel.

"So, Mr. Ripley has asked you to audition for a film," Emily prompts once the four of us are in a row of trees picking cherries, buckets hanging from our necks. Emily is tall like her father, strong enough to hoist full lugs all day long. Maisie is smaller than her older sister, though by no means small, and her curls give her extra stature. Nell is like me, or Nell is like I was. It's as if the genetic material from which these girls were made diminished with every effort, so that the eldest daughter is strapping and the middle is middling and the youngest is a wisp. They might as well have been three bears. I flick away a tiny green inchworm. "Why am I telling you this part?"

"Because you're putting together the whole picture," Nell says. "Telling us everything you previously kept from us."

"You need to go back and get a hat," I say to Nell.

She touches the top of her head, surprised. She was still half-asleep when she left the house. "I will at the first intermission."

What Ripley wanted to convey on that phone call, which cost me seven dollars and eighty-five cents in change and made me late for American History, was that he was worried about his niece finding out that he was asking me to audition. "My sister doesn't know about this particular movie. She wouldn't be happy to find out a part for someone Rae Ann's age had been given to the girl standing next to Rae Ann onstage."

Had he given me a part? I didn't ask.

"So when you leave town it would be better if you

said you had a family emergency, a funeral or something. Tell her your grandmother died."

I felt like he had stuck me with a pin. "I'm not going to tell her my grandmother died."

"Think of someone else then." Ripley's voice was incapable of concealing boredom.

Ripley-Believe-It-Or-Not asked for my parents' phone number, which I gave him, and while I was adding up how many skirts I'd have to sew to pay for the trip, the production company bought me a ticket. I was twenty years old but Ripley's assistant made the arrangements with my parents because I didn't have a phone. My parents assumed Ripley had told me that, but Ripley wasn't a man to deal in itineraries. When I called my grandmother and asked if I could borrow the money from her, I found out the problem had already been solved. My family thought it was a wonderful idea for me to leave school in the middle of the semester to go to California at the behest of a man I didn't know. I thought it was pretty swell myself, not because I dreamed of being an actress—that part of the equation was still inaccessible to me—but because it felt like I finally had a direction to go in, and that direction was west. All of New Hampshire sinks into despair in March anyway so no better time to leave. As soon as my grandmother heard the news she kicked her sewing machine into overdrive, putting together what she referred to as my ingenue's trousseau: dresses, skirts, a swimsuit coverup to match the swimsuit she ordered me from L.L. Bean. She saved this from being the chapter in which I arrived at LAX in a pair of duck boots and my dark-green Loden coat with the barrel toggles.

The buckets around our necks hang from canvas straps, and when they're full we empty them into the lugs. When we have filled enough lugs, Joe heaves them onto the flatbed of the green John Deere Gator and drives them to the barn.

"So, California," Nell says, nudging. This is the part of the story she's invested in.

I worry she's getting too much sun and give her my hat, which she tries to bat away. "It's too late for me. Save yourself." I drop it on her head.

Nell accepts it because, unlike her sisters, she doesn't like to argue. "I want to hear about the audition and then I want to hear about the movie."

She thinks I have something to teach her but I don't. Nell doesn't dominate a room or stand on a chair to sing. She is the one who watches. She has the kind of naturalness Ripley often accused me of having, an ability to be so transparent it's impossible to turn your eyes away. She works at her craft constantly. Even picking cherries, I swear I can see her thinking about how other people might pick cherries. And that is the difference between us: I was very good at being myself, while Nell is very good at being anyone at all.

"It wasn't interesting," I say.

"Humor us," Emily says. "We're working."

I try to explain. "I learned how to act from a State Farm agent in New Hampshire when I was in high school. Other people did too much, so by doing very little I stood out. Mr. Martin needed an Emily because all the Emilys were awful. By not being awful, I looked pretty good. I think Bill Ripley was in a similar situation. Every actress he'd auditioned had been acting up a storm and he needed someone simple in the part. Simple was my specialty."

"Why are you selling yourself short?" Emily asks, throwing a cherry at me. Maisie leans over and parts the grass with her hands, and when she finds the cherry she pops it in her mouth. We do not waste sweet cherries. "If one of us said that you'd smack us in the back of the head and make us do positive affirmations in front of the mirror."

"I made you do positive affirmations one time, *one time*," I tell her, "and it was good for you."

"Maybe it would be good for you, too," Emily says.

"But I'm not being self-deprecating. I'm telling you, I had a genuine talent for being myself, and for a while it worked. In fact, it probably worked better in film than it did onstage."

"You're talking like we haven't seen the movie a hundred times," Nell says. "You were really good."

I shrug. "It's like being able to sing one song perfectly. It's a great trick, but it's only going to get you so far."

Go back to New Hampshire, to Bill Ripley sitting in that darkened university theater beside his sister. Ripley wasn't new to the game, and when he saw me he understood what he was looking at: a pretty girl who wasn't so much playing a part as she was right for the part she was playing. Unlike his niece, I knew how not to ruin things.

When I got off the plane in Los Angeles, a deeply tanned man in a black suit held up a clipboard with my name on it. He took the little duffel bag from my hand and walked me out to an honest-to-god limousine double-parked in front of the terminal. You could have knocked me over with a feather, as my grandmother liked to say. Had he driven me around the airport and dropped me off in the exact same spot, and I had flown back to New Hampshire without ever seeing anything else of California, it would have been worth it because one day I'd be able to tell my children that I had ridden in a limousine. I rolled down the tinted window so that anyone straining to see who was in the back of that car would see it was me, basking in sunshine.

The hotel had a swimming pool. A small gift basket in my room contained fruits so foreign to me that I didn't know how to eat them. A note from Ripley read *Welcome! Please sign for all your meals at the hotel*, which was nice enough but hardly the same as *Welcome! Pick you up for dinner at 7.* The hamburger I ordered from room service was brought to me beneath a great silver dome which the waiter whisked away with a flourish. As far as I could tell, everything in California was something out of a movie. I ate the fifteen-dollar hamburger in a fluffy white bed and practiced my lines. The next morning a different driver in a different limousine drove me to a soundstage at Warner Brothers. For two hours people dressed me, undressed me, and dressed me again. I sat in a fancy barber's chair while a Black man wearing a pink T-shirt that fit him so exactly I was sure he'd had it tailored, took off the makeup I had so thoughtfully applied that morning and painted a whole new face on top of my face. When he wanted me to lift my chin or turn to the left, he held his finger in front of my face. "Follow my finger," he said, and so I did.

“Eyebrows?” he asked the man sitting in a chair beside mine, reading a script.

The man looked at me in the mirror, then he looked at the makeup artist. “Hold off,” he said.

A woman with hair as fine and colorless as cornsilk and no eyebrows at all brushed out my hair, then picked it up and poured it through her hands again and again. “Look at this,” she said to her colleagues. “It’s like a shampoo commercial.”

I kept thinking of that scene when Dorothy and her friends get spruced up before they’re taken to meet the Wizard. *Pat, pat here, pat, pat there, and a couple of brand new straws. That’s how we keep you young and fair.*

Merry Old Land of Oz.

When their considerable efforts were complete and I had been transformed into someone who looked like my more attractive first cousin, I was taken onto the set where I stood in front of a white backdrop. The man who’d been sitting in the barber chair next to mine took my picture. His praise was so obsequious that I first felt embarrassed for myself and then felt embarrassed for him. Another man came in with a small camera on a tripod and had me say my name (Lara Kenison) and the name of the film (*Singularity*) and the part I was reading for (Lindsay). When all that was done, they took me into the set's open space where Ripley was waiting with everyone else.

Nell's hands drop from the branches and she leaves them hanging by her sides. Idle hands, I start to say—an old family joke—but stop myself. She is standing beside me in a smocked dress covered in daisies, a dress with big pockets that had once been mine and had then been Emily's, then Maisie's. Nell's eyes are bright with terror.

"Weren't you terrified?" she whispers.

Maisie and Emily stop. All three girls watch me as I try to remember. This was a very long time ago. I look around that vast white space. Ripley is there along with the famous actress who is playing my mother and the less-famous actor who is playing her boyfriend. People with boom mics and giant lights and cameras on dollies are there, silently adjusting the angles of their equipment. The two actors and I are sitting at a table that is meant to stand in for a dining room table, and we're laughing because that's what the scene calls for. For all the times I've ever been onstage, I've never been asked to laugh before, and the laughter comes easily. I had been so afraid that day I read for Emily in high school, but when I look around for that fear now it isn't there. I understand that all I have to do is try not to act, and that's easy because I have no idea how to act. It's the reason Ripley brought me out to California.

"No," I tell my daughters. "I'm not afraid."

I don't know where I got the idea that if they liked me I'd just stay in California and make the movie, but as soon as the screen test was finished they put me in the car and returned me to the airport with my duffel, even though I hadn't packed my duffel before I left the hotel. I took the red-eye to Boston and a shuttle van back to Durham. I would have three hours to sleep before sociology.

I set my alarm and crawled into my single bed, thinking about that limousine. My roommate was sound asleep and I wasn't going wake her up to tell her, but the limousine was the thing I couldn't get over.

Two weeks later my mother called me on the hall phone and told me they needed me back in L.A.

"Did I get the part?" I had already felt bad about not getting the part. I had already gotten over feeling bad.

"Mr. Ripley said they need a second test."

"That's a lot of money to spend when they've already seen me."

"I think they have the money," my mother said.

And so back I went, this time sliding into the long

black car like someone who was used to it; the first time is luxury, the second time privilege.

The next morning Ripley and the casting director met me at a swimming pool on the lot. One of the chaise longues was occupied by a blonde in a red-and-white lifeguard tank suit. She looked up from her magazine and waved so I waved back. The water was dazzling in the sunshine. Movie-swimming-pool-water. Did studio employees swim here on their lunch break, or was this where they made movies in which people swam? Ripley and the casting director had a woman with them, older than me but not old. She was all smiles and solicitude: How was my flight? Had I gotten something for breakfast? Could I believe this gorgeous day?

"We need to see you swim," Ripley said.

"Seriously?" Right away I wondered how cold the water was because that's the first thing a person from New Hampshire thinks about when someone starts talking about swimming.

"Do you know how?"

I was in every sense still young and I was trying to put it all together. "Sure I do, but wouldn't it have been easier to just call and ask me?"

The casting director laughed and Ripley nodded. "Sure, but we've got to see you do it. Some people don't look good when they swim. Other people do."

I wanted to tell them I'd been a counselor at Camp Huckins for my last two summers of high school, that I'd completed the Red Cross lifesaving course which included a half-mile open-water swim in a lake that was not warm. I taught the water safety class after that. I had the certificate though somehow I knew they could care less. "My suit's back at the hotel."

The woman who was with them, the one who was a little older than me, smiled again. "We've got plenty of suits," she said. "Come on, I'll take you over to wardrobe."

"Take your time," Ripley said. "We'll wait."

Of course, if some girl takes you to a room and starts telling you how cute this bikini is going to look on you, you figure it out. I thought of the sturdy navy one-piece my grandmother had bought, sitting in my duffel back at the hotel, the tags still on, and felt a surge of rage for having let myself be so duped. When I went back to the pool I didn't say a word to any of them. I went to the diving board, bounced hard and high twice, then split the bright blue water with my hands. I did three laps with racing turns. Those fuckers wanted to see if I could swim? I'd show them how to swim.

They didn't tell me I'd gotten the part until I was back in New Hampshire, then said I'd need to be on the set in four weeks. The plane ticket for my third trip out was first class, which, as far as experiences go, beat the limousine by a mile. I was given a union membership and a small furnished apartment. Ripley bought me a pair of sunglasses and told me to wear them whenever I was outside or I'd get crow's feet. The girl who'd been tasked with taking me to wardrobe was named Ashby, and now it was Ashby's job to pick me up in the mornings and keep an eye on me on the set. Ashby's job was to make the weird new things seem vaguely normal, and she was good at it. Ashby wanted to be an actress.

Whatever talent I had for transparency, for smallness, was suited to the camera, where I channeled the memory of Veronica's remarkable eyebrows and was subsequently praised for my subtle insight. I knew how to smile just a little and then look away while I pushed my hair behind my ears. The cinematographer couldn't get over the fact that my ears weren't pierced. He told me it was better than being a virgin. I didn't tell him the only reason they weren't pierced was because the girl in line ahead of me at the mall had fainted when they punched her earlobe with the little gun and no one thought to catch her. You never know in life what's going to serve you; my particular magic was being from New Hampshire with hair that wasn't dyed and ears that were unpierced. I agreed to wear a two-piece but wouldn't take my top off, and while I understand that

that can be a tough combination to find, it wasn't exactly the same as acting.

Ripley had me sign with an agent who was a friend of his, and the agent negotiated a contract for $45,000, a fortune to a girl who had so recently scrambled to find change for the pay phone. Not long after I arrived, the filming was delayed because the famous actress who played my mother twisted her ankle while hiking down a trail in Topanga Canyon. She said she'd seen a snake. Ashby told me if anyone else had sprained their ankle this early in production they would have been replaced, but the famous actress was pretty much what this movie had going for it. There were only three weeks left in the semester so I asked if I could go back to school, but everyone agreed that I could not. If the actress's ankle took a sudden turn for the better, they wouldn't want to have to wait on me. People in Hollywood thought, and maybe rightly, that New Hampshire was near Mongolia. As a consolation, my agent got me a Diet Dr Pepper commercial and one for Red Lobster. They were the kind of national spots real actors would have sold their mothers to get. I drank a Diet Dr Pepper, showed off my earlobes and opened a bank account. Ripley lent me a car because directors have extra cars—a little green MG convertible that was older than I was. If this was work, then I was made for it.

The fact that the release date kept getting pushed back wasn't a problem as far as I was concerned. They decided they needed a winter scene, a flashback, but the famous actress was so famous by then that no one could find a place in her schedule, and even when she did have time and they found the snow they also had to find more money because the winter scene wasn't in her contract. That threw them off at least another year, it might have been two. There was some problem with postproduction, and then a hang-up with the distribution, none of which was explained to me. Understanding what became of the film wasn't part of my job, and I didn't care because I liked L.A. All that sunshine agreed with me. My agent got me two seasons on a forgettable sitcom called *The Finnegans* along with some more commercials. I had work, a place to live. I went to parties on the beach and ran around with boys who wanted to be movie stars. I got to go dancing. I got out of New Hampshire.

Nell sits down in the grass. "I can't stand this anymore," she says.

Emily leans over and puts a hand on her sister's head. "What?"

"The whole thing," Nell says. "That someone just knocked on your door and gave you the part in this really great movie, and when the movie didn't come out you still got jobs. You were making money even if you weren't making art. I mean, I understand you had to go swimming first and that wasn't great but did you even really want it?"

What had I wanted? To fly on a plane? To get out of New Hampshire. I sit down in the grass beside my daughter. "I did, I guess. By the time the movie started shooting I wanted it, but not in the same way you would have wanted it. I get that."

"I want to go on an audition. I want to act. I want to get the hell out of this orchard. It's like the universe conspired to make you an actress and the universe conspired to make me pick cherries."

"But you do that really well," Maisie says to her. "You have an excellent technique."

It is sentimental and useless to tell someone you would gladly give them your past because the past is nontransferable, and anyway, I would have wanted to give her only the good days. When seen through Nell's eyes it's hard not to think those good days were wasted on me, and that she would have done a better job of it. "We should stop this. There are plenty of other things to talk about. Or we can talk about nothing. Or we can go back to podcasts for a while." We could listen to podcasts until the hour of our death and not make a dent in the stories that are available to us.

"You can't stop," Emily says. "We haven't even gotten to the part that matters yet."

"The part that matters?" I ask, though I know.

"Duke. The whole reason you're telling us about the past is that you're eventually going to get to Duke."

"He isn't the reason for the past," Maisie says darkly.

Nell rests her head on her knees. "Go ahead. I'm not shutting us down. I'm sulking. There's a difference. I want you to keep going."

"Keep going while acknowledging that life is unfair and it should have been you in the movie even though you were still more than a decade away from being born," Maisie says.

Nell nods against her knees. "That's all I'm asking for."

"I have no interest in making you miserable." If the story was going to end, this wouldn't be a bad place to end it.

"The circumstances of my life are making me miserable, not the story. It's not the same thing even when it feels like the same thing." Nell flops back in the grass, spreading out her arms like a starfish, like a girl for whom hope is lost. The next thing I know we are all lying in the soft and very green grass, staring up through the branches and cherries and leaves at the Michigan sky, little clouds tumbling high above us. How many years has it been since we have lain in this grass together, beneath these trees, the four of us, discussing which of the clouds were duckies and which were bunnies?

"You should have been famous," Nell says finally. "I think that's what kills me."

I raise myself up on my elbows, taking a moment to admire the sun in my daughters' hair. "Famous? Are you serious?"

They stir the grass very slightly with their nodding heads.

I lift up my hand to the lushness of trees. "Look at this! Look at the three of you. You think my life would have been better spent making commercials for lobster rolls?"

At that moment Benny comes flying down between the rows, riding his same old bike from high school. Hazel sounds the alarm but we scramble into seated positions too late. He has seen us in repose.

Benny skids to a stop. "You're sleeping? It's not even ten o'clock in the morning."

We all know he's come to find his girlfriend's father and not his girlfriend. He wants to borrow a saw or a spool of wire, or he's come because Joe has called and asked for help fixing something none of us would know how to fix. Benny is thin because he doesn't take time to eat and his hair is a mop held up by a rubber band because he doesn't take time to cut his hair.

I wave at him. "We're solving the problems of the world."

He gets off his bike long enough to kiss Emily, and we appreciate this: Maisie, whose vet school boyfriend is stuck with his own family in Oregon; Nell, who has no boyfriend; me, who loves love.

"Don't let your father see you like this," Benny says, by which he means asleep mid-morning. He doesn't understand that it's the weight of the past that's pinned us there, and before we can explain he rides off again.

We should get up. We should get back to the trees, but we don't. We sit and watch Benny fly away, our heads still full of movies.

5

In this summer which can at times be mistaken for the end of the world, we are the ones who pick the fruit and send the fruit to the processor and tie up the branches and take the goats out to eat the weeds. We work from the moment we wake until we close our eyes at night. Sometimes one of us says something about how it would be fun to watch a movie but it never happens. We fall asleep with books in our hands. I fall asleep with a threaded needle in my hand, sewing face masks out of pillowcases. And then in the morning the whole thing starts again and we are standing between the rows of trees, telling stories to pass the time. Oh, how we miss the people who have worked on this farm year after year, generation after generation, the kids who went to school with our kids for half the year, every year, from the time they were little, always leaving and coming back, until they come back with kids of their own.

Emily's future, the one in which her father and I grow old and she takes over the farm, has been decided. Maisie's veterinary classes at Michigan State are online but she finds no shortage of practical application for her education in this neck of the woods. She takes all comers: helpfully administering deworming paste on one farm, castrating the spring kids and lambs on another, and giving Hazel a multitude of physicals. Neighbors a mile away call in the middle of the night to ask if she can turn a breeched foal, and she does, then delivers it. "Turns out I'm better than nothing," she says, walking in the back door the next morning, bloody and reeking of afterbirth.

But Nell has no such opportunities, no breeched foal equivalents. She spent her last spring of college picking cherries and reading plays in her childhood bedroom. She and her friends balance their laptops on stacks of books and practice monologues for one another. Because they want to act and to learn about acting any way they can, she begs for my stories even though they are wildly out of date. Even though they wind up depressing the hell out of her.

"What was it like?" she asks me again.

It was like being a leaf in a river. I fell in and was carried along.

Nell begins for me. "So you left Los Angeles and went to Tom Lake," she says.

We are back on our feet again, back to work. "I went to New York first. New York and then Tom Lake."

Emily shook her head. "Los Angeles, Tom Lake, and then New York."

These girls are so certain about the things they do not know. "New Hampshire, California, New York, Michigan, New Hampshire, New York, Michigan. I promise you."

When three years had passed and the movie still wasn't finished, I wondered if it wasn't time to stop relying on the charms of my unpierced ears and take some acting classes.

Ripley shook his head. "You'll ruin yourself," he said.

It had been a long time since we'd seen each other and I'd called him up, looking for advice. We were sitting out by the pool behind his house, our teak lounge chairs shaded by a giant red umbrella. It was a Tuesday or a Saturday, March or October. That was the problem with L.A., I could never remember. "You're telling me no one here takes acting classes?"

"You're fresh, unspoiled," he said. "That's your thing. People take acting classes to learn how to do what you're already doing."

"So by studying acting I'll spoil my unspoiledness?"

"Exactly." He was drinking Perrier with crushed ice and lime. A Hispanic woman came out of the house to put a bowl of kumquats on the table between us, then went back without a word.

"I just want . . ." I began. But I had no idea what I wanted. All I knew for certain was that the day was hot and the pool looked like heaven.

"What?" Ripley asked. "To be a movie star?"

I smiled. "Swimming pools, movie stars."

Ripley felt some responsibility for me, I guess, having brought me there to be in a movie that was sitting in a can. Still, he offered up his next sentence with hesitation. "I know a guy," he said. "They're starting to put together a production of *Our Town*."

Just that fast I felt the words rise up in me—clocks ticking and sunflowers and new-ironed dresses. They were always there, like some small animal hibernating in my chest. I said nothing.

"You could try," he said, making it clear that my impending disappointment would not be on him.

"Where?" I popped a kumquat in my mouth the way bored girls in L.A. will do. The sourness was akin to being electrocuted but I betrayed nothing. Maybe I was a better actress than I thought.

"New York." Then, a kumquat later, added, "Broadway. They've signed Spalding Gray for the Stage Manager."

"No!" Nell says.

"I didn't get the part."

"You tried out for *Our Town* on Broadway with Spalding Gray!"

"Spalding Gray wasn't there when I auditioned and I didn't get the part."

Emily lifts up a branch and peers beneath it, trying to decide if it needs to be tied. "I'm starting to understand something here," she says, and all of us think she's talking about the tree. "Every thing leads to the next thing."

Maisie stops to look at her sister. "That's called narrative. I guess they don't teach you that in hort school."

"I understand *narrative*, idiot, but when you see it all broken down this way, step by step, I don't know, it's different." Emily looks at me. "Your grandmother asks you to register people for a play and you wind up starring in the play, which gives you the nerve to try out for the same play in college, which means that Ripley gives you a part in his movie, but the movie doesn't come out, so you wind up in New York to try out for the play again—"

"But you don't get the part," Maisie says.

"And so you go to Michigan," Nell says, "which is how you get to us."

"It's just that I thought this was going to be a story about Duke," Emily says, her dark braid down her back, the bill of the Michigan State cap shading her eyes. "And then I thought you were just taking us on some wild-goose chase to amuse yourself."

It's still there, though you have to tune your ear in order to hear it: the last hissing ember of Emily's bygone rage and desire.

"It is a story about Duke," I say, taking in a deep breath of northern Michigan in the summer, the smell of the trees, of these three girls. Nothing will ever be like it.

"It's about Duke and it's not," Nell says.

"That's right," I say, nodding. "Yes and no."

I went to New York expecting to win. There was no George at the audition. An assigned reader sat to the left of the director's table and read George's lines, Mrs. Webb's lines, the Stage Manager's lines. When they called me back the second day, a few other actors were loitering nervously, though not Spalding Gray. We read scenes together, testing our chemistry. I had never felt so comfortable, so certain that I was an actress. The next time I saw Ripley I would thank him for talking me out of acting classes. I wore barrettes to keep the hair out of my face so the casting director could see my lovely little ears. I wore my UNH sweatshirt. When I went to leave the second day, the five men in the audition studio all stood to shake my hand. The last one double-checked to make sure he had the name of the hotel where I was staying. I went back to that hotel room to wait by the phone, and two hours later it rang. A man was asking if I could meet him at the Algonquin the following afternoon so that we could discuss the play.

I said sure. I asked when.

"What you need to remember is that everything's a fix," he told me at our little table in the corner of the very dark bar. His name was Charlie. Gray suit, a white shirt, no tie. I remembered the suit from the audition. He had a good tailor—a scant quarter-inch of shirt cuff showed beneath his jacket sleeve. "They say they want someone new but you're *too* new. If the movie was out, you'd be a shoo-in. Ripley says you're terrific in it, by the way. We certainly thought you were terrific in the audition."

I'd been formulating a brief acceptance speech in my head in which I expressed my excitement and gratitude, but Charlie seemed to be telling me I wasn't going to need it. Is that what he was telling me? I refused to believe his message was clear. Then the waitress arrived at our table and I stumbled over my choice of beverage: a Coke would make me look young, but a Jack and Coke would make me look even younger, a kir might make me look like an actress but maybe one who was trying too hard not to care. In my sudden panic I defaulted to Perrier with crushed ice and lime, which made me look like a Californian, which was the last thing I wanted to look like. "The movie will be out by the time the play opens," I said, my voice small.

Charlie shrugged, by which he meant what did I know about release dates? He was right, of course. That's when it occurred to me that I was supposed to sleep with him. He'd brought me to a dark hotel bar to talk about getting the lead in a Broadway play, which, sorry as he was, he wasn't going to be able to give me. Or maybe he could. I imagined the key was already in his pocket. I went through my options quickly, a feeling not dissimilar to my drink order: I could be indignant or offended, or I could just follow him to the elevator. Didn't everybody have to sleep with somebody eventually in this business? Would I sleep with him if it meant I'd get to play Emily on Broadway opposite Spalding Gray?

Yes. Yes I would.

"Listen, you're great," he said, resting his hands

on the white tablecloth just in front of our flickering candle. They were nice enough hands—no wedding ring—at least I would be spared that additional guilt. "But there's too much money involved. You've got to be able to sell tickets."

"Spalding Gray sells tickets."

"Well, you've got to be able to help out Mr. Gray."

I put my hands on the table as well. I kept them on my side of the candle but I thought they made my intention perfectly clear without looking like I was hosting a seance. He was twice my age, give or take. I looked at him the way Jimmy-George used to look at me. The way he used to look at Veronica. "Tell me what I need to do."

Then Charlie laughed, not a nervous laugh but a great, unexpected guffaw. Into that moment the timely waitress returned with his Diet Coke and my Perrier. He wiped his eyes with his thumb, then took a sip of his drink to calm himself. "I've known your uncle since before you were born," he said. "Did you know that? Ripley and I used to play racquetball together at the Y out in Hollywood Hills. Fierce backhand, that guy. Nearly broke my goddamn nose once."

"It was always his game." As nice as it was of Ripley to safeguard my honor in absentia, it would have been even nicer had he remembered to tell me.

"I'll get to the point." Charlie tapped the table lightly

and then took his hands away. "I've done some work with Tom Lake over the years. The artistic director is an old friend."

"You have a lot of friends," I said stupidly because, god, I was so stupid.

"You know Tom Lake?"

I nodded. I did not know.

"They're doing *Our Town* this summer."

"Seems like everyone is."

"They just lost their Emily. She did the first table read then got a call from her agent telling her to pack up. It's a big film, and the studio is covering her cancellation clause. My friend asked me to keep an eye out since he knew we're auditioning. They're going to need someone who can step right in."

"That would be me." Why was I only now remembering that Perrier tasted like salt?

"I think it *is* you. That's why I asked you to meet me. I'm sorry if I gave you the wrong idea." He allowed himself one final chuckle—this crazy business!—then brushed the smile off his face with his hand. "You'd have to go immediately. Can you do that? Do you have anything else going on?"

I shook my head. Having played easy to get, I forfeited the chance to play hard to get.

"Go to Tom Lake for the summer. Send me a postcard

and thank me. Have you ever been to Michigan? Christ, you won't believe how beautiful it is. Do the play. Once you see all the people who've come through that place you'll realize what a break this is. Everyone needs at least one season of summer stock under their belt, I don't care who you are. Do the play and then, who knows? They're starting rehearsals now and we're at least a year out. Obviously Emilys vanish, or they get bad reviews and wind up needing to be replaced. You, in the meantime, will be impressive. And you'll be seen. They've always got theater scouts there. Then your movie will come out. You never know where you'll wind up after that."

He had a way of making it sound like things had gone my way after all. I would play Emily at Tom Lake, renowned summer stock theater, and I hadn't had to go upstairs to get the part. One more lucky day.

He paid the check and asked if I wanted him to get me a cab. I shook my head. "Go back to the hotel," he said. "Order room service and wait by the phone. I'm going to have them call you."

"Thank you," I said.

"You're very good, Lara. Really, you are. I think Michigan is going to mean big things for you."

We walked out to Forty-Fourth Street where it was just getting dark. Traffic was at a standstill and I was glad I'd forgone the offer of a cab. Then, because he was a friend of Uncle Ripley's, Charlie kissed the top of my head and said good night before turning in the opposite direction.

I would go on but Joe arrives on the Gator to collect the lugs. "Sorry to break up a party," he says. "But I'm going to need at least one of you to help in the barn."

Sweets don't hold up in the sun once they're off the tree. We field run the cherries, which means sorting them on the conveyor belt and pulling any fruit that's spotted or cracked, then sending them to a packing plant in the lugs, stems and all. He needs Emily but he won't say it, fearing the appearance of favoritism. Joe would swear in front of a firing squad that he has no favorite daughter, and while there may be no favorite, one of them is indisputably more useful than the other two. Emily is faster than the rest of us put together. Maisie checks her phone and says it's time for her to go back to the house anyway. She has a conference with one of her professors and the cell reception is better there. "Drop me," she says, shifting a couple of lugs so that there's just enough space to climb onto the flatbed of the Gator, the way we never let the girls do when they were young. Even now I want to tell her no.

"Go slow," I say to Emily as she gets behind the wheel, her father sliding in beside her.

"I'm not going to risk the cherries," Emily says. When she puts the thing in drive, Hazel leaps up and Maisie catches her. Who knew?

"Don't tell anything good while we're gone!" Maisie calls, removing the hat from her head and tossing it to me.

"Don't tell anything at all!" Emily shouts.

"Where's the story now?" I hear Joe ask Emily, and Emily says, "Michigan."

"Ah," Joe says. "The good part."

I watch until they've crested the low hill, Maisie waving like the Cherry Queen on her float, Hazel safe beneath her other arm. That's another thing we've lost this year, the Cherry Festival. Any of our girls would have looked smart in a tiara.

"Two-thirds of my audience gone, just like that," I say to Nell as we wave goodbye.

"Three-fourths if you count the dog," she says.

"I should count Hazel."

Plenty of empty lugs remain and we'll leave them in the grass once they're full. Emily will drive back later to pick them up.

For a while we say nothing. I'm tired of talking, and of the three, Nell is the best at being quiet. The thing about picking cherries is that you can look only at the tree you're on, and if you have any sense, you'll just look at the branch you have your hands in. The peekaboo ladder is up, waiting for us to clean off the top. We won't look down the rows at what seems to be an unbroken field of red dots, a pointillist's dream of an orchard. If we opened our minds to all the cherries waiting to be picked, we'd go home and back to bed.

"You weren't really going to go to bed with him," Nell says after a while. It is not a question.

But I am here again, back on the farm, and for a minute I have no idea what she's talking about. "Who?"

"The guy," she says. "Charlie."

To be able to play younger is a great and fleeting gift. I had it once. I could play fourteen at twenty-four. Part of it is in the way you carry yourself, the pitch of your voice, but part of it is pure physiognomy. Nell has that in spades. At twenty-two she is slender and small, and in her faded smock dress that had once belonged to all of us in turn, she could pass for thirteen.

I shake my head. "No. I was just acting, or I had no idea what I was doing."

"But what would you have done if he'd taken you up on it?" Her face is tilted up and the sun is lighting her eyes and her eyes are the sun.

"I would have run, and he never would have caught me because he would have had to stay and pay the check."

She turns back to the tree in front of her, giving it fierce consideration. "We talk about these situations in school all the time, about how no matter who you are, there's always going to be someone with more power than you. They want us to think it out, you know, go through all the scenarios in advance of anything happening so we'll be ready."

"Nothing happened to me," I say. Things happened to me, but not on that day, and not like that. "And for the record, Charlie was a prince."

She nods but she's still looking at her hands. "It's terrifying," she says quietly, and now I see the tears in her eyes. "The idea that in order to get to do this thing you really, really want, you might be told you have to do the exact thing you'd never want to do."

I wish I could tell her, Oh, my darling, that's all behind us now. Those are very old stories about things that don't happen anymore, but instead I take her in my arms. I want to tell her she will never be hurt, that everything will be fair, and that I will always, always be there to protect her. No one sees us but the swallows looping overhead. She puts her arms around my waist and we stand there, just like that, casting a single shadow across the grass.

6

It had been my plan to go back to New Hampshire to see my grandmother after I left New York, but there wasn't time for that now. The original Emily—you haven't heard of her; her moment was brief and came to nothing—was already gone. I flew to Detroit and took a commuter plane to Traverse City. The Executive Director of Tom Lake drove the hour and a half north to collect me from the airport, which made about as much sense as Ripley sending a limo.

"It's awfully nice of you," I said, wrestling my suitcases into the trunk.

"I don't pick up actors. I had an eye exam." He briefly lowered his dark glasses to show me his dilated pupils. "But this gives me a chance to bring you up to speed."

I stared at him, then bobbed my head a little from side to side. "Can you see?"

"Enough." His name was Eric, and after that car ride I never crossed paths with him again. Just because the company was iconic didn't mean it wasn't forever on the precipice of financial ruin. Eric's job was to bring in major gifts and soothe patrons who were offended by a particular show and make sure the ticket sales were on track. In a normal season the actors weren't his problem, but so far this wasn't shaping up to be a normal season. Emily had bailed and the Stage Manager, a character actor who'd spent ten years playing the indelible Uncle Wallace on television, had transitioned from a heavy drinker to a worrisome drunk. Worrisome because Uncle Wallace, otherwise known as Albert Long, was the washed-up marquee name people drove over from other counties to see. "No Emily and a knee-walking Stage Manager isn't the best place to start," Eric said.

I said something sympathetic, but really, I wasn't listening. Who can listen to complaints about actors in the presence of so many cherry trees, miles and miles of them in full ceremonial headdress? "Look at this!" I wanted to cry as we raced down the straight country roads in Eric's old Volvo station wagon, but surely Eric had seen the trees before.

He told me I would get the other Emily's salary and

better accommodations. He'd been able to snatch back the program from the printers at the fifty-ninth minute of the eleventh hour. They'd play up my soon-to-be-released movie and two seasons of unremarkable television. "If you can think of anything else, that would be helpful," he said.

I assumed that my Red Lobster commercial (*Everybody LOVES a fried shrimp feast!*) would not be helpful. "I'll think about it."

"We deal in embellishment around here," he said, his eyes on the road, but not on either side of the road where the action was.

He said he hoped I'd stay the summer. The other Emily had been slated to play Mae in *Fool for Love* after the run of *Our Town* ended. "We could look for another actress but if you could do it that would be one less headache."

I had never seen the play, hadn't read it, but I'd always thought the title was snappy. "Don't you want to see if I can act first?"

Eric shook his head. "That's not my job. If you've made it all the way to my car it's because other people think you can act. That's good enough for me. Charlie said you were excellent, by the way. He said they wanted to cast you in the Spalding Gray production but the backers wouldn't go for it. They needed a name."

It was entirely possible that Charlie had been blowing smoke at Eric, or that Eric was blowing smoke at me, but on the off chance it was true and I could have played Emily on Broadway without having to sleep with anybody at the Algonquin, I wished he would pull the car over for a minute and let me throw up. I stared at the trees instead, that endless expanse of trembling petals. I told Eric I'd stay for the season.

"What's in the boxes?" I asked.

"What boxes?"

I pointed, thinking his eyes must really be bad. Big wooden boxes were set out among the trees. They were everywhere.

"Bees," he said.

"They come in boxes?"

He nodded. "Farmers rent bees. They come in an eighteen-wheeler, and when pollination is over, the truck comes back and takes the boxes someplace else."

"Summer stock," I said, and for the first time since I'd gotten in the car, Eric laughed.

Tom Lake turned out to be crushingly pretty. There was a huge covered amphitheater sunk into the rolling lawns. The musical ran in the amphitheater. They also had a black box theater where they staged the straight plays like *Our Town* and *Fool for Love*. There were tennis courts with a clubhouse that served iced tea and sandwiches. A smattering of lovely houses—some that had been turned into administrative offices, some for boarding the actors and designers and technicians, and some where regular people spent the summer—spread along the shore of a tremendous lake. Fruit trees bloomed, paths meandered, hills swelled, like someone had clipped pictures out of a pile of magazines and then glued the very best ones together on a single page. A couple of miles away was a small town that took most of its annual revenue from the summer tourists who came to stay in one of the two hotels, have supper, and spend the next morning wandering through the little shops before coming over with their theater tickets. The most ambitious ones walked in for a show then caught a shuttle bus back. They wore Tom Lake T-shirts and Tom Lake hats as they paddled rented canoes past the diving platform and out across the lake. The whole thing was a fragile ecosystem, as small towns and theater companies usually are, but as far as I could see it was thriving.

I had two suitcases and Eric carried the heavier one up to my room in the company housing, leaving the smaller one for me. The name of the previous Emily was still on the door. "You won't understand how nice this is until you've seen the other rooms," he said. "We need to build more housing. That's one of the sixty-two things I'm raising money for."

The room was nice in the same way the best dorm room can seem nice: a double bed, my own tiny bathroom, and a window that was open and overlooked the lake.

"I'll have someone bring the schedule by," he said. "I'm afraid you're going to have to hit the ground running."

I unpacked as soon as he left, hanging up my dresses and putting my shoes in a line on the closet floor. I arranged my travel clock and a small pile of books on the nightstand. The girls I'd gone to high school with were married now. They had little houses in New Hampshire with sofa sets and televisions, forks and knives and spoons, maybe a kid or two. During those years when they were hanging wallpaper in the nursery, I'd been living in a furnished studio in Los Angeles, a place that came with everything—sheets, towels, a dish rack. I had money but no idea of how to spend it, so I didn't spend it. I liked the lightness of my life, the feeling that I could leave tomorrow and go where they needed me: New York, Michigan. Not counting my winter clothes, which were still in the closet of my grandmother's spare room, my worldly possessions amounted to the contents of these two bags, more or less. I hadn't had any real success but every one of those high school girls knew about my life, and as much as they may have had the story wrong, they wished they were me. In their place, I would have wished I were me, because this unremarkable room with the remarkable view in Middle-of-Nowhere, Michigan, was everything that had ever been written about freedom and possibility. I pushed the empty suitcases under the bed with my foot, then stood at the window staring, thinking how nice it would be to use the word *lush* again after such a long time in California. The light was so much softer here, and still so much brighter than New Hampshire's. I would send postcards to Charlie and Ripley tomorrow. I would tell them both how grateful I was, how much I already loved the place.

Eric had left the door to my room open behind him, maybe so I could get a cross breeze, and when I turned around a tall, slender man was leaning against the doorway. He had been watching me watch the lake.

"Pretty grand, right?" he said.

My mind did that quick mental calculation women must make when they find their exit blocked by a man they don't know. How far down if I had to go out the window? Too far, I was guessing.

He saw me, he caught it, and took a step back into the hall. He held up a piece of paper. "Schedule," he said.

"Ah."

"You can come out or I can come in or I can lay it

here on the floor between us." He leaned over partway to pantomime his intention. His eyes were dark and overlarge in his thin face, his black hair long and pushed behind his ears. He stood up suddenly and very straight, the paper still in his hand. He was wearing a linen T-shirt and very long surgical scrub pants. "If you invite me in I'll tell you a story."

"Come in then," I said. His ancient espadrilles were dirty and folded at the heels. "I'll risk it."

He smiled. "Oh, good, good." But he barely came into the room at all. He left the door open wide and leaned against the wall beside it, as if it were exactly the spot he was meant for. "Who picked you up at the airport?"

"Eric."

He puzzled over this. "Eric who?"

I hadn't asked his last name, proof that I'd been in California too long. "Eric the Executive Director."

This seemed to impress him. "I've never even seen the Executive Director. I'm assuming he didn't tell you anything about the lake."

"He did not."

"He wouldn't know how lucky it is to be the one to tell it to a newcomer. Actors are all about luck. Executive Directors are all about spreadsheets. People are going to be rushing you from every direction wanting to tell you but I'm the one who got here first, or first after Eric."

"You're an actor?"

He looked down at himself: scrub pants, espadrilles. "It isn't obvious?"

"No, I mean, of course, but actors don't usually deliver schedules." No one seemed to be confined to their regular jobs in this place.

"They do when the errand is presented as a personal favor to the very busy assistant stage manager."

"Checking out the new blood?"

"I call it being thoughtful. Plus I wanted to be the one to tell you the story."

"Did you tell the last Emily?"

"Unfortunately, no. Someone beat me to it, which makes this a sort of redemption."

"Well, it wouldn't be fair really."

"What wouldn't be fair?"

"If you got to tell all the Emilys."

He nodded. "I hadn't thought of it that way. So you've seen the lake?"

"I have."

"And you know what it's called?"

"Tom Lake," I said. "But that's a guess."

He smiled again, showing off the wonkiness of his size XL teeth. I'd been told that wonky teeth, like unpierced ears, were valuable human relics from another time. "Excellent guess!" He gave a single clap. "The lake does have an official name, the name they put on maps and watertable records, but that's no concern of ours."

"I wouldn't think so."

"What you need to know is that all this land was once owned by a very wealthy family, Vanderbilts of some sort, though I'm not sure what sort. Railroad money, oil money, money money—you know the type."

I gave a slight nod, though I didn't know the type from Adam.

"They spent their summers here, or a very small part of their summers, the part when they weren't on a ship or in Scotland. They had a castle in Scotland, which isn't quite as impressive as it sounds because you frankly can't swing a cat without hitting a castle in Scotland. The many children were overseen by many Scottish nannies. I should tell you that these were the friendly ones. Scottish nannies get a terrible rap."

"They do." I sat down on the windowsill, thinking this might be a long one.

He stopped. "Would you not do that, please?"

"What?"

"The windowsill. Not when the window's open."

"Really?"

"We've already lost one Emily."

"She didn't fall out the window." I looked down at the ground, as if to check.

He shook his head and pointed to the corner of the room. "Isn't that a nice chair?"

I was sorry to give up the view but went and pulled over the chair nevertheless.

"Thank you," he said.

"What about you?" The room lacked a second chair, and the windowsill was out, and I didn't feel like offering him the bed.

"I'm a stander by nature. I do better standing."

"Okay."

"Where was I?"

"Scottish nannies." Such a big, goofy smile, I thought. A movie star's smile.

He stopped again. "You're a wonderful listener."

"Thank you," I said. "Occupational hazard."

"Hah! Well, that tells me how long you've been acting if you think actors are good listeners."

"Scottish nannies," I prompted.

He nodded. "So the family had a passel of girls and then Tom and then another boy after him, but our story is about Tom. Tom Something, Tom Scion-of-the-Aristocracy. Tom and his favorite Scottish nanny were taking a walk around the grounds. It's a beautiful day, not unlike this one, and Tom points up the hill and asks the nanny who owns the house. And the nanny says, "Och, Tom, yur father oones the hoose."

I told him I thought his Scottish nanny accent was remarkably good. Not that I'd ever met an actual Scottish nanny.

"Thank you," he said. "So young master Tom goes on, who owns the trees in the orchard, he wants to know, and who owns the horses, and who owns the hill itself, and who owns those flowers? The nanny very patiently gives him the same answer every time. 'Yur father, yur father.' It's a patriarchy, I'm sorry to say. The mother had no ownership of anything, not even herself."

"Understood."

"By now young master Tom is running low on inventory, but he likes the game, so he keeps looking around until finally it occurs to him to ask about the lake. 'Who owns the lake?' And the nanny, we'll call her Heather—not that history wrote down her name but it feels polite to give her one anyway—Heather, for whatever reason says, 'Tom oones the loch.'

"'Me?' the boy asks." The stranger propped against the wall of my bedroom let a split second of wonderment wash across his face, making himself into young master Tom, then just as quickly sent it on its way. "The moment is very touching, and maybe Heather thinks she's made a mistake but let's be honest, the whole fucking place belongs to the father and there's no reason the boy shouldn't get the lake. So he asks her what the lake is called."

"I see this one coming, " I said.

"There was an apostrophe-s back then, *Tom's* Lake, but time condenses experience."

"Sure."

"The kid's aglow. He spends a solid twenty minutes throwing stones and sticks into the water and shouting his own name. After Heather finally corrals him back to the house and down for his nap, she tells the story to the kitchen girls, and even the head woman thinks it's charming. She says Heather ought to tell the Missus, and so Heather does, and the Missus loves the story and she tells her husband and her passel of daughters, and while it's never a formal decision, they agree from there on out it's Tom's Lake."

When he stopped to make sure I was still with him, I realized he hadn't told me his name. He had told me only the name of the lake.

"Now I know," I said.

"Well, there's a small coda, if you have one more minute."

"You're the one who knows how much time I have." He had the schedule in his hand.

"You're good. Let me just finish up. Okay. Somehow the boy never catches on that the whole lake thing is a charade. We all have a blind spot, right? That bit of incorrect information from childhood that mysteriously never gets updated, the person who makes it to thirty-five believing that unicorns had been hunted into extinction."

"Wait, unicorns weren't hunted . . ."

He smiled at me, tipping his head to one side as if to say I was adorable, as in, I was to be adored. "So Tom grows up and finds himself a bride, the sister of one of his Princeton friends, and he thinks it would be nice to get married here, to show her Tom's Lake. Out they all come, the families, the friends, the massive support staff, everyone on the train. Tom hadn't been to the house in years and the place is even more beautiful than he remembers it. He can hardly wait to show her the lake."

"Does she have a name?"

He paused for a minute to consider this. "No, but for the sake of this conversation we'll call her Lara."

That same look of slight discomfort must have come across my face again because he held up the paper in his hand. "It's on your schedule."

"And your name?"

"Peter Duke."

"Peter Duke," I repeated. Such a nice sound.

"The two of them are walking hand in hand, and he's going on about the house and the cherry trees and how they'll spend at least part of their summers here, then he points to the lake, which, as you've no doubt noticed, is difficult to miss. 'Tom's Lake,' he says, and what he's telling her is that all of this is his, his and his family's but eventually his because he's the oldest son, and therefore hers in part, but of course that's not the way she hears it. She says, 'That's so sweet. But really, what's the name of the lake?' because clearly this is not the family trout pond. The lake goes on for miles. It doesn't belong to a single person. And just as Tom is about to repeat himself, he stops. He suddenly remembers that day with Heather, who was by then long back in Scotland. Heather, the first woman he'd ever loved because his mother was never really available to him. And at that moment, standing there with his bride-to-be, he realizes that this body of water he has only heard referred to by his own name was not named for him at all, and that it did not belong to him. Worse yet, he has no idea what the lake was called."

I went back to the window to look again at the lake and the day, to imagine the two of them stopping for this conversation. "Tell me they didn't call the wedding off over this." I was not a particularly romantic person but still, that would have been a disappointment.

Duke shook his head. "Quite the opposite, in fact. Something miraculous happened, something that sealed their love forever. Tom told Lara the truth."

Involuntarily, I yelped. I made the sound a small dog makes when you accidentally step on his paw. "Oh my god, I was totally with you."

Nothing in his face betrayed him. His cheeks didn't flush, his long black eyelashes, so ridiculous on a grown man, did not cast down. "He told her that he didn't know the name of the lake, and that he had only this minute realized this fact, and that his nanny, and truly, his entire family, had infantilized him, not with malicious intent, but as a sort of sweet joke that was emblematic of both their love and how he had been coddled his entire life. He told her that he didn't know the name of the lake at all."

"I believed you this entire time!"

"This would have been his Siddhartha Gautama revelation, the moment the prince casts off his wealth to go and live among the suffering and the poor to seek his spiritual path, but he loved her too much."

"Stop."

"And he loved the house. Really, he was crazy about the house. And the place in Scotland. And the triplex in New York."

"So why is it called Tom Lake?"

"No idea."

"You're not playing George, are you?" He didn't seem young enough to be George, but I thought he probably could have played the invisible chickens if that was the part he'd been given.

He gave me a casual two-finger salute. "Editor Webb, newspaperman."

"You're my father?"

"I had hoped your mother would have told you someday."

We stared at one another until the small room felt very small. I was the one who looked away.

"You've got an hour," he said, holding up a second page. "There's a map." He took one large step forward and laid the papers gently on the bed, as he might have picked me up and laid me gently on the bed.

This is a story about Peter Duke who went on to be a famous actor.

This is a story about falling in love with Peter Duke who wasn't famous at all. It's about falling so wildly in love with him—the way one will at twenty-four—that it felt like jumping off a roof at midnight. There was no way to foresee the mess it would come to in the end, nor did it occur to me to care.

I have long been at peace with Duke the famous

actor, but my feelings for the person who walked into my bedroom that first day at Tom Lake are more complicated. I've made a point never to think of him at all, except that now I am thinking of him.

I am making one part of my life into a story for my daughters, and even though they are grown women and very forward thinking, let's just assume I leave out every mention of the bed, even the two sheets of paper that are resting there on top of the covers.

"I feel like I'm on the verge of anaphylaxis," Maisie says. "I'm serious. My throat's closing up."

Emily and Nell just look at me, their throats already closed. The four of us are back among the cherry trees where the rain is falling so gently we don't even acknowledge it.

"How do you ever get over someone like that?" Maisie asks. What she means is that I must not be over him still, and I must never have loved their father as much as I loved Duke.

"Do you remember when you would beg us to take you to the county fair every summer?" I want so much to make them understand this. "How the three of you would not shut up about the fair. The fair! Oh my god, I wanted to drown the whole lot of you in a bucket. You would needle and whine until finally we gave in. Your father and I would try to get you to come to the community hall and look at the quilts and pet the angora rabbits, but you wanted to eat chili corndogs and cotton candy and then get on one of those god-awful rides that had been put together by three heroin addicts with a sprocket wrench, the rides that made you feel like your head was going to be flung off your neck by centrifugal force. One of you would vomit on the other two in the ride and then the next one would vomit on me in the parking lot while I was trying to clean you up and the next one would vomit down the back of Daddy's neck in the car. And then in the morning you were all bright as daisies, begging to go back. Do you remember that?"

"I loved the fair," Maisie says, her sisters still mute with wonder.

I turn to face my middle child. "Would you want to go now?"

"Maybe," she says, but she is twenty-four, the age I was at Tom Lake.

"Would you say that the ride was better than being a veterinarian? That you'd rather be whipsawed by something called the Zipper than you would deliver that foal in the middle of the night?" I can argue with Maisie because Maisie is logical and strong. I will always be afraid of waking up the part of Emily that has long been dormant. I will always be afraid of accidentally breaking something in Nell that is fragile and pure. But Maisie is up for it; no one will ever have to worry about Maisie.

"I don't see why you have to give up one for the other," she says.

"You don't *have* to," I tell my daughter. "You *want* to. You wake up one day and you don't want the carnival anymore. In fact, you can't even believe you did that."

Nell turns her face away. Emily is holding on to her own braid with both hands. They aren't buying it. "We're not talking about a carnival," Emily says. "We're talking about Duke. I believe in Duke."

I want to tell her she used to believe in the Easter bunny, too, but I don't. I could say that to Maisie but not the other two.

7

Wondrous god, I had the presence of mind to stick a chicken in the Crock-Pot with some onions and carrots this morning, and the kitchen garden needs only to be picked, rinsed and reassembled in order to have salad. Emily has made bread and pie and after a day of work, bread and pie are really all we want. We scrub our hands up to the elbows and throw water on our faces to dilute the paste of sweat and sunscreen and bug spray. Sometimes we will deem ourselves too disgusting to sit at the table and so we run up for a quick shower, forgetting we can't stay awake after a shower, we can't go back downstairs to eat. And so we eat first, the five of us together, something I would have sworn had gone the way of childhood—a beautiful memory forever outgrown except for holidays and the occasional birthday, but I would have been wrong because look, here we are at the table talking over the progress of the day in terms of pounds picked and rows cleaned. Benny eats with us on Wednesday nights, and Emily goes to the Holzapfels' on Sundays. Other than that they've decided to eat with their families of origin, at least during harvest, then meet up later in the bed they share.

From our never-ending conversation about stone fruit, Nell veers away. "Daddy," she says, her fork hovering above lettuce. "What did you think of Duke?"

Her sisters blink. They look at Nell, then me. They hadn't realized they were allowed to call their father to the stand.

Joe has just taken a bite of buttered bread and for that reason he is slow to answer. "He was a very talented man."

"Did you like him?"

I can see my husband remembering. Isn't that the way long marriages are? You can turn off the sound and still know the answer. "Everybody liked Duke. Everybody including me." His eyes wander back to his plate. He's starving, and I've made potato salad, potato salad being my husband's truest love.

"You 'liked' him?" Emily asks. "There has to be more than that." The girls' need for information is voracious, limitless, and Nell has just tapped what they had assumed to be a forbidden line—did their father like their mother's boyfriend?

Joe smiles. "Okay, something else about Duke." He thinks about this and then comes up with the necessary detail. "He could stand on his hands."

I look at my husband in amazement. "Oh my god, how did I forget that?"

"He could hold on to the seat of a folding chair and go up straight as a ruler. You'd be talking to him and the next thing you knew he was fully inverted. He even pointed his toes. I'd never seen anyone do that before and I haven't seen anyone do it since. Duke was an athlete, you know. It's all over his films."

Duke used to say it was better than caffeine for waking up, all that blood rushing to the brain.

"If it hadn't been for Sebastian, I bet he wouldn't have gone for acting at all," Joe said. "I think he would have played some sort of sport."

"Sebastian?" Maisie asks.

"Duke's brother," Emily says.

"How do you know Sebastian is his brother?" Nell asks.

We are so tired and still, here we are, amazing one another.

Emily fixes her sister with a look and then we remember, of course, that even if she's outgrown her condition, Emily is still the clearinghouse of Duke information.

"Sebastian was a tennis player," Joe says. "He was ranked for a minute, wasn't he?"

I nod. "Juniors."

"Wait," Nell says to me, "you knew about Sebastian?"

"I knew Sebastian."

The girls all begin to speak at once but Joe ignores them, shaking his head at the memory. "To see how good Sebastian was and to know he didn't make the pros, it always made me think how good the pros must have been. The only person who could ever make Sebastian break a sweat was Duke, and Duke could never beat him. Never. Do you remember that?" my husband asks me. "How hard the two of them went at it?"

I nod. What I hadn't remembered was that Joe came to watch them play. Everybody came to watch them, which was one of the countless reasons Duke hated to lose.

"Duke had a great game, but he wasn't good enough to beat his brother, and Sebastian wasn't good enough to beat, oh, I don't know, whoever beat him. We all take our place in the food chain."

"So what did Sebastian do if he wasn't a tennis

player?" Nell asks, though whether the question is meant for me or Joe or Emily isn't clear.

"He was a schoolteacher, wasn't he?" Joe asks.

"History," I say. Saint Sebastian.

Joe nods again, smiles. He has redirected the topic of conversation so deftly that the girls have no idea he's done it. He crumples his napkin, picks up his silverware and plate. "Good man," he says. "Good men. Now, if you'll excuse me for a minute, I have a few things left to do in the barn while it's still light."

We don't remind him that he says this every night. We don't tell him that he's too tired already and that whatever it is he thinks he needs to do can wait. We don't tell him because he doesn't listen to us.

Emily pushes back from the table. "I'll go with you."

"Don't be crazy. I know how to check on goats." He puts his dishes in the sink. "You've got your story to listen to."

There was only one table read on the schedule, and even that, I think, was for my benefit. They'd been cooling their heels in Michigan waiting for the new Emily and now that I was there they were ready to work. Duke was out of his chair the minute I came into the rehearsal room, guiding me around the table like it was a cocktail party. "Emily," he said, "this is your mother,

Mrs. Webb, and your brother Wally." He leaned over and gave the woman who would play his wife a fleeting kiss on the temple. Mrs. Webb was faded and soft, old enough to be my mother had my mother started young, which she would have in Grover's Corners.

"How do," Wally Webb said, and offered his hand. He was an actual child, maybe ten or eleven, with straight brown hair and freckles, though the girl playing Rebecca Gibbs was probably sixteen and got the part for being small. I met Doc Gibbs and Mrs. Gibbs and George. Georges were bound to disappoint me, and this one was no exception. He was a good-looking guy with a string of Pizza Hut commercials and a Saturday morning Disney show that was about to be cancelled. Instead of trying to hold my eye, he lifted himself halfway from his chair and halfway shook my hand.

Uncle Wallace though, he was another story. He leapt to his feet and planted both hands on my shoulders. "Look at you!" he cried. "Look at our Emily! Thank god you're here. I'm going to have to hug you."

Hugged by Uncle Wallace! Oh, but I had loved him as a child. The gruff and tender caregiver of his sister's orphaned brood. The carefree bachelor, dashing in middle age, had risen to the challenge, leaving children all across America to wonder how much better their lives might be if only their parents were dead.

Uncle Wallace put a rinse on his hair to keep it in the neighborhood of red, and his face had the slightly pulled-back quality I'd come to accept in women when I was in California but still found disconcerting in men. He pressed me to him a beat too long.

"This is Uncle Wallace's eleventh production as the Stage Manager," Duke said. "He's hot off a smash success at a dinner theater in Tempe."

"I can do it in my sleep," Uncle Wallace said, giving me a wink. I would have laughed had Duke not squeezed my upper arm, moving me along to meet Constable Warren and Howie Newsome and Mrs. Soames. The smaller parts went to people in the community, a strategy that resulted in good will and unexpected fund-raising opportunities. I liked Duke for taking every bit as long introducing me to one cast member as another. Apart from Uncle Wallace, none of us were famous, after all. We were on the way up or on the way out. Our audience for the table read was a collection of swings and understudies who sat at the far end of the room with their pens and scripts. The actual stage manager, as opposed to the actor playing the Stage Manager, sat with the assistant stage manager. I waved to them collectively and they waved back.

"We should get going," one of the men at the table said patiently.

"And *this* is our esteemed director, Mr. Nelson," Duke said, holding out his hand. "Our fearless leader. He's the one who has no business being here."

"But here I am," Mr. Nelson said.

"I can't remember when I last worked with a real director," Uncle Wallace said, pitching to the room. "There's always a director, of course, or someone claiming to be a director even though they have no interest in your performance. But not this one! Nelson is a man of ideas, of insight. I thought I knew everything about the part, but he's opened it up for me again, invited me into the very soul of the Stage Manager." Uncle Wallace turned to me. "Makes it feel like my first time."

George picked up his script and tapped it on the edge of the table like maybe he was thinking about leaving.

"Drinking," Duke whispered as we took our places at the table.

"I'm afraid I already gave my terrific introductory speech last week," Nelson said to me. "Went over the themes we were highlighting. I don't want to make the rest of the company listen to it twice."

"We loved it!" Uncle Wallace said. "We'd be happy to hear it again."

Nelson shook his head. "Let's go ahead and read through. Lara, I'd be more than happy to catch you up later if you'd like. I've been told you know what you're doing."

I looked at the director and smiled. I was ready.

I was sixteen when I installed *Our Town* into my brain, back when my brain was spongy and fresh and capable of holding on to things forever. Thanks to all those nights in Jimmy-George's car, I could recite George's lines as easily as Emily's, and if I didn't think about it too much I probably could do the other parts as well. Maybe not all of the Stage Manager, but most of it. *Three years have gone by. Yes, the sun's come up over a thousand times.* At not quite twenty-five, this would be my third production of the play. I kept the script on my nightstand to read when I woke up in the middle of the night. I'd spoken the lines over traffic while driving Ripley's MG down the Santa Monica freeway to spend the day at the beach with friends. I ran scenes in my head on the plane going out to New York, on the plane coming to Michigan. I repeated the words like Catholic girls with their rosary beads, clicking through Hail Marys until they were muscle memory. So it was easy for me to be there in Tom Lake, to be Emily again, to be myself. I had enough room in my brain to think about work and wonder about Duke at the same time.

Having known him for all of an hour, I assumed Duke would be a ham, but his Editor Webb was perfectly restrained, a dignified, matter-of-fact man, even when he had to say words like *Satiddy, likker.* It's hard not to make hash of those things, but Duke was the kind of natural Ripley would have liked. Not only was he natural, he remained present for the whole reading, unlike George, who managed to check out the very instant his lips stopped moving. Duke paid attention to the other actors, and I flattered myself by imagining he paid the most attention to me.

If it was my gift to play younger, Duke came off older than he was. He was twenty-eight that summer, but as my father, anyone would have thought he was on the other side of forty. Over the course of his career, Duke played older, then for a stretch he played his age, then he played younger, all the while staying in the same exact place. I never knew how he pulled that off.

It hadn't occurred to me until we started reading the funeral scene that I was now the age of Emily in the third act, and that no matter how young I looked, I would age out of the part in time because time was unavoidable. I thought of all those women dressed as girls who'd showed up to audition at my high school. No one gets to go on playing Emily forever. That's what I was thinking at the table read, how I would lose her.

I said my lines with my script closed. I thought that Mrs. Gibbs and Mrs. Webb were teary, though their voices held. Even George, who doesn't have a line of dialogue in the third act, turned to look at me. If this was going to be my last time in the part, I was, as Veronica would say, going to kill it. Plus, I held out a flickering hope that if I did my very best work at Tom Lake, word would get back to New York, and that the Emily they'd chosen for the Spalding Gray production would be gently done away with, and even after this I'd have the chance to play her one more time.

When we finished, Mr. Nelson smiled. "Friends, let us breathe an enormous sigh of relief. We're going to have a play after all."

We clapped for one another, and the swings and the understudies clapped with us. The people who'd shaken my hand three hours before came back to shake it again. My mother-in-law, Mrs. Gibbs, who'd been especially good in her part, held onto me a minute more. She told me she'd been Emily once. "Probably before you were born," she said. "I was nothing like you. You're one of those Emilys that people will talk about for years. They'll say, 'I saw Lara Kenison at Tom Lake when she was a child' and no one will believe it."

Maisie's phone rings. The house rule is no phones at the table but we've made an exception for Maisie who keeps getting calls from neighbors asking for help, and we made an exception for Emily so that Benny can text her and tell her what time he'll be back at the house, and so of course we extended the exception to Nell, because why would we let her sisters answer their phones at the table and make her turn hers off? Joe and I turn off our phones because everyone we want to talk to is here.

"Sure," Maisie says, stepping into the kitchen while we listen. "No, no, it's fine. We're finished. I'll come over." She ends the call and looks at us. "The Lewers have a calf with intractable diarrhea."

"Does it ever occur to you to try to protect us while we're eating?" Nell asks.

"Protecting you means putting my clothes in the wash and taking a shower before I come into our room. It doesn't mean I'm not going to tell you what happened." She turns to me. "Pause the story, will you? I don't want to miss the part about Sebastian."

Emily stands up from the table. "If you're stopping the story then I'm going home. You just reminded me I haven't done laundry in two weeks."

"Then I'm going to go to help Dad." Nell stands as well.

"Good night, ladies," I sing. "Good night, ladies, good night."

"Keep Hazel here, will you?" Maisie asks. "I don't want her getting into this."

"Understandable. The three of you go. I'll clean up."

They stack their dishes in the sink and head out the door together, Maisie holding the end of Emily's braid the way one elephant will use its trunk to hold another elephant's tail. Nell slips her finger through Maisie's belt loop. Joe and I used to say that if lightning struck one of these girls all three would go up in flames. "How did you never tell us Duke had a brother?" Nell says to Emily.

"At the time in my life when I found out about Sebastian I wasn't speaking to you," Emily reminds her.

Hazel rushes the door just as it's closing and Maisie turns and pushes her gently inside. "Stay, stay. I'll be right back."

But Hazel doesn't believe her. When they're gone she scratches and cries until finally I crouch down and pet her ears. "Hazel," I say to her very quietly. "Hazel. She's coming back. I'll stay here until she does. Hazel, listen to me. I'm going to tell you something important, you need to be brave." I then explain to the dog how I have told myself for so many years that my career fell apart because I wasn't any good, but now I'm starting to think it all fell apart because I had ceased to be brave. "If this were a movie, I'd be drowning in regret now. But I'm telling you, Hazel, it doesn't feel anything like regret. It feels like I just missed getting hit by a train."

The entire life span of summer stock is four months—four months birth to death—so time must move faster now. Duke was the person I knew best at Tom Lake. We had been alone together in my room. I had seen him act and felt moved and surprised by what he was capable of. He had seen me act and so waited for me at the door while the others said good night. We had known each other for a matter of hours, but they were summer-stock hours, which in the outside world would have translated to a solid six months.

"I promised I'd show you the lake," Duke said.

"Did you?"

"I know it's a lot to manage," Nelson said to me at the door, "getting thrown in this way. Let me know if I can help. Not that you need help." Nelson had a thick brush of hair that must have been blond when he was a child, and his eyes behind his glasses were blue and bright. Directors as a rule did not lead with such friendliness, and I was interested to see if it could work.

"She doesn't need help," Duke assured him. Duke who was now my agent. "Unless she needs help finding the lake."

"I think we'll all remember the switching-Emilys-debacle as a lucky break." Nelson shook my hand again. "My number's on the schedule."

I thanked him. I told him good night.

"'My number's on the schedule'," Duke said once we were well out of the building. "As if that isn't the oldest line in the book." He shook his head in disappointment.

"No," I said, "'I promised to show you the lake' is the oldest line in the book."

If the implication was that the director was trying to pick me up, I had missed it. Duke was trying to pick me up, and that was all that mattered. Uncle Wallace had given it a shot as well, saying that he knew a lot more about where the lake was because this was his fourteenth summer here. "Let me show her the goddamn lake," he said.

The lake, which stretched two miles in length and a half mile across, was right in front of us.

"Is Nelson famous?" I asked Duke as we crossed the grass, down the hill, towards the water.

Duke stretched up his neck to startling length then tipped his head. "He's not Francis Ford Coppola, if that's what you're asking."

"That's not what I'm asking." The day was just then beginning to soften towards dusk. I had woken up in a New York hotel room that morning.

"Well, all right, if you aren't asking if he's a very famous Hollywood director, if you're willing to lower the bar, then yes, I suppose Nelson is famous. By the standards of Tom Lake he's famous."

"Meaning what?"

Duke took my hand and started swinging it so as not to appear tender. I could feel the current of his life flow into my fingers and up my arm and travel into the muscle of my heart. "Nelson has directed several plays for a well-established theater company in Chicago we need not name, and last summer he directed in Sag Harbor, and he's had one play Off Broadway. Something you've heard of." He turned his face away from me and whispered the name of the play in the direction of the lake so the breeze could carry it away.

"Then what's he doing here?" Even if I had yet to establish the parameters of the assembled talent, I knew enough to know that an Off Broadway play exceeded them.

"It's a mystery. He's only directing one play, and once it opens, he's out of here. Everyone's trying very hard to make a good impression in hopes he'll take us with him when he goes." He stopped. "I don't mean us. I mean them. I'm not trying to make a good impression. Uncle Wallace is trying to make a good impression. Rumor has it he very badly wants off the dinner-theater circuit."

"How would a person make a good impression on

Nelson?" I wondered if I would make a good impression.

"Acting, I guess. Acting well. Don't tell that to Uncle Wallace though. You'd break his heart."

Uncle Wallace may have been a goose but he was certainly acting well. Based on one table read I would count him as an excellent Stage Manager, not that Duke wanted to hear that from me. Duke, I cleverly surmised, would rather hear about Duke. "So you're making a good impression if you want to or not. You were wonderful."

It was the strangest moment, like I was telling him something he hadn't heard before. He stopped and rested one elbow on my shoulder, pushing his hair back behind his ear where it belonged. "You're just saying that because of the lake and the cherry blossoms."

"No," I said. "You were wonderful."

Then he kissed me, a first-day sort of kiss, very hesitant and sweet, the way George might have kissed Emily had a kiss been written for them. It was not, however, a kiss between an editor and his daughter.

"Thank you," Duke said.

"Thank you," I said, or thought I said, then he took back my hand. We walked the path along the lake for a while and then turned back. We lacked both the time and ambition to go all the way around.

"Do you swim?" he asked me.

"Like a fish."

"Then we'll go swimming sometime."

I stopped. He knew what I wanted to do before I knew it myself, because as soon as he said it I wanted to go swimming more than anything. "Let's go now," I said. "I'll tell you, this has been one hell of a day. Let's go swimming." It was northern Michigan in the summer. There would still be enough light.

He looked at me. "We're busy now."

"We are?"

He nodded, moving a piece of hair from my forehead with his thumb. "We have plans."

It sounded so much like a line from a play. We were going to go back to my room, and to pretend otherwise would have been acting.

He took out a pack of Marlboros and offered me one.

I shook my head. "I don't smoke."

"Would you try?"

"Smoking?"

He nodded. "It's something we could do together. Just think how nice it would be to go outside during breaks and sit on the lawn. We could look at the lake and smoke."

He lit two cigarettes with a single match, and then, exhaling, handed one to me. Jimmy-George had nothing on this guy. Nobody had anything on this guy. I took a small drag and coughed. My first cigarette.

"Just a couple of puffs or it will make you dizzy," he said. "You've got to build up your lungs."

We were walking again. I had a cigarette in one hand and his hand in the other. I couldn't imagine Emily smoking, and I wondered if the director would have an objection, though surely I wouldn't be smoking by the time the audience arrived. The way the embers brightened when we inhaled made me think of fireflies. When Duke stopped again we were back at the house where I was living. He took the cigarette from my fingers and put them both out in a pot of geraniums on the porch. Maybe I was a little dizzy. I hadn't noticed the flowers when I came in or when I went out. That we were walking up the stairs holding hands seemed like the most natural thing in the world. For all I knew he had gone upstairs with the other Emily as well, the one who'd lasted only a day. He may have been taking me back to a bed he'd already slept in, and I couldn't have cared less because it was my bed now.

"This is odd," Joe says when he comes in the back door. The dishes are done and I'm on the couch sewing bits of everyone's castoff dresses and favorite sheets and the random cloth napkin into quilt squares while Hazel sleeps. Thirty years from now I'll have enough squares to make a quilt for each of our daughters.

"What's odd?"

"We're the only two people in the house."

"Where's Nell?"

"She went to Emily's. I guess Maisie's still trying to plug the calf."

It might not sound like an overture but I stick my needle in the tomato-shaped pincushion all the same. People with children are attuned to the inherent sexual possibility of an empty house. For years we tried to schedule activities for all three girls at the same time: the weekly dance class, the 4-H meeting, the algebra tutor. A scant hour of overlap was all we were hoping for, but even when those bright stars aligned, one daughter so often refused to leave. There always seemed to be one girl who wanted nothing but to crawl into my lap for an hour while the other two were away. And so I would hold her. You don't forget that, even if your daughters have grown and been gone for years and then come home.

"I would have thought they'd all rush back for the story."

"We'll pick it up tomorrow."

"How far have you gotten?"

What came after that first night? "Well, I'm at Tom

Lake, we've had the first table read, so I guess we're up to Pallace."

Joe shakes his head. "Oh, Pallace. Don't you wonder about her?" He cuts a piece of the strawberry cake I've left on the counter. I wish he'd eat the whole thing. As thin as he gets in the summer, he should eat a cake every day. "Pallace and then Sebastian."

"I never should have started."

He looks at me with that small, sad smile he has. "How? They're relentless. They would have sat on your chest until you told them everything."

"And it's not like I'm telling them everything anyway. I'm not telling them the good parts."

Joe brushes the crumbs into the sink, rinses the knife. "By which you mean sex."

I am staring at my husband from across the room, a calm man who isn't given to picking apart the past, which doesn't mean he needs to hear it. "I'm speaking in the parlance of three girls in their twenties."

"Really good sex?" He's still smiling when he comes over and takes the pincushion from my hand.

I shrug. "Who can remember?"

"You, probably. I'm betting you remember." My husband smells very faintly of hay and goats.

"I remember yesterday if I'm lucky." I'm not fooling him but still, I want to be polite.

"How tired are you?" he asks.

"Less tired than you."

For so many years I have kissed him. For so many years I have not kissed another soul, and there is a deep and abiding comfort in this. Joe is not Duke. Joe was never Duke and I would never have wanted him to be. From the couch Hazel gives a low growl.

"What about her?" Joe asks.

"She can't climb stairs."

He looks at the dog. "Really? I just thought Maisie liked to carry her."

"She does."

"Can you stay awake while I take a shower?"

"I can." I follow him up the stairs. We leave the lights on because before we know it, one of the girls will be home.

8

It's a different kind of sleep when the girls are home. Even after so many years I am asleep but also waiting to hear the back door open and close. Nell comes home first, then Maisie. When they were younger I could hear the difference in their footsteps, a job that is simplified by Hazel barking. It's strange to me that Maisie and Nell have continued to sleep in the same room now that Emily's room is available, but they've always liked being together. Even when they were children, neither of them seemed to pine for a room of her own. At thirteen, Emily nailed a NO TRESPASSING sign to her door (purchased from Ace Hardware and put up not with tape or thumbtacks but nails), and even that couldn't rouse her sisters' interest in getting in there. All these years after the end of Emily's hormonal rage,

Maisie and Nell are still opting for the familiar comfort of their twin beds.

When I go downstairs in the morning I find a cardboard box full of eggs waiting on the kitchen counter, some of them the color of milky coffee and some of them the blue of clouded sky. I'm glad we don't keep chickens because I regret the goats, but it means that eggs are always welcome. Maisie and Nell drag downstairs while I'm making French toast, Maisie clutching her dog like a pillow to her chest. I ask her if she'd been paid in eggs last night and she nods, yawns. "They tried to give me money."

"Money's nice," Nell says, rubbing at her eyes. None of our girls have money.

Maisie shakes her head. "I can't take money until I have my license. And anyway, what's a person supposed to charge for helping a poor little shitting calf in the middle of the night?"

"Three dozen eggs?" I say, guessing.

"More or less."

Animals aren't much of a thing around here. Like our goats, the occasional cow or horse or flock of chickens represents a fruit farmer's temporary insanity, the fanciful quest to make a hard job harder. Wouldn't it be fun to sell eggs at the fruit stand? Goat cheese? Butter? But it isn't fun. We know how to tend to our trees but the animals are largely a mystery to us, which is why Maisie's phone is always ringing. No one cares that she hasn't finished school. She knows more than they do and they need her now.

"Is the calf okay?" her sister asks.

Maisie nods again, thanking me as I put breakfast on the table. "I got a stomach tube down her for fluids, and they had some Albon tablets. It turned out okay." She cuts a corner off her French toast and slips it to the dog.

I brush my fingers through my middle daughter's curling hair before sitting down. Chemistry was nothing for Maisie. Sick calves are nothing. She is never afraid.

Maisie looks at her sister as if she is just now awake enough to see her. "What did you wind up doing last night?"

Nell swirls a piece of French toast in a puddle of syrup. "I went to the little house. Benny told me I could borrow his copy of *Moby-Dick*. He said by the time I finished reading it the pandemic would be over."

"You went to the little house to read *Moby-Dick*?" Maisie reads journal articles about small-animal vaccinations, and Emily reads journal articles about weed control and pesticides, and Nell reads novels and plays, each of them marveling at the other two.

"No," Nell says. "We wound up playing Pictionary." She stops because there's something else she wants to tell but she's conflicted about it. Nell is a girl without secrets. Watching her face is like going to a movie.

"And—" I prompt.

"Maybe I'm not supposed to talk about it. They didn't say I couldn't so I wonder if maybe you already know and haven't told me."

Maisie and I put down our forks.

"Let's assume we don't know," I say.

"Let's assume we do," Maisie says.

Nell takes another bite, weighing the options. "Do you know they're getting married?" she asks.

Maisie slaps the table with her open hand, sloshing her coffee, startling the dog. "They got engaged?"

Nell folds her lower lip into her mouth. "You didn't know."

"We didn't know," I say, and what I feel—and I am ashamed of this—is a very old prick of exclusion. Emily didn't come to me. Emily, who didn't tell me when she started her period and didn't tell me when she decided to go to Michigan State, didn't think to tell me that she was marrying Benny, though Emily, had she been at the table, would have said it was because I already knew those things.

"I don't think it's an *engagement* per se. I mean, it wasn't like she was holding out her hand to show me a ring. They were just talking about whether or not they should try to fit in some kind of wedding between cherry season and the apples. The only reason it even came up was because one of the pictures I was supposed to draw was 'marriage vows.'"

"Outed by Pictionary," Maisie says.

Nell looks from her sister back to me. "I shouldn't have said anything."

"Of course you should have. How else would we have known?" I can hear the petulance in my voice.

"They were always going to get married," Maisie says.

Nell nods. "When I was a kid I thought Benny must have hated his parents because he was here all the time."

The French toast has grown cold but we make ourselves eat it. We know how the morning will go if we're hungry. "Come on," I say, picking up plates. "Let's get to work. I bet your father thinks we're still in bed."

We remember our hats. The day is clear and bright as we walk out to take our place between the trees. We see the six members of the Ramirez family in the distance and shout out our greetings, and they in return wave their arms above their heads. Their family is safe and together in this cherry orchard they have come back to year after year. Our family is safe and together in this cherry orchard. Our eldest daughter is going to marry our neighbors' son, a boy she loves, a boy we love, and I am mad at Duke, who, through no fault of his own, or through only the fault of his essential Dukeness over which he had no control, tore the fabric that bound me to my daughter. And though it has been repaired, expertly, repeatedly, this lumpy seam remains between us that keeps her from telling me she's getting married. The dog has run ahead and Maisie jogs after her while Nell drops back and takes my hand. "I want to see if the daisies are up," she says.

We climb the little hill to the cemetery where to my surprise the tall grass is tangled with flowers—white petals, bright-yellow hearts. She'd called the seed and feed store more than a month ago and asked them to put a couple of packets of daisy seeds in with our order.

"I was just here," I say, amazed by the degree to which everything is changed by the presence of daisies. The girls like to bring the goats up to the cemetery in the summer—they do a beautiful job trimming around the stones—but no one's had the time this year and now we'll never do it. The place looks too pretty. The shaggy and shaded wilderness of the cemetery was always Emily's favorite place on the farm. Even when she was a tiny girl she liked to run her fingers along the tombstones, the letters worn nearly to nothing, the stones speckled with lichen. I would lie in the grass between the graves, so pregnant with Maisie I wondered if I'd be able to get up again, and Emily would weave back and forth between the granite slabs, hiding then leaping out to make me laugh. Like every other mother in the history of time, I wondered if I would ever be able to love another child as much as I loved her.

"Listen, she isn't mad at you," Nell says. "They were thinking out loud, that's all. I just happened to be at the table while they were thinking out loud."

I laugh. "I should have named you Veronica."

"Veronica from high school?"

"She knew how to read my mind."

Nell smiles. "Maybe I'll start a mentalist act, even though I think yours is the only mind I can read. Well, yours and Emily's and Maisie's. I can't read Daddy's mind."

"I wonder why not," I say. Veronica. She will always be eighteen for me. I can see her so clearly.

"He's too good an actor." She leans over to brush her hand across the daisies. "I'd make a fortune if I knew when we were getting out of here."

"Don't you sort of love it, though?" I am projecting, of course. I know this.

"Love being trapped with my family on the farm while the world goes up in flames? Not so much. I mean, I know we're lucky. I know that pretty much everyone else has it worse, but it's hard. You and Dad and Emily live here anyway, and Maisie's got the shitting calves to give her life meaning, but for me it's pretty much just picking cherries."

I can do nothing about the world and the flames beyond leaving free masks in the fruit stand, but the part in which we're trapped is joy itself. "I'm sorry."

She shrugs. "At least we have the past."

Nell and I agree that we'll come back at the end of the day and pick a bouquet for the table but for now we should get to work. Maisie has her bucket around her neck by the time we catch up and Emily's bucket is nearly full with a good six inches of cherries already in the lug.

"You knew Benny and I were getting married," Emily says before I even pick up my bucket. Just as well, since I didn't know how to start the conversation. She tilts back her head so she can see me from beneath the bill of her cap, so I can see that she's fierce again.

I glance over at Maisie but she keeps her back to me while deftly picking cherries. I understand now that the detour to see the daisies in the cemetery was meant to give Maisie and Emily a minute to talk. "Listen, I'm thrilled about this. You know we love Benny."

You know we love you.

"It's not like we were making plans behind your back," Emily says. "We were only having a conversation. If this isn't a good time for you—"

"Don't say that."

She squeezes her eyes closed. "I don't want to feel like I'm doing this wrong before I've even done anything."

"Emily." I put my arms around her from the side, the buckets dictating the shape of our embrace. She tries to pull away but I have her. I hold her, and then she starts to cry.

"Oh, Emmy." Nell touches her sister's shoulder. "Oh, god, I'm so sorry."

Emily shakes her head, covers her face with her hands.

"Somebody didn't get enough sleep," Maisie says.

That's what I used to say to the girls when they wailed over whatever it was they wanted and didn't get—another puff of cotton candy, a final spin on the Zipper. The perceived injustice of the phrase enraged them, but when they got older and started saying it to one another it was suddenly hilarious. Sure enough, Emily's sobs are disrupted by her own hiccupping laughter. She pulls up her T-shirt to wipe her face, blow her nose.

"You're so gross. You should be a vet," Maisie says.

Emily shakes her head. "I don't know how to do this."

"Get married?"

"I don't know how to do *any* of it." She turns up her face to shout at the sky. "Are we going to get the cherries picked in time? Will anyone be working at the processing plant? Is everything going to rot in a warehouse? Then Benny says we should just go ahead and get married, at least get *that* knocked off the list, and I think, why not? If we do it now we don't have to invite anyone—no relatives, no neighbors, no friends from school. We've got the perfect excuse. It can just be us and the Holzapfels. We can bring blankets and sit in the grass by the pond. I can wear something I already own and nothing will cost anything and we won't have to write thank-you notes." The breeze shifts imperceptibly through the leaves and just like that she's crying again. Maisie lifts the yoke of stone fruit from her sister's neck and Emily rubs her eyes with the heels of her hands. "Whenever I think about getting married I feel like I'm losing my mind, and maybe that's because I'm losing my mind, and then I think of poor Benny getting stuck with a crazy wife and what a burden I'm going to be for him, then two minutes later I don't feel that way at all. Getting married is bullshit, if anyone wants to know. The whole institution is designed to drive women crazy. We don't have the time or the money to blow on some princess fantasy I never had in the first place. So why can't we just get married on a Thursday after lunch and then go back to work? Done. I love Benny, you know I do, and I want to marry him. I just don't want to be a bride."

Maisie and Nell and I are staring at her, and while I've always said my daughters are capable of a perfect communion of thought, this time I'm in on it. Emily has solved the age-old problem.

"You slipped the harness," Nell says.

"You're a fucking genius," Maisie says, her voice gone soft with wonder.

Emily stands radiant before our adoration. "Dad doesn't know this, does he?"

We shake our heads.

"Hold off for a minute, will you? Let me tell him. Benny's going to want to talk to him. I want to talk to him. He'd be hurt, you know, if he thought we'd worked the whole thing out without him. We're together all the time."

Emily! I want to say. This sorrow at the thought of exclusion you wish to protect your dear father from, that's what I've been feeling all morning. But I have been here long enough to understand the difference between daughters and mothers and daughters and fathers. We promise to wait. Secrets are at times a necessary tool for peace. "Take as long as you need."

"I'll tell him," she says, then opens up her arms to take the three of us in.

When all of this is done we feel that we have lived enough for an entire day. We've done enough. Now we should be able to go home, sit on the porch or in the bathtub, go back to bed with our books and our dog and our sewing, but the truth is the sun is ticking up and we've barely started to work. Sweet cherries must be picked today and every day until they're gone. We'll start shaking the tarts before the sweets are finished. They overlap at the end. When all the cherries are harvested there will be just enough time to get the trees pruned and finish up the farm maintenance and take care of equipment repair before we start in on the apples. And the pears. Only a few acres but still, we have pears and they will have to come off the trees. Everything does.

"Did you ever think that you were going to marry Duke?" Emily asks, bringing the story back to me.

Given that marriage is Topic A, I try to remember. Did I ever look at Duke in my bed asleep, the cigarettes on the nightstand, his arm thrown out across my chest, and think, yes, you, every morning, forever?

"No," I say.

"But you loved him," Emily says.

"I was twenty-four."

"That's a yes," Maisie says.

Did I ever wonder if my parents had been in love with other people, or think of them as having lives before their lives included me? Maybe it's just that my girls are modern, or that Duke was famous, or that we're mired down in work with only the past for distraction. I have no idea.

"So you did your first table read and then you went for a walk along the lake," Nell says.

"And you smoked!" Maisie says. "We haven't talked about the smoking. I can't believe that. You'd kill us if we smoked."

I nod, picking, picking, picking. That is all I have told them, and now I can feel them bearing down on me as if they are once again crawling into my lap, pushing my book aside, trampling my sewing. *Mommy, Mommy, Mommy,* they cry.

The most amazing thing was how well I slept—in a new state with a new job and a naked man I scarcely knew in my bed—I went through the entire night without so much as a dream. The window had no curtains, and when I opened my eyes to the brightness of Michigan I felt myself to be newly and fully adult. Certainly I hadn't been an adult in New Hampshire, and in L.A. people made money by herding me around, Ripley or Ashby, my agent, a producer. But I'd gotten to Michigan all on my own, into the play and into this bed. "Hey you." I tapped the small dip in the middle of Duke's chest.

He kept his eyes closed, smiling as he pulled me to him. "Oh, perfect. This is perfect." He snuffled into my neck. "I was hoping you'd still be here."

"Where else would I be? It's my room."

"And you've been nice about sharing. What's the time?"

I lifted up enough to see my travel clock, which was on his side of the bed. His side, my side. "Eight-seventeen."

He yawned like a lion, showing me his molars, his fillings. "We start at nine." He took my face in his hands and looked at me with great seriousness. "You shouldn't be late, the star, her first morning. You've got to be disciplined. Either breakfast or sex. Not both. You have to choose."

I was making good choices these days, which meant that by the time we rolled apart there wasn't even a moment for coffee, and no time for Duke to go back to his dorm to change. "Lend me something," he said.

I was pulling my favorite dress over my head, the smocked one with the daisies and the wide pockets that my grandmother had made for me to take to Los Angeles. "You can't wear my clothes." Small female, large male, I could think of so many reasons why it was inappropriate.

"I'm not going to rehearsal dressed in something I wore yesterday."

I looked at him. "No one remembers what you wore yesterday."

He threw off the sheets, leaping up. Duke, naked

and twenty-eight, opened the dresser: underwear, socks, and two nightgowns in the first drawer, T-shirts, shorts, and two swimsuits in the second. "Your organization is impeccable."

"Put your clothes on," I said. "We have to go."

He chose my Disneyland T-shirt, just that word in swooping pink script on a bright white background. I had wanted to go to Disneyland when I first went to L.A. and so Ashby had taken me. The two of us spun in teacups and had our picture taken with giant mice. "This," he said, tugging it over his head like a butterfly trying to stuff itself back inside the papery chrysalis.

"I don't think—" I started to say, but it was already done. He was back in his surgical scrubs, his espadrilles, the T-shirt straining to hold itself together across those wide, bony shoulders where so recently I had slept. He took my hairbrush from the dresser, my toothbrush from the sink.

"You're using my toothbrush?"

He stopped his brushing. "This is not intimacy," he said, holding the toothbrush up, the toothpaste foam sliding down his hand. And he was right, of course. He was even right about the Disney shirt, which was cute on me but was on him both scandalous and spectacular.

We came down the hall behind a Black girl wearing shorts and a Boy Scout shirt. I remembered her from the table read, her face but not her name. Or not even her face—I remembered her legs. Never had one person been in possession of such preposterous legs. She was an average height—by which I mean taller than me and shorter than Duke—but all that height was in her legs.

Nell raises her hand.

"What?"

"You're objectifying her."

"Pallace? What am I doing wrong now?"

Maisie agrees. "She's a person. She isn't a great pair of legs."

"If you'd give me another minute I plan to establish that."

"But you can't just lead with a body part."

"Have you ever met dancers? Have you ever heard them talk about their legs? About other people's legs?"

Nell thinks about this for a minute. "She may have a point."

"Get back to the story," Emily says.

Pallace dropped down the stairs three at a time, and when she got to the bottom, turned around. "Are we late?" she asked Duke.

"Right on time," he said.

Then she saw me, one stair behind him. "Emily!" she cried.

"Pallace," Duke said, holding his hand out to her by way of introduction.

She looked at us standing there together. "Seriously?" she said to Duke. "She must have been here for what, twenty minutes? Did you go to the airport and stake out the plane?"

"I didn't like my room," he said, his voice oddly prim.

"That explains why he didn't try to sleep with me," Pallace said. "The dancers are in the attic. The view is great but it gets really hot up there."

"Walk, please," Duke said, lighting the morning's first cigarette.

I was trying to keep up. *My* room? "You're a dancer?" Of course she was a dancer.

Pallace extended her left leg at a ninety-degree angle from her body and lifted up on the ball of her right foot, her little red tennis shoe straining in the point.

"Showboat," Duke said.

"Not *Showboat*, you fool, *Cabaret*. But I'm studying acting, too. Right now I'm studying your acting."

"Pallace is your understudy," Duke said.

I hadn't thought about that. Of course there would have been an understudy in place already. "So why aren't you playing Emily?"

"Because then I'd be in *Cabaret* four shows a week and *Our Town* three shows a week and at the end of the summer I'd be dead. Anyway, Tom Lake's idea of racially progressive casting is to let me be the understudy, not the lead. It's a big step for them."

"Better not get sick," Duke said to me.

"That last Emily—" Pallace began.

"Piece-of-work Emily," Duke offered.

Pallace nodded. "That piece of work dropped out soon enough for the company to find a nice new white Emily." She held an open hand in my direction.

"New and improved." Duke put his arm around my shoulder.

"*Very* improved." Pallace tossed me a smile. "And anyway, can you imagine it? A stage full of Caucasians with me standing right in the middle looking all lonely?"

Duke lowered his eyebrows, lowered his voice. "Whose town is this, anyway?"

"Not our town," Pallace answered brightly.

"I don't think—" I started to say. What was I going to say?

"If you like things just a little weirder, I'm also your understudy on *Fool for Love.* Oh! and I'm the understudy for your mother, which is stupid. Your mother should have gone to a swing."

"My mother?" My mother in New Hampshire?

Duke took back his arm. "I didn't know that! That means if Mrs. Webb gets sick you'll be my wife." The kiss he gave her then had more intention than the kiss he'd given to the woman who was presently playing my mother. "Someday we'll have to tell Emily she's adopted."

"What happens if Mrs. Webb and I are both sick on the same night?" Mrs. Webb, my mother. I couldn't remember her name.

"Then whichever one of you is less sick will pull your shit together and go on anyway," Pallace explained. "Dancers always go on. If you ever see a notice that a dancer's out, you can bet money that she OD'd on whatever painkillers they gave her to keep dancing."

"The show really must go on," Duke said.

I stopped on the path. We were almost to the theater, actors arriving from every direction, understudies and swings, all of them with coffee in hand. I would have given a lot for a coffee. "Do you two know each other?"

Duke and Pallace looked at each other. "Do we?" she asked him.

"No more than we know anyone else."

"But not less than we know anyone else," Pallace added.

"The way you talk." I turned from one to the other. They were both beautiful, unusual, overly animated, the way actors and dancers are. This was something else though. "It's like you've come out of the same improv group."

Pallace laughed, her teeth as perfect as Duke's were stricken. "Do you think? Maybe that's because we came out of the same improv group."

"The great state of Michigan," Duke said.

Duke and Pallace had known each other a week but they were both from Michigan.

The small New Hampshire town where I'd grown up was as white as Grover's Corners. In my class at school we only had Aly, who came in the ninth grade. We treated her the way we might have treated an alpaca, which is to say with fascination and solicitude but no actual friendship, so while I could give a comprehensive description of her hair, clothes, and patterns of speech (she said pop instead of soda) I had no idea why her family had moved there or where they had come from or why they had left abruptly in the middle of our junior year, though that last one probably wasn't such a mystery. The University of New Hampshire was only slightly better than our high school, and Hollywood was only slightly worse. The Black makeup artist at my first screen test turned out to be an anomaly. Hollywood had nothing on New Hampshire when it came to the intermingling of the races.

So I followed the dancer in the snappy Boy Scout shirt towards the building, running ahead to open the door because the way she and Duke were talking they would have walked straight into it. I was going to have a boyfriend who crackled like a downed power line and a girlfriend who was Black. I was even more of an adult than I could have imagined.

It turned out the summer stock in the middle-of-nowhere, Michigan, beat both the University of New Hampshire and a Hollywood backlot by a mile when it came to diversity. A low bar but still, Tom Lake won. As all of us hustled off to our various rehearsals, we nearly resembled an American city. Most of the actors came from Chicago and Detroit, a few had come from as far away as D.C. and Pittsburgh. The cattle-call auditions for summer stock—the auditions I had been spared—drew from conservatories and regional theater companies. Theater people were always looking for work, and while they might not have chosen to build a life in Tom Lake, they were happy to get out of the city for the summer. Gene, the assistant director of *Our Town,* was Black. Gene checked to see if we had our scripts. Did anybody need a script? Auden, one of the other understudies, was Black as well. He was also a dancer, and he and Pallace started dancing at the far corner of the stage, executing an intricate, old-fashioned swing without benefit of music. They looked only at each other and didn't seem to care that we were watching. Whether they were rehearsing for something that wasn't *Cabaret* (which I was pretty sure didn't include swing dancing) or killing time because Uncle Wallace had yet to arrive, I couldn't say.

I did know that diving into *Our Town* without a Stage Manager on the first day of rehearsal would be a trick, and after waiting for twenty minutes (in which we all finally just sat on the floor and watched Pallace and her friend dance, hypnotized by the regular squeak of their tennis shoes), Nelson dispatched Gene the A.D. to find out what the hell was going on.

"He might have misread the schedule," Duke offered, even though the top of the schedule said REHEARSALS BEGIN PROMPTLY AT 9:00 A.M. in a typeface large enough to be scolding.

The collective desire of every person in that theater was for the play to succeed. Emily had skipped out. Emily had been replaced. New day, let's get to work. The A.D. returned, too quickly I thought, and the director met him in the aisle for a brief consult. The director, Nelson, already looked tired.

"Okay, people," he said, clapping twice even though he had our full attention. Pallace and her partner let go of one another's hands. "We're going to get started.

Albert will be here momentarily. Let's go ahead with the understudy. I want a full day. Lee?"

A man in a light-blue golf shirt raised a tentative hand.

"Do you need a script?" Gene asked.

We were all looking at him. "I—" he said, then stopped and held up his script.

"That's good," Nelson said.

"I don't know the part yet," Lee said.

"It's early. You'll be fine. Hopefully you're just going to read for a few minutes. Nothing gets an actor out of bed like the knowledge that the understudy is reading his part."

Everyone laughed politely except the man in the golf shirt. We were meant to sit in the row of chairs on either side of the stage whenever we weren't in the scene. We went to sit in them now, leaving Lee out there alone. When the moment came for one of us to talk at the kitchen table or the drugstore soda fountain or in the cemetery at the end, we were to carry our chairs across the empty stage and put them in places marked with gaffer tape on the floor, but for now everyone was sitting on either side, waiting. When we had taken our places, Nelson told the understudy to begin.

Lee was in his sixties, his hair gray, his glasses heavy. He had the sunburnt look of a man who took his golf shirts seriously. When the play opens, the Stage Manager is alone. "This is a play called *Our Town*," he says. "It was written by Thornton Wilder." He then goes on to name the director, the producer, the actors in major roles, but Lee read the script exactly as it was written. "Directed by A," he said, and then later, "In it you will see Miss C . . ."

I'd seen a lot of people read the Stage Manager, but I had never seen anything that approached this. I wanted to go back to New Hampshire and tell those men with their handkerchiefs and pipes what a good job they'd done. Surely Spalding Gray was speaking these same words in a rehearsal now. I willed myself to hear his voice, even though I'd never heard his voice before. Here in Michigan, the words were clearly painful for Lee to say, and they stuck a needle into the confidence of every person in the room. Maybe I wasn't the adult who'd won the lead at an important summer stock in Michigan; maybe I was a talentless kid who'd been hustled out of the room because I was taking up too much of the air. "Send her to Michigan!" is what they'd scribbled on their notepads during my audition. "She won't know the difference."

Duke, in the chair next to mine, ran one finger lightly up my thigh while looking straight ahead, slipping past the hem of my daisy dress like a spider on a mission.

Things were just about to get better in Los Angeles, that's what Ripley had been trying to tell me. I was supposed to stay true the course, be patient. I had failed.

This was what a bad reading of the Stage Manager could do to the room.

So when Uncle Wallace miraculously appeared at the very end of the first act, I once again loved him the way I had loved him as a child: *In the face of tragedy our uncle has come to save us.* What did I care that he looked like an unmade bed, or that he was walking the line between hungover and still actively drunk? He was there to lead us into Act Two, and I would no longer have to listen to Lee in his golf shirt telling me that the sun had come up over a thousand times.

"Alarm clock malfunction," Uncle Wallace announced, applauding generously for the man who had made him look like a Barrymore. "But I'm here now. We can begin."

"Aren't you being awfully hard on Lee?" Emily asks. "It was only the first day. He wasn't planning to go on."

Nell agrees. "I wouldn't have wanted to do it, and anyway, they wouldn't have hired an understudy who was *that* bad. We know Nelson's too smart for that."

It is already hot. I am already tired of cherries. "Funny you should say that, because the understudies were great as a rule. The company was very rigorous about the understudies. Except for Lee. Lee was horrible."

"Why would they hire someone horrible to cover the lead?" Nell asks.

"Because Lee owned a trucking company. His family had a big house right on the lake. They hosted fundraisers—real money, major donors. Lee loved the theater, god bless him for that. He didn't want to be an actor, he just wanted to hang out with us. Maybe it was strange. He used to bring popsicles and prosecco to rehearsals sometimes. Everybody loved him then."

"So they sold him an understudy part?" Maisie asks.

"That would be a crass way to put it, but yes. They sold him the part."

"Nelson?"

"No, no," I said. "He wasn't given any choice in the matter. Of this I am certain."

"But why did he have to be the Stage Manager?" Nell says. Nell, who takes all injustice to heart. "The Stage Manager is too important."

Joe and I have taught our daughters how to grade a plum and pick a stone from a goat's hoof and make a piecrust, but I fear we have taught them nothing of the world. "Because you don't go around at a cocktail party telling people you're the understudy for Constable Warren."

"Wasn't he at least smart enough to be afraid Uncle Wallace might get sick?" Maisie asks.

"Lee was talentless but he wasn't stupid. Uncle Wallace had been at Tom Lake for fourteen consecutive summers and had never missed a performance. That man was like a dancer. He always went on."

"He went on drunk?" Emily asks.

Big old blustery Albert Long, red-faced and red-haired. My heart seized with unexpected affection at his memory. "Drunkish. He found a way to make it work."

"And what about the George?" Nell asks.

"The George? What about him?"

"Was he bad?"

"Forgettable," I say.

"As bad as Lee?" Maisie asks.

"Oh, no, nothing like that. I'm sure he was fine. I only mean that I've forgotten him."

"Which means what? You can't remember his performance?" Nell is concerned that this is further proof of my diminishment. To my children I am unimaginably old.

"I mean the kid who played George is gone," I say, but they don't understand what I'm talking about. Duke is as close as the cherries on the tree, as is Uncle Wallace, for reasons that are no doubt connected to how things ended. Lee I remember less as a person and more as a story, and George I do not remember at all. There is no explaining this simple truth about life: you will forget much of it. The painful things you were certain you'd never be able to let go? Now you're not entirely sure when they happened, while the thrilling parts, the heart-stopping joys, splintered and scattered and became something else. Memories are then replaced by different joys and larger sorrows, and unbelievably, those things get knocked aside as well, until one morning you're picking cherries with your three grown daughters and your husband goes by on the Gator and you are positive that this is all you've ever wanted in the world.

9

Yes, it was true that Uncle Wallace was a drunk, and his understudy hid in the farthest corner of the theater where not even the light could find him, but plenty of other things were true as well, such as the fact that Albert Long embodied the Stage Manager as completely as he had embodied that long-ago bachelor uncle. Duke might have made fun of him—dinner theaters, bombastic speeches, lecherous asides—but when he was onstage there was nothing to complain about. Uncle Wallace never had to reach for a line because the lines were written inside him, just the way Emily's were written into me, the difference being he'd found a part he wouldn't age out of. When, in the third act, Uncle Wallace took me back to my mother's kitchen, he looked at me with so much compassion it stung my eyes.

So what if he smelled like gin? So what if he went out for a cigarette and wandered away? The A.D. always managed to find him, guiding him back like an errant lamb. On the stage he was able to bring himself into focus, so that even as the people who knew him said he was different this year, said he was so much worse, we continued to bank on the fact that he had never missed a show. Why wouldn't the past be the future as well?

After rehearsal, Duke and I stretched out on the grass beside the lake, sharing a cigarette and a beer. "The man takes every bit of joy out of alcohol," Duke said, tipping the bottle back. "I could hate him for that alone."

"Somebody told me he plays Lear at another summer stock at the end of the season, that he's always trying to get them to do a production of it here but he can't get anybody at Tom Lake interested in Shakespeare."

Duke lifted an eyebrow. "He's the one who told you that."

"Maybe." I took another drag. One week and my smoking had already vastly improved. "I think he'd make a wild Lear, stomping around screaming. He'd be completely heartbreaking in the end."

Duke sat up and pulled me into his lap. "And you'd be his little Cordelia, is that what you're thinking?"

"I wouldn't mind."

"Put down the cigarette."

"Why?"

"Because you're dead. You're Cordelia and you're dead and I'm going to show you how Uncle Wallace plays Lear."

I twisted the cigarette into the grass and died right there in his arms. Duke held my lifeless body against his chest, rocking me gently as his hand snaked up under my T-shirt. "Never, never, never, never, never," he whispered in my hair, squeezing my left breast gently with every declaration. Truly, it was all we could do to make it back to the room.

Our Town contains a single kiss and it's not between Emily and George but between Emily and her father, the newspaperman. She pecks his cheek in the first act. There's also exactly one erotic moment in the play, in the second act, just before George and Emily marry. Emily begs her father to run away with her so that they can build a life together, just the two of them. "Don't you remember that you used to say—all the time you used to say—all the time: that I was *your* girl! There must be lots of places we can go to."

I couldn't tell you how many times I'd planted that kiss, said those words, and never given any of it a thought.

Nelson interrupted the scene. Nelson who showed up for work in a collared shirt with the sleeves turned back and nice khaki pants, while the rest of us wandered the stage in cut-offs and Phish T-shirts. "Peter, Lara," he said calmly. "If you could come up with a slightly more wholesome interpretation, it would be appreciated."

Everyone laughed. Uncle Wallace, waiting to officiate the union—by which I mean the union of George and Emily as opposed to the union of the editor and his daughter—cleared his throat. Nobody was pretending that Duke and I weren't happening. They were only asking that we tone it down.

Every day at Tom Lake was a week, every week a month. We spent hours in a dark theater, saying the same things to the same people again and again, finding ways to make the world new. In high school and college I'd gone to rehearsals a few times a week, but at Tom Lake rehearsals were our life. Where we stood and how we stood and how we placed our chairs and looked into the lights and spoke to one another and listened, all of it mattered. Uncle Wallace had been right about Nelson. Every day he directed each of us towards a better performance.

Our schedule included precious little free time but we made excellent use of what we had. We wore our swimsuits under our clothes and ran to the lake in lieu of eating lunch. With advanced planning we could get from the stage to being nearly naked and fully submerged in four minutes flat. I owned two suits, the one my grandmother had ordered me from L.L. Bean and the bikini I had not returned to costume the day I was instructed to swim in the backlot pool. I never questioned which one to wear. Pallace came to the lake with her dance partner, Auden, and Auden's Korean American boyfriend, Charles, who we called W.H. because we never saw one without the other. W.H. was another dancer and also a swing. Mother Gibbs and Mrs. Webb swam in the lake but Mrs. Webb wouldn't put her head under water and neither would Pallace. They swam like women in classic Hollywood movies, smiling, with lip gloss. Some days Pallace even wore a hat. The water was cold and none of us cared and all of us screamed. Duke was always the first one in. Maybe that's all that needs to be said about Duke: he was forever the first one in, cutting long strokes out to the swim platform while the rest of us waded in up to our knees then stopped to watch the little fish trying to make sense of our enormous feet. He would disappear and then pop up again someplace far away, pushing his wet black hair out of his face. "Where's my girl?" he bellowed. "Where's my birthday girl?" It was his favorite line in the play and he got to say it twice in the third act. He said it at night when he folded back the sheet and slipped into my bed.

I swam out to Duke, looped my arms around his neck, looped my legs around his waist in the deep water. He held me up.

"You two are going to break something," Pallace said, swimming past us. "The people in the first ten rows are going to have to wipe their glasses off."

"Jealous girl," Duke said.

She laughed, then glided away. When Duke started acting like he was being eaten by a shark, I untangled myself and swam after Pallace. I was in love with the play and in love with Tom Lake, and maybe I was in love with Duke, and certainly I was in love with Pallace, her red bikini every bit as insubstantial as my own.

"You must be bored to tears having to sit there all morning," I said when I caught up to her. Just our heads were sticking up above the water. The blue sky was her backdrop and the sunlight was her lighting; it caught the gold hoops in her ears.

"Nothing boring about it," she said. "I'm watching you."

I thought about those auditions in high school, and how I put together my idea of Emily by watching people play her wrong. Wouldn't it be a different thing entirely to watch someone doing her right? If, in fact, Pallace thought I was doing her right. "Now I'm going to be nervous."

"You are many things, Emily Webb, but nervous isn't one of them."

"You seem pretty relaxed yourself." My arms worked back and forth across the surface of the lake.

She shook her head. "Dancing and singing is all about working your ass off so that people think you just roll out of bed dancing and singing. I mean, acting is like that too, but it's less physical for the most part."

Duke and I had missed breakfast again. We were perfecting the craft.

"Anyway, being your understudy is teaching me things," she said. "Half the day I'm playing a little country girl in a town full of white people, doing the whole thing in my head, then the other half of the day I'm playing a hooker in a German night club and I'm doing the whole thing in my body. That's why I like to swim in the middle. It helps the transition." The water was so clear I could watch the graceful mechanics of her legs as she treaded.

"*Fool for Love* is going to be a lot more work," I said, though she was the understudy for that as well so she already knew.

"Or a lot more fun. You and Duke in *Fool for Love*." She laughed, swimming a gentle lap around me. "That's a lucky piece of casting if I've ever heard one. They'll have to hose out the theater. Good thing you're not going up against that dopey George again. Not the guy you'd want slinging you into bed every night." She shaded her eyes with her hand and watched Mother Gibbs as she walked out of the lake. "Is it time?" Pallace called.

Mother Gibbs shook her head. "Fifteen minutes," she shouted back. "I want to dry off and put my underwear on."

Lee was sitting there on a beach towel the size of a picnic blanket, watching us swim.

"So what happens if you end up having to play Emily?" I asked her.

Pallace gave me a squint. "Are you trying to tell me something?"

"No, no, nothing like that. I just wonder how it would work."

"Tuesday night *Our Town*, Wednesday night, *Cabaret*, Thursday night, *Our Town*, Friday night, *Cabaret*, Saturday, *Our Town* matinee with *Cabaret* at night, Sunday is *Cabaret* at night but no *Our Town* matinee, so there's a break. Monday I sleep."

"That's not possible."

Pallace disagreed. "It's possible, not optimal. I'd like to play Emily once or twice, only if you had a UTI or something, but other than that I pray for your health." She was looking back at the shore. "Do you know who that is?"

Mother Gibbs was gone and in her place a man now stood at the edge of the water, waving his arms over his head. "*Pee*dee," he called. "*Pee*dee!"

I looked over my shoulder to see who he was looking

at—Duke on the swim platform was wet and shining like a god. There should have been a golden trident in his hand, a crown of seaweed and starfish in his hair. He waved his arms wildly in return then dove into the lake. It was straight out of a movie, the elegance of his dive and then his swimming, clean and fast, none of the splashing around he'd been doing before.

"Must be his dealer," Pallace said. "We should go in anyway."

Off she went, but for a moment I stayed behind treading water, watching all the actors and dancers as they swam to shore. Lee folded up his towel and walked away. I wondered if anyone had ever prayed for my health before. My grandmother, probably. She would have done that for me.

"It's Saint Sebastian, isn't it?" Emily says. She is Emily again, fully restored, taking cherries down at twice the clip of the rest of us.

I nod. "He used to drive up when he had days off."

Maisie looks at Emily. "How could you possibly know who it was?"

"I like reading interviews, that's all. Sebastian was always there. Don't you remember when Duke won his Oscar? The first word out of his mouth was *Sebastian.*"

None of us remember that, but I'm more than

a decade into convincing myself that Emily's attention to the details of Duke's life isn't something to be alarmed about.

"So even if you know he was close to his brother, how do you know that his brother's come to Tom Lake?" Maisie asks, pushing. "Break's over, time to get back to work. Why don't you just think it's Gene the A.D. calling him in?"

Emily sighs and I worry that Maisie's going to set her off. "Sebastian was the only one who called him Peedee. Peter Duke. And Duke was the only one who called him Saint Sebastian."

"The first part is right," I say. "But pretty much everyone who knew Sebastian called him Saint Sebastian."

"To his face?" Emily asks.

I nod, picturing Sebastian's face in my mind, as restful as Duke's was restive.

"I've been looking forward to Saint Sebastian ever since Dad told us about him playing tennis," Nell says, as if Sebastian were a character who had just made his entrance in the play. "Where did he live?" It's Emily she's asking, not me.

"In 1988 he would still have been in East Detroit."

"Wait," Maisie says. Maisie could not care less about her sister's mood. "First off, what the hell is *East* Detroit? And secondly, is there a biography of Sebastian Duke that I failed to get my copy of?"

Maisie wouldn't have known the details of Sebastian's life, and she surely wouldn't have heard of East Detroit, seeing as how it was renamed in 1992, but Emily knows everything, and she lays out the facts like a state historian: East Detroit renamed itself when Detroit proper was circling the drain; the city council of East Detroit tried to bolster eroding property values by changing its name to Eastpointe, that fancy silent "e" at the end an indicator that the white people lived over here and the Black people lived over there, on the other side of Eight Mile. Emily's obsession with a movie star had given her this particular knowledge. In her role as the living archivist of Duke, she is also the archivist of the vanished East Detroit.

"You've just been walking around with this in your head all these years and you never told anybody?" Maisie asks.

"You'll be surprised to know that this is the first time it's come up." Even though Emily's face is impassive, I think she's pleased we've finally knocked on the door of her vast storehouse of data.

"Was Saint Sebastian still a tennis player then?"

Emily looks at me.

"Go ahead," I say.

"He was done," Emily tells her sisters. She never stops picking cherries, her hands on autopilot. "He'd made the National Sixteen and Under in Kalamazoo. He played the Future Challenger circuit, but he didn't make the pros. Tennis costs a lot of money and their family didn't have it. But he was still coaching then. Duke used to say Sebastian couldn't have been much of a coach if he couldn't even make a decent tennis player out of his own brother, but Duke was pretty good, wasn't he?"

"Duke was a great tennis player," I say. "He just wasn't as great as his brother. And Sebastian was a very good coach. He taught me how to play."

"You can play tennis?" Emily looks at me, surprised. They're all surprised.

"I played that summer. Pallace and I both played. Sometimes we played doubles with the boys but that was a joke." What Pallace and I never did was play each other because what would have been the point in that?

"It was just the two of them, right?" Nell asks. "Just the two boys?"

Emily shakes her head. "They had a younger sister."

"There wasn't a sister." Only Duke and Sebastian, raised by wolves, but even as I'm saying it, my mind is scrolling backwards: late nights, rehearsal breaks, floating in the water holding hands. What did Duke ever tell me? That he was hungry, that he wanted me to take my swimsuit off in the lake, that he needed a drink? For as much as the feel of Peter Duke's hair slipping between my fingers is mine, the facts of his life more accurately belong to my daughter.

"Sarah was the youngest," Emily says. "She died of Ewing's sarcoma when she was four."

Was it possible? Duke was always saying he'd take me home with him, back to East Detroit, so he could show me where he came from. Surely the little girl's photograph would have been on the mantel in their parents' house. I would have asked who she was.

"Sarah Duke," Emily says.

"I didn't know."

"He never talked about her."

"But you knew," Maisie says, because it was starting to feel like Emily had gotten Duke's number after all, that she had somehow called him from her bedroom when she was fourteen.

"Some journalist went through every piece of information in the public record about his family. I think it was for *Vanity Fair*. Anyway, he found the death certificate and then he sprung it on him in the interview, just to see how he'd react. Apparently Duke walked out. He wouldn't finish the interview, wouldn't sit for photos."

Good for you, I want to say to him. I who knew nothing and have nothing to say. I can remember very clearly when Emily was eight and Maisie was six and Nell was four, the big girls were in school all day and Nell came home from preschool after lunch. The sweetness of those hours when it was just the two of us never left. What would life have been without Nell? Who would Emily and Maisie have confided in once they were grown? *We had a younger sister.*

Nell puts her hand on my shoulder, Nell who reads my mind. "Go back to the lake," she says to me. "Tell us about Sebastian."

I didn't know Duke had a brother, and while later I could see some resemblance, it wasn't immediately evident. When I was close enough to really see him I didn't think, he must be my boyfriend's brother; I thought, this guy's not a drug dealer. He was talking to Pallace, making her laugh, and Duke had on his biggest possible Duke smile. My swimsuit was seersucker, blue and white, with a tiny, heart-shaped button sewn between the cups with red thread, a lovely, unnecessary detail that spoke to how much the stupid thing must have cost. I shivered slightly when I walked out of the water even though the day was so hot. Pallace had to get to her *Cabaret* rehearsal and it was late but she waited for me. She took the towel from around her waist and draped it over my shoulders, like she knew I'd forgotten my towel. Maybe she did know. We were so naked, the two of us.

Duke put his arm around me. "This is the one!" he said. "This is Emily. Emily, this is my brother, Sebastian."

"Lara." I shook his hand.

Sebastian smiled. "He forgets."

Sebastian was a man, that was the thing. Sebastian, scarcely a year his senior, was a man and Duke was a boy and Pallace and I were girls.

Everyone else had already left. Pallace tugged her sundress over her head and I was trying to pull up my shorts, suddenly envying Mother Gibbs her dry underwear. I rubbed quickly at my torso, my hair, so I could give Pallace her towel back.

"Maybe I could have come at a worse time?" Sebastian asked.

"Are you kidding me? It's the perfect time!" Duke said, his voice exalted. "We're working on the third act after lunch. It's all Emily. You won't believe how great she is."

"Are you in the third act?" Sebastian asked Pallace.

"Not the third act you're talking about. I'm in a different third act and I'm going to be obscenely late if I don't leave right this second."

I gave back the stripey beach towel. "Go."

She looked at all of us, making it clear she wanted to stay. She smiled at Sebastian. "I'm so late," she said, and then she turned around and ran. She was wearing flip-flops, a bag over her shoulder. She bounded off to the rehearsal studio while the three of us stood there, watching her go.

"My god," Sebastian said. "Is she a runner?"

Duke gave the question serious consideration. Was Pallace a runner? "I would say she is everything."

We headed back up the hill to the theater, Duke lit up in his happiness. He carried his shirt and espadrilles in one hand, and kept his other hand on his brother's back. How was the drive and had he had lunch? Sebastian could sleep in his room in the dorm because he was bunking with me. Duke hadn't dried his feet and now they were coated in dust. He never brought a towel to the lake because he always just used my towel, but today, for whatever reason, I'd forgotten.

"Are you in the third act?" Sebastian asked Duke as he held open the door to the theater.

"Where's my girl?" Duke called out as we walked into the darkness. "Where's my birthday girl?"

None of us knew we were at the beginning of anything but this was where the four of us started. After rehearsal, Duke took his brother back to his room to get him settled, and for the first time it struck me that I had no idea where Duke's room was. My room—he was always telling me this—was so much better. I walked out of the theater alone and thought about what I should do with my time. I never had time. I should write letters, or at the very least postcards, and let everyone know how well things were going. My intention was to go straight to my room but I heard music through an open window. "What good. Is sit-*ting*. A*lone* in your room?" the singer asked. The accompanying piano felt tinny and stale, exactly right. The words were less a question than a directive. "Come *to* the *Ca*-ba-*ret*, old chum . . ." I went inside and stood against the back wall of the rehearsal room.

I'd left Grover's Corners, where we sat in a row of chairs in the cemetery, staring ahead, and arrived at the Kit Kat Klub, where the dancers straddled their chairs with intention, stood on chairs bending forward, asses offered to the light. Pallace draped backwards across the seat of one, the top of her head touching the floor, her legs scissoring up in time with the music. She was still wearing her red swimsuit, all the dancers were wearing some variation of swim wear, and it all looked vaguely obscene so far away from the lake. Upside down and sideways they were singing, dancing, grinding away while a man at an upright piano played along, darting up a hand to turn the sheet of music then coming right back to playing again.

It would be easy to describe Pallace as the most beautiful, most talented person I had ever seen, but Tom Lake was bristling with her equals. I suppose a few attractive duds had snuck in here and there, the kid playing George being one, but for the most part the performers had a magnetism that required no practice whatsoever—either you've got it or you don't. Duke had a truckload of it. He had it when he spoke the dullest lines of Editor Webb, or ordered coffee, or took me to bed. If Jimmy-George from high school knew how to look at a person, Duke knew how to make a person look at him. The Kit Kat girls were no slouches in that department either. I had come in to watch my friend, but confronted with the whole lot of them I hardly knew where to rest my eyes. They all looked hungry. I went from Pallace to some others I'd met at dinner or in the lake, a few I didn't know, and finally came to rest on Sally Bowles, who stood in the middle of the stage like a diamond set in a ring. Sally Bowles, her leg slung shamelessly over the back of a chair, extended an invitation to the cabaret that no one could refuse.

Just as I'd started to think I could act, I found myself wishing I could sing and dance. I wanted to climb up on one of the Kit Kat chairs, to be a woman rather than a girl.

When they were finished, Pallace used that same

striped towel to dry herself again, laughing with the other dancers as she pulled on her dress. I waved to her, and when she saw me, she smiled like I was the person she was most hoping to see. "You're here!" she said.

"I want to be your understudy," I said.

She fell breathless into the folding chair beside me, bending over to unbuckle her high-heeled shoes. "How much do you know about the brother?"

"Until a few hours ago I didn't know he had a brother. That's how much I know about the brother."

"Did he say anything?"

"He's staying for a couple of days."

"Did he say anything about *me*," she said, the perspiration shining at her hairline.

I thought for a minute. What had Sebastian said? "He was impressed with your running."

She smiled. "I'll take that."

"You want Duke's brother?"

"He's not a dancer and he's not an actor and he doesn't work in a theater and he has very nice shoulders."

It turned out that was what she was looking for.

"I understand what Pallace's talking about," Nell says, speaking from unreferenced experience. "Nobody should date actors."

"Except for Mom," Maisie says. She and I pick up the ladder together and carry it down the row to the next tree so one of us can climb up and clean the top, and by one of us I mean Maisie. Maisie loves to climb. We were always pulling her off the curtains when she was little.

"Why should Mom have to date an actor?" Nell says. "It's not like it turned out so well for her."

"It wasn't that bad," I say. Was it that bad? Yes and no.

Emily ignores this. "If Mom hadn't dated Duke then what would we be talking about now? Fungicides?"

"We'd go back to listening to the news all day," I say.

Maisie shakes her head. "No more news."

Nell agrees. "We'd rather talk about your wedding than a global pandemic," she says to Emily.

Emily's wedding. I have not said a word about it to Joe.

"Well, that's reason enough to date an actor right there," Emily says, "because we sure as hell aren't talking about my wedding."

It is as if every action in my life has been planned for the pleasures of this very afternoon.

Nell takes the bucket from around her neck and dumps her cherries in the lug. She gives herself a minute to roll her shoulders before putting it on again, then turns her face towards the sun, closing her eyes. Sometimes I wonder if the work isn't too much for her, though she'd sooner die picking cherries than be the weak sister. "I would have dated Saint Sebastian," she says.

"You're telling me that you would have turned down Duke, arguably the greatest actor of his generation and certainly the most famous, so that you could date his brother who didn't make it as a tennis player?" Emily says.

Maisie disagrees. "Oh, come on, that's not fair. It's impossible to make it as a tennis player, not to mention the fact that Saint Sebastian was, you know, a saint. That's a very attractive quality in a man. And even if Duke was famous he didn't have a happy life."

"You don't know that," Emily says, picking, picking.

I might not have known much about Duke but I knew his life wasn't happy. I put my arm around Nell's shoulder. "As insane as this conversation is, I think you're making the right choice. And anyway, even if Sebastian didn't make the pros he was still an excellent tennis player. He played McEnroe."

The three of them drop their hands and I know I've finally said something of real interest. I can hear Joe telling me not to get them overexcited. They have to keep working.

"Did he win?" Maisie's voice is hushed, and Maisie's voice is never hushed.

"No," I say. "But it was something he was proud of, just that he got so far as to even be on the same court with him. They were both seventeen. McEnroe was a big deal at seventeen."

"What was the score?" It was a scrap of information for Emily to add to her collection.

"Six-two, six-o."

Nell covers her face with her hands and moans. "Oh, Saint Sebastian! I can't bear it."

"What are you talking about? He was happy!" I say. "Sebastian never expected to win."

"He did," Nell says. "Even if he never admitted it, he thought he might. He wanted to."

Maybe she's right. Saint Sebastian was twenty-nine when we met, and it was Duke who told me the story about McEnroe. At seventeen, Sebastian must have thought of himself as someone who would make it. The number of things I'd failed to grasp back then was as limitless as the stars in the night sky.

10

For three seasons of the year, Saint Sebastian was the tennis coach at the University Liggett School in Gross Pointe Woods where he taught U. S. History and World Civilization. In the summers he worked at the Grosse Pointe Yacht Club in Grosse Pointe Shores, where the fact that he had once squared off against Johnny Mac made him the stuff of legend. At the yacht club, that match was spoken of in terms of victory, with the score widening in Sebastian's favor over time. When Sebastian corrected them, and he always did, they took it as further proof of his humility and loved him all the more. He ate his dinner in the bar of the club's grill where he wasn't allowed to order steak or the crab cakes and anyone who wanted to rattle on about the game could pull up a chair and join him. Dinner at the grill was part of Sebastian's job. After work he drove home to East Detroit, because there was still such a place as East Detroit, and whenever he could work enough doubles to swing a few days off in a row, he made the three-hour drive to Tom Lake to see his brother.

I loved it when Sebastian was with us. Tom Lake had a good court far from the amphitheater and they kept it lit at night. Pallace and I would drag out canvas folding chairs and sit and watch the two of them play. Sometimes we were the ball girls, Pallace running for Sebastian, me running for Duke. Pallace and Sebastian happened quickly after they met, though if my relationship with Duke were the benchmark of courtship, they had proceeded with Victorian decorum.

How beautiful those brothers were beneath the floodlights, the two of them dashing across the green rubico. Duke used twice the energy Sebastian did, maybe three times more, smashing out his serves, lunging for balls he could never return, making deep animal sounds that were not unfamiliar to me whenever his racquet connected. All Duke wanted to do was play tennis when Sebastian was there, though I imagine for his brother it must have made Tom Lake a busman's holiday.

"Doesn't he get tired of it?" I asked Pallace, our heads moving right to left, left to right, as we followed the bouncing yellow ball.

Once Duke lost the set, Pallace would be up. She hadn't played much before but she had the strength for it, the grace. I, on the other hand, was hopeless, though Sebastian would bring me on to hit a few at the end of the night, praising me every time I returned his easy lob. Soon enough Duke would get restless watching girls play, and start to make noise about wanting to go back to the house for a drink.

"Sebastian loves it," Pallace said, her eyes never leaving him, when what she meant was, *Sebastian loves me.*

Oh, Pallace, I thought. This is summer.

But that wasn't what I thought about Duke. Duke threw his entire life into everything he did, into every backhand, into the modest role of Editor Webb, into me, into us. He was so sure of us that we'd decided to go to L.A. together once the summer was over. We could rent a furnished apartment in the building where I used to live or in one of the hundred buildings like it. I had talked to my agent, who said he'd have no trouble finding work for me. I told him that surely he could find something for Duke as well. I'd written to Ripley about him twice, asking him if he had any parts. No one in Hollywood looked like Duke, and if anyone had his particular brand of charisma, well, I'd never seen it.

But Sebastian was the actor when it came to the game—a play in three acts—so that he was one tennis coach with his competitive brother, another tennis coach with his athletic lover, and a third tennis coach with his brother's inept girlfriend. He didn't throw points, but he made it all look harder for him than it was, running and reaching when he didn't need to do either. He slammed the ball at Duke, hit the ball directly into the center of Pallace's racquet, and all but handed me the ball in a cup. I bet he did the same for the yacht club wives, for their husbands, and the kids he taught at school: power in accordance with need. At the end of the match his shirt was dry, whereas Duke had pulled his soaking T-shirt over his head and thrown it into the corner of the chain-link fence. Under the bright lights I could see the sweet indentations of his ribs, and how they cast the smallest shadows across his pale torso.

It was the very busiest time. *Cabaret* had already opened the season at Tom Lake and *Our Town* was a week out from following them. The rehearsals were all in tech now, ten out of twelve. They put a stiff pomade in Duke's hair and pinned it in the back so that he looked less like the lead in *Jesus Christ Superstar* and more like a respectable newspaperman in 1901. At the same time, we'd started the table reads for *Fool for Love* and at night we ran our lines in bed. Duke had played Eddie once before at Detroit Rep. His Eddie was the reason he'd been hired for Tom Lake. Even as he lay there on his side, his hand on my hip, I could see how scary good he'd be in the part. How it thrilled me to think of going straight from *Our Town* to that run-down motel room, going from the father and daughter we'd imbued with too much chemistry, to a pair of half siblings who had enough chemistry to burn down a barn. We'd show Tom Lake a thing or two about what it meant to be dark and complicated and grown-up.

We ate and drank and slept our art, pounded our art into the mattress. Actors and dancers, designers and techs of different races from different states and wildly different backgrounds strolled through a utopia of cherry trees when they weren't being worked to a nub. Men held hands with men. No one gave Sebastian and Pallace a thought. Michigan! Who knew?

"Let's see you take me home to East Detroit come fall," Pallace said, her head in Sebastian's lap. We had just come out of the lake and the four of us were lying on an old cotton blanket Sebastian had brought from home. Duke's beautiful head was in my lap, his face pressed against my bare stomach.

"Let's see you take me home to Lansing," Sebastian said to her.

Pallace shook her head. "I'm not going back to Lansing. I've already told my folks if they want to see me they can come to Chicago." Pallace had stayed in

Chicago after finishing her training at the conservatory, though she was hoping Tom Lake would be her ticket to New York.

Duke reached out a finger and ran it down a few inches of Pallace's thigh and Sebastian leaned over and brushed his brother's hand away. "Scoot over here," he said to Pallace, tapping her hip, and she laughed. She stayed where she was, sandwiched between the two of them.

Duke was so happy when Sebastian was there, we were all so happy, but still, Sebastian's visits unsettled things, almost as if his calmness allowed Duke to be crazier than he usually was, like a kid who'll throw himself off of ladders once he knows someone's there to catch him. Duke was showing off for his brother because showing off was Duke's nature, but the way Sebastian watched him, it was almost like he was waiting for something terrible to happen, and that made me look for it, too. Sebastian was trying to anticipate Duke's craziness in the hopes that he could circumvent it, and by craziness I do not mean talent or eccentricity but something deeply nuts. When Sebastian was there to see it, it became much harder for me to pass the whole thing off as Duke simply being Duke.

Maisie holds up her hand. "I'm sorry, I have to interrupt. You can't say crazy."

"And you really can't say nuts," Nell says. "Unless you're talking about pecans."

"But he was crazy. Nuts. He really was."

"Duke had things to overcome in his life but he wasn't crazy," Emily says firmly.

I shake my head. "I'm going to overrule you on this one."

"It's not that you can't say *Duke* is crazy," Maisie explains. "I mean you can't use that word anymore. It's pejorative."

"I know crazy is pejorative. I mean for it to be pejorative, insofar as I don't mean it was a positive attribute."

"You need to find a better word," Nell says.

"Insane?"

The three of them shake their heads.

"What am I allowed to call it then?"

Maisie gives a long exhale, which means that I am old and she can't explain anything to me. Nell tries to explain. "You could refer to whatever was wrong with him by using his diagnosis: He had schizophrenia, for example. He had a bipolar disorder."

"But you really shouldn't talk about another person's diagnosis," Maisie says. "Unless he wanted you to."

"He wasn't schizophrenic *or* bipolar!" Emily is suiting up for battle. I can see it.

"You can't say a person *is* schizophrenic anyway,"

Maisie informs her sister. "He wasn't a disease. You wouldn't say 'He was cancer.'"

"I might," I say.

"Stop it." Emily is in no one's corner but Duke's.

"So you want me to tell you about Duke without mentioning that he was crazy? I'm already leaving out the sex. I'm not sure how much of a story is going to be left."

This brings us to an impasse. They very much want to know about Duke having sex without ever wanting to know about me having sex, which is fine because I'm not telling them.

"I think it's okay to say mental illness," Nell says.

"Maybe," Maisie says. "If it's just the four of us."

"We're in a cherry orchard." Emily raises her voice. "Who's going to cancel us? The dog?"

"Maybe you should just tell us what happened," Nell says. "Just the facts, without attaching any judgment to it."

And so I relate the following without the attachment of judgment:

—I would wake up in the middle of the night to an empty bed and go downstairs and find him on the love seat in the front hall, writing furiously in a notebook, page after page after page of notes on Editor Webb: his childhood, the girl he'd liked in middle school, his newspaper route, his secondary education, his college years majoring in English, what his parents thought about him going to college to major in English, that his parents wanted him to stay and work on the farm, his first job on a newspaper in Concord, the books he read, when he met Myrtle who would later become his wife, the birth of their daughter Emily, the birth of their son Wally. He was on his third notebook. I'd found the first two in the nightstand, his handwriting a microscopic block print, all caps. I got a headache trying to read it. Then I found the notebooks on Eddie and *Fool for Love.*

—He forced himself to stay awake for an entire weekend because he'd heard it was a better high than getting high. Then he tried to punch Sebastian when Sebastian wouldn't give him the car keys so that he could drive to the all-night diner in town for coffee. He didn't succeed in punching Sebastian though, because all Sebastian had to do was step aside and then catch Duke when he pitched forward, like some sort of unfunny comedy routine they'd been rehearsing for years.

—The four of us came back to the company housing late one night after playing tennis to find that the front door, which was never locked, was locked. While three of us discussed our best course of action, Duke punched out one of the small panes of glass beside the door. He didn't sever an artery or cut a tendon, though it took Sebastian half an hour to tweeze the shards of glass out of his hand and get it wrapped. "Saint Sebastian, Saint Sebastian, Saint Sebastian," Duke repeated as he watched his brother work. He refused to go to the hospital. "That's the way they do it in the movies," he said, pleased with his own decisiveness.

"In movies the glass panes are made out of sugar, you fucking moron," Pallace said, waiting up with us even though we'd come home because she was tired and wanted to go to bed. We had to act in the morning. She had to dance.

"And the guy punching the window out always takes the time to wrap his hand in a towel first," Sebastian said.

"And the door wasn't locked anyway," I said, because it wasn't. I tried it and found it was only stuck.

Duke thought this last bit was hilarious.

—He put out a cigarette on his arm one night, looking right at me as he did it. I jumped up and batted it out of his hand. "What in the hell is wrong with you?" I shouted, and then ran downstairs for ice. When I came back to the room I could smell it.

"Tell me," I said, holding the dish towel to the burn. But he wouldn't tell me.

Benny is here, even though it isn't Wednesday night. His arm is around Emily's waist. He and Joe must have had the daughter's-hand-in-marriage conversation because here comes Joe right behind them, beaming.

Emily looks at her boyfriend in horror. "You *asked* him for me?"

"I begged him," Benny says.

"They haven't agreed on the specifics of your dowry yet," Maisie says.

Nell nods. "Dad's insisting that Benny take the goats."

"I'm not taking the goats," Benny says.

"That's between me and your father," Joe says to him.

I get another placemat, another plate. Benny's been in this house for as long as I can remember, trying on Halloween costumes, watching movies from the movie basket, talking us into another strip of raffle tickets for 4-H. Benny all but vanished from our lives in the years of his early adolescence, but those years were followed by his later adolescence, when Maisie referred to him as The Fixture. He and Emily started living in the little house when they came home from college, though they swore it was a platonic arrangement between two young farmers desperate to escape their parents. We pretended to believe them, though we knew that Emily and Benny had been making use of the little house for a long time.

Nell goes to the sideboard and takes out the pale-blue linen napkins we use at Thanksgiving and Christmas and Easter lunch. Joe reaches into the high shelf to bring down the good glasses, filling them with wine so that we can toast the marriage. "Benny and Emily eternal," we say, raising our glasses to love. They don't know when they're getting married, but they know that they are, and now we know it, too. Anyone looking in the window would think the wedding is tonight, here in this very kitchen.

"Maid of honor." Emily points to Maisie. "In fact, you will be the only maid at all."

"What about me?" Nell asks.

"Officiant," Emily says.

Nell clutches a dish towel to her heart. "Seriously? I get to marry you?" She throws herself into Emily, wraps her arms around her sister.

"You'll have to get ordained on the internet," Benny says.

Maisie smiles, glad to see Nell cast in a speaking role.

"What about the two of us?" Joe comes to stand beside me.

Emily shakes her head. "You've done your work already. Now I think you should just sit back on a blanket and enjoy yourselves."

Joe and I will enjoy ourselves. For reasons of love and stability and property, we've hoped for this day. We believe that marriage will be good for both of them, all of us. Benny is laughing, kissing Emily's cheek. When is the last time I looked at Benny Holzapfel? When he was twelve? Sixteen? His college graduation? I see him tonight. Benny, so bright and full of ideas, Benny attentive to everyone, Benny who smiles at Emily even when she's turned away, Benny who I just now realize has grown to look like someone I used to date.

Maybe I've missed it all this time because the resemblance is vague, or maybe I missed it because you'd be hard-pressed to find a man less like Duke. Benny opened his retirement account at twenty-three. He's drawn up plans for his family's orchard and for this orchard that go out twenty years. But damn me if there isn't something about his neck. It's not the kind of likeness that would make a girl in a mall run up for an autograph, or make an old woman at the grocery checkout ask if people tell him he looks like Peter Duke. It wouldn't have occurred to me had we not been spending our days immersed in this story, but now that I've seen it I can't unsee it. Even his hair, which he wears in a bun, is hair that is familiar to me. And I wonder if this was how Emily finally gave up her obsession with Duke when she was in high school: She learned to see just a bit of her beloved in the boy next door.

"I wish we could have a proper party," Joe says to Benny. "At least get your parents over here."

"Well, we can't," Emily says. "As much as I enjoy a good party with the Holzapfels, everybody's got too much work to do."

It is less about work than it is Gretel Holzapfel's asthma. Kurt and Gretel are careful to only see people outside and at a distance. In the morning I'll get up early and make Gretel an apple cake to leave on her back porch. That will make her laugh. Emily, the eldest of three, is marrying Benny, the youngest of four. The Holzapfels already had three children when we moved to the farm. I remember Gretel coming to the house the day after we moved in, an apple cake in her hands, three young Holzapfels marching behind her. Two years later when she found out she was pregnant with Benny, she sat at my kitchen table and cried great tears. "We were done!" she said. They had given away the baby clothes years before. They had given away the crib. All of their children were finally in school and Gretel had part of her days to herself again. Now she would be straight back to diaper pails and booster shots, leaky breasts and the pervasive smell of spit-up. When, four months later, I found out I was pregnant with Emily, Gretel said I did it just to keep her company. That's how far back our children go.

The eldest three Holzapfels are scattered now, one daughter teaching English in Milwaukee, one daughter a nurse practioner in Petoskey, a son at the Marine Corps base at Camp Pendleton. None of those grown-up children had any interest in the farm. The Holzapfels' midlife mistake alone will save them. Maybe Benny thinks he owes them that much.

"This must be how England felt when Henry II married Eleanor of Aquitaine," Maisie says.

Nell looks at Emily in horror. "You're giving him *France*?"

"I'll take the goats if I get France," Benny says.

"Aren't any of you afraid I'm going to run out the door screaming?" Emily digs through the refrigerator for the pizza kits I'd ordered for the occasion.

"We always know where to find you," Maisie says ominously.

"By the time Richard the Lionheart is born, the two of you will rule all of northern Michigan." The history of the British monarchy is Joe's winter hobby, and it thrills him to see that his girls have been listening, in the same way I imagine it would thrill me if they could sew.

Emily and Benny turn their heads towards one another. They don't raise their eyes. Maisie and Nell are busy with the salad but Joe sees it and he looks at me, thinking the same thing.

"Are you pregnant?" As soon as the words are out of my mouth I wish I'd waited until after dinner, wish I'd pulled Emily into the pantry and whispered the question in her ear, but I have asked her and so we all stop, hold our breath, those wineglasses still within reach.

The blush rises straight from Emily's heart, and even though I would have sworn that Benny had been standing on the other side of the table, he is there beside her, his arm around her shoulder. "Nope," he says, pressing his hip lightly against hers.

Emily looks at Benny. She is saying nothing but is also asking him a question and without answering he is saying yes.

"We're getting married and we're not having a baby," Benny says. He picks up Emily's wineglass. "Proof."

"We're not having a baby," Emily says, and I understand that she's telling us there will be no babies.

"Plenty of time for all of that," Joe says.

The happiness in his eyes makes my eyes fill up, and I hope for his sake we can leave this alone, talk about whatever it means on some other, less celebratory day, but forestalling conversation is not a skill in our family's wheelhouse.

"Or not," Emily says.

"Or not what?" Joe asks, teasing her. "Not enough time? Is this going to be a very long engagement?"

Everyone is waiting now. Hazel is waiting. Emily opens her mouth but nothing comes out.

"We're not having children," Benny says.

Joe shakes his head. "You don't know that."

"I know that," Emily says.

We should have one night that is not about the future or the past, one night to celebrate these two people and nothing else but we've blown it. "You don't want children?" I ask her.

Emily tips back her wineglass. She drains it. "I don't know if I want them but I'm sure I'm not going to have them."

I am making our three daughters quilts from my grandmother's dresses, from their grandmother's dresses and my dresses and the dresses they wore when they were children. I started collecting the fabric when I was a child because even then I knew I would have daughters one day and I would make them quilts. My daughters will give these quilts to their daughters and those daughters will sleep beneath them. One day they will wrap their own children in these quilts, and all of this will happen on the farm.

"I know this isn't the way you planned things," Emily says. "I know it's not what you want."

"It isn't about what we want," I say, but that's a lie. These children we've never spoken of? We want them very much. We long for them.

"Crops used to fail once every fifty years," Benny says, his voice quiet because all of us are silent. "The crops have failed twice since I was born. The winters are milder, the lake is warmer, the trees aren't staying dormant long enough. They bloom too early, the freeze kills the buds."

Joe holds up his hand. "Why are you saying this? What do you think we don't already know?"

But Benny doesn't stop. His voice comes without drama or demand and still, he keeps talking. "Sooner or later we're going to have to stop putting in cherry trees."

"No," Joe says.

"I really cannot stand this," Maisie says.

"It's not going to be cold enough for them anymore. We're going to have to start thinking about wine grapes, strawberries, asparagus."

"So plant the grapes," Joe says. "It doesn't mean you don't have children."

"It sort of does," Nell says. "Once you think about it."

"You, too?" Joe asks. "Have the three of you signed a pact?"

"I have no idea what I'm going to do," Nell says. "But I'll tell you, I think about it."

Maisie tightens her arms across her chest. "Who doesn't think about it?"

Emily sits down on a kitchen chair and Benny stands behind her, his hands on her shoulders. We are all so tired.

Emily picks up a fork and balances it on one finger. She looks at nothing but the fork. "I can eat vegetables and ride my bike and stop using plastic bags but I know I'm just doing it to keep myself from going crazy. The planet is fucked. There's nothing I can do about that. But I'll tell you what, I'm going to spend my life trying to save this farm. If anybody ever wonders what I'm here for, that's it."

Nell reaches across the table and takes her sister's hand, and Joe, Joe who never walks away from us, goes out the kitchen door. He is standing at the edge of the garden, his back is to the house. He is looking at the trees.

11

Joe didn't want to talk about it last night when we went to bed, and when I wake up in the morning he's already out there. He's wondering if Maisie or Nell will have children, and if those children who won't grow up here will want to take over the farm someday. He's thinking about what will happen to the farm without another generation of family to protect it after we're gone, after Emily and Benny are gone. He is thinking about Emily and Benny being gone. He is thinking about the developers who relentlessly sniff the perimeter of our land, the strangers who knock on our door in February to ask if we wouldn't rather spend the winter in Florida. They are the enemies of stone fruit. They would leave just enough trees in the ground to justify calling the place Cherry Hills or Cherry Lane, then pull the rest up and build pretty white summer houses with picture windows and wraparound porches, places we could never afford. And that's the good scenario. The bad scenario, the one where the trees eventually die? Joe isn't thinking about that one and I know this because I'm not thinking about it either.

When Maisie and Nell come downstairs for breakfast I can tell they've been staring at their own bedroom ceiling for most of the night, running through the same worst cases. Maybe we should start a family mentalist act, see if we can make a living reading one another's minds. Maisie's phone dings at the table and she takes it out of her pocket and stares at it for so long that Nell and I stop and wait for her to tell us.

"What?" Nell says finally.

"Someone's trapped a litter of feral kittens in their barn and wants to know if I can come by and kill them this afternoon." Maisie puts her head down on the table.

"Who?" I reach for her phone but she grabs it away.

"We'll have to see them again," she says. "You're better off not knowing."

"Let them kill their own kittens," Nell says tiredly. It's true: Ignore the kittens and you'll wake up one morning to find the cats outnumber the mice. But still, people need to kill their own kittens. You don't ask your neighbors to do that for you.

Maisie sighs. “I can’t think about this right now.”

The back door opens and Joe is there looking so worn out I wonder if he got any sleep at all. Joe pretty much never comes back to the house in the morning once he’s gone out. Hazel raises her head and issues a single bark of acknowledgment.

“We’re taking the day off,” he says, jingling the keys in his pocket. “We’re going to the beach.”

We stare at him like he’s someone we’ve never met. “We can’t go to the beach,” Maisie says. “There’s too much work.”

“There’s always too much work and I’ve decided we aren’t doing it today. I’ve already sent Emily home to get her suit.”

We continue to sit. Nell pours milk in her coffee to cool it.

“Go on.” He stands there like a teacher who’s just announced *Class dismissed.* This is the part where we’re supposed to fly out the door.

“Let’s pick for a while,” I say, looking for the middle path. “Then we’ll knock off early and go to the beach.”

Joe shakes his head. “We never knock off early, in case you haven’t noticed. That’s why we have to do this in the morning, first thing. Go.”

“It’s Tuesday,” I say. “Since when are we off on Tuesday?”

"It's Thursday," he says.

Thursday? I wonder if this could be true.

"Are *you* going to the beach?" Nell asks her father. She tests the coffee. Still too hot.

"I'm going to go check on a couple of things and then I'll come down."

"So we'll work until you're finished then we'll all go together." I meant it to be helpful, Joe can't do everything by himself, but my suggestion flies all over him.

"Could someone in this family listen to me for a change? I just went through this with Emily. She's crying. She's useless. All of you are tired and useless and I want you to go and have some goddamn fun."

"'Some goddamn fun'?" Maisie says. "Oh, well, when you put it like that. I'll go kill the kittens and then meet you at the beach."

"Kittens?" Joe asks.

"We'll go," I say to him.

He turns around to look out the window above the sink. "Do it now. I don't want Emily down there by herself."

This is the fire that ignites us because none of us wants Emily to be at the beach by herself. We clump together in our sorrow. In joy we may wander off in our separate directions, but in sorrow we prefer to hold hands. I head upstairs for my swimsuit, towel, and hat.

When I come back down Joe's gone and the girls tell me to go.

"We'll clean up and make the sandwiches," Nell calls as I am out the door. "We're right behind you."

I take the two-track away from the orchard and towards the woods until I find the smallest break in the trees, a path I know to look for only because I've come this way a thousand times. It's like stepping into a book, one turn and everything changes: cool instead of hot, dark instead of light. Instead of cherry trees, eighty-foot hemlocks and red oaks and white pines, and between those hemlocks and oaks and pines are giant rocks dressed up in mossy sweaters. The girls loved nothing more than to lie on those rocks when they were little, press their faces into the cool, shaggy green and pretend they were mermaids flung from the sea by a towering wave. They squeezed their legs together and flopped them like sad tails. A century ago these very rocks must have been in the orchard, and those ancestors who are buried up the hill beneath the daisies must have dug them up and dragged them here. They had already cut down all the oaks and pines, planed them into boards and sent them out into the world to be reassembled into houses and ships. Tired as they were, the ancestors took the time to pull the stumps and burn them. Then they planted the fields with cherry trees. Maybe they had left the half mile of woods that stands between the orchard and the beach because they'd lost the strength to cut it down. Maybe the men lived to be fifty before a rock or a tree or a horse tipped over and crushed them. Maybe the women died at forty-five giving birth to their eighth or ninth or tenth child. Maybe they never went to the beach in the summer, not even once. Maybe picking cherries really is the least of it.

At the edge of our woods is the shore of Grand Traverse Bay, our corner of the choppy, gray-blue behemoth that is Lake Michigan—the dark stand of woods, and then a dozen feet of pebbly, sandy beach, and then the water that stretches out forever; the trees and then our eldest daughter alone on the beach, hugging her knees. I sit beside her and she tips herself into me, her head on my shoulder, her glorious hair falling across my chest, and for what feels like a very long time we watch the cormorants skim the water.

"Everything should stay like this," she says.

I tell her that I wish it could, even though I know she means the temperature of the lake and I mean this summer, everyone home and together. As sad as I am for the suffering of the world, I wish to keep this exact moment, Emily on the beach in my arms.

"We didn't mean to tell you last night. I'm not even sure we were going to tell you at all. Lots of people don't have children, you know. I could have just waited until I went through menopause and then said I'd forgotten."

"You never know." I try to make my voice neutral. "You might change your minds later on."

I feel her head move sadly against my neck. "It's bad enough having to worry about what's going to happen to the farm. I can't imagine worrying about what would happen to our kids."

"Every generation believes the world is going to end."

She raises her head. "Is that true? Did you and Dad think it was all going up in a fiery ball?"

She is so close to me. I can see the faintest remnants of long-ago freckles on her forehead. "No. I said it to make you feel better." Joe and I thought about the plays we wanted to get tickets for, the price of rent, whether or not we should go out to dinner, how soon we could afford to have a baby. We didn't think anything would end, any of it, ever.

Emily returns her head to its comfortable spot. "I know it seems like I'm upset that Benny and I aren't going to have children, but I don't even know what that means, really. I want to marry Benny but if I have a biological clock it hasn't kicked in. Maybe women don't have biological clocks anymore."

"It's not like humanity's stopped having children, you know. It's still going on."

"That's because humanity doesn't live with Benny Holzapfel, and if I didn't live with him it wouldn't be any less true, I just wouldn't have to think about it."

"We couldn't begin to list all the depressing things we're not thinking about—all the things that have happened in the world, the things that are happening right now here in Michigan, the things that are going to happen in the future—no one can hold it all."

"Emily died in childbirth," my daughter says.

"What?"

"She died giving birth. I remember thinking about that when we read the play in high school, like it was a bad omen."

We had named our daughter for the plucky girl in the first act, the smartest girl in her class. We had not been thinking about the third act at the time.

Emily shakes her head. "I'm just talking. I don't think I'm going to die in childbirth."

Which doesn't mean I can get the thought of her dying out of my head. "So it really is the cherry trees?"

She nods. She still isn't looking at me. "I'm going to tell you something I probably shouldn't tell you."

"This would be the day."

She takes in a deep breath, giving me just enough

time to flash through every horrible thing that might have happened to her without my knowing it. "I never forgave you and Dad for burning those trees."

"Which trees?" We have burned a great many trees over the years.

"I think I was nine. I don't know, I might have been younger. If it had happened before, I don't remember. I think you used to burn trees when we were in school or else you sent us to the neighbors' or something. Dad said they were old, they weren't putting out enough fruit anymore so he had them pushed out." She turns to me then, her cheeks wet with tears. "Look at me!" she laughs, rubbing at her nose. "I've been to hort school and I still can't talk about this. We *begged* him not to do it. I said I'd bring out buckets of water. Fuck." She pinches the bridge of her nose and waits. "I've burned so many trees since then but that first time I couldn't stand it. You set them on fire like it was some kind of party. 'You've outlived your usefulness! Time to die!' The neighbors were standing around drinking cider. All I wanted to do was save them and I couldn't save them. I'm sure I'm going to miss having children. I'm sure in twenty years I'm going to feel awful about it, but for now all I can think of are all these trees that aren't going to make it and how we're going to pull them all up and burn them."

The men had come in the afternoon with a 4WD loader. They sank the tines down into the ground and then bulldozed the trees, pulling them up to shake off the dirt before piling them to burn. By the time the work was done it was nearly dark and we set the fire. I remember it now, our girls screaming as if the plan had been to throw them into the blaze as well. Had they just not remembered, or had they really never been there before? Those fires are enormous and I worried about keeping up, all three of our girls were runners. I had to keep them safe. Maybe we did send them away before that. Maybe this was the time we decided they were old enough. Old trees have to be pushed out but we didn't need to turn it into a party. We'd told the girls that the trees were our life and how good they were to us and how they took care of us because we took care of them. The night air was bitter on that autumn night but one by one we pulled off our jackets. The flames shot twenty feet over the pile of branches, throwing bright-orange sparks up to the stars. Joe couldn't leave, he and the neighbors had to make sure the fire didn't get out of hand, so finally I pushed the girls into the station wagon and drove them around until it was done, until they'd cried and kicked and slapped at the back of the seat for such a long time that they wore themselves out, falling asleep against their will. When we got home Joe lifted Maisie out of the car and I took Nell, but Emily was awake. That night she said she hated us, and that she had always hated us, that she would always hate us.

Hazel runs out of the woods and right away starts frantically digging a hole in the sand next to Emily. She digs and digs, then sticks her head in the hole she's made to see if it fits, then takes it out and digs some more.

"Here we are." Nell throws herself down beside us. "Our day off."

"Let me try to ruin it for you." Emily wipes her face with a towel.

"What's your dog looking for?" I ask Maisie. When Hazel stops digging long enough to look up, the sand-colored dog is covered in sand.

"Treasure," Maisie says.

"If we're going to be miserable and cry, let's do it in the lake." Nell stands up to pull off her T-shirt and shorts. The girls had taken the time to put their swimsuits on under their clothes. I take mine out of my bag, glancing up and down the beach.

"We can hold up our towels," Maisie offers. "Make you a towel tent."

But I decline, taking my clothes off where I stand and then struggling into my one-piece. They have seen me and I have seen them, even if they've forgotten. They follow me into the water, screaming at the cold.

"You said the lake was getting *warmer*," Maisie yells. "If all hope is lost we should at least get a decent swim out of it."

The four of us go out straight and strong. We don't have a swim platform, we don't have any destination at all; with a little orienteering we could swim to Wisconsin. I drop beneath the surface and open my eyes. It's as if someone bought up all the diamonds at Tiffany's and crushed them into dust, then spread that dust across the water so that it sifts down evenly, filtering through the shards of light that cut into the depth. We are swimming through eternity, my daughters' bright mermaid legs kicking out towards deeper water. I stay beneath the surface and marvel for as long as my lungs can hold.

"Swimming is the reset button," Pallace used to say. "Swimming starts the day again."

We swim and we swim and we swim, and when we've exhausted ourselves we turn and head back to shore. Duchess the German shepherd is there now, having bunched one of our towels into an unsatisfying bed while Hazel keeps an eye on the cheese and mustard sandwiches Maisie made. We shake out the remaining towels and crowd together.

"Tell us the happiest day of your life," Nell says.

"You and you and you," I say, looking at each of them, their dripping swimsuits and wet, tangled hair.

"No, seriously," Emily says. "You have to keep it in the context of the story. What was the happiest day of your life at Tom Lake?"

"The happiest day of that summer wasn't at Tom Lake."

They deem this to be an acceptable variant, as long as it's the happiest day within that limited period of time. They stretch out on their towels in the sun to listen and dry.

"There's a small setup before we get to the day itself," I say.

"Certain scenes require setups." Nell covers her face with her hat.

Duchess emits a sigh of unspeakable boredom then gets up to leave.

"Really?" Maisie says to the dog.

Duchess goes and stands in the lake, gulping at the water before turning to cross the narrow beach. We call for her to come back, come back, but she doesn't listen to us. She follows the path into the woods and is gone.

After opening night the director's work was done, which had not been the case in the community theater, nor the case in college. But Tom Lake was professional theater, which meant that Nelson would take a bow after the first performance and be off to his next job in the morning. All of us wondered what that next job would be but as far as I knew, none of us had asked him. That was why I stuck around at lunch break one day shortly before we opened, when everyone else ran off to the lake to swim. I wanted to find out where Nelson was going. He was younger than many of the actors in the play but he had never been one of us. He never came to the lake. He was the adult and we were the children rushing off to swim.

"Traverse City," he said when I asked. "Have you been?"

"I flew into the airport there," I said.

"Airports don't count. Traverse City is very pretty, not that that's saying much. It's very pretty everywhere around here." He was sitting alone in the front row of the theater with his notebook and a bag lunch. He offered me half his tuna sandwich, which was incredibly generous. I couldn't remember the last time I'd eaten lunch.

The blossoms were off the trees and the fruit hadn't fully come in and the boxes of bees had been taken away to their next job and still, everything was beautiful. "What are you directing in Traverse City?"

"Nothing." He opened a large bottle of seltzer then looked around as if hoping to see a glass. "There isn't a glass," he said.

"I'm fine."

"Do you mind sharing?" he asked. When I shook my head he took a drink from the bottle and handed it to me. "I have an aunt and uncle who live there and I promised to come up and be helpful. I've been saying I'd do it for a couple of years now but I keep getting diverted."

"By plays?"

"Things too good to pass on kept coming along, and then I'd be on the wrong side of the country. So when Tom Lake asked me to do this, I thought, that solves the problem. I'll finally be in exactly the right place. That's a long answer to a short question: Once we open I'm going to spend the rest of summer in Traverse City."

"What kind of help do they need?"

"They need all kinds of help but my first priority is to sort out their finances."

"You're good at that?" I wished that I was good at something as useful as bookkeeping. I very nearly told him I could sew.

He shrugged. "I wouldn't say good. I'd only say I'm better at it than they are."

I asked him what his aunt and uncle did for a living while eating his sandwich and drinking his seltzer.

"They're cherry farmers. Have you ever been to a Michigan cherry farm?"

I shook my head.

A little light broke over Nelson's face, the same quiet light the actors saw whenever we did something right. "You should come and see it."

"The cherry farm?" I was thinking about that first drive down from the airport and how I'd wanted to stand in the middle of the road and do one slow rotation. It felt like years ago.

"Do you have a car?" Nelson asked.

"Pallace does." Sebastian was up for a couple of days and if Pallace wanted to get somewhere, Sebastian would take her. Pallace would lend me her car.

Nelson opened up his notebook and started drawing a map: the roads, the mileage counts, the names of the farms I would pass and the name of the road where I should turn. "Come tomorrow," he said. "Come for lunch and I'll show you around. You can swim in the lake if you want."

Tomorrow was Monday, our day off. Opening night was Thursday. I was going to see the director's family's cherry farm.

Uncle Wallace was muttering when he came back from break and everyone else was laughing. Who could keep their mind on another rehearsal? Not even Nelson's persistent calm could snap us into focus. Uncle Wallace wove around the stage in the pointless configurations of a squirrel. George dropped his lines and then stared at me as if it were my job to pick them up. The whole thing was a disaster, which meant good luck. Sebastian was around more often now that *Cabaret* had opened. He claimed he was in danger of losing his job, though I think he said it to impress Pallace. No one would fire Sebastian. As soon as rehearsals were finished, Duke and I hustled out of our costumes so we could find him.

"You weren't at the lake," Duke said to me, sliding the pins from his hair as we walked. He put them in his pocket. "I even went down and felt around on the bottom. You weren't anywhere."

"I talked to Nelson. I asked him where he was going next." I must have looked happy because Duke stopped short, folding his arms across his chest.

"Did he offer you a part?"

Oh, Duke of the wide dark eyes and thick black lashes. Duke who had gotten too much sun even though we'd been told not to because it made more work for the makeup people. I shook my head. "Nothing so glamorous."

"Then what's with the smile?"

"His family has a cherry farm in Traverse City. He invited me up to see the farm tomorrow."

"I bet he did."

I laughed. "I'm excited! Haven't you ever wanted to see a cherry farm?"

"I'm from Michigan."

Somehow I hadn't thought of there being cherries in East Detroit. "Well, I'm from New Hampshire and I'm going."

"How are you going to get there?"

I knew what he was thinking. He didn't want me in the car with Nelson. Men were not impossible to decipher. "Pallace will lend me her car." I wasn't certain of this but the more times I said it, the more it seemed true.

He looked at me another minute and then finally smiled. Maybe he was happy for my happiness. Maybe he still hoped Nelson would give him a part in another play later. Maybe he really just wanted to keep an eye on me. "If it's going to be that much fun we should all go together, the four of us. That would be all right with you and Nelson, wouldn't it? If it's not a date?"

I rolled my eyes at the stupidity of it all. "It's not a date." And it wasn't. But that didn't mean I was supposed to show up with three extra people.

"Good!" Duke cried. "Then it's settled. We'll all drive up in the morning to see the director's cherry farm."

"The cherry farm!" Emily cries, and Maisie and Nell raise their fists in the air.

Parts of this story they already know, and this is one of them. The stories that are familiar will always be our favorites.

12

It had rained all morning but by the time we'd finished breakfast the sun was out. Sebastian said that he should drive to Traverse City, his Plymouth had a big back seat, and so we piled into the car, boys in front, girls in back. We rolled down the windows, waving goodbye to everyone we passed. Goodbye, Tom Lake! None of us had been farther away than the coffee shop in town since we arrived, none of us except Sebastian, who had an entire life about which we had no curiosity. Ubiquitous fruit stands lined the road and I wanted him to pull over so that I would have a gift to bring to Nelson's aunt and uncle, a pie or some flowers, something more than three uninvited guests.

"These people own an *orchard*," Duke shouted, the wind reaching inside the car to carry his voice away.

"All that stuff at a fruit stand is the stuff they're trying to get rid of."

"What good. Is sit*ting.* A*lone* in your *room,*" Pallace sang absently. I could see Sebastian's eyes go to her in the rearview mirror. The sound of her voice called him like a bell.

"You should have been Sally Bowles," I said, because even though that German-looking girl who played Sally was pretty extraordinary, I had no doubt Pallace would have been better.

Half of Pallace's face was hidden behind her enormous black Jackie Onassis sunglasses. Who knew what she was looking at. "I should have been a lot of things," she said.

"I coulda been a contender." Duke said it like Brando, *conTENdaah.*

It was fun to be in the car, fun to be together and going somewhere other than rehearsal. I saw an antique store up ahead and leaned forward to tap on Sebastian's shoulder. "Stop, please."

"No!" Duke cried. "Antique stores are worse than fruit stands. They're full of things the grown children had to sell off when their parents died so they could put the farm on the market."

"You just keep raining on that parade," Pallace said.

Sebastian stopped the car.

Duke turned to Pallace, leaning over the seat. "Don't let her out."

But I was out. I'd been invited to lunch by our director and I'd be damned if I was going to arrive without a gift. Just inside the door, on top of a glass display case, a dozen linen napkins with cutwork around the edge were sitting in a basket waiting for me. They were a blue nearly pale enough to be white, nicely ironed. I knew very little when I was young but I knew the role of Emily and I knew fabric. These were good napkins. I counted them slowly, looking for stains and finding none. As a bonus, they were expensive, and that pleased me more than anything.

"You must have come in looking for these," the woman at the cash register said when I handed them over.

Two minutes later I was back in the car.

"Let me see!" Pallace held out her hands. Sebastian turned in his seat to look.

"Napkins!" Duke cried. "They must have seen you coming. Napkins are for tourists. First they try to unload a tractor on you, then they bring out the napkins." He clutched his head as Pallace held a single napkin up to the light.

"I can't imagine anything nicer than these," she said.

Sebastian waited until the napkins were back in their

bag so they wouldn't all blow out the window once we started driving again. Pallace sang single lines of show tunes along the way and we guessed the musical. ("Because it's *JUUUNE*! June-June-June.") Duke recited pieces of dialogue and we guessed the play. ("Always tell the truth, George; it's the easiest thing to remember.") Duke was crackerjack at memorization. He believed in memorizing any part he wanted, both for the discipline of it and to make sure he would always be ready. "You never know when something's going to open up," he said.

"What's your secret talent?" I shouted to Sebastian.

"Driving," he called back, leaning his elbow out the open window.

By the time we got to Traverse City, the sky was clear. The rain had given up and gone to Canada. Duke read Nelson's directions aloud—a complicated series of poorly marked turns onto twisty roads. Finally up ahead we saw a small sign reading NELSON nailed to a post beside the drive. "He named the place for himself?"

"It's his aunt and uncle's farm," I said. "Their last name is Nelson."

Duke stuck his head out the window like a dog. "So I can call my cherry farm 'Duke Acres'?"

"Dukedom," Sebastian said.

The rutted drive was filled with rainwater. Every leaf and blade of grass was shining. Once we turned we quieted down. The towering woods to our left, the white clapboard house with blue shutters up ahead, the gentle hills of fruit trees to the right that spread out behind the house past where we could see—it looked like a sampler stitched by an eighteenth-century girl.

"They have a barn," Pallace whispered.

It wasn't as if I'd grown up in Los Angeles. I'd seen plenty of farms in my day, but never had I seen a place that made the tightness in my chest relax. The order in the rows of trees and the dark green of the lush grass beneath them soothed me like a hand brushing across my forehead.

Sebastian parked the car beside the gray Chevy we knew to be Nelson's. Then the screen door of the house opened and Nelson came onto the porch and waved.

"Go tell him you invited us," Duke said quietly, his eyes straight ahead.

I shook my head. "Not on your life."

"He didn't invite us?" Pallace lifted her sunglasses.

"Emily invited us," Duke said.

I might have looped my purse strap around Duke's neck but Nelson came to the car smiling. "You found us!" he said. "Those roads can be tricky."

"You draw a good map." I held the package lightly.

The napkins weighed nothing. I suddenly thought how nice it would have been to have brought a gift for Nelson as well, for all he'd done for us, but I would have had no idea what to get him.

Sebastian held out his hand and introduced himself.

"You're the tennis player," Nelson said, smiling. "The other Duke. I've seen you at rehearsals."

"I think we may be crashing the party," Sebastian said.

Nelson laughed. "There is no party, or there's always a party, depending on how you look at it. People on farms love company. The more people showing up, the better." Pallace walked right up to Nelson and kissed his cheek like they were best friends. She kissed our director, who, in his blue T-shirt and jeans, looked nothing like the person who'd been telling us where to stand and how to speak for more than a month now. I wasn't sure I'd ever seen Nelson outside before.

Duke was making the slow rotation I had wanted to make the first day I came to Traverse City, and when he stopped he looked at Nelson. "I'm from Michigan," he said.

"So am I," Nelson said.

"But I'm not from this Michigan."

Nelson nodded. "This is my uncle's farm. I worked here in the summers when I was growing up. I took the bus here when school let out and then my parents would drive up from Grand Rapids at the end of the season and bring me home. As far as I was concerned, August fifteenth was the saddest day of the year."

"I'll bet it was." Duke cast his gaze out over the cherry trees.

"It's like Tom Lake," Sebastian said, by which he meant we weren't exactly driving over from Flint. We were trading beauty for beauty.

"I've got nothing but praise for Tom Lake," Nelson said. "But it's not like this."

That was what Duke had meant. For all of Tom Lake's splendor, this was superior by an order of magnitude. Nelson turned and led us up the stairs and into the house.

"Stop," Emily says, raising up on her elbows. "Are you saying that Duke came to our house? You brought him to the house?"

"It wasn't our house then but yes, he was here."

"The happiest day of your life was the day Duke came to our house?"

"Maybe you could just shut up and listen to the story?" Maisie suggests.

"Why wouldn't you have told me that?"

"Maybe," Nell says, choosing her words judiciously,

"you were a maniac who was in love with a movie star and Mom didn't feel like throwing gasoline on it."

"I wasn't in *love* with Duke," Emily says. "I thought he was my father."

"Right. Your father. Forgive me." Maisie pulls the towel over her face. "Please proceed."

"None of you think she should have told us this before?" Emily says, looking at the three of us in disbelief.

"I'm starting to think I shouldn't have told you this now." I wonder if the red in Emily's cheeks is sunburn or rage.

"I just can't believe—"

"Please," Nell shouts. "Please! Mom is about to go into our house for the very first time and it's the happiest day of her life. Can this not be a story about you for two minutes?"

"The happiest day of the summer of 1988," I remind her. "Not the happiest day of my life. Not by a long shot."

"All I'm saying is that I think it would have helped me to know," Emily says.

Beneath the towel Maisie shakes her head. "It would so not have helped you."

The long oak table in the kitchen was set for four but Nelson's aunt Maisie was already pulling more placemats out of the drawer. She was a tall woman with short, curly hair, an oversized laugh and oversized feet she housed in blue Keds. "It's the first time we've ever had a movie star come to lunch," she said. "You'll just have to forgive me if I say anything stupid."

For all the world it appeared she was looking at me. "Me?"

"A huge star," Nelson said. "Once your movie comes out."

"Joe can't stop talking about how good you are," his aunt Maisie said. "Joe says you're the best actress he's ever worked with, and you know he's worked with a lot of good ones. We're going to drive down on Thursday to see you. Opening night! And Uncle Wallace, I can't believe we're going to see Uncle Wallace."

"Uncle Wallace is really something," Duke said.

I held out my package to her and she looked so surprised. "You didn't need to bring me anything," Maisie said.

She put it down on the table and folded back the tissue. Such a genuine pleasure lit her face. I could imagine that it had been a while since someone had brought her something so impractical and pretty. She ran her fingers over the cutwork. "Oh, Lara, will you look at these," Maisie said quietly.

***Maisie, look,** the white canisters are still on the sink, the whole row of them including coffee and rice. I broke the sugar the year we moved into the house. My hands were wet when I picked it up and it slipped right through and smashed on the floor. I stood there crying and crying, until Joe told me it was just a canister and it didn't matter. But they were yours. Everything was yours. I'd forgotten how small the kitchen was before we pushed out the back wall. You would have loved it the way it is now. I can stand at the sink and keep an eye out for Joe and make dinner and talk to the girls. There's so much space. The first day I came to the house the kitchen was so small and we were all crowded in together. Look how beautiful we all were, Maisie. Can you believe it? Look how young.*

"Maisie, this is Peter Duke," Joe said. "He's Editor Webb in the play. And Pallace Clarke, she understudies Lara's part. Pallace is in *Cabaret* too, so she's the busy one. And this is Sebastian Duke. He's Peter's brother."

"What part do you play?" she asked Sebastian, holding his hand.

"I play the brother," Sebastian said.

"You wouldn't believe how good he is at it," Duke said.

Maisie laughed. "You're going to tell me everything," she said to Sebastian. "We'll sit down and you can tell me what it's like to be the brother of a famous man."

And Duke, who knew he was destined to be a famous man, smiled.

Joe was dispatched to the orchard to find his uncle but as soon as he turned to leave his uncle walked in the kitchen door. Maisie's husband was Ken. Ken and Maisie Nelson. Their nephew, Joe. A bouquet of pink and yellow dahlias sat in a green drinking glass on the table. I didn't know how there would be enough food for everyone but Maisie brought out plenty. Maybe we ate their dinner, too: fried chicken and biscuits and butter beans and corn cut from the cob and baked apples. We ate like children, greedy and unconcerned, and Maisie acted like nothing in the world had ever made her so happy.

"When I was growing up I used to lie in bed at night imagining what other people's families must be like," Duke said once the pie was served, cherry pie, which he told her was his favorite. "I would picture their houses, their furniture, what they ate and how they spoke to one another, and what I always pictured was this." He turned to Joe. "Turns out I spent my entire childhood picturing your family."

Joe smiled. "You were picturing this particular branch of my family."

"I was, too," Pallace said, setting down her fork. "Ever since I walked in the door I've been trying to remember what this place reminded me of and that's it. This is where I wanted to live when I was a kid."

"We would have been happy to have you," Ken said.

"Except in my fantasy the family was Black," Pallace said. "But other than that it's a very similar vibe."

Pallace and I tried to help with the dishes after lunch but Maisie shooed us away. "Let Joe show you around. Come back later and help us pick cherries. That's when we'll put you to work."

The kitchen was small so off we went, because of course the work was not really for us. Maisie kept a cutting garden in the backyard, zinnias and dahlias and foxgloves and coneflowers. The bees made such a racket we thought at first the noise must be coming from someplace other than bees.

"In my vision of the perfect childhood there were no bees," Pallace said, and Sebastian moved her to his other side so that he would stand between her and the menacing insects.

Joe walked in front of us, pointing out trees. "Those are the Montmorencys."

"Tart or sweet?" Pallace asked.

"Tart," he said. "Pie cherries. They're mostly sold frozen. The pie today was from last year's frozen cherries. You can take some back with you if you want."

But we didn't have a freezer to keep the cherries frozen or an oven to bake a pie.

"And those?" She pointed to a very different group of trees on the other side of the road.

"Plums," he said, shaking his head. "The plums are a disaster. We're going to have to take them out."

"How can plums be a disaster?" I asked.

"Gerber told the farmers they wanted more plums for baby food, but by the time the farmers put in the trees and grew the trees and picked the plums, Gerber said they didn't want plums anymore."

"Can't people just eat them?" Pallace asked.

"I eat them. You probably wouldn't. No one buys a bag of Stanleys at a fruit stand."

I had no idea that a Stanley was a plum, or that one plum was made into baby food while another was eaten over the sink. I didn't know that a Napoleon was a cherry. What I knew was that the four of us were strolling through an orchard with our director, who, after Thursday, would come up here for the rest of the summer to do the work of sorting out his family's finances. The show would go on. He would go on.

"How long has your family owned the place?" Sebastian asked.

"One Nelson or another has been here for five generations. Either they hate it—my father hated it—or they were like Ken and couldn't imagine doing anything else. All Ken ever wanted out of life was Maisie and the farm."

"So who's up next? Do they have kids?"

Joe walked over and pulled an errant weed near the base of a tree then dropped it in the road. "That's the question. Their daughter Alice lives in Phoenix. Alice is out. She's got a husband and kids. They're settled there, they like the heat. I don't think she even eats cherries. My cousin Kenny is a forester in the U.P. Everybody's looking to Kenny to save the day but nobody knows for sure if he's going to do it, including Kenny. There might not be anything to save anyway."

Pallace was walking ahead of us in her little yellow shorts. She turned around to face us and started walking backwards. "Are they broke?"

"Pretty much," Joe said. "This business runs on a very small margin. The crop is bad one year and you're broke, or the crop is good, which means that everybody's crop is good, and so the prices drop and you're broke. Gerber tells you to put in twenty acres of plum trees so you sink all your capital into plum trees—"

"—and Gerber doesn't want the plums," Sebastian said.

"And you're broke."

"That's so depressing." I sounded like a petulant schoolgirl but the day was too beautiful to think that anything could change. Five generations of Nelsons had lived on this farm. Surely the sixth generation would live here as well.

"Farming is depressing," Joe said. "But once it gets in you, you can't put it down."

"Farming is the new acting," Duke said.

"Couldn't they sell off part of the land to pay the debts?" I said this as if it were an original thought.

Joe laughed. "I'm glad you didn't float that over lunch. Maisie would have handed you your napkins back."

"So no one sells land."

"Land gets sold when people die and the kids refuse to come home and take it over. Otherwise you keep the land."

Duke put his arm around my shoulder. "As you know," he said in a voice both animated and conspiratorial, "your cherry orchard is to be sold for your debts; the auction is set for August twenty-second, but don't you worry, my dear, you just sleep in peace, there's a way out of it. Here's my plan. Please listen to me."

Then Joe Nelson was walking on my other side and slipped his arm around my waist. The director's arm around my waist! Nothing but me in between him and

Duke. "Your estate is thirteen miles from town," he said. "They've run the railroad by it. Now if the cherry orchard and the land along the river were cut up into building lots and leased for summer cottages, you'd have at the very lowest twenty-five thousand rubles per year income."

Pallace was laughing her head off. "You've *got* to be kidding me. Where were you people raised?"

"I understand why I know *The Cherry Orchard*," Joe said to Duke. "But I don't understand why you know it."

For the record, neither man removed his arm from me.

"I like Chekhov," Duke said. "All the boys from East Detroit like Chekhov."

"It's true," Sebastian said.

"And I always wanted to play Lopakhin."

Lopakhin was the rich son of a peasant who was looking to install himself in Lyubov Andreevna's cherry orchard, in her family—new money legitimized by shabby aristocracy. Joe shook his head, letting me go so that he could take a step back to look at Duke. "You're too handsome for Lopakhin."

Duke disagreed. "It's all in the performance," he said. Suddenly I wondered if the afternoon had been one long audition. I wondered if Joe might take Duke with him come the fall, cast him in a bigger play.

Small orange butterflies tossed themselves through the air in front of us, one of them lighting on my wrist. "That means big change is coming," Pallace said. Even when I held up my arm it stayed. I'd forgotten how many butterflies there were back then, how many bees.

"What's up there?" Sebastian asked, staring at the hill ahead of us. From where we were we could just make out the pretty iron fence. Joe didn't answer, he just started walking in that direction and we followed him, exactly as we had all summer.

It was the first time I had seen the farm, had seen the Nelsons' house, had called Joe by his given name. The first time I had seen the cemetery and stood in its benevolent shade. The hill and the breeze and the shade always made it feel ten degrees cooler up there. "The Whitings are north," Joe said, pointing to a farm a mile away. "And on the other side are the Holzapfels. And here we have all the Nelsons." He opened up his hands to include the generations of his family.

"You don't even have to leave when you die," Duke said. Maybe it was part of the life he had imagined as a child: everlasting inclusion.

We looked at the pond and the rows upon rows of trees. We looked at the house and the garden, which was just a stamp of color from where we stood.

"What's that little house?" Pallace asked.

"It's an extra. Workers stay there sometimes. I stay there."

"An extra house," Pallace said in wonder, because none of us could imagine having one house.

"It's very small," Joe said, as if he were embarrassed.

Duke lay down on one of the graves and closed his eyes. "Does this bother you?" he asked. I didn't know if he was talking to Joe or the residents.

"Be my guest."

"I'd like to come back here. Could I? Do you have any vacancies?"

"I think you'd have to marry a Nelson," Joe said. "Alice would be too old for you."

"Your cousin is already married," Duke said. "And she doesn't want to leave Phoenix. I wouldn't want to break up her marriage and then find myself buried in Phoenix." He shook a cigarette out of the pack and put it between his lips.

"Hey." Sebastian nudged his brother with his shoe. Sebastian wore canvas tennis shoes all the time, the way a tennis player would. "Get up."

Duke shook his head, fishing his lighter out of his pocket. "I like it here."

"Peedee," Sebastian said. His voice wasn't stern but we all understood his seriousness. Duke got to his feet and put the cigarette behind his ear. Pallace brushed some pine needles off his back.

"There's one more thing to show you," Joe said. "You can stay all afternoon if you want but after this I need to get back to work."

We followed him down the hill, Duke coming last and closing the gate. "Wasn't that something?" he whispered, leaning close.

"Beautiful." It was the word I used for the entire day.

We walked back a different way, past a long stretch of apple trees and a smaller stand of pears, Joe telling us the names of every variety and which ones were for eating and which were for processing and which trees were past their usefulness and needed to be pushed out. That was another thing he was planning to do if he found time. We were back on the main road that ran alongside the woods, and when he reached a break in the trees that he alone had seen, he stepped inside.

Into the dark woods we followed.

"Look at this!" Pallace cried, her head craned back to see the place where the leaves cut the sunlight to thread.

"Keep going," Joe said. He went past the hemlocks and white pines and the red oaks that were never felled or burned, past the giant rocks in mossy sweaters. We could smell the cherry trees and then the moss and then the water, and then the woods opened unexpectedly and let us out on a beach of the Grand Traverse Bay of Lake Michigan. He had brought us to the edge of the world.

"How much have I missed?" Joe asks, taking his place on the towel beside me. He is wearing his plaid cotton work shirt and jeans, his steel-toed boots. His hair is much the same, as is his smile. His back is straight, his blue eyes still bright behind his glasses. Of all the things in life that have changed, Joe has changed the least.

Nell gets up to sit beside her father, wraps him in her skinny arms. "You've just been freed from your cloak of invisibility and are now revealed to be the hero."

Joe shakes his head. "Believe me, I wear the cloak of invisibility for a long time in this story."

I admit that I was slow.

"Did she tell you the part about bringing a date on our first date?" he asks Nell. "She brought her date and her date's brother and her date's brother's girlfriend."

"You in no way posed the invitation as a date."

"That's because you were dating Duke. I was just putting out a feeler to see if I stood a chance."

"Too subtle," I say.

"I was playing the long game," he says.

Nell, tucked beneath his arm, looks up at him. "You were in love with her then, weren't you?"

There's a question I'd never asked.

Joe is not a man to lie, even when the lie could be categorized as harmless and polite. I can see him digging around in his memory. Did he love me then? It was such a long time ago. "I like the thought," he says finally, "but probably not. I don't think I could have been in love with a person who was so clearly in love with someone else. That would be self-defeating and I wasn't the self-defeating type."

"I wasn't in love with Duke," I say.

Joe makes a ridiculous sound, an eruption of laughter and incredulity.

Nell keeps her attention on her father while making an effort to soften the blow. "So you weren't exactly in love with her but you liked her very much and thought she was a wonderful actress."

"Your mother was the best actress I ever directed," Joe says. "If she had decided that that was what she wanted to do with her life, she would have been brilliant at it."

"Shoulda, woulda, coulda," I say, lying back on the sand, though it is true that his estimation touches me.

"No one was better," he says.

"Well, actually, someone was better," I say.

"That was your opinion," Joe says.

I open one eye and stare at him. I use my amazing powers of mentalism to tell him to shut up, which he does.

Nell rests her chin on her knees. "What I don't understand," she begins.

"Here it comes," Joe says.

"What I don't understand," she says again, looking at her father, "is how a person can grow up in Michigan, love the theater, become a famous director, and then ditch it all to come back and grow cherries."

"I've wondered about that myself," Maisie says. She is scratching her dog's stomach with both hands and Hazel stretches out her four legs as far as she is able.

"It's nice to see them turn their attention on you for a change," I say.

"First off, you grew up on a cherry farm in Michigan and you want to be an actress," he says to Nell.

"What choice did I have? You read us Chekhov at bedtime," she said. "No *Hippos Go Berserk* for the Nelson girls."

"Secondly," Joe says, ignoring her, "cherry trees come equipped with invisible leashes. Just when you think you're free they start to pull you back."

"Emily inherited the cherry leash, not me," Nell says.

Emily nods. "Thanks for that."

"Are there more sandwiches?"

Maisie rifles through her bag and hands him one. We are partial to cheese and mustard, all of us.

"I had two lives," Joe says, unwrapping his lunch. "Maybe more than two. I got to do everything I wanted. Who can say that?"

I raise my hand.

"So what happened to Duke?" Emily asks.

We look at her. The four of us are forever turning as one to look at her. "You know what happened to Duke," I say.

"I don't mean what *happened* to Duke. I mean what happened to him that day, that summer?"

"Duke liked the farm better than anybody," Joe says, glad to be back on topic, glad to be thinking about anyone other than himself, glad to have a sandwich. "By which I mean he liked this place more than pretty much anybody who ever visited. Duke would have quit acting to pick cherries, at least on that day he would have. If Ken had offered him a job he would have taken it. I remember him running up and down the beach like a kid. He was crazy. That was the first time I ever saw him do a handstand."

"Was it?" I ask. He used to do them on the chair in our room.

"But when did things change? Did it happen the day you brought him to the orchard?" Emily asks me. "The happiest day of your life?"

"Let's strike the whole happiest-day-of-my-life motif," I say. "You three refuse to understand what I'm saying."

I can see that Emily is both irritated and making an effort not to be. We've had a good day so far, some real sweetness, and we both want to keep it that way. "You come up to the farm with Duke and Sebastian and Pallace and you leave with Daddy. Something must have happened."

Joe looks over at me as if he might have missed some pivotal piece of information himself.

"I came up with Duke and left with Duke. I didn't leave with your father."

"Okay, so maybe not on that day but eventually you did. You were with Duke and then you were with Dad."

I shake my head. A child's ability to misunderstand is limitless, even when she is no longer a child. "I didn't leave Duke for your father. Your father and I were never together at Tom Lake."

Now Maisie is squinting at us as well. "But you and Dad met at Tom Lake. You fell in love at Tom Lake."

"We met at Tom Lake and didn't fall in love, and then we met again a long time later and we did fall in love," Joe says to them. He looks at me. "I feel like I need a lawyer."

Because now we feel the shift from Lara and Joe and Maisie and Nell on one side and Emily on the other, to Lara and Joe on one side and Emily and Maisie and Nell on the other. The jury does not believe us.

"You fell in love at Tom Lake," Nell says, of this she is certain. "That was always the story."

"It was never the story!" I say. "It may have been the story you told yourselves but it wasn't the story we told you." Over the years I told them I had dated Duke at Tom Lake. Over the years I told them their father and I met at Tom Lake. What I realize in this moment, and Joe realizes it too, is that maybe we've never told them more than that. Or maybe they are children looking at their parents and so our lives began when they began and everything else they colored in with fat crayons any way they wanted.

"The four of you can sort this out. I'm going for a swim." Joe pulls off his boots, his shirt, his jeans. He had gone to the house and put on his swim trunks before coming to the beach, proving once and for all that these girls are his.

13

Duke was somewhere. He was getting his hair pinned, or he had already gone outside to read over his obsessive Editor Webb notebooks and smoke a final cigarette and then stand on his hands. He said it cleared his mind before a performance and I wouldn't doubt it. All the actors were in costume, swinging their arms around, trilling through scales. Only Uncle Wallace and I were still. If we were not exactly standing together we were very near one another. We were waiting to begin.

"I still get scared," Uncle Wallace said. He was looking straight ahead and his voice was so quiet I barely heard him. I don't think he was talking to me anyway. Backstage was dark and the houselights were up. From where we stood we could see the people milling around, looking for their seats. They always made me think of chickens, like a truck had backed up to the theater door and emptied four hundred chickens into the house. They pecked and clucked aimlessly, found one place to roost then changed their minds and went off in search of another. *Our Town* does not have a formal opening; when the audience enters the theater the curtain is up and what little set there is is in place and soon Uncle Wallace would wander out and wait for the chickens to settle, even though the very fact of him standing there, the much beloved television star of another era, impedes the process considerably.

"You're the Stage Manager," I whispered to him, "same as I'm Emily."

He reached down and took my hand in his large, warm hand and we didn't say anything else. That will always be my memory of Albert Long, the two of us holding hands in the dark until it was time for him to go on.

Nothing about going out onstage as Emily scared me, but playing Mae in *Fool for Love* made my feet cold. The expression came from a literal condition: every time I spoke her first line, which was nothing more than the single word *No!* all the blood in my body surged to my heart in an act of self-preservation. My heart needed the blood in order to survive, and so my bloodless extremities were left to freeze. Fear would be another name for it. I was told the last Emily—the one who'd dropped out and made a space for me—had had to audition for both parts. Her Mae, from all accounts, was searing. Pallace had auditioned to understudy both of the parts, and I had no doubt she had been searing as well. But I had never been asked to audition for anything at Tom Lake. I'd been asked to plug two holes in the summer schedule. "Look how good she is!" was what the management said when they came to those first rehearsals of *Our Town*, not realizing there was a difference between a first-rate Emily and a first-rate actress.

We had started rehearsals for *Fool for Love* the week before *Our Town* opened, and now I had some sense of what Pallace had been talking about. During the day I played a grown woman who was damaged and clear-headed and afraid, then three nights a week I was Emily again. The result was whiplash, and not just because the characters were so wildly different, my *ability* was so wildly different. I'm not sure Duke fully understood how bad I was. He was a full fathom five into his own performance. Duke was Eddie through and through, swinging his lasso, walking like he'd just come off a horse. He radiated his talent and intensity all over me but it did not make me better. The director, a Sam Shepard enthusiast named Cory, saw my failures clearly enough, as did the other two actors in the play, but it was still very early. Everyone regarded me as talented so maybe it was just taking me a minute to shift gears. But I didn't have another gear. Ripley had told me not to take acting classes, but he'd also given me a part in a movie in which I was essentially Emily again, and a part in a sitcom in which I was essentially Emily. Even hawking Diet Dr Pepper I was Emily, because she was the only thing I knew how to do. I had the range of a box turtle. I was excellent, as long as no one moved me.

But one of the very best things about playing Emily was that, at least for the duration of the performance and for maybe an hour or two on either side, she was all I thought about. After opening night Joe had gone back to Traverse City for good. Gene the A.D. was in charge of us now but we all knew what we were doing. We were well-trained horses: the starting gate flung open and we ran the race.

More and more I had seen Uncle Wallace struggling, not in any way the audience would have noticed, and truly, the cast might not have seen it either. He never dropped a line but he often missed his marks by a foot or more and the light board op had to scramble to keep the light on him. His voice was good, maybe he lacked his usual boom but we were all wired so it didn't matter. On the night of his disaster I saw him clenching and unclenching his teeth, like he was taking in an electrical shock. I even looked down to see if he was stepping on something. In the second act, just before Emily marries George, and Duke and I were having our moment—Duke holding me too tightly; Duke's hand on my ass in a way that was not visible to the public—I really thought Uncle Wallace was going to cry out.

I tried to find him at the second intermission but he was nowhere. He had stepped into the wings and vanished. I couldn't ask Duke because Duke stayed in character between acts. He would have answered me as Editor Webb and I would have killed him so I just skipped all that. I wished Joe were there. Somehow I felt that going to Gene would have been ratting Uncle Wallace out, saying that something was off about the job he was doing when that wasn't it at all. If Joe had been there I could have told him I was worried, that's all, just worried, and he would have searched Uncle Wallace out and found some way to gentle him. Joe was no doubt with his aunt and uncle now. I bet they'd already finished dinner and washed the plates and put them away.

When the call came for places, Uncle Wallace reappeared as mysteriously as he had left. He looked better, pinker. I stepped towards him but he held up his hand and looked away. *Not here* he was telling me, so he knew I had seen him. I nodded and stepped back.

He was holding it together and I needed to let him do that. He was a professional, Uncle Wallace.

The third act of *Our Town* takes place after Emily's death. She has died giving birth to her second child, though there's no mention of whether the baby has died, or if her father-in-law, Doc Webb, had been the doctor in attendance. The dead of Grover's Corners sit in straight rows across the stage, and when Emily joins them I couldn't help but think about the cemetery at the Nelsons' farm—the shade and the breeze and the stones that were very nearly rubbed clean of names. Duke had been right, the place had a peace that made a person want to stay. I had never thought about a cemetery that way before, and it helped me. I sat down next to Mother Gibbs and we both stared straight ahead, though in that moment I was remembering her getting out of the lake to put on her underwear.

The nice thing about having an entire script tattooed inside your cell walls is that you can pretty much play your part regardless of circumstances. Uncle Wallace and I went through the third act same as always. But when he brought me back to my mother's kitchen so that I could see how blindly the living go on, he didn't step away as he should have. In fact he tucked me into his armpit like a crutch. He was a big man, and I am small, but I held his weight for him, his cold sweat soaking through the shoulder of my dress. We both said our lines as perfectly as we ever had, and maybe we were better, because when we turned to go back to the cemetery on the other side of the stage it was death we were thinking about.

Why did we do this, both of us? Why didn't we simply pass the row of chairs and keep walking? In a sold-out house of four hundred, some small percentage of the audience were bound to have been doctors. But we soldiered on, stopping in front of my empty chair. I looked at the woman playing Mrs. Soames and mouthed the word *up*. She got up and moved to a chair in the back. Whatever was happening, we were all in it now. Not the audience, they were too far away, but all of the actors onstage were with us. I helped Uncle Wallace sit and he kept his arm around me. This was not the way the play was meant to be staged but people told me later it was very affecting, the Stage Manager sitting there among us, saying his final lines. And he did say the lines, every last word of them, even though the electrical current I had seen before had him in its teeth now. I didn't move, none of us did. We used the full force of our lives to listen to what he was saying, as if the purity of our attention was holding him up. Uncle Wallace talked about the stars and how the earth was straining, straining to make something of itself and how it needed to rest. In all my life I had never heard anything spoken so beautifully, and I felt certain I never would again. No sooner had the curtain come down that he pitched into my lap, bringing up an endless convulsion of blood. Blood poured from his mouth and pooled in the fabric of my white wedding dress, spreading, soaking. I had no idea how a man could lose so much blood and still be alive. I did my best to hold his head up while the rest of them ran to call for a doctor in the house.

An ambulance was called but even if they drove flat out the hospital was still fifteen minutes away. Uncle Wallace and I were sitting in those same two chairs with two doctors in front of us. One took his pulse while the other asked him questions, mostly as a way of making themselves feel useful. Uncle Wallace was able to remark on his level of pain between retching up another mouthful. He was holding on to me with both his bloodied hands. When the ambulance arrived I said I wanted to go with him. The stage manager—which is to say Pete, the actual stage manager for the show—said no, and the doctors said no, and the paramedics said no, until finally Uncle Wallace let go of me and they took him away. The entire cast was still on the stage, plus the deck crew and runners. Cat, the wardrobe mistress, was shaking when she came back to the dressing room to help me get undressed. She poured hydrogen peroxide on the dress. She had bottles of it, and in the end she got the stain out, even though the stain was more or less the entire dress. I wouldn't have believed such a thing was even possible.

People told me later how well I had handled the situation but I remembered it with nothing but shame. I could see him sinking and I let him go down. He said his lines, I said my lines. I did nothing to save him.

"How do you think you could have saved him?" Duke asked that night in bed. I had spent twenty minutes in the shower, the water as hot as I could stand it. Even after I took my costume off I had blood all over me. I scrubbed out my bra and underpants with bar soap.

"I could have walked him offstage and driven him to the hospital."

"Which would have bought him what, twenty minutes?" The lights were off and the moon was reflected in the lake. The moonlight spread across the clean white sheets of our bed. I had finally done the laundry the day before. "He didn't start vomiting blood because he spent an extra twenty minutes onstage when he didn't feel well. He started vomiting blood because he's been an unrepentant drunk for his entire adult life."

I shook my head, unwilling to relinquish my responsibility. "I should have made him stop. He shouldn't have kept going."

"He shouldn't have kept going, you're right about that, but it was his decision. You couldn't have gotten that man off the stage with a crane."

"Don't," I said quietly.

"Nothing against Uncle Wallace," he said, kissing my forehead. "Nothing at all. But he was teaching you a lesson you'd be wise to learn: you can't save them that won't save themselves."

And the thought of that stark reality, for whatever reason, was the thing that finally got me crying.

No one mentioned my poor performance in rehearsal the next day. They thought I was stiff and halting because Uncle Wallace had vomited blood all over me the night before, not because I'd been stiff and halting all along. *Fool for Love* only has four characters and really, only two, Mae and Eddie. Me and Duke. Pallace was my understudy again, and a guy named Nico was the swing for all three of the male parts. I wanted to go swimming at lunch. I wanted to stay under the water for as long as was possible. Cody, the director, came with us and I wished I'd worn the one-piece. He swam around behind me, telling me about the other Maes he'd seen over the years and how they'd played the part. He recited different lines in their voices so that I would have clear examples of how he wanted me to sound. I wanted to learn, I desperately wanted to be better, but all I could think of was what a good director Joe had been. When we were finished swimming and heading back to the theater, Cody said he was calling off rehearsal for the rest of the day.

"Just go," he said. "We're not getting anywhere."

It was so shocking to me, so shaming, and still I was grateful.

Pallace gave me the keys to her Honda and I went back to my room to change. She couldn't come with me because it was *Cabaret* night, and while it might have been nice if Duke had offered to ride along, we both knew Uncle Wallace wouldn't care about seeing him.

"Which brings us to the subject of Lee," Nell says over dinner.

"Wait, who's Lee again?" Maisie asks.

Joe nods solemnly. "Who is Lee, indeed."

"The understudy?" Emily scoops green beans onto her plate. "The rich guy?"

"The talentless, unprepared understudy," Nell clarifies. "He's like one of those crazed axe murderers who's hiding in the basement. I've been waiting for him to reemerge this entire time."

"Are you serious?" Maisie says. "Poor Uncle Wallace

is in the hospital having practically bled to death on our mother and you're thinking about the understudy?"

"He was something to think about," Joe says.

"Stop it!" Emily says. "For all we know, Uncle Wallace is dead."

Joe and I shake our heads in unison.

"What happened to him?" Maisie asks.

"Esophageal varices," I say. "It's a rupture in the vein that runs along the bottom of the esophagus. Truly, something you do not want to happen."

"How do they fix it?" Maisie asks, and I know that before she goes to sleep tonight she will be looking up esophageal varices to see if it can happen to dogs, to pigs, to rabbits.

"They put something called a Blakemore tube down the throat. There's a balloon on the end." I stop myself. "Forget it. You don't want to know."

Emily puts down her fork.

"I don't mean to be insensitive," Nell says. "You know how glad I am that Uncle Wallace pulled through."

"He only pulled through until the fall." Just saying it makes me catch my breath. So many years ago! Dear, stupid, intractable Uncle Wallace.

"He had cirrhosis as well," Joe says. "He didn't stop drinking."

"They put a balloon in his esophagus and he kept drinking?" Emily asks.

Joe and I nod as the girls sadly shake their heads.

"Was that his last performance?" Nell asks. "That night with you?"

Funny how we never know. Uncle Wallace didn't go onstage thinking it would be his last night. When my last night came I didn't know it either, my last time to play Emily, my last swim in the lake. "I guess it was, the shape he was in. He went home after he got out of the hospital, back to Chicago."

"Nell's right," Emily says. "Tell us about Lee. You can finish up with Uncle Wallace later but I need a break if I'm going to eat dinner."

Joe sighs, tents his fingers. "Talking about Uncle Wallace bleeding out onstage will ruin your dinner but talking about Lee will ruin mine." He looks at me but I shrug. I've done most of the telling around here. If Joe is forced to reminisce about Lee, so be it.

"Okay," he says. "First off, this wasn't my problem. I had gotten the play to opening night. That was my contractual obligation. Lee was Gene's problem now."

"Whatever happened to Gene?" I ask.

"Children's television," Joe says. "Last I heard he'd made it to *Sesame Street.* Gene was a talented guy, but that didn't mean he was up for Lee. He went to find

Lee as soon as the ambulance pulled away. They were still mopping up the stage when Lee had gone back to his house. It must have been eleven o'clock at night by the time Gene got to Lee's and started knocking on the door."

"The only person in the company who left the theater was the understudy," Nell says.

"That's a bad sign," Maisie says.

Their father nods. "Gene doesn't stop knocking. That's what I liked about Gene. He came across as very mild but he was tenacious. He'd been there maybe fifteen minutes when finally a light goes on upstairs."

"Tell me he didn't send his wife down." I've never heard this part of the story.

"He sends his wife down."

The girls do their unison groan.

"She opens the door six inches, tells Gene it's late and Lee has gone to bed. He's very tired after the performance."

"He wasn't *in* the performance!" Nell cries. I can see now that her dinner will be ruined as well.

"Gene tells her to please wake him up, tells her it's important, a man is very sick. She wants to know if he's dead, and when Gene says 'No, Missus'—" He looks at me again. "What was his last name?"

I can't remember. I've blocked it. Joe nods. "Missus

says if Uncle Wallace isn't dead then Gene should call in the morning after ten. Gene tells her that Lee can just open the door at ten because he isn't leaving."

"I'm assuming there was a . . ." Emily pauses, searching for the correct word, "a *dynamic* at work here."

"Black man, white woman, huge house, middle of the night," Joe says. "Yes, there was a dynamic. In fact I would hazard to say it was the dynamic that sent Gene into a career of directing puppets. But into that dynamic walks Lee himself, glasses on, fully dressed, asking his wife who had come to see them so late. *Oh, Gene, goodness, I didn't know it was you*, so then they have to go through all of that."

Maisie pushes away her plate.

"Lee sends his wife back to bed and steps out on the front porch, closing the door behind him. Gene tells him he'll have to go on as the Stage Manager, day after tomorrow. Then Lee asks if Uncle Wallace is dead. When Gene says no, Lee completely relaxes. He claps Gene on the shoulder. 'He'll be fine,' he says. 'It might not seem like it but trust me, I've known this guy a long time. He always goes on. If he has to walk here from the hospital, he'll do it. He won't miss a show.'"

I pound my hand on the table. "He's missing the show!" I say this as the person he bled on, the person who went to see him in the hospital.

Joe nods again, a marvel of restraint. "They go in circles for a while, Gene explaining and Lee demurring until finally Gene, who doesn't feel like he's been hinting at anything, becomes explicit: The company will not allow Albert Long to return, and as his understudy, Lee will perform the role on Thursday night."

Then suddenly I do remember. Joe told me this story eons ago. I remember all of it. "This is the best part!"

"Lee just stares at him and finally he says, 'I would prefer not to.' Then he goes inside and closes the door."

"Bartleby!" Nell shouts. "He Bartlebied him."

Her sisters, smart women both, stare blankly.

"'Bartleby the Scrivener,'" Nell says. "Herman Melville. Look it up."

"How do you remember these things?" Emily asks her sister.

"Trust me," Joe says. "It was unintentional on his part."

"So what happened?" Nell can scarcely stay in her chair. "Who played the part?"

"Your father," I say, beaming.

"You were the Stage Manager?" Emily is incredulous. They all are. I think Joe is the obvious choice but if we'd made them guess all night they wouldn't have come up with the answer.

"Gene drove up here the next morning. He said I had

to do it, which meant driving down to Tom Lake and back three times a week for the rest of the run. Poor Gene, I wanted to punch him but it wasn't his fault."

"Why you?" Maisie asks.

"I knew the part."

"You knew the whole part?" Nell is in love with her father, her actual father who has saved the play.

Joe gives the back of his head a ferocious scratch, the way Hazel would have scratched her own head with her paw. "I played it in college and then with a summer rep outside Chicago."

"You wanted to be an actor?" Emily asks.

"For about ten minutes," he says.

"So wait." Nell looks at me. "You dated George, and then you dated Editor Webb, and then you married the Stage Manager."

"I never thought about that." I look over at my husband and smile. "I married the Stage Manager."

The hospital was small and cheerful in the way hospitals never are anymore: red brick, red geraniums. I asked for Albert Long's room number and the woman at the information desk could not have been happier to give it to me. I found Uncle Wallace lying flat on his back and sound asleep, wearing a blue and yellow University of Michigan football helmet. Not a jersey, a helmet. A fat red tube was coming out of his mouth and the tube was tied to the face guard. Had it been a brain tumor that had caused him to bleed? Had they scooped the contents of his skull into a football helmet for safekeeping? I tiptoed to the edge of the bed to see if it was really him.

"It's disturbing," the woman in the next bed said, "but you'd be surprised how fast you get used to it."

In fact, it was so disturbing that I'd failed to register the room's second occupant, a smartly dressed blonde holding an open copy of *Architectural Digest.* Her bed was cranked to the angle of a chaise longue, poolside.

"Hello!" she said in a stage whisper, then smiled. She was wearing lipstick. She looked so familiar I wondered if she was an actress. We have an ability to spot one another.

"How is he?" I whispered back, not entirely sure I wanted to know. Uncle Wallace was a smaller man in a hospital bed, in a Wolverines helmet. He looked old.

"I don't know," she said. "No one around here can tell me much more than he isn't dead." The steady beeping of the heart monitor confirmed this.

"Why the helmet?"

She nodded as if to say, Oh, that. "As best as I can understand it, the tube coming out of his mouth is connected to a balloon inside him that's keeping his esophagus from bleeding. They have to tie the red tube to the face mask of the helmet to keep everything in place."

I nodded, putting my hand on his wrist. I didn't like to think about tubes and where they went. No one does.

"Were you at the play last night?" she asked.

I nodded again.

"Turns out one of the doctors from this hospital was in the audience. He said it was a mess. Poor Albert. I'm Elyse, by the way." She gave a little wave. "Second wife."

Uncle Wallace had a wife, two wives? "I didn't know he was married," I said.

She reviewed me then with an entirely new level of seriousness. "The two of you? What are you, fourteen?"

I held up my hands. "No, no! I'm Emily in the play. We work together, that's all."

She closed her magazine and then, for a moment, closed her eyes. "I'm sorry. He doesn't always make the best choices." She looked at me again. "Which isn't to say you wouldn't have been a delightful choice. It's just—"

"I understand," I said. I didn't understand, but I was tired.

"He's got a young wife now, or she's younger than me but she's nowhere near as young as you."

"Is she coming?" The second and third wives in one hospital room, that would be something. For all I knew the first one would be showing up as well.

"They're in the process of disentangling, Albert and his third wife, which, I'm guessing, is why he put me down as his personal contact. Or maybe Tom Lake just never updates their intake forms. Anyway, I got the call and so here I am."

"Do you think the other wife knows what happened?"

She shrugged as if to say that wasn't her problem, which I suppose it wasn't. "My plan is to get him out of here as soon as I can, take him back to Chicago and get him into a grown-up hospital. No disrespect to Tiny Town here but I think he may need something more advanced than a football helmet."

"That's so nice of you." All I knew about divorce was what I'd seen in movies or read in novels. I couldn't remember any cases where the second ex-wife steps in to take her former husband home from the hospital.

Elyse turned on her side to watch his labored respiration. "We've got kids," she said. "They're in their twenties now but they're still kids, you know? They love him. They grew up watching Uncle Wallace. They think he's a fantastic father because he played one on TV." Why should I know this? Why should I know anything? Because we'd spent six weeks standing so close together, saying the exact same words day after day? I knew how naive it made me look to be shocked by everything. Uncle Wallace didn't have kids. He had his sister's orphans, and the Stage Manager, well, the Stage Manager didn't have anyone because he was essentially God. I asked her if I could do anything to help.

"Maybe you could pack up his room for him. That would be helpful."

"Sure, I can do that."

She stretched out her legs and yawned. She must have driven through the night. "I'll tell him you came when he wakes up. I'll tell him the sweet girl from the play came to see him. What did you say your name was?"

I told her it was Emily.

"When did he die?" Emily asks me. There is so much tenderness in her voice. Had we told this story earlier in life, Emily might have grown up convinced that Uncle Wallace was her father, though really, that might have been worse.

I look at Joe. "Fall? Winter maybe? I can't remember."

Maisie takes out her phone and taps in his name. "July twenty-eighth, 1988." She reads the names of his three wives, his two children, his major roles. "The actor will be remembered as the beloved Uncle Wallace. The second wife was Elyse Adler. She played his girlfriend on the show for two seasons."

I looked at her tiny picture on the phone. "Oh my god."

Nell and Emily lean in to see her pretty face.

"So he died just a couple of weeks after I saw him." So much had happened that summer, and in the confusion, I had forgotten him. "How old was he?"

Maisie takes a moment to scroll, stopping to admire the other two wives. "Born January twentieth, 1931, died July twenty-eighth, 1988. Fifty-six."

"What?"

She holds up the screen to show me. There he is. No picture of his own children, just those little orphan actors in his arms.

"He was my age," I say.

Emily shakes her head. "You're fifty-seven."

14

I am fifty-seven. I am twenty-four. After dinner the girls head out with Hazel, some blankets, and a six-pack of beer. They have plans to sit in a field far away from their friends and watch *The Promised Man* just as the last of the fireflies flickering in the tall grass turn out their lights. The movie is a cause for merriment, not because it's happy—in fact, I remember it as soul-crushing—but because activities unrelated to work are few and far between these days. Benny will meet them there. On this windless night, the Otts have strung a king-sized sheet between two trees and pulled it taut. They have a video projector. They call to ask if Joe and I would like to come, but I decline. They have no idea we're living our own version of the Peter Duke film festival over here.

"That one?" Joe stacks the dishes in the sink once the girls have gone.

"I don't even like to think about it." I open the back door and shake out the placemats, wipe off the table.

"It's a beautiful piece of work, though. Certainly Duke's best."

My husband's sleeves are rolled and the hot water steams his glasses. It's so easy to forget what Joe is capable of, so easy to remember. "Were you ever sorry?"

He laughs. "We could be living in Los Angeles now."

"You could be on your third wife."

"Come dry." He holds out a towel to me.

It's not as if I don't understand. It's exactly what the girls have been saying to me: *Are you sorry? Don't you wish?* But Joe was better than I was. Sometimes I wonder what he would have done had he stayed. "You were so good."

He shakes his head. "You *are* so good," he says, correcting me. "That's what you're supposed to say."

"Were and are, both things are true."

"You're spending too much time in the past." He passes me a dripping Pyrex casserole dish.

"So tell me how to get out of it."

He shakes his head. "There's no way out but through."

"You were a very good Stage Manager."

"I was no Uncle Wallace."

"You were different, that's all. You were your own man." It's true that no one else would ever be the Stage Manager for me—Uncle Wallace took the part with him—but Joe had a radiant optimism and health that no amount of gray shadow beneath his eyes could diminish. No one thinks of the Stage Manager as a young man but why shouldn't he be? God can be anything. "You were strapping."

"And you—" He turns and looks at me, a wet plate in his hands.

I start to put the glasses away. I wait for him to finish his thought but nothing comes. "What was I?"

"You were Emily. I could have watched you forever and never understood how you did it. I believed you every minute you were on the stage. Everyone did."

I stretch up on my toes to kiss him and he meets me. "We were in that play together. It really is miraculous when you think about it."

"Those drives back and forth three times a week." Joe takes the towel from me and dries his hands. "I wanted to kill Uncle Wallace for drinking and I wanted to kill Lee for being himself."

"So why did you do it?" I ask. "I mean, I know Gene was leaning on you and everyone was in a pinch, but we were living in a summer town full of actors. You can't tell me that no one else at Tom Lake had ever played the Stage Manager before. Somebody could have pulled it together. You could have done one performance and then made Gene take the part."

"That was the plan."

"What was the plan?"

"I told Gene I'd do it once, two times at the most. I said I'd give him that much time to find someone for the part and then I was done."

All the help that Ken and Maisie needed: the books, the trees, the taxes, the house, every piece of it called for his attention. I understand it now in a way I could never could have understood it the summer I met them. Joe was a life raft coming to save them. He didn't have five minutes to spare, much less three shows a week. "So why did you change your mind?"

My husband stood there. How many performances had there been between the time when Uncle Wallace dropped out and when I dropped out? How long were Joe and I in the play together anyway? A week? Not two weeks. "Me?"

"I liked being on the stage with you."

"You liked being on the stage with me but you weren't in love with me?"

He closes his eyes, smiling. "I was young. I don't remember what I was."

"You were in love with me!"

He shrugs. "I might have been," he says.

Uncle Wallace's room turned out to be a small cottage behind the company housing where we lived, a fairytale bungalow made for sheltering iconic television stars. I'd never seen it before, but then my room faced the lake. If Duke was sleeping with me in order to upgrade his accommodations, he would have done better to sleep with Uncle Wallace. The cottage had a fireplace in the sitting room with a comfy chintz sofa and a television. Who knew such inequities existed in the world? A painting of a greyhound in profile hung over the fireplace. There was a bathtub, a kitchenette, a small stone terrace ringed with red poppies. Duke had no interest in going to the hospital but he couldn't wait to get inside the cottage.

The door was unlocked because everything at Tom Lake was unlocked. The place was so tidy that my first thought was that the management must have already sent someone over to take care of things. But after a few minutes I started to see what was his: a copy of *The 7 Habits of Highly Effective People* on the nightstand, a wristwatch beside it. Uncle Wallace carried a pocket watch in the play. His black leather dopp kit was on the bathroom sink. Duke poked through the contents with one finger and came up with two bottles of interest.

"Put those back," I said. "He might need them."

"I might need them." Duke fell back on the bed, his arms stretched wide, an orange prescription pill bottle in each hand. "Uncle Wallace is in the land of limitless refills now."

I opened the dresser drawer, found his underwear, his socks.

"Come here." Duke rattled the bottles like little maracas.

I went to the bed, then got down on my hands and knees to look beneath it, finding two empty suitcases.

"Since when are you no fun at all?" he asked, lifting his beautiful head.

For whatever reason, I took this to be a serious question. Had I been no fun at all since Uncle Wallace vomited a bucket of blood in my lap? No, wait, it was before that. Since I realized that I didn't have the talent to play Mae but I was going to play her anyway? Since I realized that soon I'd be too old to play Emily, the only part I was good at?

"Jesus, are you crying?" Duke put down the pill bottles and sat up to take my hand. I shook my head. He pulled me into his lap, kissed me.

"Okay, cricket," he said. "Here's the plan: first,

we're going to smoke a cigarette. Ah! Don't look at me like that. He's never coming back so he isn't going to know, not to mention the fact that Uncle Wallace smoked a few himself. Listen to me. We're going to smoke a cigarette and then we're going to pack everything up. Judging by the looks of the place that should take all of four minutes. Once we've got his stuff in the suitcases we're going to put this bed to use as it has never been put to use before. Okay?" He gave me a squeeze and then a better kiss. He bounced me on his knees. "Doesn't. Take. Much."

He lit two cigarettes and gave me one, and when we'd finished he got up according to plan. He opened the first suitcase and put in the book and the bedside clock, though for all I knew the clock belonged to Tom Lake. He wrapped the watch in Kleenex and snugged it in the side pocket of the dopp kit so nicely I thought it made up for taking the pills. I opened the closet and took out the two suits, the dress shirts, the casual pants. I found a tidy stack of twenties in the nightstand and folded them in his suit pocket. I found his pajamas. I swear they were the same pajamas he'd worn on television, or at least the same style, a crisp blue and white stripe. He was wearing those pajamas when the orphans brought him breakfast in bed on Father's Day. He was wearing them when the little girl woke him in the middle of the night, crying from a dream about her dead mother. "Come on," he'd said, and held up the covers, scooting over to make a place for her in his bed.

I continued with the dresser drawers and Duke went to the kitchen. I wouldn't have thought to check the kitchen. Then I heard him whistle, long and low.

"What?"

The freezer was full of vodka, proud Russian soldiers standing shoulder to shoulder beside the ice maker. I came and stood next to him to see. The cold air was beautiful. "Therein lies the problem," I said.

Duke peered inside. "I always thought he was a gin man."

"I think he is. I think that's why the vodka's still here."

Duke took out an open bottle, twisting off the cap to drink. He closed his eyes and shivered. "To Uncle Wallace," he said. "*Za lyubov.*" He raised the frozen bottle in salute then handed it to me. The day was hot and I touched it to my forehead before bringing it to my lips.

This would be as good a time as any to talk about alcohol.

Duke's drinking did not distinguish him from anyone else at Tom Lake that summer. Drinking was what we did to pass the time when we weren't onstage, and while he would be the first to say he drank more than most (though less than Uncle Wallace), he wasn't in imminent danger of rupturing anything in his esophagus.

But *Fool for Love* tipped the balance. *Fool for Love* could just as easily have been called *Fool for Tequila*, the bottle being the central prop in much of the action. It's Eddie's bottle, and it starts the play full and ends the play empty. Eddie drinks a lot; Mae, who's on the wagon, drinks a good bit, and the other two characters, the Old Man and Martin, both drink some. Duke believed that if the stage directions said the character was drinking tequila, then it was his responsibility as an actor to drink tequila.

I was a lousy drinker.

"That's because you don't practice," Duke said. "Look how much better your smoking has gotten!"

Everybody smoked through rehearsals now. Ten o'clock and I was halfway through my third cigarette.

"Eddie has a problem," he said to Cody in rehearsal. "Mae has a problem. The Old Man has a problem but he also has his own bottle." The Old Man drank whiskey, though he gets a shot of tequila along the way.

"What about me?" the guy playing Martin asked. "Do I have a problem?" The guy playing Martin was a Sault Ste. Marie Chippewa named Homer. He was cracking himself up. "You need to find your own backstory." Duke handed him the bottle he'd bought for rehearsal.

Cody was stumped. Cody took Sam Shepard's stage directions to be the Nicene Creed. He listened to Duke's madness while having no clear understanding of how a group of actors could function on that much booze. "Are you wanting to do this in rehearsals, too?" he asked.

"Rehearsing means getting ready to play the role," Duke said. "No one drinks their first bottle of tequila on opening night and expects to survive. That's what I've been telling Mae here. You have to work up to it."

I wanted this to work. I would have done anything to be good in the part, to be as good as Duke was. I even wanted to please Cody, who I couldn't stand. I just didn't want to drink tequila first thing in the morning.

Cody, nibbling the end of his pencil, was intrigued. "It's verisimilitude."

"It is *not* verisimilitude." I looked to him to be the adult in the room, like Joe had been the adult. "Verisimilitude is the *appearance* of something being real. Verisimilitude means putting tap water in an empty tequila bottle." The problem with being the only woman in a play in which the three other characters were men and the playwright was a man and the director was a man was that no matter what I said, I sounded petulant, female. "It's one bottle. It isn't one bottle for Eddie and one for Mae. If you're drinking yourself blind then you're consigning the rest of us to the same fate."

Homer shrugged, and the Old Man, who was played with great authority by a former junkie named Sal, said he was all in. The prop master should bring him a bottle of whiskey, preferably Jim Beam.

"I guess it wouldn't kill us to try," Cody said. Early as it was in rehearsals, Cody already hated me.

Duke smacked the table. "Now you're talking!"

I looked over at Pallace, who was sitting in the corner doodling on her script. "Help," I said very quietly when she raised her eyes.

She shook her head. *Doomed,* she mouthed to me.

The introduction of Jose Cuervo into morning rehearsals made me even worse in the part than I was, if such a thing were possible. Instead of tossing it back and slamming it down, I fiddled with my glass and tightened my lips. As hard as I tried to relax, I never stopped looking like I was faking it, because I was faking it. I was thinking about the evening's performance of *Our Town.* Nobody wanted to see a drunk Emily.

The men, however, were another story. All three of their performances were radically improved by alcohol. They blossomed. They were lit. They raged when rage was called for, and then retreated to their moody silences. Duke, who'd been good in the part all along, was roaring now. He was taller, looser, stronger. He was dangerously real. He lassoed the bedposts one at a time. He threw me to the ground and covered me with his body. I could feel his erection pressing into my leg through his jeans. I was miles behind.

"*Try* drinking," he said when I screamed in frustration.

And so I tried. I drank a fraction of what the men drank and still I wobbled and forgot my lines. Cuervo didn't have those sad little worms curled up in the bottom of the bottle but I thought about them every time I tipped the bottle back, the bile rising in my throat.

I won a single battle in that war, and it may well have been the battle that saved us all. The directions say a bottle of tequila but they don't say what size it is. Duke swore it was a fifth. I said a pint.

"A pint?" Duke asked.

"Or maybe it's a half gallon," I said. "Get something with a handle."

Cody, for once, took my side. "I think a pint makes sense."

Duke put up a little argument then let it go. A fifth was hard to control, even if he wouldn't admit it. I wasn't drinking my share and he was left to pick up the slack. Like it or not, the bottle had to be empty by the end of the show. "Drinking is a muscle," Duke liked to say. "And you have to keep that muscle in shape." He had no end of theories as to how to avoid the repercussions, though mostly it came down to gallons of water and three prophylactic aspirin, which he insisted on chewing for best results. After his incandescent rehearsals, he took a long swim and pulled himself together for the evening's performance of *Our Town*. I always went with him to the lake to make sure he didn't drown, having no idea what I would do if he did. My swimsuit was never completely dry in those days. Whenever I pulled it on it was still clammy from the swim before.

I had no idea how Duke managed to drink so much and be so good. I was desperate to be good, but all that did was make me look desperate.

After we finish cleaning up, Joe says he's going to check on the goats and just take care of a few more things out at the barn. He says he'll only be a minute and I say, okay. I say, tell the goats good night for me. After a respectable amount of time has passed, I take a flashlight from the basket by the door and head in the direction of the Otts.

The leaves on the cherry trees are silvered with

moonlight, with flashlight, the branches bent beneath the cherry weight. They make me think of cows aching to be milked. I take the quickest way, not on the road but through the orchard, feeling like I'm doing something I shouldn't be doing. But what shouldn't I be doing? Going to see a movie? Joe wouldn't care. Joe would have come with me had I asked him, and the girls would gladly make room for me on their blanket. But I want to have a thought, an action, a memory that I haven't run past anyone. I want to see a little bit of the movie by myself.

At the bottom of the hill I go past the pear trees, those difficult, unlovable pears. The Otts have five children, and when they were young each of my girls had an Ott of similar age to play with—sleepovers back and forth, campfires and homework dates, all of them ultimately disrupted by the gnarled pear trees. One by one our girls became evasive about the Otts. They loved them in the summer, but as the days got shorter and colder, they started to cancel their plans at the last minute, and in the winter they would have nothing to do with the Otts outside of school. I might have suspected something amiss at our neighbors' house were it not for the fact that the seasonal disenchantment worked in both directions: Young Nelsons would not visit young Otts, and young Otts wouldn't come to see young Nelsons once the weather turned cold. One day I picked up two of the Ott girls from school and brought them home with us. I don't remember why but it wasn't an uncommon situation: We all picked up other people's children and they picked up ours. Maybe Patsy Ott was taking her older boy to have his braces tightened or maybe two of our children had partnered on a science project, but when it came time to go home they cried. They could not stop crying.

"What?" I asked them. "I'll walk with you."

They would not be walked and would not be consoled. Finally, Maisie, who might have been nine, gave me a high sign to follow her to the bathroom. She shut the door quietly behind us and sat down on the toilet lid, pulling up her knees to make herself small. "Drive them," she whispered.

"Drive them next door?"

She looked at me, her green eyes huge. Maisie was about to cry herself.

"Why? What's out there?"

Some kind of oath was involved in all of this. I never got that part straight. The dangerous thing was infinitely more dangerous if you spoke its name. But Maisie was hard up against it now, and she wanted to save her friends. "Pear trees," she said.

"What about them?"

She closed her eyes, shaking her head in despair. "We can't walk past them and there's no other way to get there."

It was true, they weren't allowed to walk on the road.

In the summer the pear trees were fine. In the summer, all that is hideous about a pear tree is hidden by leaves and pears. But once those disguises were removed they were nothing but acres of murderous psychopaths emboldened by darkness. To cross the naked pear orchard at night was to run the gauntlet of death. The branches jutted with dark knives: child snatchers, child killers. Turns out it wasn't just the Nelson children and the Otts who believed this about pear trees. Nearly everyone who grew up on an orchard in Grand Traverse County had had issues with them at one point or another, and then they forgot, or, worse, remembered and thought it was funny. I gathered up all the children, theirs and ours, and told them we were going to the Dairy Bar for soft serve. A week from now the Dairy Bar would close for the season, and so we needed to get in all the frozen custard we could, even if it meant spoiling our appetite for dinner. When all of us were sticky and full, I drove the Ott children home, their dignity intact.

"It's the pear trees," I whispered to their mother at

the handoff. I could see the memory cross Patsy Ott's face, *pear trees.*

Maisie announced her plans to sleep between us that night, certain the trees would march up the hill and smash their horrible branches through her bedroom window to carry her away. But as soon as the lights were off she bolted up. "They'll take Nell!" she cried.

Joe, who had come in late to the story, put his arms around her. "They won't take Nell," he said. "Not if they're looking for you."

"Daddy, they're *trees*," she gasped. "They don't know the difference."

So Joe got up and brought back her sister, sound asleep. We made a space for both of our younger girls in the bed. We didn't think of Emily because Emily had her own room and surely, pear trees knew better than to mess with her. It all comes back as I walk through the orchard at night, the four of us in bed, and how quickly we fell asleep.

When I crest the hill it's Duke I see, his enormous face rising like a moon in the distance. Across the Otts' field the farmers and their families and the pickers all sit apart from one another, one family to a blanket, maybe two dozen blankets spread around, the light of Duke pouring over them. I'm too far away to hear what he's saying but I can make out the sad cadence of his voice, which blends into the soundtrack, which folds into the evening saw of crickets. He is a movie star, an actor. He is incalculably more than the person I knew, and he is that person as well.

I don't remember exactly what part of the movie we're in. He's staring out at a barren landscape. He says something to the woman beside him without facing her. Her hair is long and tangled and it blows in her eyes. I saw *The Promised Man* ten years ago when it first came out and I never wanted to see it again. I don't remember the character's name, but everything we need to know about the trouble he's in is there in his face. He loves his wife, his two beautiful daughters, of this I am certain. His family doesn't know he's lost his job. They don't know how much he's been drinking. He's been making mistakes, then stealing to cover them up. The action of the film takes place in the brief window of time between the people Duke is working for finding out what he's done and his family finding out. He's trying to give his family a few perfect days before it all goes to hell, or he's trying to maintain his denial for as long as he can. Even this far away I cannot bear to see how afraid he is. That had always been Duke's magic, that with all his beauty and charm he was able to let the audience see how small he was, how terrified, how deeply in love.

We never had time to go to movies when the girls were young, or not the kind of movies that required a babysitter. The concept of date night had yet to reach northern Michigan, so the few movies we saw in the theater revolved around singing cartoon dogs. Because Emily was at the height of her fervid misconceptions about her paternity then, she insisted on seeing Duke's new film, and since it was rated R, we said no. Every morning she'd leave another review on the kitchen table that she'd printed off and highlighted so I would know that not only was it Duke's *best* film, it was a culturally *important* film. He was long past his stints in cop shows and family features by then. He was a serious actor, and this was the picture that would forever cut his ties to that earlier career we had all enjoyed.

I told Emily she wasn't going.

"How can you tell me not to see it when you don't even know what it's about?"

"That's why there's a rating system, because parents don't have time to see every single movie in advance of their children."

"I'm not asking to see *every single movie.* I'm asking to see this one."

Around and around. I used to wonder if this was what parents felt like trying to shield their daughters from Elvis. Duke was everywhere: His picture in the paper, his voice on the radio, his reruns on television, his movies in the movie basket. I don't know why I tried to fight it. Maybe I should have taken her to the theater and bought two tickets, because I had no sense of whether I wanted to keep her from seeing an R-rated movie, or if I wanted to keep her from seeing another Duke movie, or if I just wanted to prevent her from having something she wanted because she tortured me every minute of the day.

"Let's just go and find out if it would be okay for her to see it," Joe said finally, the two of us in bed. "It wouldn't kill us to go to a movie."

"That movie?"

Joe folded me in his arms. "We've seen *Swiss Father Robinson* seven hundred times and it didn't kill us. At least this one is supposed to be good."

And so we drove to Suttons Bay for a noon matinee on a Tuesday when the girls were in school. You can do things like that when you're the ones who own the farm, and anyway, it was winter. We thought our biggest risk was that a foot of snow would fall while we were inside and bury the car. We never considered that the movie might destroy us. I started crying halfway through and kept up a steady weeping until the end. Joe handed me his handkerchief in the dark but then later took it back. We stayed through all the credits, the closing song, trying to pull ourselves together before walking back out into the blinding winter sun.

"I didn't see that coming," Joe said, using a stack of thin paper napkins he had taken from the concessions stand. He gave half to me and I mopped my eyes.

"Was it sad because we knew him or would anyone have been destroyed by that?"

"Both," he said.

What I had felt, standing out in front of the Bay Theater with the wind whipping off the lake, was that I had seen Duke's end, his shame and his failure, his letting go.

But of course that wasn't it at all. It was a movie, an incredibly convincing performance in a movie. Duke was nowhere near his end. He was an actor at the top of his game, and the fact that he could make me so believe him when I knew better only proved how good he was. This was the role he'd win his Oscar for. Viola Davis opened the envelope and said his name. He took the stairs two at a time and embraced her, whispered something in her ear that made her laugh, then turned to the audience, holding the golden statue above his head.

"Sebastian!" he cried.

I remember it now.

We never told Emily we saw the movie. We stuck by our original answer: It was R rated and she couldn't go. So when she managed to talk the Holzapfels into taking her and Benny, telling them she had our permission, she didn't tell us either, at least not for a long time. We all carried around the shattering grief of that performance by ourselves.

Times are hard in Michigan, as times are hard everywhere. The Otts have had the wonderful idea to arrange an activity where people could do something together other than harvesting cherries, but they might have shown *The Popcorn King* instead. I understand that *The Promised Man* is a better film, but so was *Taxi Driver*, so is *The Deer Hunter*. That doesn't mean we're up for it.

The woman projected up on the sheet has sold Duke crack. He has lost his job but he still has his family. He is an alcoholic but he still has his family and they love him. They would gladly reach down into the darkest hole and use all their strength to pull him up. But he doesn't go to them. He goes to this woman instead. And when he is back in his car we realize that things are much worse than we had understood. He has a pipe and he lights it and when the flame pulls down we can see the drug hit him, the color draining from his face, his nose and eyes streaming, and then the look of relief that breaks over him, a violent gratitude, like he wasn't sure it would come for him this time and it came.

I want someone to tell me how that was acting. I want someone to tell me how many people were on the set, and how many of them understood what was happening. They had to wait until the golden hour when the light was perfect because there could be only one take. He couldn't do this thing twice. I wonder if Sebastian was there, but he couldn't have been. Sebastian would never have let that happen.

All these years later, I feel like I let it happen. I didn't refuse to drink even though I knew what the drinking was doing to him. I didn't pour out the tequila and replace it with water. I didn't walk Uncle Wallace off the stage. It's nothing but foolish self-aggrandizement, I know. No summer girlfriend ever changed the course of a movie star's life. But still, I am sorry I didn't try.

The evening air is sweet and the warmth of the day rises up from the grass. When I can't stand to look at Duke's face another second I look out over the dark field, trying to find four people and a small dog, but I can't find four people and a dog because it's five. Joe is there. For once he's put the goats to bed and left the barn as planned. Emily, Maisie, Nell, Benny, and Joe, all of them together, with Hazel wandering off to sniff at other people's picnic dinners. I stand on the hill for a long time and watch them instead of the movie. I think about walking down to join them but I remember how the movie ends and I don't want to see it. I don't want to walk home past the pear trees when it's over, each of us dissecting the merits of Duke's performance. I want to be asleep when they get back. I want them all to keep their voices down for fear of waking me.

15

No one's around when I get up in the morning. When does that ever happen? I make so many sandwiches and take them to the barn, then head to the orchard where I find my girls already hard at work. The work is always biting at our heels. "Good morning," they say, keeping their eyes on their hands. We talk about how many rows we mean to pick today. We talk about the weather. Emily says some neighbors have posted that they'll be selling whitefish this afternoon and we decide that whitefish is today's answer to the eternal question of dinner. No one says anything about the movie. My guess is that they can't make sense of what they saw, or maybe it just made them too sad. Maisie's already been back to the Otts' early this morning because the Otts think that Happy, their ancient yellow Lab, has had a stroke. She's walking in circles, Maisie tells us, holding her head at an angle, one eye closed. She's vomiting, falling over.

"Oh, not Happy!" Emily says. "She came by the blanket last night."

"It's not a stroke," Maisie says. "At least I don't think it is. I'm pretty sure she has old-dog vestibular disease."

"Happy's dizzy?" I ask.

Maisie nods. "I called her vet and they're going to fill some prescriptions for her. She should get straightened out, unless I'm wrong, in which case it's probably a brain tumor."

"You saved Happy's life!" Nell says. The girls have known Happy since earliest puppyhood. No one is interested in the possibility of a brain tumor.

Joe comes by on the Gator to collect the first round of lugs. He whistles at our productivity.

"We haven't been talking as much this morning," Nell says.

"Well, that's a first," Joe says. "I would have thought you'd be taking the movie apart."

The three girls look at him, stricken, and it occurs to me that they must have stayed up half the night doing exactly that.

"I can't blame you," he says, answering what has not

been said. "I have regrets about seeing it again myself." He looks at me. "Was it that sad the first time?"

"It was," I say, and then wonder if he knew I was there.

We help him put the lugs in the back, grateful to use our bodies some other way even for a minute, then he waves and is gone.

"Was Dad a good Stage Manager?" Nell asks, watching the Gator crest the hill.

"Excellent," I say.

Maisie pulls over the ladder and goes to clean off the top of her tree. "He's not what you'd call theatrical," she says. "For someone who used to work in the theater."

"That's what made him good. Your father was a relief. He never tried to call any attention to himself. He acted the same way he directed: He was there to set up our scenes and move us around. But he was very steady, very—" I stop. "What's the word I want?"

"Trustworthy," Nell offers.

Never has a word been so exactly right. "Trustworthy."

"It must have been strange though, to be onstage with Uncle Wallace one night and Dad two nights later. They must have been so different."

We are nearing the end of my brief career as an

actress, and I'm still trying to remember what acting was like. "They were as different as chalk and cheese but they were both right for the part. I stood so close to them. That's what I remember. The audience is far away but the people you're acting with are so close. You can smell them. Uncle Wallace smelled like mouthwash and Royall Lyme cologne. And then your father—" What did Joe smell like? It was nothing like mouthwash and cologne.

"Daddy smells like this." Nell closes her eyes for a minute, sniffing the breeze.

"Like what?" Emily asks.

"He smells like the cherry orchard," Maisie says.

"Yes." I'd been too young to understand it then. He smelled like the cherry orchard.

When it came to breaking rehearsal early, Cody was the uncontested champion. Maybe he was right to let us go. The entire cast was only four people after all, one act, and if those people were all drinking tequila and if the director wanted to run a scene a second time, a great deal of thought had to go into marshaling resources. On the days we had *Our Town*—Tuesday, Thursday, Saturday—he had to be especially careful to keep the drinking in check. Other people knew what was going on over at *Fool for Love*, and while some actors might have found our methods gritty and inspired, the management saw us for the ticking time bomb we were. We could not slip up, which was to say Duke could not slip up. He drank his flooding amounts of water and shook the aspirin straight from the bottle into his mouth. He dove down into the bottle of tequila, dove down into the glittering lake, then swam back up, breaking the surface with the full force of his life.

We never knew when Sebastian was going to be there. Probably Pallace knew. Everyone wanted to play tennis in the summer. The Grosse Pointe Yacht Club was right on Lake St. Clair and the breeze blew gently across the courts, just enough to dry the sweat from a player's brow but never enough to alter the trajectory of the ball. Every hour of Sebastian's weekends was booked in advance, so weekends were out, but as soon as he could cobble two days together he drove up to see us, or he drove up to see her. I don't even think Duke had much to do with it anymore. Sebastian must have gotten up in the dark to be there so early on a Tuesday morning. I saw him sitting in the back of the theater with Pallace, his arm around her, her head tipped towards him, the two of them watching us drink and slam and scream at one another. I didn't care about the rest of them anymore but I hated that Sebastian was there. I suspected that Cody called the rehearsal early that day because he couldn't stand to see me act anymore, but maybe it had something to do with Sebastian. Like Pallace, Cody had a weakness for quiet, handsome men who weren't actors.

"Saint Sebastian!" Duke shouted when he saw his brother. "Tennis!"

"Too hot," Pallace called from the comfort of her boyfriend's shoulder. "I want to go swimming."

"He was mine first," Duke said. "And anyway, you're off tonight. You can swim all you want." One night *Our Town*, one night *Cabaret*. We worked and then Pallace worked and on Monday everyone was off. It dawned on me then that Sebastian must have driven up last night. He'd come in and hadn't told us.

"Okay." Sebastian leaned over to give Pallace a kiss. "We'll play a game."

How could he have stood all that tennis? It was hot and I wanted to swim too, but like Pallace, it never occurred to me that we could have just gone without them. If our boyfriends played tennis then we would sit at the edge of the court and watch them play. Cody tagged along for the first set but Pallace and I ignored him so completely he finally said something about having work to do and went away. Duke was getting creamed. Sebastian pulled back as convincingly as possible but Duke was missing the lobs. This must have been what every day was like for Sebastian—hitting balls to talentless automotive engineers hellbent on winning. Duke stopped abruptly, his racquet straight down, his head tipped back. The yellow ball bounced twice then rolled away.

"Peedee?" Sebastian asked, all of us thinking that Duke was about to start screaming, but instead he went briskly out the gate and vomited in the grass by the walkway. I understood. The heat of the sun and the fast-moving ball made everything tilt. I went to stand beside him. I was getting good at this.

Turned out an afternoon swim and an afternoon game of tennis registered differently when the morning had been spent drinking tequila. Duke hadn't known that before and now he did. Sebastian appeared with a bottle of water and Duke rinsed his mouth then vomited again, his hands braced against his knees, his black hair wet and clinging to the sides of his face. Sebastian waited another minute before giving him a towel. Tennis pros had bags like doctors.

"Let's get you back to the room," Sebastian said.

Duke shook his head very slowly so as not to upset his equilibrium further. "I'm going to lie down for a minute," he said, meaning on the ground.

I thought Sebastian would object but he patted his

brother's back and then walked him onto the court where Duke stretched out parallel to the fault line.

"Keep playing," he said, his voice subdued, his hand making a little circle in the air. "I don't want to ruin the afternoon for everyone."

"Too late," Pallace said.

"Do you want to play a set?" Sebastian asked her.

She shook her head, lifting up her leg to flex and point her foot. "Ankle," she reminded him. Pallace had a flare-up of tendinitis in her left ankle and if she wasn't dancing she tried to rest it. She was sitting on the court near Duke's head but had nothing to do with him.

Sebastian turned his racquet at me. "You're up."

I hadn't had that much to drink but it took very little. Despite Duke's predictions, my muscle for consumption remained weak. "Let's go to the lake."

Duke had his arm across his eyes, the tender underside of his wrist turned towards the sun. "You can't move me and you can't leave me here. You might as well get a lesson out of it."

Now I was sorry for having chased Cody off. Cody would have sold his mother to play a game of tennis with Sebastian. I asked Duke how he was feeling.

"Potentially better. Not better right this minute but I can see how this could really help in the long run."

"Oh, fantastic," Pallace said. "Now you're bulimic on top of everything else."

"Quiet," Duke whispered.

"Come on." Sebastian handed me a racquet. "Unless you've been drinking, too."

"A little bit," I admitted.

Duke gave his head a very slow shake. "She fakes it."

My beloved, sick and stretched out on the ground, how I felt like kicking him. Not hard. Only once. I told Sebastian I would play.

On that day I was a bad girlfriend, a bad actress, a bad drinker, but by god I could play tennis. The magic that tequila had brought to the performances of Duke and Homer and Sal came to me on the tennis court. Who knew? I started slow and built my game. I knew that Sebastian was probably operating at two percent of his ability and I didn't care. I was confident, loose. I gave him everything. I slammed my return to the opposite corner of the court and got one honest point off of him. Pallace whooped and called my name. Duke turned gingerly onto his side and opened one eye. I remembered myself in that backlot pool, in the bikini I still wore. They had wanted to see if I could swim.

"The cricket's coming for you, brother," Duke shouted, inasmuch as he could shout.

I was running, reaching. I didn't care how I looked.

Again and again I found a way to get the ball back over the net. The universe had conspired to grant me a single decent game of tennis, and I went in with everything I had. I could see the light change in Sebastian's eyes. He was taking me seriously, not as an opponent, but as a person on the other side of the net, and the attention enlivened me. He shouted instructions, encouragement. He was a wonderful teacher, and he was doing his best to improve me. I leapt for a serve beyond my range, leapt and lunged and was felled by something like a gunshot I hadn't heard. That was my exact thought, not that I had fallen but that I'd been shot. I crumpled onto the hot surface of the court. Duke was still there, lying a dozen feet away. He wiggled his fingers at me. How had he been lying on the court all this time? It was hot like a cookie sheet straight from the oven.

"You get used to it," he said.

Sebastian was crouching down beside me, his dark eyes warmed by concern. All summer long I had conscientiously failed to notice his beauty but having his face that close to mine made it unavoidable. "Hey," he said, putting his hand on my shoulder gently. "Just stay there a second, catch your breath."

"I'm fine." I blinked. I was fine, more surprised than hurt. "I didn't scrape my knees."

"Is she okay?" Duke raised up on one elbow for a moment then eased himself back down.

"I don't know yet."

"She might be faking it," Duke said. "She doesn't like it when I get too much attention."

Pallace was there, her hand on my face, her face so close to my face. "Are you very hurt?"

Everything had stopped and everyone was watching. I felt so foolish. I pushed myself up to a seated position. I swayed at first and then sitting seemed fine. Still, the question of what had happened, the explosion inside my calf that had very clearly come from outside my calf, was unresolved. "Did someone shoot me?" I asked her.

Pallace rocked back on her heels. "Oh, fuck."

"Oh fuck what?"

"It's her Achilles," Pallace said to Sebastian.

Sebastian squeezed my shoulder. He did not disagree.

"You ruptured your Achilles?" Maisie asks.

"How did we never know this?" Emily asks.

I lean over and pull up my right pant leg, show them the thin white line that runs from my heel up the middle of my calf. "Apparently they're much better at this now. Now they only make a tiny incision."

Maisie leans over, runs the tip of her finger down the scar. "How have I never seen this before?"

"I've had this scar a lot longer than I've had any of you."

"How did Pallace and Sebastian know what had happened?" Nell asks.

"Dancers and tennis players know about legs. If someone falls over and says they think they were shot, chances are they've ruptured their Achilles."

"Partial or complete?" Maisie is still marveling at the neatness with which her mother was reassembled.

"Total rupture. Go big or go home."

"Could you walk at all?" Emily asks. Why does it matter so much, the way she's looking at me this minute? Like I am on the tennis court curled on my side and she is there, her hand on my shoulder.

Maisie shakes her head. "She can't walk."

"Wait," Nell asks. "This happens to dogs?"

"Yep."

"So you had to go back to the hospital," Emily says. "Was Uncle Wallace there?"

I shook my head, smiling. "Elyse had already taken him back to Chicago. That would have been something though, wouldn't it? Uncle Wallace and me in a double room."

"Pallace had to take your part," Nell says. "She had to go on that night."

Sapphire sky, diamond clouds, emerald leaves, ruby

cherries. The magic with which Nell understands overwhelms me at times. Her sisters turn and stare. "You're doing it again," Emily says.

"What?"

"You're thinking about the performance, the understudy, and not your own mother lying on the ground with a ruptured Achilles."

"You did the same thing with Uncle Wallace," Maisie says.

Nell won't bite. "She's on a tennis court. Sebastian is there. It's not like she's facedown in the dirt."

Emily is irritated with Nell, which is noteworthy because none of us get irritated with Nell, the sweet one, the small one, the baby. "But why do you always care about the understudy? Why is the most important thing in life whether or not the show goes on?"

Nell is standing beside me. She puts her arm around my waist in solidarity. "You're not getting it," she says. "This is when everything changes. This is the beginning of the second act. She can't walk. She can't walk for—" She stops to look at me.

"A long time," I say, though walking can be defined in different ways. "No cast, no crutches, it was probably six months."

"So it's not just Emily Pallace is going to play. She's going to play Mae, too. Pallace is going to finish out

Our Town and do the entire run of *Fool for Love.* Why can't you understand that?" she asks.

"We can understand it," Maisie says. "But we're more worried about Mom than we are the play."

Just like that Nell is crying and then sobbing, a fierce storm blown up out of nowhere. She turns her back on Maisie and Emily in shame and presses her face against my breastbone, both of her arms tight around me now. I don't for a minute think she is crying because of her sisters, though surely part of her is crying for herself. She has lost these months to the pandemic, being stuck on the farm with no idea how much longer she'll have to stay. She is losing this time when she is beautiful and young in a profession that cares for nothing but beauty and youth. But really, she is crying for me. While her sisters stand and stare in utter bafflement, Nell the Mentalist has snapped all the pieces together. She knows I am finished.

I insisted on trying to stand, and so Sebastian got on one side with Pallace on the other and together they lifted me like a marionette whose string had been cut. My leg was rubbery, almost liquid. "I need to rest it for a minute," I said.

Sebastian shook his head. "You need to go to the hospital."

"She doesn't need to go to the hospital," Duke said, his voice clearer now. "She just tripped on her tiny feet. Give her a minute."

He had vomited and I had fallen and in just a minute, everything would be fine.

A minute, a minute, a minute. I could feel Pallace shifting beneath my arm. "Let's put her down," she said to Sebastian.

And so they sat me down again and Pallace sat beside me. She looked at me hard but kept hold of my hand. "I wish we had more time," she said. "But we don't so I'm just going to say it: You're not going on tonight, and I'm going to have to go get ready."

Emily. I had forgotten her.

Duke was sitting up now. "What?"

"She can't walk." Pallace looked at Duke like maybe I had been shot and maybe he was the one who'd shot me. "She's not going to be able to walk. I've seen this happen." She looked at Sebastian. "Have you seen this happen?"

He nodded, the sun behind his head lighting up his black hair.

Pallace touched her finger to my ankle so lightly I couldn't feel it. "It doesn't matter if you go to the hospital right this minute or if you wait three days, I'm telling you the truth. You're going to go to the hospital and they're going to sew your tendon back on. Like it or not, I can pretty much promise you that's the way this is going to go."

Now Duke was on his feet, leaning noticeably to the left as he came towards us. I expected him to make a joke, to say that Pallace was scheming for my part, but instead he leaned over and patted my head. He asked his brother if he could drive me to the hospital. Duke and Pallace wouldn't be able to come with us, of course. They had to get cleaned up. They had to be onstage in a couple of hours, the two of them, Editor Webb and his daughter Emily.

Sebastian leaned over and picked me up like a towel, a tennis bag, and again, I waited for Duke to make a joke but he didn't. Maybe he was already Editor Webb, maybe he was going over his notebooks in his mind, or maybe he was worried about me, I guess it was possible, maybe he didn't know what to say. The parking lot where Sebastian left his car was nowhere near the tennis courts and so he carried me, past the path that went down to the lake and past the path that would have taken us back to the theater. He carried me all the way to the company housing. Would Duke have carried me under different circumstances? No, Duke would have gone and gotten the car. That was the difference: One brother would take the girl to the car while the other would bring the car to the girl. It was such a strange sensation to be carried, to be so high up. I looped my arms around Sebastian's neck and gripped my wrist, trying to somehow make myself lighter. I could smell my own sweat. Pallace went ahead to get my purse and came back with the nightgown I hadn't worn all summer, two pairs of underpants, socks, a clean T-shirt and shorts, hairbrush, toothbrush, all in a plastic bag.

"Don't worry about anything, okay? It's going to be fine," she said once I was settled in the passenger seat of the Plymouth.

I nodded, though I didn't know if she was talking about my leg or the play. I knew she was anxious to get away from us. She had so much to do, and if she was excited—and she would have been excited, wouldn't she? after so much waiting around—she wouldn't have wanted me to see it. Duke and Pallace stood beside one another and waved as we drove off, like they were my parents sending me into the world.

I rolled down the window, my mind remarkably blank. I understood what was happening but not that it was happening to me. The cherry trees at Tom Lake were shaggy and didn't have much fruit; feral cherry trees left over from some other time. No one bothered to pick them, much less prune them. "What do you know about the Achilles tendon?" I asked Sebastian.

"Can you flex your foot back then point your toe?"

I could not.

He nodded as if that were the entire conversation. "I played mixed doubles once with a woman who swore I'd sliced the back of her calf with my racquet even though I was nowhere near her. From what I've been told, it feels like something exploded inside your leg."

"That's it."

"So they'll reattach the tendon, and after a while you'll walk again, and a while after that you'll play tennis again." He looked over at me. "If you ever want to play tennis again. I'll tell you, you were killing it today."

"Damn it," I said, closing my eyes.

"What?"

"I forgot to tell Pallace good luck for tonight. I don't mean good luck. I mean 'break a leg.'"

"You mean, 'rupture your Achilles'," he said, and we both laughed because what else was there to do?

16

"Daddy would have taken you to the hospital," Nell says that night at dinner. She will not let this new turn go.

"Daddy would most certainly have taken you to the hospital," Joe says. He is tired. He is grateful for the deviled eggs and green beans and the whitefish. Every year since we first came to the farm he's wondered how we'll get the cherries off the trees in time, and now it seems all of his previous fears were in preparation for this year when we're down dozens of picking crew, which of course means we'll be down dozens to shake the tarts off the trees in a few weeks.

"Maybe you passed each other on the road," Emily says. "Dad coming down from Traverse City, Mom on her way to the hospital. You might have. You would have been going north on 196."

"We *did* pass you!" I say, flush with memory. "I told you that."

"You most certainly did not." Joe pops half an egg in his mouth.

"I said it to Sebastian. I said, 'Look, there goes the Stage Manager on his way to 'work.'" I remember how much I wanted to tell him to turn around. My leg was just a dull ache by then. Sitting on the wide bench seat of the Plymouth it was easy to believe it had all been a silly bit of drama on my part.

"How did anyone survive without cellphones?" Maisie asks.

"We survived very nicely."

Joe nods. "I can believe it. Our entire relationship was like that back in the day."

"Two cars passing in the late afternoon," I say.

"Did you go see her in the hospital?" Nell asks.

"I was only there two nights," I say.

"I came," he says.

"No you didn't." I turn to him. "Did you?"

"After the play, on my way back here."

"I don't remember."

"You don't remember because you were asleep. You'd just gotten out of surgery."

"You came after the play? It must have been too late for visitors. They let you in?"

"I told them I was your brother and that I'd come as fast as I could. The nurse let me sit by your bed."

Joe, who never lied, could lie fluently when it was necessary.

"Did you leave her a note?" Maisie asks.

He shook his head. "If I'd left her a note she would have known I was sitting by her bed like some kind of weirdo, thinking how pretty she looked when she was sleeping."

Oh, Joe, working all day on the farm and then driving down to play the Stage Manager and then coming to the hospital to sit in a vinyl chair and watch me sleep. And I had missed him. "Sebastian didn't stay?" Emily is disappointed. She needs Sebastian to be better than that.

But Sebastian was better than everyone. He parked the car and carried me into the emergency room, and all the while I was thinking how romantic it would have been had Duke been the one to do the carrying. More romantic, though less practical, as Duke would have played it as a screwball comedy or hospital drama whereas Sebastian told the doctor what had happened with so much specificity they must have thought he was a doctor himself. "He stayed until they got me in a room but then I told him to go back. I knew he wanted to see Pallace and I knew she would want him there."

"How was Pallace?" Nell asks her father. She cannot help herself.

"Pallace was just fine," he says diplomatically.

"She was excellent," I say.

"Were you scared?" Maisie asks me.

"Of Pallace?"

Maisie rolls her eyes. "Of being in the *hospital*, of surgery."

There is no scenario in which one of our girls would be in a hospital without us. We would find a way to get there and they know this. But I was the girl who'd left college for Hollywood, who'd lived alone in a furnished apartment in L.A., who'd offered to sleep with the wrong person in her efforts to get a part in a play, who came to Michigan with two suitcases. It never occurred to me to call my parents and tell them what had happened. I was an adult, after all, with good insurance through the Screen Actors Guild. "I was scared later," I say. "I wasn't scared then."

"Were you scared of Pallace?" Nell asks.

"Later," I say.

I woke up in the morning to a fat beige rotary phone ringing on my bedside table. I didn't know where I was or what the phone was doing there. I didn't have a phone in my room at Tom Lake. When it finally occurred to me that the only way to make it stop was to answer it, I picked up the receiver. A man said, "Lara?"

"Ripley?"

"Believe it or not."

The room was sunny. The shades were up. The second bed was mercifully empty. "Ripley, I'm in the hospital."

"Why do you think I'm calling you in the hospital?"

"Why are you calling?"

"One of the camp counselors at the lake said you had an accident."

"Do they know you?"

"No."

"Then why did they call?"

"Lara, are you on drugs?"

"Probably. I'm just waking up."

"Waking up? It's nine o'clock out there."

I turned my head to look at the nightstand. There wasn't a clock. "I think I had surgery yesterday. Be sympathetic."

"I am sympathetic. That's why I'm calling."

My ankle was encased in a mound of plaster and laid out on a stack of stiff pillows. Everything about it looked like a prop, a movie cast. "I still don't understand why they called you."

"You put me down as your person to contact."

Had I done that? The form must not have been very clear because really, why would Uncle Wallace have listed his second wife? "I must have thought they meant professional contact, like if I was offered a great part and they needed to get ahold of someone." Is that what I was thinking?

"Well, I'm touched," Ripley said. "Are you okay?"

"I think so." Why was the cast so big? I fell on a tennis court, that was all. "I ruptured my Achilles."

"You don't want to do that," he said, like I'd been offered a part in a teenage slasher film that would ultimately diminish my career.

"Well, I wish you'd called yesterday morning and told me."

"You aren't the easiest person to get on the phone."

"Have you been trying?"

"No, but I was going to. There's serendipity in this."

I pushed the button on the guard rail that made the top of the bed go up. I held it until I had achieved the angle I thought of as Elyse Adler. "I want to hear how my ruptured Achilles is going to work in your favor."

"I need you to come back to L.A."

I planned to go back to L.A. in the fall when summer stock was over. Duke and I were going together, but somehow hearing Ripley say it, I didn't want to anymore. I looked out the window of my hospital room, across the parking lot to a row of trees. Even the parking lots had trees! For the first time I realized that I didn't want to leave Michigan. "I have a contract."

"Okay, one, it's a contract with a summer stock theater. That's easy enough to take care of. Two, you can't walk, which means you're no good to them. They'll be thrilled to get you off the payroll."

"If that's one and two I can't wait to hear three."

"Three," Ripley said, pausing to indicate drama. "Three is that your movie is coming out."

"*Singularity*?"

"Unless you've made another one."

I had thought it was a wash, a tax write-off for someone. "Oh, Ripley, that's great. I'm happy for you." It had taken such a long time.

"Be happy for yourself. The film editor fell in love with you. When he cut it all together he made you the star."

"I'm not the star."

"Wait till you see it. It's a sharp bit of work, kiddo. You're fantastic. I need you out here for publicity. Publicity is all about sitting down, you know. Plus the injury makes you relatable. How did it happen?"

"Tennis."

"Tennis in the summer in Michigan. Beautiful."

My toes were sticking out of the plaster, a pale row of little mushrooms. I could move them, which I took to be a good sign. "Always glad to be picturesque."

"Did you ever wonder when things were going to change?" Ripley asked. "Well, now they are. This is it."

I hadn't wondered when things were going to change. I had wondered when things were going to stop changing. "Ripley, I'm in the hospital. I'm on Demerol. I'm not going to walk away from my commitment." I didn't know if I was on Demerol but it seemed possible. I was definitely on something.

"Are you listening to me? You can't walk and you don't have any commitments in Michigan. You've got a commitment to this film."

"The nurse is here," I said, because surely if it was after nine o'clock a nurse would be here any minute.

"Don't go cagey on me."

"I'm not," I said. "I have to go."

"Do I need to come get you?"

"Ripley, listen to me, I'm hanging up now. Say goodbye." I said it but then I didn't give him the chance. I hung up before he did.

Ripley's announcement that I wasn't going to be acting on one foot was my first glimpse into the future. The second came by way of the doctor making morning rounds. He told me I would be non-weight-bearing for a minimum of six weeks. I had raised the bed up to sitting, thinking it was more polite.

"Meaning what, exactly?" I wished there had been someone with me so I didn't have to ask all the stupid questions myself.

"Meaning the cast"—he stopped and pointed to the cast with his pen—"does not touch the ground for a minimum of six weeks. Do you want a wheelchair?"

I shook my head.

"Okay. I'll have someone from P.T. come up and show you how to use the crutches, how to transfer."

"I'm going to another hospital?"

He paused for a minute, looking back at my chart. "Okay. So. Transfer means getting in and out of a car, in and out of a chair, in and out of the bath. You do those things differently when you're trying to keep your foot off the floor."

It wasn't until he'd left that I realized he had mistaken me for an idiot.

I never thought about New Hampshire in those days, though I missed my grandmother. I wrote her postcards, and every now and then she'd send me a dress.

Sometimes she put molasses cookies in the box, sturdy, reliable cookies that were well suited for mailing. I'd offered to send her a plane ticket a couple of times when I was in L.A. but my grandmother didn't believe in planes, at least not for personal use. She'd been made in New Hampshire and planned to die there, that's what she always said. I would have liked to have her with me in the hospital. I bet she could have made it as far as Michigan if I told her I needed her. I bet my parents would have come too, or either of my brothers. Even if we weren't a particularly close family, they were decent people. They would have taken care of me. The problem was they couldn't have done it on intuition alone and I wasn't about to call and make them worry. In fact, I couldn't call and make them worry because the phone was rigged for local and inter-hospital calls only. I could call the patient in the room next to mine but could not call my mother, who I hadn't called all summer anyway. I was fine. I was taught how to transfer, how to get to the bathroom by myself. A girl in a pink striped smock came around with a book cart and I found a copy of *The Bridge of San Luis Rey* by one Thornton Wilder. Imagine that. It was about a bridge that snaps and sends a group of strangers careening to their deaths. I'd never read it before.

I had some trouble with swelling and the doctor

wanted to make sure he wouldn't have to change the cast so they kept me for a second night. I thought about all the time I'd spent sitting in my apartment in Los Angeles on the days with nothing to do, and how those days had prepared me to be alone with my thoughts. I had a knack for it, not everyone does. I ate my dinner off a tray and read my slender novel and practiced crutching to the nurses' station and back. I looked out the window as the sun was going down and realized that Pallace would be going on right about now. Mrs. Webb and Mrs. Gibb would be calling their children to breakfast from the opposite sides of the stage. I ran the whole scene in my mind. I wondered if Pallace would be nervous, but then I thought of her dancing on that chair in her red two-piece. I couldn't imagine Pallace getting nervous about anything.

Because I couldn't call my grandmother, I called Tom Lake and asked if they could send somebody to pick me up in the morning. Jeanne, the morning nurse, washed my hair while I sat on a stool in the shower, my foot in the cast, the cast in a plastic bag. I was brushed and braided and ready to go when Sebastian arrived.

Sebastian! "I thought you'd be gone!" I cried, by which I mean tears filled my eyes at the sight of him. Had I been able to jump out of the bed and throw my arms around him I would have done it.

"I called the club and told them my transmission was out." Sebastian said. "I'm in big trouble."

"Big trouble for me? You could have sent your brother."

"Let's just say the rest of the team was in no condition to drive, and they very much wanted to drive. The last thing anyone needs is Peedee wrapping my car around a tree trying to bring you home from the hospital."

"And Pallace?"

He patted the front pocket of his jeans. "I took her keys."

So Pallace was already Mae. You'd have to take the keys away from Mae. She was drinking all day with the men. As sorry as I was to miss my last week as Emily, it was almost worth it to know that I would never be Mae. I would never again endure Cody's disappointment or my own lousy acting or my inability to fill out the red dress. Pallace could wear the dress. "How are the rehearsals going?" Sebastian claimed to like the rehearsals more than the finished product.

"They don't let mc in."

I was sitting on the bed, wearing the outfit Pallace had grabbed from my room in the rush of leaving: khaki shorts and my Disney T-shirt which never did fit right again. My foot was up. They had told me to keep it elevated whenever possible. "You were there when I was doing it."

Sebastian shrugged. "The problem seems to be that my brother has to kiss my girlfriend. They say I make them self-conscious."

I could so clearly feel Duke lying on top of me on the stage, pinning my hands to the floor. Duke as Eddie and me as Mae. Duke as Eddie, Pallace as Mae. I stopped there. "Will they let you see the play?"

"They can't keep me from seeing the play," he said. "I have tickets."

Jeanne swung through the door with a wheelchair and then stopped short. She actually blushed when she saw Sebastian there. "You're the actor," she said to him. I'd told Jeanne all about Duke while she washed my hair.

"I'm the brother," Sebastian said.

"He's your *brother*?" she said to me.

Now we were all laughing. "Can you believe it?" I said.

Jeanne wheeled me to the elevator with my crutches and painkillers and an antibiotic and seven typed pages of instructions. Outside, she made me transfer from the wheelchair to the car just to make sure I knew what I was doing, then she stood there and waved as we drove away. I rolled the window down to wave at her.

"By the way, you've been upgraded," Sebastian told me. "They moved you to the cottage."

"To Uncle Wallace's?"

"He isn't coming back and you can't go up the stairs so it all works out."

For my troubles I got the bathtub, the kitchenette. I tried not to be excited since the whole thing was the product of disaster. "Did Duke bring my clothes down?"

He shook his head. "They sent over a couple of interns. The whole job took them two minutes."

Even if Duke was busy he could have found two minutes, especially since his clothes had to be moved as well. He would come for the better room, for the vodka I was betting was still in the freezer. Now I had to think about unpaid interns going through my underwear drawer. "Wait, wait!" I said. "Pallace was Emily. How did she do?"

"Conflict of interest," Sebastian said.

"Meaning what?"

"Meaning you were Emily and you were great and Pallace is my girlfriend."

"You know I'm not the only person who's ever played Emily, right?"

"You were the only person I'd ever seen play her until last night. You're the gold standard."

"Sebastian," I said, "seriously, how did she do?"

And then he smiled, a great, toothy grin of the sort I had never seen from him. He had exactly one word and it was *spectacular*.

True fact: I had seen only one production of *Our Town* and that was when I was in seventh grade. The high school put it on and I thought it was *spectacular*. Every line in the play was new to me. I had no inkling that Emily would die in the third act. I cried so hard when the Stage Manager takes her back to her mother's kitchen that I had to cover my face with my hands while my grandmother fished through her purse for Kleenex. All of which is to say you don't see a play when you're in it. You might see pieces, but you don't know how it looks from a distance, the whole thing put together. Aside from the Emily I saw in seventh grade, and the Emilys I saw auditioning years later in our high school gymnasium, I didn't know how other people played the part. That night I was going to see Pallace in *Our Town*.

Sebastian parked on the street and came around to give me my crutches. I crutched heroically, halfway up the drive, holding that Christmas ham of an enormous cast behind me until I had no choice but to stop. My arms were shaking.

"Come on," he said, his steadying hand on my back. "I'll carry you."

It was one thing to have been carried off the tennis court or into the hospital, but something else entirely to just be carried around. I was sweating as I stared up the steep pitch of the driveway. I had done this to myself. I drank the tequila I knew not to drink, played the tennis game I didn't want to play. It might not sound like much but it cost me everything.

Sebastian picked me up, letting the crutches clatter to the ground. He gave me a bounce to get me situated in his arms and once again I clasped my arms around his neck like a bride. "Lucky for me my brother fell in love with someone small," he said.

Love, he said. It was the single mention of that word during my relationship with Duke.

This was how we entered that sunny cottage, Sebastian using his foot to push the door open, Sebastian taking me straight to the bed and laying me out, using the extra pillows to elevate my foot. Someone had cut a bunch of poppies and put them in a drinking glass on the nightstand and I didn't ask who had done it for fear the flowers would be from him as well.

"I'm going to find you a wheelchair," he said.

"I don't need a wheelchair." What I needed was a minute of sleep.

"Think about how far away the theater is. I really do have to go back to work now, and Duke and Pallace can't come and get you. It's the only way you're going to see the play tonight."

Sebastian went back for my crutches and leaned them against the foot of the bed. He put my pills and my book on the nightstand. Sebastian kissed my forehead with kindness, the same way my brothers had kissed me as a child. He would get me a wheelchair. He would make sure someone took me to the play. I think I was asleep before he was out the door, and then I was awake again and Duke was kissing me, the startling taste of tequila filling my mouth. He must have come straight from the lake and into my bed. He covered me with his pervasive dampness. "You've been gone forever," he said, pushing off his espadrilles.

"Did Duke come and see you before the play?" Emily asks, her brow knit with concern. Joe has gone off to the goats while the girls and I wash dishes. Cherries, cooking, goats, dishes, the past. Days are endless and the weeks fly by.

"He did." I lean into the pan to scrub off bits of whitefish. "In between rehearsal and the performance."

Maisie shakes her head. "Knock yourself out, Duke."

"They were busy days," I say.

"Not that busy," Nell says.

I smile. "No, you're right. Not that busy."

"Your girlfriend's laid up in bed," Maisie says.

"And she doesn't get to finish her run of *Our Town*," Nell says.

"In fact, she never plays Emily again," I say, joining them for a moment in the third person. Nell had already come to this conclusion but I can see that Emily and Maisie didn't know.

"Never?" Emily asks.

I shake my head.

"It's just like Uncle Wallace," Nell says, then catches herself. "I don't mean that. It's nothing like Uncle Wallace."

Emily puts down her dish towel. "Never Emily or never anything else?"

"I stopped acting after that."

"When you were twenty-four?"

"Twenty-five. I turned twenty-five in the hospital."

"I really can't stand this," Maisie says.

"It redefines the quarter-life crisis," Emily says.

"The what?"

"Quarter-life crisis," Nell says. "It's when your life falls apart at twenty-five or thereabout. The pandemic is our quarter-life crisis."

"Ah."

"But yours was so much worse," Nell says.

"Not getting to act in *Our Town* again is not worse than the pandemic," I say.

"Did you really go and see her be Emily?" Emily asks.

"Sure I did. All my friends were in that play. I had to be there for them." I can't remember if this is true, if this is the person I was at the time or the person I became later. Certainly we preached it to the girls growing up: Work for the good of the collective, root for the team, get over yourself.

"You went in a wheelchair?"

No one is doing dishes now, and I clap my hands the way their father does to restart their engines. "I went in a wheelchair. One of the swings from *Cabaret* came to get me. This isn't a Dickens novel."

"So how was Pallace?" Nell asks. This is the question all three of them want answered: How was Pallace?

I tell them the truth. She was spectacular.

I knew Chan from the lake. He was easy to be around, a good swimmer with a solid connection to a guy who sold top-quality weed in Detroit. He made me feel like he just happened to be walking past the cottage with an empty wheelchair in case I felt like riding along because he was going to the theater anyway. The world isn't full of people who can pull that off. The sky was tipping into pink as he wheeled me down the path, what was left of the daylight shimmering gold on the lake.

"People are saying that you returned the serve and that it was totally magnificent," Chan said to me as merrily we rolled along. "It cost you your leg but you did it."

"It isn't true," I said.

"Doesn't matter. All that matters is what people say. Hey, do you want some cherries? We don't want to be the first ones there."

I did want some cherries.

He set the brake so I wouldn't roll backwards, down the grassy hill and into the lake. "I found this tree last week," Chan said. "Sweet cherries. I don't know what it's doing here. I mean, somebody must have planted it and then not stuck around. Can you imagine bringing a sapling out here with no one to look after it? *Good luck, little tree.* Maybe it was some kind of performance art." He went to a tree and picked off a few handfuls, then came back and put them in my lap. I thanked him. I was new to the idea that trees were things that needed looking after.

"You look nice." He stepped back to look at me in the golden light. "But not too nice. Not like you put too much thought into it. You look exactly the right amount of nice."

That was the look I'd been going for and it had taken a great deal of effort, considering how hard it was to get dressed with a cast on your foot. The part I hadn't considered was that other people would know, Chan would know, but I couldn't do anything about that. I ate cherries all the way to the theater.

We arrived with the chickens, all looking for their seats. The curtain was up and Joe was sitting on the stage reading a book. There were steps down to the rows of seats so Chan parked me behind the back row and went to get me a program. Duke's hair would be gelled and pinned by now. He would read through his maniacal Editor Webb notes for the hundredth time and then go smoke a cigarette and stand on his hands. Two slips of paper announced the change of cast: the role of the Stage Manager would be played by Joe Nelson, and the role of Emily Webb would be played by Pallace Clarke. I folded them up and put them in my pocket. *I am ready, I am ready, I am ready* I told myself, until finally the lights came down and it didn't matter if I was ready or not.

"This play is called *Our Town,*" Joe began, the Stage Manager began. He might as well have raised a lantern because we knew we would follow him. You listened to Uncle Wallace because he was mesmerizing, but you listened to Joe because he was telling you what you needed to know. I thought about our first day of rehearsal—years ago!—and how it was the same thing then. We knew he was trustworthy. Joe had seen the entire story and stitched it together for us. Now there he was as the Stage Manager, doing the same thing. "This play is called *Our Town*."

Emily doesn't come on for a while, and when she does she only has a single line. I could see Pallace dancing in the chorus of the Kit Kat Klub, her leg flashing up and over the back of her chair and then sitting down hard. I could see her in the lake, laughing, keeping her head above water. I could see her stretched across a blanket by the shore of the lake, a tree above her, her head in Sebastian's lap. But I could not see her as Emily because when I thought of Emily I was still seeing myself. Had I come with a knife I would have sawed the cast off my leg right there. I could have made do without it. Only three more performances after this one. I could have managed.

But then all the children were there—George and Rebecca Gibbs having breakfast stage left, which represents their house, Emily and Wally Webb having their breakfast stage right, which represents their house. Pallace was a good head taller than I am, and she was Black, but Pallace was Emily. I believed her from the moment she made her entrance, when she sat down at her mother's table, saying she's the brightest girl in school for her age. Every sentence she spoke was sitting in my mouth.

I learned so many things that summer at Tom Lake and most of those lessons I would have gladly done without. The hardest one had nothing to do with Duke or plans or love. It was realizing that I wasn't Emily anymore. Even if I'd gotten to play the part on Broadway with Spalding Gray, there still would come a time when I'd be finished and someone else would take the role. Many someone elses could do it just as well, because look, Pallace on her second night was every bit as good as I had been after years of practice. Day after day she had watched me in rehearsal and then made the decision to do the part her own way. She stamped her feet at times, found places to laugh I'd never seen. She kissed her father, who was also my boyfriend, and when he says in response that he has never had a kiss from such a great lady before, he meant it. When Pallace had come to her audition for Tom Lake, she wanted to sing and dance, but she wanted to play Emily as well. People who could sing and dance and act and play the ukelele and walk on their hands were legion in summer stock. You couldn't swim in the lake without brushing up against one. Pallace had practiced, studied hard. With the exception of Lee, the understudies ran neck and neck with the actors they were set to replace. The only disappointment the audience felt was when someone like Uncle Wallace didn't show. His name was the draw, but they didn't know a Lara from a Pallace. So when that first Emily took off, why hadn't they just given the part to the understudy?

"Emily isn't Black," I heard the woman in front of me say very clearly to her husband at the first intermission. Programs rustled all around, a collective murmuring like wind in leaves. Where was the slip of paper that had fallen out of their programs? What had it said?

All those hours she had endured me, day after day as she watched from the back of the theater, all those lines she had wanted to speak for herself.

You don't see the play when you're in it, and you miss the chatter of intermission entirely. *Our Town* has an intermission after each of the first two acts, and the second one felt like a break in a political rally or a tent revival. The disbelievers were starting to lean forward. They were listening. The message had made no sense at first but this Emily was eroding their notion of what was correct. Her wedding day was played not for eroticism but for fear. She didn't want to leave home, keep house, make meals, endure childbirth, because childbirth would kill her. She wanted to be her father's girl, his birthday girl. Growing up was a terrible thing—a clear path to the third act. Emily showed us that, all those moments in life we had missed and would never get back again.

The remaining few who'd managed to hold on to their belief that Emily could not be Black were destroyed by the third act. We all were. When she went back to her mother's kitchen I cried like I had never seen the play before. I cried because she was that good. I cried because I would never play Emily again. I cried because I had loved that world so much.

17

We do not stop for snow in northern Michigan. Schools open, buses run. Knuckling under to snow means condemning yourself to an uneducated populace. Joe gets up early to drive the tractor with the blower attachment down the rutted drive while I shovel the steps. All those years I pulled the girls out of their beds one at a time and rushed them to the warm kitchen to begin their layering, red tights beneath pink long underwear. What difference did it make? I filled them with oatmeal, gave them hot chocolate, finished them off with hats and mittens and boots, then sent them out into the drifts. Had it been snowing this morning we would be in the orchard now, pulling frozen cherries off the trees.

But on this July morning it is raining, great white

sheets of water pounding every side of the house. The lightning flicks like a strobe, filling the kitchen with a single second of blinding brightness before flicking off again. We wait for the low crash of thunder, counting *one, two, three* before it comes. We will work in the rain, but every member of our family has sense enough not to stand beneath a tree in lightning, which means that lightning, at least for an hour or so, is our favorite weather of all.

"Will you look at it," Nell says.

I look just in time to see a jagged bolt split the sky in half, leaves torn from the trees shooting sideways. "Do you have to stand right in front of the window?" I say to my youngest. She clasps her hands behind her back, cutting a small silhouette in the frame.

"Do you think the lightning's going to get me?"

"No, but I think the pear trees might. Didn't you tell me once that pear trees are agitated by lightning somehow? Don't they come through the window?" All year long we stare out this window—the tissue-thin blossoms, the birds, the cherries and the apples, the bright-red autumn, the sweep of snow, the resulting mud, and then the blossoms again. French Impressionism has nothing on our view. We put the window in when we expanded the kitchen and built the family room. Michigan farmers like houses they can keep warm, and so for months we debated the question of warmth versus beauty and in the end beauty won. Neighbors come into this room and shake their heads at such decadence.

"You're awful," Nell says, stepping away. She says to me, "Does your ankle tell you when it's going to rain?"

"You mean my Achilles? No. It has no weather predicting abilities."

"Does it ever hurt?"

I shake my head. "Never. I would say an entire decade can go by without my thinking of it."

Maisie is lying on her stomach in front of the sofa, one side of her face pressed to the floor. "Hazel," she pleads. "Sweetheart." She reaches out her arm to no avail. She reports that the dog is now the size of a cantaloupe, obstinate and trembling in the farthest corner where no one can reach her without moving furniture. "Will one of you bring me a piece of cheese?" Maisie asks, not looking up.

I put down my sewing and go to the refrigerator. Joe and Emily are no doubt in the barn, sorting, stacking, repairing. They will sit in the barn office, which is full of spiders and hay, placing orders and writing checks. They know how to make good use of an hour of lightning, and so do we, but our use is different. I will get the mending done. Nell will make a spinach pie for dinner. Maisie will continue to try to coax the dog from under the sofa.

"So when did Duke start sleeping with Pallace?" Nell asks, pulling out the mixing bowls.

I laugh. Maisie sits straight up, banging her head on the edge of the coffee table.

"Ow!" I say on her behalf. "Are you okay?"

She rubs her head with her fingers then checks them for blood. "Have the two of you been talking without us?"

"No." Nell comes over to look at her sister's head in another flash of lightning. "But you know where this is going."

"I swear to you, I have no idea where this is going."

"That's where this is going," I say.

"I didn't think Pallace *liked* Duke."

"Sometimes that makes it all the more compelling."

Nell nods in sad agreement and I start to think that when this is over, and it is very nearly over, each of my daughters should be asked to serve up their own brief pasts.

"Well, we can't talk about it when Emily's not here," Maisie says. "We promised."

"We sure can't talk about it when she is here," Nell says. "She's not going to want to hear anything bad about Duke."

"How did you know if Mom didn't tell you?" Maisie asks. "Did Dad tell you?"

Nell groans.

"That's a horrifying thought," I say.

"I know that Duke's sleeping with Pallace because that's the way it works." Nell has put on red lipstick this morning though I cannot for the life of me imagine why. "The guy likes the star of the show. Then later on he doesn't like her because she's the star of the show. Then there's a new show with a new star and he realizes the new one's better."

"For the record, I didn't know any of this at the time." I raise the shirt I'm mending to my lips, bite the thread.

"And you want to be an actress?" Maisie asks Nell.

"Because it's so different in vet school?" Nell replies.

Now Maisie's quiet. Her long-distance boyfriend has recently told her he needed space, as if there had been some shortage of space. Nell has told me this in strictest confidence. From Maisie I've heard nothing. She lies back out on her stomach. "Hazel?" she says.

"Emily doesn't understand anything about the way the world works," Nell says. "Benny's been in love with her since she was three."

"Faithfully in love," Maisie adds.

"She says, 'You're so lucky. You get to date lots of

people. You get to go out and have experiences and all I'll ever have is Benny.'"

Maisie stretches her arm further, the cheese in her upturned palm. "Which is like calling a marine in Afghanistan to tell him that you wish you got to go to war, too."

Nell shakes her head. "She's only been in love with Benny and Duke."

"So maybe it would help her to know that Duke was unfaithful," Maisie says.

"Maybe we don't need to talk about it at all," I say. "That works for me. Duke ended up with Pallace for a while. What else is there to say?"

"I feel so bad for Sebastian," Maisie says.

"I feel bad for Pallace," Nell says.

I smile to think that neither of them feels bad for me because here we are, together in this tight house with the rain lashing at the trees.

"Did it happen right away?" Maisie asks.

"I don't know. What constitutes right away?" We are still on summer stock time, after all, four performances of *Our Town* left when I came back from the hospital, *Fool for Love* opened four nights after *Our Town* closed. I would say within the first five minutes of *Fool for Love* I knew they'd already had sex and were planning on having sex again as soon as the curtain came down. I knew it, Sebastian knew it, the audience knew it. When she tipped the bottle of tequila back, I could see it going down her throat. When he threw her to the floor and covered her with his body, I could hear people gasp. Sebastian and I gasped. "I think by the time *Fool for Love* opened things had changed," I say diplomatically. "I'm not sure. They never told me."

"What do you mean, they never told you?" Nell asks.

"I mean one night Duke was there and the next night he wasn't. I couldn't exactly go out and find him. Having a giant cast on your ankle really does impede your ability to hunt your boyfriend down. They don't do casts for Achilles ruptures anymore, did you know that? They put you in a walking boot that you can take off in the bath."

Did it happen before *Fool for Love*? Did it happen while I was in the hospital? Would it have happened if my ankle hadn't swollen and I had stayed only one night instead of two? Two nights was one night more than Duke could sleep alone. They don't even keep you one night now. It's outpatient surgery. These were the things I used to think about, how with a slight shift in circumstances the outcome might have gone another way. Then I realized it would have gone that way eventually. Then I stopped thinking about it.

"So what did you do?" Nell asks. She abandons the spinach pie before she starts it, coming out of the kitchen to sit across from me in the big green chair. Her red lipstick makes her look French. Maisie gets off the floor and lies down on the sofa. When the next round of thunder shakes the floorboards, Hazel darts out and cries to be picked up.

I look at my girls, my brilliant young women. I want them to think I was better than I was, and I want to tell them the truth in case the truth will be useful. Those two desires do not neatly coexist, but this is where we are in the story.

I'd latched on to *Our Town* when I was sixteen and stayed fastened tight until the hour Pallace took the stage and said the words I'd thought of as mine. After that the whole thing just blinked out. Ripley thought a good therapist could turn me around but I never tried. My confidence had snapped and left me self-conscious, semiconscious. I don't think much could be done about that. I needed to come up with a plan, not for my life necessarily, just for these days, something that would justify my staying at Tom Lake until I could walk out on two feet.

I wheeled myself over to the wardrobe department to talk to Cat. Cat was the busiest person I knew that summer. She made the costumes, altered the costumes, mended the costumes, and did it with half the staff she needed. She made the calico dress I wore in the first and second acts, and the white wedding dress for the second and third acts, then she made replicas for Pallace on the off chance I would rupture my Achilles on the tennis court. Once when she was zipping my dress, Cat told me she'd stayed up half the night sewing spangles back onto the glittery bits of the *Cabaret* wardrobe. She said no matter how tightly she knotted the sequins down, the cast would dance them off again.

I had believed that Tom Lake was more enlightened than the average small town in Michigan, but the longer I stayed, the more I could see how it operated like the rest of the world. The directors and the choreographers were men. The men chose the plays, made the schedule, and ran the lights. The women made the food, styled the wigs, and glued false eyelashes onto eyelids. Cat was the woman with the needle and thread.

There were three steps going up to the large room full of sewing machines and dressmaker's dummies where she worked behind the scene shop. I tried to calculate a way to get out of the wheelchair and onto the ground and then scooch up the stairs backwards on my rear end while keeping my cast more or less off the ground. That's when a girl walked by in a striped T-shirt, she couldn't have been twelve, and asked if I needed help.

Where to begin?

Cat and I didn't know each other long, but her help was immeasurable. I still sent her a Christmas card every year. For her part, she claimed her fantasy had always been that someone would knock on her door one day and volunteer to do the mending. For mending I had credentials. I knew how to tailor and cut patterns and replicate simple things without patterns, though I couldn't do any of those things without standing. Mending, however, was work for sitting down. She made me a sewing basket on the spot, put in a beautiful pair of Fiskars like the ones my grandmother had. She gathered up the costumes in a laundry basket, put the sewing basket in the laundry basket, then put the laundry basket on my lap and wheeled me home.

"They put you in the cottage?" she said, looking around in wonder at just how nice it was.

"Just since this." I nodded at my foot. "Uncle Wallace was here but they say he isn't coming back."

"I wouldn't think so." Cat, of course, had been there that night. She sat down on the little chintz sofa. I didn't know how old she was, maybe my mother's age, but at that time in life I thought every woman over thirty was my mother's age. Cat had sad green eyes and hair that must have been blond when she was young. I won't say she was pretty but she had a dreamy quality about her, something soft. "I've been here before," she said, pulling a throw pillow needlepointed with violets into her lap. "A long time ago."

"With Uncle Wallace?" I meant it to be funny but she nodded.

"He always stayed in the cottage. Nowhere else. The first couple of years he came to Tom Lake he'd invite me over sometimes, maybe once or twice a week. He always said he needed me to hem his pants. He called me his wardrobe mistress. He got such a kick out of that."

I smiled because I wanted Cat to think I understood the ways of the world. One person's endured lechery was another person's cherished summer affair.

"He was a lovely man," she said, as if he were already dead.

Every day I took a jumble of snags and tears and turned them back into clothes. I found the work extremely satisfying, as I imagine Rumpelstiltskin must have gotten a kick out of spinning all that straw into gold. Did actors destroy everything they touched? Cat brought a new basket over in the morning and by the afternoon I had finished. Sometimes when there was an extra minute she brought a couple of sandwiches and told me stories about Albert Long, nice stories about him being funny or thoughtful, never the things I didn't want to know. She said she had wanted to visit him in the hospital after his esophageal disaster but she was afraid. After those first couple of years he never seemed to remember who she was, who she had been to him, even when she was on her knees pinning a hem in his trousers. I told her about meeting Elyse Adler and then she was glad she hadn't gone. Elyse was the wife Uncle Wallace had been cheating on in those days.

I had Duke open all the curtains before he left in the morning. I loved to sew in the cottage, the light was so good. I could sit in bed with my foot up and my mountain of mending and manage to stave off panic for hours at a time, my mind settled by the work in my hands.

"When are you going to call Ripley back?" Duke asked before he left for rehearsal. He had shaved in the shower, the way he did. His hair was dripping on the edge of the bed where he perched, naked. Maybe I did love him.

"It's impossible to get to a phone around here."

"They have phones all over the place. He keeps leaving you messages at the office."

I had made the mistake of telling Duke about Ripley

calling me at the hospital. He saw the movie as the answer to everything: the loss of Emily, my one-footedness. "Why should I call him when he never listens to me?"

"If you're saying something stupid he shouldn't listen."

"I don't know what's going to happen," I said.

"Welcome to the world. You've got a movie coming out. This isn't the part where you start burning bridges."

I touched his arm, the silky skin stretched over muscle. The round red scar where he had put out the cigarette still had the last vestige of a scab. "Would you do me a favor?"

"What?"

"Do you think you could rig up some sort of ironing board over the bed?"

"What are you talking about?"

"I want to iron the mending. That's how you finish the job. But I can't iron if I can't stand up. If I had an ironing board that went over the bed, just a little one—" I was thinking of the Veit ironing table with suction and blowing my grandmother and I used to dream about. What I was asking for was nothing like that. I had just finished sewing the sash on a muslin apron that I knew belonged to Mrs. Gibbs. I wanted to make it look nice.

He pushed my hair back from my forehead with the flat of his hand "You're losing your mind, cricket."

I looked at him, his crazy beauty. "Go," I said kindly.

Duke was so happy now that *Our Town* was almost over, now that he was almost Eddie full-time, now that he was taking Pallace back to the room that had once been mine after they swam in the lake. I didn't know the last part at the time but I understood that everything was shifting. Duke was on his way up and I was on my way out. Neither of us could have said those words but we knew.

Pallace came to see me but found the floor of the cottage to be blistering hot. Try as she might, she couldn't stand on it for more than a minute. She arrived with a bottle of Orangina from the cafeteria, a bag of pretzels: small offerings to lay on her altar of guilt. Clearly, she was tortured, and I was foolish enough to think she felt bad about taking my part—two parts! A low fog of tequila settled around her.

"When's Sebastian coming back?" I turned the open bag of pretzels in her direction but she shook her head. Pallace was thin and getting thinner. I knew because I'd already taken in the red dress she would wear in *Fool for Love.* Sebastian was very much my hero in those days, and I'd be so much happier once he came back. If Sebastian were there the teams would be even: two actors and two non-actors.

Pallace tipped her head, bit her lip. “He took too much time off. He got in trouble at work. He’s going to be busy for a while catching up on the lessons he missed.” She shifted her weight from side to side, very nearly lifting her feet to keep them from burning. “I should go,” she said, her face aglow. “I’ve got so many lines.”

“Practice here!” I patted the empty space beside me where Duke slept. “You can climb up in the big fluffy bed and we can run lines.”

Oh, Pallace, such a good actress, and yet she couldn’t fix her face to make me think that things were fine, that she was my friend and would return. She all but ran to get away from me.

In retrospect, my inability to put it together was its own sort of gift. I would understand what they were doing soon enough, at which point I would finally understand what I had done to Veronica. Veronica had such a small part in the story and still I loved her more than everyone at Tom Lake put together. She stayed with me after the rest of them had faded, maybe because we remember the people we hurt so much more clearly than the people who hurt us.

Attending those three remaining performances of *Our Town* was an exercise in endurance. I watched George and Emily up on ladders, talking about their homework, talking about the moon. George and Emily at the soda fountain talking about their future. There they are at their wedding ceremony and Pallace is asking Duke to take her away. Hadn't he always said she was his girl? The next thing you know it's the third act and she's sitting in the graveyard with the rest of the dead. For all the times I was in the play, I don't think I ever fully understood just how fast it went. Chan very kindly came back to the cottage and wheeled me over for all three performances, but after that first night I told him he didn't have to stay. I could ask any stranger to push my wheelchair back across the campus of Tom Lake when the night was black and full of stars. Over time I would have built up my confidence with the wheelchair but it was so hilly and the thought of tipping over in the dark when I was alone and breaking a shoulder or cracking a knee put the fear of god in me. Duke loved to set me on the front stairs of the company housing late at night when he got home, then race around in my wheelchair, making it spin in crazy circles. Then he would take it down the hill, going faster and faster until he threw his up hands and screamed, his head tipped back, his eyes closed. I couldn't stand it. I couldn't stand to watch him and so I closed my eyes.

The part of this story in which I lived in the cottage and sewed for Cat, the part where *Our Town* was still in performances and *Fool for Love* was still in rehearsal and Duke was still in my bed, couldn't have lasted much more than a week, eight or nine days at most. But they were long days, summer stock days. For me, it may as well have been a geological age.

Saint Sebastian returned for the opening of *Fool for Love.* Oh, how I'd missed him! It is so clear to me now that he was the best of us. At first glance a person would have thought it was Duke who ruled the orbit, with Sebastian and Pallace and me as the circling moons. But Sebastian was the one who was necessary. His interest in what we said made us interesting, covered up our deficits. I missed the four of us and all the places we were together—the lake, the tennis court, the car. So often my mind went back to that day at the Nelsons' farm.

"Look at you!" Sebastian held out his arms to me when I crutched to the open door to meet him.

But look at him, his white Oxford shirt starched and ironed, his navy summer blazer. No doubt it was the same shirt and blazer he wore to the bar of the Grosse Pointe Yacht Club, but tonight he was wearing them for Pallace, for the opening of the play that starred his brother and his best girl.

Sebastian brought the wheelchair around and knelt to lift my cast onto the footrest. "It's going to be so much easier for her now," he said, reflecting on Pallace. "When it was *Our Town* one night and then *Cabaret* the next night and then rehearsing *Fool for Love* all day, I thought, she's never going to make it."

Why hadn't I thought of it this way? All the pressure she was under because of me, her boyfriend made to stay at work because of me. Small wonder she could barely stand to be in my room. "Pallace is tougher than the rest of us," I said, by which I meant Duke and myself, not Sebastian.

"That's why she told me not to come up for a while," he said.

"She told you not to come?"

"I understood. She didn't have the time. I mean, when you think about her schedule there wasn't one minute. I wanted to see her in everything. I can tell you that. I really wanted to see her in *Our Town* again, even if it meant driving up and turning around to drive back after the show, I would have done it but she said it was too much." He was so careful to avoid any obstacles or breaks in the walkway as he wheeled me to the theater.

"It would have been a lot."

"Joe did it."

Joe Nelson! I hadn't said goodbye to him after the last performance. I forgot that I wasn't going to see him again. "Maybe we can all go back to the Nelsons' farm," I said, thinking I could get another chance. We could live the entire day again! Lunch with Maisie and Ken, the napkins, Sebastian and Pallace holding hands when we went into the woods, Duke running across the beach, Duke lying down in the thick cemetery grass to smoke. I would take all of it.

"We can go anywhere you want as long as we get her here in time for the curtain."

Her, he said, not him. So recently it would have been Duke's schedule Sebastian kept his eye on. "Let's go to the Yacht Club for lunch," I said. "The three of us could come down in Pallace's car and meet you." Duke loved to talk about the Yacht Club, he loved to say the word *yacht*, to say how Sebastian ruled the world in his tennis whites.

Sebastian stopped at the place where the view of the lake was best, the place where you turned off to take the path to the theater, the place we ran past day after day as we barreled down the grassy slope in the afternoon heat to throw ourselves into the water.

"The club is no place to go," he said.

A heron raked across the surface of the lake just as we

were watching, wetting his toes and coming up empty. "Look at that!" I said. We were both so excited to see the bird. I could have asked him what was wrong with having lunch at the Yacht Club but I already knew. Sebastian wanted to protect her from everything, including the place where he worked.

Unlike Chan, who left me parked behind the last row, Sebastian picked me up and carried me down the stairs. To be fair, it never crossed my mind that Chan might offer to carry me anywhere, and I don't think it occurred to him either, but it was comforting to be in Sebastian's arms again. "You know I wouldn't do this if you were a normal-sized person," he said, and I laughed, glad for once to be small. This was the big night, and we'd come early for the privilege of sitting in the center of the second row.

The lights were up as the house started to fill. I told Sebastian about the sewing I'd taken on and the things I'd found in people's pockets. He asked where I learned to sew and so I told him about my grandmother and how I'd been in her shop since a time before memory. Then he told me about his lessons for the week, about a fourteen-year-old boy named Andy with a canny backhand who was the best student he'd ever had. The boy's parents had joined the Yacht Club just so he could take lessons with Sebastian. The excitement in his voice when he talked about this kid was moving to me. More than once he told me Andy was his best.

I don't think Sebastian and I had talked about anything much before he took me to the hospital but we were different now, we counted each other as friends. I was, for those few remaining minutes, happy just to be with him. When in the future I would think of Saint Sebastian it was always at that moment in the theater before the curtain went up, his white shirt and navy blazer, his smile as he leaned over to whisper something about the woman who was standing in the aisle, complaining that all the good seats had been taken when the play was set to start in five minutes.

Fool for Love is complete in one act. Sam Shepard in his infinite wisdom knew that, if given an intermission, too many people would make a run for the door. I don't mean the play was bad. As much as I hated it, I knew it wasn't bad, but it ran a person ragged, both the actors and the audience. Even if you weren't the two people in the second-row center waking up to the fact that everything you loved was lost, it was hard to watch. When Eddie and Mae started kissing, Sebastian covered my wrist with his hand and kept it there for the rest of the performance, his eyes straight ahead. Duke was gone and Pallace was gone and all we could do was sit there and wait for the show to be over.

But while we waited we watched them. We understood that there had never really been a world in which Pallace would have stayed with a tennis coach from East Detroit, never any world in which Duke would stay with anyone at all. We were members of the audience and they were slender gods, brilliant and terrifying. They lit the room with the lightning of their drunken grief and extravagant love. How could they get to the end of that show without going home and slamming one another up against the wall, the floor, the bed? Surely some actors in the past had managed, the same ones who swapped the tequila for water, but Duke and Pallace were just kids. Prodigiously talented kids.

When finally it was finished, the audience leapt to their feet to applaud and Sebastian pushed his way down the row and was gone. It was the last I would see of him. I sat there in the pale blue dress my grandmother made and my enormous plaster cast and waited. I hadn't understood that Pallace and I were in a race but we were, and she had won. The cocktail of grief and humiliation and longing battered my heart with such violence I was sure I could feel the muscle tear. When people asked if I needed any help I told them no, my friend was coming right back, but after another half hour, after every other person had trickled away, I had to concede that not even good old Saint Sebastian was coming to get me. That was when I saw how the backs of theater seats could provide a stable means of transfer. I stood and held one and then the next and the next, hopping my way to the aisle and then hopping my way up the stairs row by row, all the way back to where my wheelchair was waiting. I used the chair as a walker, pushing it through the door until I got outside and got myself seated and got myself very slowly back home in the dark. Funnily enough, this turned out to be the thing that saved me: the knowledge that I could get back by myself.

18

The storm is all but played out, the thunder rolling off to a place so far away that not even Hazel is alarmed. It's only rain now, and not the kind of rain that will drown you if you look up. Maisie and Nell are staring at me, drunk with disappointment.

"Sebastian just—" Maisie swallows. "Didn't come back?"

"He went to the greenroom to find them. There was some sort of fight."

"Who told you?"

"Cat came over with the mending in the morning."

"You had to sew their clothes?" Nell's romance with her mother's summer of summer stock exhales its final breath.

I shake my head. "Cat would never have asked me to

sew their costumes. She knew what was going on. Everybody knew what was going on. She said there had been a lot of shouting and shoving and accusations. She said the whole thing was like a Sam Shepard play. Sebastian punched his brother in the face." Had he ripped Duke's shirt as well? Anything was possible.

"What about Pallace?" Maisie asks.

"Apparently she hadn't been drinking that much in rehearsal and then on opening night she went all in. Cat had to get her out of the dress."

"So two brothers are slugging it out over her and she missed it?"

"She might have missed it." Cat said Pallace was facedown on that nubby yellow couch in her bra and underpants, crying her eyes out. She wouldn't let Cat help her get dressed again. Sebastian stormed off and Duke was on the floor and the A.D. was hunting up an ice pack for the side of Duke's face. Then the A.D. said the face was going to need stitches so he drove Duke to the hospital. Pallace was too drunk to sit up. Duke had been evangelical when it came to the consumption of alcohol being a matter of practice but maybe she hadn't listened. "I know I shouldn't be saying this to you," Cat said to me, "but I felt sorry for her. I wished the tennis player had just picked her up and put her in the car. He could have forgiven her later. That girl's not up to Duke." I'd wanted to ask her if she thought I was up to Duke, but whatever the answer was it wouldn't have been helpful.

"So when did you see Duke?" Maisie asks.

I shake my head. "I didn't see him."

"Meaning what?" Nell says, looking like a mad little Frenchwoman. "He ghosted you?"

"We didn't have the terminology but yes, that's the general idea."

Maisie covers her eyes with her hands. "Son-of-a-bitch. I want back every hour of my childhood I spent watching *The Popcorn King.*"

I stand up. *The Popcorn King.* What a thought. "Thus concludes the story of the summer your mother dated a famous movie star. Fill your sister in however you see fit. I'm not doing this part again."

"But he *wasn't* a famous movie star," Nell says, straining to control her voice. "Not then. He was just some asshole actor like all the other asshole actors."

I shrug. "Some of the actors were nice. Your father was very nice."

"Which is why he became a cherry farmer."

Maisie is still sitting there, the dog in her lap asleep. "I want to kill him."

"Well, you can't, he's dead, and anyway, it happened a long time ago." The rage dissipates along with the love, and all we're left with is a story. Peter Duke is dead and I'm telling them my small corner of what happened.

"So how did you get out of there?" Nell asks.

I turn to the window. Even the rain has reached its conclusion. The sun is everywhere. "Come on. Back to work."

"You'll tell us, won't you?" Nell says to me. "You promise?"

I tell her yes, I promise, but she isn't going to like it.

Maisie and Nell get their hats, their bug spray, and go out into the great dripping world wearing muck boots. I stay behind to make the lunch, which I should have been working on while I was talking all this time. The past need not be so all-encompassing that it renders us incapable of making egg salad. The past, were I to type it up, would look like a disaster, but regardless of how it ended we all had many good days. In that sense the past is much like the present because the present—this unparalleled disaster—is the happiest time of my life: Joe and I here on this farm, our three girls grown and gone and then returned, all of us working together to take the cherries off the trees. Ask that girl who left Tom Lake what she wanted out of life and she would never in a million years have said the Nelson farm in Traverse City, Michigan, but as it turned out, it was all she wanted.

Once I finish with the sandwiches and put the bags of cookies and chips in a backpack, I walk out past the kitchen garden. The lettuce and tomato plants and zinnias are already straightening up from the beating they've taken. Those tiny periwinkle butterflies are working their rounds. Where do the periwinkles go in rain like that? It's not that I'm unaware of the suffering and the soon-to-be-more suffering in the world, it's that I know the suffering exists beside wet grass and a bright blue sky recently scrubbed by rain. The beauty and the suffering are equally true. *Our Town* taught me that. I had memorized the lessons before I understood what they meant. No matter how many years ago I'd stopped playing Emily, she is still here. All of Grover's Corners is in me.

By the time I drop off the food in the barn and kiss my husband, the girls have put their buckets around their necks like horses ready to plow a field. They are fully at work.

"He left you!" Emily cries when she sees me coming.

"All caught up," Maisie says from the ladder.

Hazel has found a filthy tennis ball, god knows where, and brings it to me. I throw it as far as I've ever thrown a tennis ball and she tears out down the row of trees, Hazel, who cannot climb the stairs.

"We opted for the abridged version," Nell says.

"You should have told me this years ago," Emily says. I don't know exactly what her sisters have told her but she is miraculously indignant on my behalf, her entire being trembling with sympathy and rage.

"You would have taken Duke's side," Maisie says, but she says it lightly.

Emily comes over and hugs me. "What did you do? Did you stay?"

Hazel is back with the tennis ball and after a brief tussle and growl for show I throw it again. She is not a young dog. This will not be our entire day. "I didn't stay."

"Are you going to make us guess?" Maisie asks from her high perch.

I start to say no, there's no guessing this one, when Nell raises her hand like a schoolgirl. "Ripley came and got you."

"No!" Emily shouts.

I look at my youngest child in disbelief. Nell in her lipstick has figured it out. "How else could you leave? You can't walk. You don't have a car and even if you did it's your right foot so you can't drive. You haven't told your family. You just said you didn't see Sebastian again."

"Wait, you don't see Sebastian?" Emily looks up at Maisie. "You didn't tell me that."

Sebastian. This is an uncomfortable point on which I have meant to be evasive, but since I have lied I decide to let the lie stand. I have staked out a single day of privacy in the light of this merciless interrogation.

"I would have thought Sebastian would get you out of there but he didn't. Cat can't leave Tom Lake in the middle of the season. Elyse Adler isn't coming back. I don't think Chan gets you out even though I bet he was in love with you."

"Give up acting," Maisie says to her sister. "The FBI needs you."

"And Ripley wants you back to do publicity. I mean, he really needs you to come to Los Angeles so he's leaning on you anyway. You're the star of the movie."

"I'm not the star of the movie."

"We've seen it a hundred times. You are. So Ripley's been calling and Duke's been collecting the messages at the office." She stops herself to think things through and we wait with her in silence. "Oh my god, Duke called him, didn't he? Duke called Ripley and told him to come and get you. That's why Ripley came to Michigan. Otherwise he would have sent the girl, the-what's-her-name, Ashby, to fly out and bring you back."

"Why couldn't it have been Ashby?" Emily asks her. "It doesn't make any sense that Ripley would be the one to get on a plane." Emily, who we used to be so afraid of, is trying to put it together.

"Don't be such a dope," Nell says.

The day after *Fool for Love* opened I stayed in bed with my foot up on pillows, smoking cigarettes, sewing spangles and drinking the syrupy frozen vodka from the stash. I had so much to cry about I could have broken it into segments: nine to ten, cry over Duke and Pallace's betrayal; ten to eleven, cry for wanting Duke back; eleven to noon I would split between the loss of Sebastian and the loss of Pallace, very different feelings yet intermingled; noon to one was the loss of Emily and my acting career; one to two, the frustration of not being able to walk to the bathroom; two to three, the terror over what to do with my life, by which I meant the next day and all the other days. That led nicely back to betrayal, which had kicked the whole thing off. I fell asleep but couldn't stay asleep; I didn't eat; I repeatedly pricked my fingers with the needle in my efforts to both sew and cry, which meant hopping to the sink to scrub little dots of my own blood from the fabric. Who knows how long I might have sustained this state had Ripley not arrived, though my guess would be a long time. I picked up a Kleenex, they were everywhere, and blew my nose. "Please don't be here," I said to him.

"Hello to you, too." He stood in the doorway of the cottage, taking measure of the wreckage.

"I'm serious. I'm not my best self right now. I can't negotiate."

"Well, that's fine because I'm not here to negotiate. Do you have any idea how fucking far away this place is? From anywhere? I flew to Detroit, the worst goddamn airport ever built. It took me an hour to walk from the gate where we landed to the gate where I got a flight to someplace called Traverse City in a tiny plane. I hate those tiny planes. Then your maniac boyfriend picks me up at the airport in a Honda that's missing third gear. He told me he had to shift straight from second to fourth and that I shouldn't think he didn't understand that he was supposed to use third, only that third was nonoperational. Somebody's pounded him, by the way, I'm sure you know that. His right eye's shut, that would be the eye that's facing me in the car. It's got stitches in the corner. Three gears on the car and one eye and the drive takes an hour and a half during which time he never shuts up."

"Did he say he was my boyfriend?" I ran the edge of the sheet under my eyes. There had been no news of Duke beyond what I'd heard from Cat.

"That's your question?"

"Just tell me what he said."

Ripley shook his head, no doubt disgusted by my decimated state. "He said you needed to go to California, that's what he said."

"It's nice that the two of you agree."

"Well, you're going. I didn't come out here for my health. Boyfriend says you're wrecked, what with your foot falling off and losing the part in the play. He says this place is finished for you, which I took to mean he's finished with you and would like to see you vacated but that's not my business."

I didn't take this gracefully, and Ripley did his best to avert his eyes. "Who the hell thought it would be a good idea to put a theater in the middle of nowhere anyway?" he said, looking out the window to the courtyard and its poppies.

I sniffled, buried my head in a pillow. "It's pretty here."

"It's pretty in Santa Barbara. Put the summer stock in Santa Barbara so people can find it."

"Ripley, seriously. I'm sorry you came all this way but I need you to leave me alone."

This seemed to hurt him, though I wouldn't have thought Ripley capable of being hurt. Maybe he was tired. He sat on the edge of my bed then, rapping lightly on the cast with his knuckles. "They don't spare any expense on plaster in these parts, do they?"

"It can't possibly matter if I do interviews. Nobody knows who I am." I rubbed my face with the sheet.

Ripley patted my leg, the space between my knee and the top of the cast. "You need to do the interviews. It's a good film. You'll see. It'll be good for you."

"I'm not going to be an actress anymore."

"You're twelve, you don't know what you're going to be, but you have to come back and finish what you started."

"You flew out here to tell me that?"

"You don't return my goddamn phone calls, and anyway, I have a sense of, I don't know—" He stopped to take in the bright mound of costumes covering the bed. "What's with the clothes?"

"I'm doing the mending for the costume department."

He picked up the edge of a silvery leotard then dropped it. "I have some responsibility to you, as crazy boyfriend explained to me on the phone. At the very least I have a responsibility to get you out of here, and that will benefit both of us."

A bit of clarity seeped into my swollen brain, a sliver of light. Duke had set this up. "He wants you to see the play. That's why you had to come here."

Ripley shook his head. "He didn't even tell me about a play."

An hour and a half in the car and no mention of Sam Shepard. Duke knew that if he could get Ripley to Tom Lake, I would get him to *Fool for Love.* Even if I hated him, he knew I'd come through, because he knew I was exactly that kind of fool. Duke was going to be a movie star, but to be a movie star you've got to find someone who's willing to look at you. His brilliance would not be readily evident on a résumé, a headshot, a three-minute audition. He needed to be seen in a play, in this particular play and in its entirety. He was as good as anyone had ever been in Michigan, and now the trick was making sure that someone who wasn't from Michigan knew that.

Ripley went to *Fool for Love* without much convincing. Going to see plays was what he did. He asked me to come but I said if we were leaving tomorrow I'd have to pack. I was like one of those clever crows who could use a stick as a tool. I sat in my wheelchair and knocked things off the closet bar with the crutch. What I'd brought didn't amount to anything more or anything more meaningful than what Uncle Wallace had: a modest amount of clothing, a handful of books I'd already read, a clock. I left my scripts in the freezer with the vodka Duke and I hadn't gotten around to yet.

I took a careful bath, finished the mending, wrote Cat a note. Ripley had his secretary arrange for a car service in the morning, saying we sure as hell weren't going back to Traverse City in the Honda.

"Sure as hell not," I said.

I pushed my two swimsuits into the corner of my suitcase. Everything at Tom Lake was finished for me. For all my protesting, I understood that I was wildly fortunate that someone, anyone, had come to pull me out.

The next morning Ripley carried my suitcases to the car as I crutched behind him, leaving the wheelchair in the cottage since it belonged to the prop department. We sat in the back seat in silence, both of us preoccupied by thoughts of the same person for entirely different reasons. The driver put the crutches in the trunk with the bags. I couldn't quite believe I hadn't said goodbye to any of them, by which I meant Duke. I hadn't said goodbye to Duke, who hadn't said goodbye to me.

Goodbye, theater. Goodbye, cherry trees and cigarettes and vodka. Goodbye, lake.

"How crazy is this guy?" Ripley asked when we were almost an hour into the drive. He'd been staring out the window, probably thinking about how he'd never see Michigan again.

"Crazy," I said.

"But crazy worth it?"

He wasn't asking me about my love life but it was hard not to think of it in those terms. "You saw him."

"What's his face like, when it's not bashed in?"

I told him it was a very good face.

He was quiet again for another ten miles or so. "I don't like working with the crazies," he said.

"No one does, but if you got rid of them I don't know who you'd have left."

Ripley nodded. "I'm assuming the two of you came to a bad end."

"We did."

"And that it had something to do with the girl in the play?"

As I have said, their truth was widely evident.

"She was good, too," he said absently.

"She's very good, and she dances." I don't know what I was trying to sell him, only that I'd spent the long summer marveling at the glory of both Pallace and Duke. I had no idea how a person was supposed to stop that on a dime.

"I might have a part for him." Ripley didn't ask me if I minded.

I nodded, wondering if there would be any pleasure in this in the future, the knowledge that I had contributed to something that was bound to happen anyway. I was a conduit in the start of Peter Duke's meteoric career, a single, shiny cog.

"I don't love the way he did this," Ripley said. "Getting me out to fucking Michigan to see him."

"How else were you going to see him?"

"I don't know. I suppose he could have troubled himself to come to L.A. like everyone else in the world. Except for you. I had to go to New Hampshire to find you." Everything had been plotted for his maximum inconvenience.

When we got to the turnoff for Traverse City, I started to think I might call Joe Nelson from the airport to say goodbye. I would tell Joe how I'd lost them, Duke and Sebastian and Pallace, all in one shot.

"What about Pallace?" I asked Ripley.

"Who's Pallace?"

"The girl."

He shook his head. "I don't need a girl. I have too many girls as it is."

And there went Pallace, tumbling off in the breeze as Duke came with us. I knew what he was telling me, and I didn't say another word about it.

Ripley put me in the pool house. In the afternoons I sat on a chaise beneath an umbrella in my one-piece and read novels. Ripley's house contained no end of novels. He said agents sent them to him in boxes, hoping he'd turn the books into movies. "If you come across anything decent, write a treatment," he said. "You can earn your keep."

"I'm already earning my keep." Ashby was still on the payroll, still hoping to be an actress. She took me to have my nails painted and my eyebrows plucked and a few subtle highlights woven around my face. There was a stylist and a media trainer who schooled me in the ways of talk shows and newspaper interviews. I had been made up to get into the business and I would be made up to get out.

"You're not getting out," Ripley said.

"That's a line from a horror movie if ever I heard one."

"I'm sure it is. So what are you going to do with your life if you don't do this?"

"There is no this. This is gone. No joke. I'm only here to do you a favor because you did me a favor. When we're done I may go back to New Hampshire, work in alterations. Maybe I'll finish college. I wanted to be a teacher before you came along."

He rolled his eyes. "Give me a break," he said.

Ripley and I struck up an odd little friendship in the month or so I was there. I never got the story on his personal life other than he didn't seem to have one. He was good to me though, in spite of my moods. I never knew if it was because he felt sorry for me or grateful because of Duke or if he felt like he needed to keep an eye on me until the movie came out. Maybe he was just a decent man. I had started to think of him as my uncle, just like Charlie had told me he was in the Algonquin all those lifetimes ago. Ripley went out and picked up salads from one fancy restaurant or another and we ate them together in the evening, drank Chablis. Sometimes we watched a movie but just as often we didn't. He liked to play honeymoon bridge and I knew how. "The only ingenue in Bel Air who plays honeymoon bridge," he liked to say while I shuffled the deck. I always wanted a cigarette after dinner but the property had been scrubbed of tobacco. Everyone who worked for Ripley had been instructed not to buy them for me. "You look like an eighth grader when you smoke," he said. "It's not attractive."

Which was how I quit. I didn't mind too much, as smoking made me miss Duke. Ripley didn't talk to me about Duke but I knew things were in the works. He'd sent a casting director out to Tom Lake to see the play and the next week a stack of headshots were left on the kitchen counter after a meeting and Duke's was in there, just another pretty boy in a thick stack of pretty boys. I took the picture back to the pool house and cried on it. I was always thinking that he might come for me. He must have known where I was, and showing up was the kind of thing he would do, walking into the pool house in the middle of the night, especially a pool house Ripley owned. "Where's my girl?" he'd call. "Where's my birthday girl?"

Ripley told me to keep the door locked but I never did.

My agent got me an appointment to see some big-time California hand and foot specialist who cut off the plaster cast, x-rayed my ankle, examined the incision, and reported with no small amount of wonder that everything looked fine. He replaced the plaster with a lightweight fiberglass cast and gave me a walker, which made me feel born again. I used the crutches for interviews because, as Ripley explained, crutches were sexy and youthful and walkers were walkers.

After two or three days, Ripley arranged a screening on the studio lot and we watched *Singularity* together with some friends of his and some studio people and some of the people in the movie, though not the famous actress, who was shooting in Quebec.

"She's not in Quebec," Ripley said, not bothering to lower his voice. "She just got wind of how good you are."

I was good, or the person in the film who strongly resembled me was good. She had just finished playing

Emily in the University of New Hampshire production of *Our Town.* She had taken a leave of absence from school four weeks before finishing her junior year and still had every intention of going back. She had never heard of Duke or Sebastian or Pallace, did not know Tom Lake existed. Seeing the movie made me think that it wouldn't be so hard to get back to that place. Three years wasn't such a long time.

I did the interviews on crutches and everyone was charmed. I crutched out on *The Tonight Show* in a hot-pink sleeveless dress, my good foot in a ballet slipper, my arms all muscle and sinew. I crossed a stage with a nice, rhythmic swing and dropped down in the chair next to Johnny Carson. Carson was old by then, tired of the job, but my crutches and cast sparked something in him. "Wow! Will you look at her?" he said. Then I smiled and waved. I'd nailed it before I ever opened my mouth.

The next morning when I called my grandmother she started crying on the phone. "Everybody's calling *me*," she said. "Like I did something."

I did help the movie, Ripley was right about that. Even if it wasn't a summer blockbuster, it did better than anyone thought it would and I got the credit, me and my ruptured Achilles. Every interviewer wanted to talk about my tennis game, ask if was I planning to take on Steffi Graf once the cast came off, and every time I laughed like no one had ever made the joke before. Publicity was the most acting I'd ever done in my life, and it did nothing to dissuade me from the idea that I was finished. I didn't want anyone curling my hair or straightening my hair or telling me to look up while they applied my eyeliner. I didn't want anyone touching me. All the things that feel reasonable when you're trying to be an actress feel unbearable once you've stopped. Jane Pauley said I was America's daughter, and I said that was good because I was going home.

Ripley took me to the airport himself in the MG. He was being nostalgic. He never drove the MG. He parked the car and walked me in, pitching ideas all the way to the gate. "You're making a big mistake," was the very last thing he said to me. I didn't know if he meant it or if he was lonely. I knew he liked having me around, but surely other actresses could be found for the pool house. I was done. I gave him a kiss and crutched off into the sunset.

19

A cool breeze stirs the trees and brushes off the rain left clinging to cherries and leaves. The orchard is glistening, and I am done. I've laid out the entire summer at Tom Lake with bonus tracks on either side. I've given my girls the director's cut.

Nell shifts her feet in the wet grass. "You don't ever think you made a mistake?" she asks.

"Oh, come on. All that and you still think I should've been an actress?"

"I think being an actress sounds like a nightmare," Emily says.

The three of us look to Maisie to break the tie. "I'd take the shitting calf any day," she says.

So I have won over two of my girls. As for the third, Nell thinks everyone secretly longs for the stage.

"Did Ripley wind up giving Duke a job?" Nell asks.

"*Rampart*!" Emily is forever astonished by the depths of our ignorance, though I knew the answer to that one. "It was Ripley's show. It won ten Emmys."

"Did Duke win?" Maisie asks.

Emily shakes her head. "Two nominations, no wins. No one understood him in those days."

I can remember watching the awards show with my cousin Sarah back in New Hampshire, the two of us sitting in my grandmother's bed because the better television was in her room. The camera panned regularly back to Duke. Even in a roomful of television stars he was the glittery thing. "Him!" I pointed to the screen. "That's the guy I used to date." They showed him in profile, laughing, his tuxedo slim and immaculate, the tie undone.

"Then who's the girl he's with?" my cousin asked, like Duke had been busted for cheating.

"I'm not dating him *now*. I have no idea who she is."

She is a creature of inestimable beauty, I wanted to say. That's who she is.

"What I want to know," Nell says, the bucket around her neck half-full of cherries, "is what became of you." She is wrestling with the knowledge that I'd been given everything she'd ever wanted, and that I'd given it away.

Emily and Maisie look over at their sister, then they look at me.

"What do you mean, what happened to me? I married your father. We came here. We had the three of you."

"But how? I always thought you and Daddy fell in love at Tom Lake, that you dumped Duke for Dad and then the two of you went from there. But you left Michigan without even calling Dad from the airport. When you went to Los Angeles, did he stay here?"

"He stayed the rest of the summer helping Maisie and Ken, then he went to Chicago to direct a play." Was it Chicago?

"Did you write to him?" Emily asks.

I shake my head. I didn't know enough to write to Joe in those days.

"How long was it before he found you?" Maisie asks. Something in the construction of her question touches me, as if Joe had gone door to door, searching for me all that time.

"Three or four years," I say. New Hampshire was its own eternity, as was New York. I did not tally up those days.

"So tell us about going back to New Hampshire," Emily says, cheerful at the thought of additional chapters. "Tell us about New York. Tell us about when you met Dad again."

"No, really, I'm done." They are reminding me of the years when they were small and it was just me in the house beneath all that snow and Joe was in the barn trying to fix a tractor he didn't know how to fix, and I felt like the children would eat me. Nell was eating me, still at my breast, and the other two rushed to crawl in my lap whenever I sat down. I thought, Joe will come home and find the three of them framing out a playhouse with my bones.

"You said it wasn't a story about a famous man," Nell reminds me. "It was supposed to be a story about you."

"It *was* a story about me, the whole thing. But I can't tell you every minute of my life. We'll die of boredom."

Maisie faces down the long row of trees, every one of them covered in cherries. "We'll die of boredom anyway."

I would pull off every last bit of fruit myself rather than go back there.

"A sentence," Nell says, as if this were an improv class. "Start small. See where it takes you."

I think about it. Those hard years can, in fact, be distilled to a single sentence, and so I try. "I went back to New Hampshire and stayed with my grandmother until she died."

I was her favorite and she was my favorite. My grandmother married my grandfather when she was eighteen, and had her first child, my mother, at nineteen. My grandfather worked for the railroad and she could sew and together there was enough to keep them going. They had five children, the fourth of whom was a sleepwalker. Brian got out of bed one night when he was six, went down the hall and down the stairs and out the front door into the snowy night. Even asleep, he knew to close the door. When my grandmother went to get everyone up in the morning, Brian wasn't in his bed. She looked all over the house and then went outside without her coat. She found him down at the end of the driveway by the mailbox, frozen to death. Her remaining four grew up fine. Over the years they brought fourteen grandchildren home from the hospital. Go look us up—Kenison—we're everywhere. My parents met in high school and also married young, everybody married young back then. They had their two boys straightaway: Heath, who they called Hardy because he was, and Jake. That was the family. That was what they'd wanted. But when my mother was thirty-five I came along. Thirty-five sounds like nothing now, it sounds young, but being pregnant when she already had two big boys, one of them playing football on the varsity team, mortified her.

I would say nothing against my parents or my brothers. They were good to me, but there was from earliest memory an understanding that I would live mostly at my grandmother's house six blocks away. My grandfather had died of emphysema and everyone said she needed company, insofar as a very small child can be company. I suppose I didn't live completely with her but I was mostly with her, playing with fabric remnants and ribbon wound onto spools while she worked. The alterations shop had a small selection of needles and yarn because we didn't have a knitting shop in town. When I got older, my mother would watch me knitting a sweater at the breakfast table and say she was sorry she hadn't paid more attention to her own mother's attempts to teach her things. I tried a hundred times to teach her myself but my mother was like a border collie. She couldn't sit still for it.

My grandmother and I though, we were the absolute masters of stillness. She taught me to play honeymoon bridge, how to watch movies while silently keeping up with my stitch count. Those were the days before audiobooks, and she asked me to read to her while she sewed, following my progression from *The Little House in the Big Woods* all the way through *Moby-Dick,* which I never would have finished were it not for her insistent requests to hear another chapter. Every book I had to read for school, along with all the ones I read for pleasure, I read to her. This was probably the origin of my acting, as I can remember her telling me to be a little more interesting, and then later on to be a little less interesting. When I played my first Emily in high school, she helped me memorize my lines and I helped her make the costumes. We each had a copy of the play and we read it through breakfast, lunch, and dinner.

"She's just like you," my grandmother said. "The smartest girl in the class."

My grandmother had been the smartest girl in her class as well, everyone said so, but there wasn't much to do with that distinction once she'd married on the Saturday after graduation. Five children made for a full life, and then four children did the best they could to make life full. Her math was sharp, it had to be to make patterns and run a business. She kept the red leather-bound dictionary her husband had given to her on their first anniversary on the bedside table where another woman might have kept a Bible. She wanted me to go to college, and then she wanted me to go to California and be an actress. She wanted me to have everything I ever thought of wanting. "Look at her getting up on that stage like it was nothing," she said to her friends. I went off to the University of New Hampshire, and after that I got on a plane to California and checked into a hotel room all by myself. I amazed her.

She never once made me feel bad about leaving. I don't know that I would have gone if I'd thought she'd be lonely. But she was so cheerful about everything, so happy for me. She had plenty of family around her still, and she knew everyone in town, so off I went. I don't regret that. She would never have wanted me hanging around for her sake. She meant for me to do something with my life, the kinds of things she hadn't been able to do herself. But when I think about what those years away added up to, I would rather have spent them with her.

My grandmother closed Stitch-It around the time I moved to Los Angeles. Even when she used her brightest light she had trouble with her eyes, which turned out to be the early stages of macular degeneration. She couldn't do the fine little stitches anymore, though she could manage plenty of other things. Even without the shop, people brought their clothes to her. She kept the yellow tape measure around her neck and did the work as long as she could because she believed that was her role in our town. Neither of my brothers settled in New Hampshire after college, and then my parents moved to Florida because my mother suffered terribly with arthritis in the winter. They invited my grandmother to come with them but that was never going to happen. She had other children, and they had children, and, in a few cases, those children had children. When I came back, my foot still locked in the fiberglass boot just the way it had been on television, it was clear to everyone that I was the person my grandmother wanted. Why not stay? I had money and no plans. I moved back into my room, which now housed two sewing machines and the button-holer and racks of thread and the Juki serger which, after me, was her pride. I helped her with the sewing. She would talk me through whatever needed to be done if she couldn't quite manage it herself. In the evenings I read aloud. I told Ripley to have his secretary mail me any books he didn't want to deal with and she shipped them out in boxes. People stopped me on the street to tell me what a good job I'd done in the movie. I was easy to spot: the crutches, the cast. They thought I was famous, and so were amazed that I'd come home at all. The leaves turned red. The cast came off. I was sure there had been some terrible mistake since now I was in excruciating pain all the time. I couldn't put my foot flat on the ground, but the doctor said it would happen and after a while it did. I started physical therapy and then I finished it. My sweaters came out of the cedar chest. I found my boots. I wondered about Duke and

Pallace and Sebastian, sure the three of them had gone their separate ways. More than anything, I wondered if they ever wondered about me. I tried to find Veronica but she was gone. Veronica, her mother, her brothers, all of them. Those were the days when people could move away and not even the post office knew where to find them.

My grandmother said I should open Stitch-It again, there would be plenty of business. I believed the part about the business, I just didn't know if I was ready to sign off on a life in New Hampshire spent sewing. Then one night a report about breast cancer came on the news, all about mammograms and early detection, women talking about finding a lump in their breast. We were making dinner. We always turned the television off when we sat down to eat but we could watch it while we were cooking. That was the rule.

"I have one of those," she said to the television set.

"You had a mammogram?"

She shook her head. She wasn't looking at me. "A lump."

I had been cutting up a head of broccoli and I put down the knife and washed my hands. "What did you do about it?"

"I didn't do anything about it."

"What did the doctor say?"

She looked at me then. "The whole thing scared me to death."

"So what happened?" My brain insisted on hearing it in the past tense, *I had a lump in my breast once.* I couldn't understand that this was something that was happening.

"I thought I'd wait for you to come home," she said. "You're always so good at figuring things out."

"I've been home three months."

But she had found the lump a year before, and taped a gauze square over it when it started to leak. When I looked at her again I could actually see a disruption in the pattern of her dress. That's how big it was.

Once we started making the hopeless rounds of oncologist appointments, the past broke away. All the things I'd thought about myself before—*I am an actress, I am not an actress, I was in love, I was betrayed*—disintegrated into nothing. I made bowls of Cream of Wheat she wouldn't eat and then scraped them into the trash once they turned cold. I managed the schedule of people who wanted to come and see her, her two sons and two daughters—one of those daughters my mother—my father, my brothers, all my cousins, all her friends. I made sure no one stayed too long. I sat by her bed and read to her. I read her *Our Town*, doing all the parts, and we cried at the end when the Stage Manager talked about the planet straining away to make something of itself and how we were all so tired. I told her about Uncle Wallace then, not that he had died but what a wonderful Stage Manager he had been. She held my hand and later I held her hand. I called her Nell in those days because Nell, which was her own name, was all she answered to.

"You know who's here?" Nell said to me, her eyes closed. She had been asleep all afternoon and I was sitting there turning hems because, unbelievably, people were bringing their sewing by, thinking it would give her something to do while she was dying. She wanted me to finish it.

"Who?" So many people came in and out.

"Brian. Whenever I wake up now he's sitting at the foot of the bed."

"That's good," I said.

"He hasn't changed. I always wondered if he would grow up but he didn't." She was looking out the window at the snow, or maybe she wasn't. Her eyes were clouded.

"Do you want a pill now?"

She nodded a little and I poured a glass of water and helped her sit. When she was asleep again I went to the kitchen and called my mother to ask her who Brian was and she told me the story of her brother who had died in the snow. All those years and I'd never heard of him.

"It was too sad," my mother said.

I found Brian in the cemetery once I knew to look for him, one more Kenison among the many. We buried Nell beside him. I stayed in New Hampshire for a long time after that. There were things to look after, of course, and I didn't have anyplace to go. The family took what they wanted: a sewing machine, a Christmas tin full of buttons, the dining room set. I cleaned out the rest. I found the five copies of the *Monitor* in the bottom of her blanket chest, the review of the play, the picture of me as Emily in high school. The cousins came over and we painted the house room by room, fixed the floor in the bathroom, paid someone to fix the roof and paid someone to take down the half-dead oak that had leaned precariously over the back porch for so many years. We did all the things we should have done while she was still alive. I was in good stead with my family and had plenty of invitations to stay once her house finally sold, but once her house was gone that was that. The one person I'd stayed in touch with from Tom Lake was Cat, and Cat knew a costumer in New York who was looking for a seamstress. After I got the job, one of my uncles packed my things in his car and drove me there.

Of the years in New York there is nothing to say. I worked hard. I had a few friends. I went to rehearsals sometimes with the designer to take the actors' measurements, the yellow tape measure around my neck. I made costumes, refreshed costumes, got house tickets to plays if there were seats available an hour before curtain. I sewed on countless thousands of beads. I thought about night school or even going back to the University of New Hampshire. Every now and then someone in line at the deli would look at me hard and ask if I wasn't the girl in *Singularity.* I told them no. I told them I got that question all the time.

Then one day I was in a theater basting long clumps of tulle to the waistband of a young woman's skirt because the costumer wanted a sense of how things would look from the back of the house if her skirt were fuller, and I heard a voice say, "Emily?"

I took the pins from my mouth and slipped them into the pincushion corsage I wore on my wrist. I couldn't see anything because the house was dark and the stage lights were on. I didn't know who was out there or who he was talking to. For all I knew the girl I was pinning was named Emily.

"Emily," he said again, but this time it wasn't a question.

And I knew, and I had never been so glad to hear

the sound of another voice saying a name that wasn't mine.

"Did you know right away that you loved her this time?" Maisie asks.

Joe has come by on the Gator to pick up the lugs. Once he realizes we aren't talking about Tom Lake anymore, he switches off the ignition and stays. "This time, yes," he says. "Right away."

I nod in agreement. In the city where people thought I might have been the girl in a movie, I'd been found by Joe Nelson, the one person who actually knew me, the one person I knew. When we left the theater together that afternoon we were laughing. He told me he'd been brought in the week before to try to save a lousy play. I told him it had never been my intention to work in theaters, to be with actors, but I needed a job and this was where Cat had sent me. We felt like we were picking up something that had started a long time ago. But we hadn't started, had we? I told him I could just as easily have been taking measurements for some other show, or been pinning tulle on the underskirts of wedding dresses in a bridal salon. He said he should have been back in Chicago but then he never would have found me. And then what? It would have been a different life, one that I will never be able to imagine. A life without Joe and the farm, without Emily and Maisie and Nell.

"Did you come back to Michigan after that?" Emily asks. She is sitting in the grass, we all are, and no one minds that the ground is damp.

"Not right away," Joe says. "I didn't ask her. I was always afraid of scaring your mother off."

"When we came back to Michigan the next summer to see Maisie and Ken they pretended I'd been your father's girlfriend all along, like we'd been together for years. God, she was good to me. She put out those napkins I'd brought her."

"Did you stay in the little house?" Emily asks.

I look at Joe. "We did, didn't we?" We slept in the lumpy double bed that Benny and Emily got rid of. We kept the windows open. The noise of the frogs would wake us in the middle of the night and then sing us back to sleep.

"Did you ever get the books straightened out?" Maisie asks.

"I still haven't gotten the books straightened out," Joe says.

"Your father gave them the money to stay afloat. He gave them all the money he had, and when that wasn't enough, he directed a couple of very lucrative peanut butter commercials."

"Don't tell them that," he says.

"He directed iconic peanut butter commercials to make the money to pay off Ken and Maisie's bills." Money that, over time, resulted in his buying out their interest in the farm, though that had never been his intention. Ken kept a record of every cent, then one day called Joe up to say he owned the farm.

"Which peanut butter?" Nell asks.

"Skippy," I say. "He made one for crunchy and one for smooth." They nod in silent appreciation for his gifts. Looking at so many trees decked out in cherries, it's easy to understand how it might have all gone another way.

"What if we didn't do this anymore?" Joe asked me one morning when we were sitting in a diner on West Thirty-Eighth Street, eating pancakes.

"I stopped doing this a long time ago," I said.

"They were my bills, too," Joe tells the girls. "My father owned half the farm even if he didn't work on it, so if you inherit the land you're going to inherit the bills. By 1995 we already owned the place. Ninety-five was the year that wiped people out. All summer long it was perfect—the perfect temperatures, the perfect amount of rain, not a single blight on any tree on any farm. The crop was huge, like nothing anyone had seen in decades, and the price went through the floor. I was just glad Ken and Maisie were in Arizona already."

"If your father hadn't paid off all the bills and put the rest of the money away we would have lost the farm," I say, but Joe gives me a look and I stop. I know better. We do not talk of losing the farm.

And there will be no talk of our meeting again at that theater, about the years spent dating, living together, deciding to marry, moving to Michigan. Joe has thrown the switch that takes the train from love to the precipitous decline in crop prices. He has seen to it that when he leaves we will be contemplating cherries and not our courtship, which is fair, because the courtship is ours alone, and there is work to do, and we've already lost half the day to lightning.

"I should get back to work." Joe gets up stiffly, the backside of his jeans muddied and wet. Then we all get up and start hefting the lugs into the Gator. The neighbors never thought that a couple of New York theater people had come to take over the farm. Joe Nelson and his wife had come. Joe Nelson who'd been there since he was a boy.

And for his efforts, the farm we took over was in better shape than we expected, by which I mean better shape financially. The main house, the little house, the barn, the trailers where the summer crews stayed, the fences and the trees themselves all existed in varying degrees of disrepair and decay. Ken and Maisie took what was theirs and left for Arizona to live near their daughter. After Ken died, Maisie spent the summers with us, providing a stupendous amount of help. "All that sunshine," she'd say to me as we stood side by side in the kitchen, the girls crawling and toddling and walking around us. "A person can only take so much."

"So Dad saved you," Emily says.

I keep picking. I will not stop for the rest of the day. "I guess he did. Unless I saved him. I might have saved him, too."

"It's a good story either way," Maisie says. "And to think if it wasn't for Duke we might never have asked."

"I wouldn't have asked because I thought I knew it already," Nell said. "And I had every part wrong."

"To tell you the truth, I just never thought about it," Emily says. "I mean, I thought about the Duke part but I don't think I ever wondered about you and Dad."

"We weren't particularly interesting," I say. Good marriages are never as interesting as bad affairs.

"Did you ever go back to Tom Lake?" Nell asks.

"You mean, did we ever drive down to see a show?"

"A show," she says, "or, I don't know, did you ever just walk around for old times' sake?"

I do not explain that "old times' sake" is a condition of fond nostalgia. "We never did. You know how it is in the summer."

"I guess Duke never went back either," Maisie says. Maisie has never been as interested in Duke as her sisters. She has no trouble letting him go.

"Duke was too famous to go back to Tom Lake after that summer," Emily says.

She's right about that. "On your way up or on your way out."

"So you never saw him again." Emily has made her peace with this, and I give serious consideration to leaving that in place, peace being a hard commodity to come by in this world. But one thing is left, the part of the story I wouldn't have told her when she was young because there would have been no context for it, the part of the story I couldn't have told her when she was a teenager because she would have submitted it into evidence against me. And so I've held it all these years, the random thing she would most want to add to her collection of ephemera.

"Once," I say.

He came to the house in October of 1997. Dates near the end of the last century are easy for me to remember based on the season and who I was pregnant with, in this case Nell, who was due in a matter of weeks. That meant Maisie was two and Emily four. I liked being pregnant. I was good at it. Joe and I had decided that two was the right number of children, but once we'd had them for a while, we wanted more. One more baby, we whispered to each other when the snow was starting to melt, one more under the wire, a terrible extravagance we could in no way afford, but we did it anyway. We went back to bed.

There was no best time in northern Michigan, only the time that best suited you. I was partial to fall because I liked the sharpness of the air and the brightness of the light on the leaves. The kitchen was still small in those days and I kept the girls in there with me while I peeled potatoes for dinner. They were making jam tarts, which meant they were smearing jam into their hair. I picked Maisie up when I heard the knock on the door, giving her my stomach for a perch. Emily, my big girl, followed on her own. Someone was always knocking, a neighbor needing me to watch a baby for an hour or a neighbor bringing a pie because I had watched the baby the day before, someone from the picking crew needing Band-Aids or eggs or butter or salt, or it was a stranger driving by who wanted to know our price on apples because the fruit stand was closed.

The enormous black SUV with black-tinted windows idling in front of the house called to mind drug lords, federal agents, movie stars. Duke had knocked on the door and then stepped back to admire the pumpkin patch Joe had planted for the girls. His sunglasses were tortoise shell, round. If time had marched for the rest of us, it had left Duke alone. He was exactly the same, or he was lovelier, his complexion all snow and roses, his hair curling gently at the collar of his navy peacoat. I guess the cop show was a long time ago. Circumstance would dictate that I should have been the one who was surprised, but Duke took the honor for himself. He didn't have the slightest idea what I was doing there. When I opened the screen door and said his name he looked back down the drive like maybe he'd taken a wrong turn into the past, then looked at me again, me and my girls, I wouldn't say *in horror* because it wasn't horror, exactly, more like acute discomfort. "What are you doing here?" he asked finally.

"I live here." Whatever he'd come for, it wasn't me.

"This is the Nelson farm?" Was he even thinner now? Somehow taller? Was it possible that every part of him had been polished?

"Duke," I said, "this is weird. Why are you here?"

He took off his sunglasses and I saw the tiny scar at the corner of his right eye where his brother had hit him. He pressed his eyes closed, then covered them with his hand as if maybe he expected that when he took his hand away again I'd be gone. He was wearing a wedding ring.

I was still there.

And so he tried to restart the moment, begin again. "These are yours?" he asked. Maisie pressed her sticky face into the side of my neck. I hoisted her up to resettle her bones on top of the baby inside me. Emily looped one arm around my thigh and with the other hand gave Duke a charming wave. I made the introductions and he said their names aloud, bent from the waist. He was still making children's movies in those days, or he was just at the end of that era, I couldn't remember, but he had a very nice smile for children, a completely different smile from the one that was familiar to me, or maybe it was just that his teeth had been fixed. Those beautiful, wonky teeth had been ground off and replaced.

He straightened up. "A couple used to live here, the Nelsons."

I nodded. "Ken and Maisie. They moved to Arizona to live with their daughter. Well, Ken died a few years ago, but Maisie comes back every summer."

"I met them a long time ago, and I was just—" He stopped to scan the fields again, as if the word that eluded him was out there. "I was nearby."

"You met them with me." Maisie was getting heavy and I set her on her feet. The girls went straight down the steps and started kicking leaves. "Remember? You and me and Sebastian and Pallace? We drove up here for lunch."

He thought about that for a while and then I saw the light click on. It was as if he had just come into his body. "You wanted to stop and get them something," he said. "We swam in a lake."

"Right."

"And you live here now?"

I nodded. I was wondering if he would put it together but I doubted it. He had no incentive.

"Can I look inside?"

"Sure." I held the door open, turning my stomach at an angle. When he walked past me I expected something, a kiss on the cheek? He went right to the kitchen. "It's messy," I called out. "I'm making dinner." Then I was irritated with myself for anything that sounded like an apology. What the hell, Duke? That's what I should have said. I stayed on the threshold, keeping an eye on the girls. I could see him, his hand on a chair, taking it in.

"It's just the same," I heard him say, though he may have been talking to himself. "I remember this table."

"We want to make the kitchen bigger."

In a minute he came back. "Don't. It's perfect. Did you buy the place?"

"I married in." The girls were rolling now, then stopping to flutter their arms and legs. They were putting on a leaf show, which required an audience. "I married Ken and Maisie's nephew."

"Oh," he said. I could read nothing into that. Not disappointment or relief or surprise.

"Did you come to see Maisie?" My daughter, who we called little Maisie in the summers when big Maisie was here, lifted her golden head.

"It was such a good day," he said. "The day I was here. Someone told me years ago that I should always have a place in my mind where I could imagine myself happy, so that when I wasn't so happy I could go there. Anyway, this is the place I go."

"Me, too," I said.

"It's funny, I'd forgotten you were with us."

"Understandable," I said.

He shook his head. "I didn't mean it like that. I'm tired, that's the thing. I've been tired a lot lately, and so I'm here a lot, you know, in my mind. I just wondered if I could find the farm again. To tell you the truth, I've thought about buying the place, just to make sure that nothing changes."

"Nothing changes," I said. "Unless you count the conveyor we put in the barn to sort the cherries."

He shook his head. "I don't count that."

"I don't think my husband would sell," I told him. I don't think my husband would sell you the orchard if you offered him the entire state of California.

"Is your husband here?"

I nodded. I would have guessed it would be strange if I ever saw Duke again. I would not have guessed it would be strange in this way. Every sentence that came into my head began with the phrase, *Do you remember?* but clearly, he did not.

"Maybe I'll try to find him. Would you mind if I just walk around?" His hair was shining like a Pantene ad and he raked it back with his hand. I was sure that Duke's hair never looked like that before, but then I don't think he used shampoo when I knew him. I think shampoo was one of the things he didn't believe in.

The girls were sitting on the lawn throwing handfuls of leaves in the air and then letting those leaves affix to them with jam. They were laughing like hyenas. "I don't mind at all but seriously, can you just wait a minute? I haven't seen you in a long time. Tell me something."

"What do you want to know?" Suddenly he looked as tired as he claimed to be. Suddenly my mind was blank of questions.

“Is there a person in the car?” I asked. The windows were so dark it was impossible to tell but the motor was running.

Duke nodded.

“Should we invite him out?”

Duke shook his head.

Then I remembered the thing I did want to know, the person I had wondered about for years. “How’s Sebastian?”

His eyes had been wandering but they came back to me then and he smiled. “I always thought you were in love with Sebastian,” he said. “At least at the end.”

“Of course I was in love with Sebastian. Everyone was.” Pallace was, I wanted to say, but I couldn’t say her name without sounding punitive or hurt and I was neither of those things. I was the luckiest person in the world. “Is Sebastian still teaching? Is he still in East Detroit?”

“They got rid of East Detroit,” Duke said. “It’s Eastpointe now.”

“I don’t know why I can never remember that.”

“Sebastian works with me. He runs the production company. No more world history.”

“But he still plays tennis.” It wasn’t a question. Of course he played.

Duke nodded. "We play, the two of us. Sebastian is the constant. Everything is change except Sebastian."

For a brief, horrible moment I wondered if it was Sebastian in the car, if Sebastian had driven him here, but that wasn't possible.

He turned and looked at my girls spread out in a pile of red and gold leaves. "Do either of you know where the cemetery is?" he asked them.

Emily sprang up like puppet. "I do!"

"That's where I want to go. Can you walk around like that?" he asked me, making reference to my stomach.

"I can."

Duke went down the steps and into the leaves. When he leaned over, Emily held out her arms to him. "Oh, you are lovely," he said, picking her up. Then he looked back at me. "I should get one of these."

"Easiest thing in the world," I said, Maisie climbing into my arms.

I didn't walk him to the cemetery. I took him in the direction of the barn instead. "We'll pick up Joe," I said.

"Who's Joe?" Duke asked Emily, his eyebrows turned down, his voice suspicious.

"Daddy!" she cried, laughing at his hilarity.

Duke had a look on his face as if he were working

a particularly complicated math problem in his head. Then he found the answer. "Jesus. Joe Nelson?"

"Joe Nelson," I said.

"You married Joe Nelson?"

"Who on the Nelson farm did you think I married?" Maisie put the end of my braid in her mouth and started chewing.

"That's right. His family owned the farm. I forgot that part. Joe Nelson." He shook his head. "It makes more sense now. Is he still directing? I haven't heard his name in years."

I shook my head. We owed him no explanation, Joe and I.

"Do you live out here all the time?"

"We do," I said, a decision that was feeling better by the minute.

"Are you coming to live with us?" Emily asked.

Duke started walking again. "I haven't been invited."

"I invite you!" she said gleefully. "You can sleep in my room. I have my own room."

"You have tremendously friendly children." He bounced my girl up and down on his hip, his walk becoming exactly the kind of exaggerated canter the girls were always begging me to do.

I could see Joe in the distance. He was out in front of the barn, wiping his hands on an enormous dirty rag. I waved. I had never loved anyone more than I loved Joe Nelson at that moment. "Look who's come to visit," I called to him.

"As you know," Duke said to Emily, his eyes two inches from her eyes, "your cherry orchard is to be sold for your debts; the auction is set for August twenty-second, but don't you worry, my dear, you just sleep in peace. There's a way out of it. Here's my plan. Please listen to me."

The Chekhov wasn't funny now that we were the ones who owned the cherry orchard, but Duke wouldn't have known that. Joe was coming towards us quickly now, stuffing the rag in his pocket. "Nelson!" Duke called to him, his voice brimming with joy. "Hail fellow well met." He was shaking Joe's hand as Joe was taking Emily from his arms.

It was years later that Joe told me how he'd thought his heart would stop when he saw Duke there in the middle of the road, holding Emily.

20

The way Emily is sitting in the grass, her head against her knees, I wonder if she's going to be sick. Maisie is on one side of her, Nell on the other.

"Should I have told you this when you were fourteen?" I ask. "Should I have said, Duke isn't your father but he came to the farm once and thought you were the most beautiful child in the world and swung you around and recited Chekhov to you? Would that have made it better or worse because I'm telling you, I don't know. Maybe I did exactly the wrong thing." It's true that she met him once and was besotted with him, and it's true that he, at least for those minutes, was besotted with her. Duke had looked straight into her eyes after all. Even if she was only four it left a mark.

Emily pulls up her T-shirt and wipes her face. "I

wouldn't have believed you," she says finally. "I would have said he'd come to get me and you refused to let me go. I would have gone out of my mind."

"Impossible," Maisie says, rubbing circles on her back.

"I would have refused to let you go," I say. "Even if you were his, which you weren't."

"Maybe you remember him," Nell says to her.

Emily considers this, looking into her own memory for Duke. "It's like watching a movie," she says. "I can see the whole thing now that you've told us. So yes, I remember Duke, but I also remember you and Veronica sitting at that table registering people for auditions, and I remember Ripley standing by the swimming pool, and I remember your grandmother. I mean, it's not the same thing."

"Still," Nell says encouragingly. "It's something."

"It's not. It's nothing." Emily's beautiful eyes fill up again. "I just wish he could go back to being a famous movie star who I wanted to be my father when I was a teenager. I wish he could have waited out the pandemic on a yacht in Capri."

"Everybody wishes that," I say.

Maisie takes Emily's braid into her hands. "But then we'd have spent the rest of our lives thinking that Duke played George in *Our Town* and Mom dumped Duke for Dad. I never would have known that Mom used to spell her name with a 'u,' or that she wanted to be a vet for a week in high school, or that she ruptured her Achilles. I never would have known that Dad played the Stage Manager. I'm not saying Duke needed to drown so that we could get our facts straight, but I'm not sorry to know. The truth is I've never been one hundred percent positive who your father was and now I am. I mean, I knew it was probably Dad, but didn't part of you think that paternity was going to be the big reveal?"

I look at Maisie, aghast. "Are you serious?"

She shrugs. "The only thing she ever said to me when I was a kid was that Duke was her father."

"She told me the same thing and I never believed it," Nell says. "Didn't you ever watch her in the barn with Dad? It's like they're the same person."

Joe started taking Emily with him to work after Nell was born, at least for a few hours in the morning, affording me the luxury of having only two children under the age of five instead of three. He showed her which green plants were weeds and taught her how to take those weeds out by the roots. He laminated a small picture of the dreaded plum curculio beetle for her to keep in her pocket so she could be on the lookout. Emily has always been Joe's.

Emily stands, then reaches down to pull her sisters to their feet, one with each hand. "Is there anything else we need to know about the past?" Back to work, is what she's telling us.

"I think that's everything."

"Then tell us what happened when Duke died," Emily says.

Emily, Emily, stop. I shake my head. "You know that story already." Talking about Duke as I knew him when he was alive has kept him alive this past week. I'd just as soon leave it at that.

For a good ten minutes we work without talking, which may be the new family record, but then Maisie breaks down just after emptying her bucket. "I was at the Minties'," she says. "Lauren Mintie called me in the middle of the night because Ramona had gone into labor and she was barking and whining."

"Doesn't every living thing whine during labor?" Nell asks.

"Lauren said she was afraid something would go wrong and the kids would wake up in the morning and the dog would be dead and the puppies would be dead and then they'd be traumatized. Like dogs have never done this without human supervision before. But births are a good experience so I told her I'd come. Plus she said Ramona was in the bathtub downstairs and she'd leave the door open and the lights on but they'd all stay upstairs so I wouldn't have to see anyone but the dog."

"Contactless whelping," Emily says.

"Ramona's a nice dog," Nell says.

Maisie nods. "She was very good. She had seven puppies so it took a long time. I got the window open and turned on the overhead fan. You can't believe how awful puppies smell."

"Everything you do smells," Nell says.

Maisie ignores this. "The third one came out sideways so who knows, maybe it was a good thing I was there. That one died. I found a baggie for it in the kitchen and took it with me."

"Don't tell us that," Emily says.

I wonder if there's a puppy in the freezer somewhere.

Maisie keeps going. "I was just rubbing puppies, trying to get them stimulated to nurse, trying to get them to latch on. By the time Ramona was finished and I'd wiped the mess out of the bathtub and put the dirty towels in the laundry it was really late. Lauren left out extra towels and I made a new bed in the tub and brought Ramona some food and water. It must have been two o'clock before I got out of there. I drove home with the windows down because I was covered in puppy stink. I came up over the hill in the pitch-black dark and saw Duchess in my headlights, standing in the middle of the road. I swear to god, if I'd turned my head for a second I would have killed her."

Emily turns around. "What?"

"Duchess was in the middle of the road."

"You didn't tell me any of this," I say to her.

"I didn't even think about it then but what are the chances?"

"If you were leaving the Minties' then she was a long way from home," Emily says.

"Right? And if she's just standing in the road in the dark, somebody was going to hit her. So I pulled over and got her in the car and she was practically in my lap, licking my sweatshirt, going out of her mind over the puppy slime. That's not a small dog. I drove her back to the Whitings' and put her in the yard. I was all keyed up. By the time I took a shower and looked at my phone it was three o'clock. That's when I saw the news about Duke." Maisie looks at me. "I don't know why I woke you up. You'd been working all day. I should have let you sleep."

"Of course you woke me up."

She shakes her head. "He was still going to be dead in the morning."

That night when I opened my eyes, Maisie was sitting on my side of the bed in the dark, scrolling on her phone. It was the light of the phone that woke me up.

"What are you doing?" I whispered.

She ran her hand over my leg, over the summer quilt that covered my leg, and I knew it was bad. Joe was asleep beside me. I asked her where the girls were.

She shook her head. "Everyone's fine." Then she told me Duke was dead, and I thought for a second she was talking about a dog because Maisie was always going out in the middle of the night for one animal or another. And then I understood.

"How?" I whispered.

"He drowned. He was on a boat in Capri and he drowned."

She meant both the famous actor and a young man I'd known a hundred years ago, the one who hadn't crossed my mind in such long time. The two of them died together. I remembered how he would shake me gently awake at four in the morning, his hand running up my arm in the tangle of our sheets. *Wake up, wake up*, he'd say. *It's time to smoke.*

"Mom and I went down to the kitchen and looked at our phones. There wasn't any update in the news but the internet was flooded with pictures of him. There must have been a thousand pictures, and I said, one of these days, you're going to have to tell us what happened."

"I was worried about you finding out," I say to Emily.

"We talked about going over to the little house but we didn't want to wake you."

"We decided to go over there first thing in the morning but by then you'd already looked at your phone." Maisie is apologetic. This has been weighing on her.

"You were worried about me?" Emily asks. "I met the man for what, twenty minutes when I was four years old, and I somehow managed to make the entire story into something that happened to me." Emily lifts the bucket of cherries from her neck and upends it into the empty lug on the grass. After all these years of begging her to put him down, I can hardly believe the time has come. Emily knows everything now, and she is done.

And I am done, except for this: I saw Duke one other time, and of that time I will say nothing to my girls. His brief reappearance came in the period after my grandmother died but before Joe returned. It was years and years before that day in Michigan when he showed up on our porch. This was when I was living alone in New York and sewing for a costumer. He called me at seven in the morning. Not a Duke hour.

"Cricket," he said. "It's your past."

This was in the *Rampart* days and Duke was already famous. Not the kind of famous he'd become, but anyone who saw him kept their eyes on the screen. I didn't have a television, but a sports bar on my block had twenty of them and the bartender was not averse to letting me watch the small one he kept next to the ice machine. I'd show up on Thursday nights a little before nine o'clock even as I promised myself I wouldn't. Not that it mattered. The bar was full of people who promised themselves they weren't coming again.

"That guy," the bartender would say, shaking his head. "Somebody explain it to me." But I didn't have to explain anything because half the time he was leaning over my beer, watching.

Duke told me he was in a hospital outside of Boston.

Had he said he was at a diner down the street and could I meet him for breakfast, I might have hung up the phone. But say the word *hospital* and everything changes. "Are you okay? What happened?"

"What happened," he began, and then was quiet. "That's a long one. That's maybe a whole lifetime."

So it wasn't the kind of hospital I was picturing.

"What I was wondering is if you could visit me here. We get two visiting hours every afternoon before dinner. We're supposed to write down a list of people we want to see. It's an assignment, they're very big on assignments here, and I'm having a hard time coming up with an answer. Then I thought of you, and how you'd always been a such regular sort of girl, very sensible. I have a memory of you sewing."

"You need me to sew something?"

"Phone calls are limited and brief in this neck of the woods, so let's not waste our minutes hashing out the past and feeling bad. It's pretty much a binary situation, yes or no. I just thought it would be nice to see someone who knew me from before. The Mythical Kingdom of Before. You knew me, didn't you?"

"How did you find me?"

"Your uncle," Duke said.

My uncle. Of course. I hadn't been in touch with Ripley since I left New Hampshire but he could find the proverbial needle in a haystack, or he could pay someone to find the needle for him.

"Could you please tell me yes or no because I'm a little desperate to end this conversation before I change my mind. They've told me it's important I have a visitor, therapeutically speaking."

"I live in New York."

"I know that."

And so I told him yes, because yes was the only word I had for Duke. Yes was the only word I knew.

Buses were cheaper than trains, and so I took a bus from Port Authority to Boston, then in Boston I found the bus to Belmont and in Belmont I took a cab. This was exactly the sort of thing that would have floored my grandmother: I'd done all of it by myself. The hospital wasn't a hospital at all, at least not in my experience of hospitals. It was more like a charming college campus in New England, one that had been rented out to shoot a movie about college. The signage was maddeningly discreet but I managed to find the administrative building and told the woman at the front desk, which was not a hospital front desk but a college front desk, that I was there to see Peter Duke. It was the sort of place where poets and academics came to dry out and/or work through their suicidal tendencies. They must admit just enough gentle actors to fill a quota because the woman at the desk was clearly no stranger to famous. The name Peter Duke didn't quicken her pulse at all, she just opened a file and asked for my name.

"Lara Kenison."

But even as she was tracing her finger down the list I knew I wouldn't be there. He would have forgotten or changed his mind. He'd already told me he was close to changing his mind. She got to the end, and then went back to double-check herself. "I'm sorry," she said.

It was cold outside and the light was already coming in through the leaded windows at a slant. The bus ride had been long and irritating, and now I was going to take the same trip back in the opposite direction and it would be too dark to read. "I don't suppose you could call and ask him if he wants to see me?"

She shook her head. "There are a lot of rules about visitors."

My bag was heavy on my shoulder, the copy of *Middlemarch* sitting in the bottom like a brick. I wondered if I could walk back to the bus stop and save the cab fare. I had been paying attention. I had not been paying attention. Duke hadn't taken me to the hospital or visited me or brought me home. His brother did all that because Duke was very busy with his important work and he was drunk and the hospital was fifteen minutes away.

"Emily Webb," I said.

"I beg your pardon?" The woman at the desk found me sympathetic. I knew that. Being small is helpful sometimes.

"Emily Webb. That's the name I'm under. We were in *Our Town* together."

And because it was a mental hospital and treatment center for the noble and literate outside of Boston and not that far from New Hampshire, she did not tell me that in this life a person gets only one chance. She checked the list again and made a tick with her pencil. "Miss Webb," she said. "I'll need to look inside your bag." Then she gave me a map and told me she would call ahead to let them know to expect me.

Duke was housed in a looming brick manse with wide stairs and oak doors. Even with the seriousness of the situation, I couldn't help but notice the maple trees that lined the walkway were in full flame. Leave it to Duke to break down on the most beautiful day of autumn in Massachusetts. He called me two years after I had stopped waiting for his call, but times were tough and he was down and I was there.

I rang the bell on the locked front door and when the voice on the intercom asked my name I said Emily Webb and the door clicked and buzzed and I went inside. Except it wasn't exactly inside, I went into a human-sized fish tank, a glassed-in holding pen big enough for one. I watched as scruffy, sad-eyed folk wandered by in sock feet, smoking cigarettes. I tried the glass door in front of me but it was locked, and now the door behind me had locked as well. A couple of the residents lifted a hand to wave. The sight I presented was not new to them. A woman with a clipboard walked briskly past and when I tapped she held up a finger. "One minute," she said, or appeared to say. I couldn't quite hear. I waited because waiting was the only option. A man with a dark beard leaned down to put his face close to mine then opened his mouth.

I turned my back on the sight of his tongue writhing against the glass.

This was never going to happen to me. I don't suppose that's something a person can ever really say but I said it anyway. *This will never be me.* I took comfort in that.

A good ten minutes went by before a member of the staff arrived with a security guard to let me out. My bag was searched for a second time and then he checked my pockets and shoes. I signed the visitor log and was escorted to a large den full of ratty couches and little tables. It was like one of those beautiful old mansions that had been destroyed by generations of fraternity abuse. Duke was sitting on the floor in a circle of men, a two-liter bottle of diet raspberry ginger ale in the center of the group with little paper cups all around. The last time I'd seen him he was up onstage, making his exit in *Fool for Love.* He was wearing spurs. He said, "I'm only gonna be a second. I'll just take a look at it and I'll come right back. Okay?" Not to spoil anything but he doesn't come back.

"Cricket's here!" He gave me a wave, then he patted an open space on the carpet beside him. "Alex was just telling us about a halfway house in Illinois where he found a friend in Jesus."

Alex didn't look up but he nodded. I remained

standing. "We listen to one another's stories," Duke said.

"Sure," I said. I didn't know how long he'd been in there but he looked better than his compatriots, which probably had more to do with the fact that he looked better going in. He was a famous undercover cop on television and I was a seamstress and very likely the biggest fool God ever made. I wondered if it would be easier to exit through the fish tank than it had been to arrive.

"We need to finish," he said, as if it were surgery they were performing with their little paper cups.

"I've got a book." I went off to a free spot on a couch on the other side of the room.

"She's always got a book," he said to his friends, and when I turned to shoot him a look I saw that the men in the circle were watching my retreat sadly, pulling on their cigarettes while Alex resumed his tale of love.

The room was smoky and crowded with people hunched into corners, trying to exchange sentences without being overheard. It was the saddest bar in the world, the one in which no alcohol was served and everyone was waiting for the check so they could settle up and go home. Two women with clipboards were making the rounds, asking questions, marking people off. Magazines were piled on every surface and I picked one up because no one could find communion with George Eliot in those circumstances. The caption beneath the picture of the famous model on the cover said she was looking for honesty. Beneath the room's only floor lamp I thumbed through the pages that had already been thumbed to thinning velvet: an article about a former child star fallen on hard times; an article about a beagle who nursed an orphaned chipmunk in with her own litter of puppies; a picture of Peter Duke on the Santa Monica Pier, eating an ice cream cone and holding hands with someone named Chelsea who was identified as his wife. The only gossip I knew about Duke I knew from standing at the checkout in the grocery store. I didn't buy the magazines because they were not good for me, but a certain amount of information entered my consciousness by proximity. Somehow, miraculously, Chelsea had not come in. I closed the magazine, closed my eyes.

"You could have been friendlier." Duke dropped down beside me, taking my hand.

"I could have been—" I started and then closed my mouth, suddenly overwhelmed by the knowledge that I would cry.

He leaned over and kissed me, missing my mouth by several inches. Let it be known that the last person to kiss me with romantic intent was this same man. Despite the daily offers I received while walking to fittings in Times Square, I had remained alone. "I'm glad you came," he whispered.

I could not say I was glad. He seemed to understand this.

"Do you want to smoke?"

I shook my head. I asked him how the marriage was working out.

His fingers gently picked at the knee of my tights. "The marriage is no more. The lawyers have seen to that, or they are seeing to that." He tilted down his head. "Where's my girl?" he said quietly. "Where's my birthday girl?"

Truly, I did not think I would survive.

He pulled me up from the couch. "Come on, I'll show you around. The full ten-cent tour." He kept his arm around my shoulder, pressing me into his chest as if to keep me safe. We went back to the reception area. A man who looked like someone's sad father was in the fish tank now, and when I caught his eye he looked away. Duke stopped in front of an empty room with a circle of yellow folding chairs and an enormous chalkboard. "This is where we have the meetings. Lots and lots and lots of meetings. And that's the snack pantry." He pointed to a wide closet. "They're very generous with snacks but we aren't allowed to take them ourselves. We have to ask for them so that everything can be properly inventoried and recorded. I would like a bag of Cheez-Its, please." He steered me back across the lobby to stand outside the open door of a large, dark room where seven single beds were arranged in a haphazard manner. "This is where the dwarves sleep. I'm Happy, but only compared to the other six. We're not allowed to go into the bedroom until bedtime. We may not put our foot in there. Sleeping in the daytime is bad for depression. Did you know that? No closing the door either because there is no door."

A yelping came from the room we'd just been in and I was glad I wasn't there to see who it was.

"That's the bathroom." He pointed to a white door. "No lock there either but people are respectful about knocking. Make a mental note of that." He walked me in a slow circle around the reception again.

"Do you have to stay here?" I asked, when what I meant was, Do I have to stay?

Duke nodded vigorously. "Oh, I do, I do. If I don't stay I lose my job. I lose my contract. I become uninsurable, which means the movie can't start, which means I can't be in the movie. I'm going to be an astronaut. Did I tell you that? I'm going to be in a big white suit with a glass bubble on my head, floating in the darkness. Every single day feels like research for that one. People start taking you seriously once you've been an astronaut. Have you noticed that? It's a rite of passage. It means you've really got something going on."

"I never thought about it."

"Well, you need to. You need to get back in the game. They're plenty of good parts for women in space these days but you're going to need to put yourself out there."

"I'm done," I said, though I imagine the scope of those two words were lost on him.

He shook his head. "I saw *Singularity.*"

"You did?" I couldn't imagine it.

"You're very beautiful, cricket, and by that I don't just mean you're pretty, which you are. You have a real beauty that shows up on the screen. Pow. I found you mesmerizing. I find you mesmerizing." He was pressing me closer now, holding on to me like a raft. I was holding him up.

"We're going to go back and sit on the couch," he said in that same low voice used by every inhabitant of the room who wasn't screaming. "In two minutes you'll get up and go to the bathroom and I'll stay where I am. We get checked off every fifteen minutes. It's almost time. Once I get checked off I'll come and meet you there."

I looked at him in horror but he ignored it. Clearly it was an emotion whose expression had lost its impact in this place.

He squeezed my arm gently. "Do this for me." There was so much need in his voice. Then he went back into the den. I suppose I could have gone back to the glass door and banged on it with my fists until someone came to let me out, but instead I went to the bathroom and took off my tights. I thought about that first day when he said he was going to show me the lake, and then I walked into the lake and I swam, farther and farther away, until I couldn't hear anyone anymore.

I stood with my back to the sink, to the mirror. There was no condom dispenser in the bathroom. I'd bet there never are in these places. For this event I relied on the birth control favored by all women in such circumstances: luck. It works maybe half the time.

Duke came into the bathroom a minute later and lifted me up on the sink. He was facing the mirror. I couldn't stop thinking about that. He was looking at himself. "Not exactly ladies' night," he said once he had finished. He kissed the top of my head and then hustled back to make his next fifteen-minute check off. I straightened myself up as best I could, then found a woman with a clipboard to let me out of the building.

The light had shifted while I was inside and I was trying to get my bearings, trying to make a space in my mind for bus schedules while my mind kept wandering back to Duke trying to make a list of who he could call who might come to New England on a cold autumn night and fuck him in the unlocked bathroom of a locked ward. Pallace? What a preposterous thought. Chelsea? I didn't know her, but why would she come if there were already lawyers involved? So many actresses and makeup artists and wardrobe mistresses to choose from, so many fans, and still, I was the only person he could absolutely count on.

My hands were shaking and I thought it was from the cold so I dug through my bag to find my mittens. A spectacular orange light reflected off the windows of the building in front of me that made the glass look like beaten sheets of copper. A man in coveralls was raking leaves while another man bagged them up and put them on the back of a John Deere Gator nearby. I wanted to go and open up every bag and dump them out because didn't they know the leaves were the nice part? I stood there, taking in the sharp air and waiting until the feeling passed so I could walk by them without speaking. Another man sat on a park bench on the other side of the open lawn and watched me watch them. Maybe he had special privileges. Then he stood and I remember thinking how tall he was.

"Lara?" he said.

There were two ways to go: I could have run or I

could have cut a straight path towards him, straight into his arms. I was crying when I walked into his arms.

Sebastian was on the visitors' list but I got there first and a patient could have only one visitor at a time. The night was cold and clear but he had a warm coat. The traffic had been bad driving from Boston where he was staying for the month, and so he decided just to sit and wait, see who came out. Sebastian visited his brother every day.

"Do you want to go in?" We were sitting in his rental car in the parking lot. "I can wait." That wasn't true, I couldn't wait, but I could leave while he was inside and that might be the best thing anyway. I had stopped crying and I was trying very hard to keep it together.

Sebastian shook his head. "I'm hungry. Are you hungry?"

I was starving. He drove quite a way, out of the small town the hospital was in and into the small town beyond it, like we were scraping the whole thing off our shoes. When we walked into the restaurant an old man with a white short-sleeved shirt and black tie smiled to see us. He took two menus from the rack and led us into the dim room. "I've got a nice booth in the back," he said. "All the young lovers want a booth in the back."

Sebastian's hand was on my shoulder and he took it away. We laughed like a couple of lunatics but we were glad for the booth, glad for the privacy, glad most of all to be together in some Italian restaurant in a town I didn't know the name of.

"Here's to drinking." He raised his glass of wine to me. The old man had been quick with the wine. He brought it without our asking.

"To drinking," I said, and touched my glass to his. I was desperate for a drink.

"There's something about the place. I seem to sponge up everyone's desire for alcohol and carry it with me out the door."

I drank down half of what I had and let the warmth spread through me. I had never been so cold, not even in New Hampshire. Sebastian refilled my glass.

"The list of things I feel like I can't ask you," I said, shaking my head. "I wouldn't even know where to begin."

"Let's see how far I can get without you asking then. I never went back to Tom Lake. I didn't see Pallace again, never heard from her. Duke and Pallace, I don't know how long that lasted. I know that when Duke went to Hollywood on a ticket your friend Ripley paid for she didn't go along. Once *Rampart* caught on, Duke started getting in over his head. He was going on ride-alongs with real cops at night and he kept making friends with the guys in the back of the car, the criminals. Duke wanted me to come see him but I was teaching and I was still . . ." He stopped. "It's very hard to put a word to it. Duke's my brother and I love him. You think the thing that hurt you is going to hurt you forever but it doesn't." He looked at the menu because he couldn't look at me anymore. I believed that he was my true friend.

"Eggplant parmesan," I said.

He nodded. "It's good."

"How do you know it's good?"

"This is my place. Whenever we go to a new town I find a place."

Wood paneling halfway up the wall, black and white photographs of Frank Sinatra and Robert De Niro and Jimmy Durante. His place. "Do you miss teaching?"

He didn't answer the question. The little candle in a bumpy red glass globe burned between us. "You know what I think about all the time?"

I shook my head. "It doesn't matter."

"It does matter." He picked up a book of matches and tapped it on the table. "I was an hour on the road going home before I even thought about you sitting there, waiting for me to take you back up the stairs."

"I worked it out."

He nodded. "You were the smart one."

Oh, Sebastian, if you only knew, though he'd been

around from the start. Maybe he did know. I opened my hands. "Look where it got me," I said.

We had been given an opportunity to make things so much worse, Sebastian and I, and no one would have blamed us except for Duke, and Duke never would have known. The flame of that little candle sat between us for the rest of the night but through some holy kindness we felt for one another, we let it burn out. He drove me all the way back to New York, four hours in the car that went a long way towards setting my life to right. I told him about my grandmother dying and my time in New Hampshire, how I stayed around too long and became embarrassingly proficient on the monogram machine. I told him about not being an actress anymore. He told me about not playing tennis, or not playing tennis as a job. He still liked to play. And he liked California. He said Ripley had been good to him. He was getting him work on projects that had nothing to do with Duke. "He's trying to make sure I stick around."

"I bet he is."

"Man, was he ever in love with you."

"Duke?"

Sebastian glanced over, taking his eyes off I-95 for just a second. "Sorry, no, Ripley."

I laughed.

"I mean it. Maybe I shouldn't have said anything.

He told me once he was waiting for you to grow up, you know, so it wouldn't seem so weird."

But everything was weird, everything but me and Sebastian in the car, the lights of Connecticut shooting past us. We had chosen not to make a hard thing harder, which made it slightly easier when I counted up the days six weeks later and realized that my luck had run out. I still had enough money in my savings account left over from when I made actual money. I didn't have to call anyone. I didn't have to ask anyone for permission or help. A nurse stood beside me and held my hand and I'm here to tell you, I felt nothing but grateful. There was always going to be a part of the story I didn't tell Joe or the girls. What I did was mine alone to do. I tore the page from the calendar and threw it away.

21

There are always four or five days when picking the last of the sweet cherries overlaps with the start of shaking the tart cherries, when things get so busy you can't find your own hand. The crew we have kept our distance from this summer, the crew who has kept their distance from us, comes closer as we bring out the giant mechanical shaker. Together we unspool the tarps beneath the tree and then attach the shaker. Ten violent seconds later all the cherries are on the ground. The tarps are then rolled back, dumping the cherries into a long, mobile conveyor belt so the whole operation can move forward—unroll, shake, roll up—tree after tree, acre after acre. When the conveyor belt fills, the cherries progress into a giant tank full of water. We climb to the top and use our old tennis racquets to skim off the branches and leaves that have fallen in. There is no talking over all the noise, no extra moment in which to remember the past or examine how we feel about anything. There is work and only work, and with a lot of help, we get it done.

At the end of the first week of August, after all varieties of cherries have been harvested and sent off to the processing plant, we spend the day at the lake—me and Joe and Emily and Benny and Maisie and Nell and Hazel—swimming a little but mostly sleeping on our towels because we are that tired and the next day the pruning will begin. We've got six weeks to get things ready before apple season and there's a year's worth of maintenance around the farm to attend to. There's a wedding to think about.

It is during this season of maintenance that Maisie leaves work in the late afternoon to go back to the house for a phone meeting with her advisor. Ten minutes later she returns, a tall, gray-haired man at her side. "Mom!" she calls out in a loud voice, and I turn in her direction. Six weeks have passed since Duke drowned in the Tyrrhenian Sea, four weeks since I finished telling the girls the story of when I had known him. There are no visitors in the orchard, no one but the people who work with us, but as I get closer I can see that it's him.

"Sebastian!" Maisie says, and in her excitement she waves. She might as well be hopping up and down. I can tell that he means to be sheepish but he's not, he's glad, and I walk straight into his arms.

He puts one hand on either side of my head and looks at my face. We are both so much older now, and we are alive. "I didn't think you'd be here," he says.

"I'm always here," I say.

He smiles. "I met Maisie."

"He was on the porch swing," Maisie tells me. "Just sitting there. I knew exactly who he was."

"She opened the door and said, 'Sebastian Duke?'"

I look behind me. Emily and Nell are hanging back like shy children. I introduce my girls.

"Emily!" he says. "My brother used to say, 'Someday I'll live on an orchard in Michigan and have a daughter named Emily.'"

"It's not all it's cracked up to be," she said, her cheeks red.

"Did you know that your mother was the greatest Emily of all time? Your father was a very good Stage Manager but this one was in a class by herself."

"He's basing that on two Emilys," I tell the girls, but I will admit it, I am grateful.

Sebastian shakes his head. "I went on to have an entire life after I knew you," he says. "You have no idea how many actresses I've seen."

"She should have stuck with it," Nell says. "We tell her that all the time."

"It looks like your mother did just fine," Sebastian says.

"One of you go get your father," I say to them. "Tell him who's here."

But miraculously, they all go, because in some ways they are grown-up women who understand.

Duke was sixty when he died, which makes Sebastian sixty-one, which makes me fifty-seven. "I look at you," he says, "and I can see the whole thing, you and Duke up there onstage, Uncle Wallace. You're still that girl."

I shake my head. "I'm so sorry," I say. "I've thought of you every day since we heard but I didn't have any idea how to find you." Which is true, but it also never occurred to me to try. We knew each other such a long time ago.

"Duke loved it here," Sebastian says, looking out over the trees. "He was always talking about the day we all came out and had lunch with Joe's aunt and uncle. The place hasn't changed."

"I could tell you all the ways it's changed but you're right, essentially it's the same farm."

"Did you know he tried to buy it? I found him a lot of other orchards over the years but he always said no. This was the place he wanted."

Even now it's such a strange thought, Duke picking cherries on the Nelson farm. "He showed up one day in a big black car. The girls were so little then, in fact Nell wasn't even born."

Sebastian nods, and I understand that he knows every story about his brother. He sees Joe and the girls coming out of the barn and he waves, then we start up the road towards my family.

Generations of Nelsons had cleared the trees and planed the boards and pulled out the roots and the enormous rocks and planted the orchard. They looked after the cherries and the apples, the peaches and pears. They weren't about to sell this place to anyone. He called them for several years making offers, and after so many polite refusals he suggested a compromise: Would they sell him a place in the cemetery? Just a little place under the oak tree, he said. Duke would be cremated, after all. How much room would he need? Maybe just a small stone with his name but maybe not even that. The privacy appealed to him, along with the memory and the view. Duke told Maisie and Ken if he couldn't live here he would at least like the right to be dead here. "Why are you even thinking about that?"

big Maisie had asked him. He was so young! But she liked his television show, and even though she knew it wasn't real, Duke had so many people shooting at him and pushing him out of speeding cars. That had to wear a man down after a while, put him in mind of his own death. The price he offered them for a corner of their cemetery came to more than what Ken and Maisie had cleared in profit for the last five years combined. The money bailed them out. Duke bailed them out, and we never knew it. The lawyer came to the house with a check and a nondisclosure agreement. They were told that Duke would like to come and sit from time to time if they didn't mind, and of course they didn't mind. They would be thrilled to have him visit, stay for dinner, sleep in the guest room. He was welcome. That's what Duke told Sebastian. The Nelsons liked him. But after he bought a piece of the cemetery they didn't hear from him again, and he never came to visit, except for the one time he did.

We are all sitting down to lunch as Sebastian explains it. I put out the good plates, the good napkins.

"I never knew how they did it," Joe says. "How they came up with the money to get out of here."

"So he's going to be buried in our cemetery?" Emily is trying to find a place for this piece of information but there isn't one.

Sebastian nods. “There weren’t many places he felt comfortable.”

Ken and Maisie are here now, their ashes together beneath a single stone. I miss them. I miss especially the summers when Maisie came when the girls were small, and how we would fill a bag with sandwiches and tramp up to the cemetery to sit and watch the clouds billow overhead. Sometimes we would go to sleep in sleeping bags and wake up in the middle of the night to see the stars. I try to imagine Duke up there with Maisie and Ken, and then I try to think if it matters at all. It doesn’t matter, and it doesn’t have anything to do with me. It was always about the farm, and how he thought he knew what it would be like to stay here based on just that single day. We all wanted to stay, me and Pallace and Sebastian and Duke and Joe. The difference being that Joe was a Nelson, and he did the work to make sure that there would always be Nelsons, some Nelson or another, on this land. The difference being I had the good sense to marry him.

“Duke didn’t have any children?” Nell asks Sebastian. “I feel like movie stars always have children, you know, all those wives.”

Sebastian shakes his head. “He saw himself as a liability.”

“What do you mean?” Joe asks.

"He just thought it would be better not to extend the line."

Emily is sitting next to Sebastian at the table. "Everybody's got their reasons," she says to him.

Then Sebastian puts his arm around my daughter's shoulder like he's known her forever. "I always thought so."

"Were you ever in love with him?" Joe asks me that night when we're in bed. We've put Sebastian in Emily's room, in the twin bed beneath the sloping ceiling stickered with planets and stars. He had planned to stay in a hotel in town, he had booked a room, but the girls wore him down with their insistence. He was ours for now. They told him so.

"Duke?"

Joe snorts, shakes his head. "I know you were in love with Duke."

"I was and then I very much was not."

"Which doesn't answer my question."

"Was I in love with Sebastian?"

"The better brother."

The better brother, indeed, but I was young, and it was years before I could see the merits of kindness. "No," I say. "I wasn't. I was in love with you."

"You weren't in love with me then." But he pulls me

to him and I put my head on his chest, I rest my head on the old blue T-shirt he wears to bed.

"But that's how it feels now, looking back. Now I think that I was always in love with you."

After Joe falls asleep I stay awake, thinking about Capri and the sea and the boat, about Duke, and the moon on the water. It's a place I've never seen and still it comes to me so clearly, the light and the dark and the quiet sea, and how he jumps from the bow feet first, straight as a knife, and how the hundreds and thousands of tiny bubbles break across his skin, his hair floating up. He lets himself go deep before he starts kicking up towards the surface, and then he swims away, from the boat and from me and from Sebastian. I think how hard it must have been for him to not turn around but he kept swimming for as long as he could go. I let him go. Not that he was ever mine but still, I let him go.

Emily carries a shovel and Benny, that genius, brings a post-hole digger. Hazel follows along. Sebastian carries what is left of his brother. He picks a spot beneath the red oak and together we make a place for him. The daisies held on all summer, becoming a wild tangle over all the graves. Sebastian turns the canister into the hole and then packs in the dirt with his hands. Joe says the lines about the earth straining away, and how every sixteen hours we all need to lie down and rest. After that we all sit down. Nell sits beside me, then stretches out, her head in my lap. We stay in the cemetery a long time, thinking of Duke, and then after a while we start talking about other things, mostly the wedding. Emily and Benny promise to choose a day, maybe the first of the month because that way they'll always remember. "You'll remember anyway," Joe says to them and it's true, at least as far as he's concerned. He never forgets. We were married in the house that later became our home. Ken and Maisie were Unitarians and said that their minister could come the next day after lunch and they would stand up with us and we both said that would be fine, which was how we finally decided to get married. Joe, the greatest good fortune of my life, these three daughters, this farm, I see it all and hold it for as long as I can, my hand on Nell's head. I think of Uncle Wallace holding my hand, and then of Duke again, his long hair gelled and pinned, waiting for me to walk off the stage so that we can change out of our costumes and swim in the dark. Like Uncle Wallace, Duke had three wives, and like Uncle Wallace, he wasn't married to any of them in the end. For all his glory, he is left with us and the wide blue sky and the high white clouds and the straight lines of trees stretching out towards the dark woods and then, on the other side, the lake. We can see everything from here. I would say that there has never been such a beautiful day, but I say that all the time. I can see how right Duke was. He only needed such a little space. There is room up here for all of us, for me and for Joe and our daughters, for their partners and their children, because this is the thing about youth: You change your mind. Despite everything we know there may still be children living on this farm and someday they will be buried here with us. Sebastian can come, too. I will remember to tell him this later. Joe will tell him. Where would he be in the world except with his brother, here with us?

Author's Note

I thank Thornton Wilder, who wrote the play that has been an enduring comfort, guide, and inspiration throughout my life. If this novel has a goal, it is to turn the reader back to *Our Town*, and to all of Wilder's work. Therein lies the joy.

About the Author

ANN PATCHETT is the author of novels, works of nonfiction, and children's books. She has been the recipient of numerous awards including the PEN/Faulkner, the Women's Prize in the U.K., and the Book Sense Book of the Year. Her novel *The Dutch House* was a finalist for the Pulitzer Prize. Her work has been translated into more than thirty languages. *TIME* magazine named her one of the 100 Most Influential People in the World. President Biden awarded her the National Humanities Medal in recognition of her contributions to American culture. She lives in Nashville, Tennessee, where she is the owner of Parnassus Books.